In the Town of Joy and Peace

Zdravka Evtimova

Fomite

Burlington, Vermont

This is a work of fiction. Any resemblance between the characters of this novel and real people, living or dead, is merely coincidental.

In Bulgarian and other Slavic languages, the word "Radost" means "joy", and "Mir" means peace. Hence the title of the book.
Cover photo: © Danny Wood
www.dannyjwood.com

ISBN: 978-1-94251-70-8
Library of Congress Control Number: 2016963551

Fomite
58 Peru Street
Burlington, VT 05401
www.fomitepress.com

1.

IT WAS A DAUGHTER AGAIN, the third one in a row. Fuming, Tano looked at the dirty heap of swaddling clothes in which the baby bawled. He wished the newborn would die under the blankets, kick the bucket here and now on the dirty mattress. He bent down and glowered at the narrow face as shriveled as a rotten apple, smaller than his fist. Yesterday, he had tried to sell the tot to a Greek man or if worse came to worst swap it for a cow, but the Greek gave him the slip. The skunk didn't show up. Then Tano tried to sell the wailing thing to a childless woman from the town of Pernik; she had promised to give him money plus her old TV set, but then she wanted documents, certificates and papers. Tano didn't have them and the woman beat a hasty retreat on him. Why don't I break its arm, he thought, enraged. The little snake screamed and he couldn't sleep. Tano felt like pouring some brandy down his throat. After the baby was born he tried to leave it with the barman at The Two Slippers Café, and he was very modest: a bottle of brandy was all he wanted. He was about to strike the deal, unfortunately for him a police car crawled along the street and the barman backed away on him.

"Take your runt away," he said.

"O, come off it," Tano thundered. "You sell this runt to the Greeks and you pocket two grand. You give me two bottles of brandy, ok?"

A nasty place, this God forsaken town, Tano thought. You can sell a donkey and you get what? No two measly bottles of hogwash brandy, no Sir. You grab two gallons of first-class cognac for your beast of burden. What do you get for your baby? Runt or no runt, the Greeks are willing to cough up two grand, but you get nothing, zilch. Tano was not sure the little one was healthy: the Greeks bought nothing but strong and vigorous tots. This one here wailed as if its tummy was full of leeches. Yes, he should have broken its arm after the thing was born. If the runt doesn't die right away it will grow up with a warped arm and that's a huge advantage, Tano thought. She'd go begging in the streets and she'd come back home with her pockets full of money. He couldn't stand the bawling heap of swaddling clothes anyway. The doctors in the hospital told him his wife was to kick the bucket any minute now: was it blood poisoning or something else went wrong after she went into labor? The bottom line was she'd meet her maker. Good riddance, Tano thought. But she worked for that stocky Greek guy, Nickos, at his sewing workshop, and it was she that put bread on the table in the kitchen, and the social workers gave her the money for the other two daughters: puny little beasts so grubby and soiled Tano could neither see their faces nor distinguish who was who. Well, if he could get his hands on her on the days she'd got the dough, he beat her black and blue, took everything to the last cent from her pockets and got uproariously drunk. She grew crafty with time—hid the money, buried it under bushes or benches, or stuck it under a loose board in the kitchen. Tano could not find a single coin, nor could he catch her. She ran more quickly than he did; she jumped through the window of their house and furtively, noiselessly like a beaten dog, ran to the forest. There were huge branches of brown trees that clawed at his face as Tano chased her. The children traipsed around the neighbors' houses; the younger one was two, the elder one three. When he trudged back home the two of them vanished: did they hide under the linoleum or in the cellar he wondered. At a certain point his wife would come back home too. He didn't know if she walked back from work, or she'd got drunk with some driver of the big trucks that headed for the Greek border.

Some days his wife drove back home carrying a bag full of twenty lev bills. Then the house would smell of roasted meat, the light bulbs shone both in the kitchen and in the two rooms, the TV babbled on and Tano, content, his stomach full, watched his daughters play on the bare floor. The two tots did not get on his nerves. On the contrary, they were quite pleasant because their mother had washed them and their white faces looked like liquor in a clean glass. He liked his elder daughter: she was half-witted and didn't wail as much as the younger one. She pissed in her pants all the time. Her mother had had enough of that and in the end she tied a piece of cloth around the kid's waist and let the girl piss as often as she liked. The tot splashed barefoot in the mud and Tano didn't think it was necessary to buy her shoes. He didn't even remember the children's names. Why should he bother? He imagined he could sell the kids to the barman and these dreams kept him alive and kicking when he was down and out until finally his wife drove back home with another bag of twenty lev bills.

Then love began, wild and savage bumping and groaning, amidst the tattered shirts of the kids, the empty beer bottles, forgotten putrid sausages, right there, on the linoleum, the two girls watched Tano and his wife on the floor, their chocolate-smeared faces glowing happily, their tummies full of food, their eyes full of stars.

"You stay at home and look after the children," his wife would say. "I'll find another driver and I'll make some more money."

Tano looked after the girls an hour or two, then suddenly he felt like a glass of brandy. He threw a loaf of bread on the floor, left two bottles—of lemonade and milk—in the middle of the room and went out to see some friend in the pub. He often happened to fall for the coat or the sturdy pair of walking shoes a drinking buddy of his had put on. Tano drank as much as he could pay for, then left the pub and ambushed the drinking buddy. He usually didn't thrash the guy within an inch of his life. Tano would just hit him on the back of the head with a brick or with a piece of wood, and calmly take the item he had been attracted to. He was a colossally strong man. He'd take a job once in a blue moon. So far, he had not got on with his bosses. Kids or women would stumble on a man all bruised and bloody not far from the place where Tano had quarreled with him.

… A neighbor hesitated, scratched her head then stepped across the threshold.

"Tano, your wife breathed her last in the hospital," she blurted out, turned her back on him and dashed out of the room. That was all Tano could remember.

His daughters—the two elder ones bawled on the floor, the baby howled at their feet wrapped in its filthy swaddling clothes. What a pity he couldn't sell it to that fat Greek, or swap it for a bottle of brandy with the barman. The eyes of the little one were blue, and if she didn't die and grew up, she'd attract drivers like a bitch and she'd bring him a purse stuffed with money at the end of the day.

Tano kicked at the baby thinking it would be a pity to break the arm of a blue-eyed kid. If it didn't bite the dust too early perhaps it would grow up to look like its mother. Men ran after her like hungry rats and gave her money of their own accord. But he couldn't tell if the baby was healthy. Maybe it was feeble-minded like his eldest. His first daughter would never wail even if she had pissed on her blanket, was hungry, or her face was grubby and no one washed her. She would sit quiet in a corner and sob herself quietly to sleep. Tano didn't want to sell his first-born daughter because she was the mildest one and because he still remembered the way he'd got drunk with joy after she was born. But now what? What was he to do after their mother had been pushing up the daisies? He had no money for brandy, he was hungry and he wanted a woman. He would readily give away the three kids to the Greek for a loaf of bread.

He lost count of days. He didn't know when his wife had died. He didn't go to claim her body from the hospital. A dead woman is good for nothing, he thought. There's no love or pleasure in her. At a certain point he felt like drinking and he robbed the pub but the owner of the joint was after him with a band of thugs who beat the daylight out of him. So Tano went and sold his blankets, the stove and even the old TV set, the only thing he loved more than women and sex. He didn't exactly know what he watched, but he stared wide-eyed, and he thought he was happy he had drunk a lot of expensive brandy in his life.

He sold everything, beds, pans and all. He ripped the linoleum off the floor and sold it to a junk dealer for a handful of small change. He sold the mattresses and the kids' clothes, then he tried to sell the girls to an old Gypsy man. Gypsies loved to have girls with fair complexion in their families, but he and Tano couldn't meet over the price. Other folks would take the kids for thirty leva or if worse came to worst they'd give Tano an old motorbike for them. They'd even add some barrels of fuel to the bargain. Tano would have agreed to anything, but they beat a hasty retreat. Somebody must have tipped them off that his eldest daughter was dim -witted, and who'd care for a softheaded kid? She wouldn't be able to steal the way you'd expect her to, nor would she try to make money with men. Even if she would, she'd forget to collect her money. In the end Tano undressed the kids. They crawled stark naked on the floor and one could see their skins were as white as fresh snowdrifts, glowing like anisette in a perfectly clean glass. The third child, the smallest one, gave an ear-piercing shriek. It must have been cold.

"What? Stop it! Cut that out!" Tano shouted at it, spat on the floor and left the heap of bare bluish legs and arms and feet to writhe on the floor. The eldest one, his favorite, the feeble-minded girl—she was the only one that didn't whimper—grabbed at his trouser leg as she tottered to her feet. For a split second he felt sweet over her. This naked kid was the best thing in his life. It never bothered him. It didn't whine or snivel. In the evenings when its mother went to the freeway and got money from truck drivers, the kid buried its dimwitted head in his shoulder and the two of them would be unhappy together in front of the old, dead TV set. The thing didn't work because they'd cut off their electricity again. His wife had not paid for it and that was a shame.

For a split second, Tano was tempted to take his softheaded daughter along with him. If worse came to worst he could sell her to a dealer. He'd heard dealers looked for crazy kids on account of their livers, kidneys or something or other they had in their eyes. Then a question crossed his mind: if his daughter was retarded did she have liver or such valuable things in her eyes? Besides how was he to take a naked kid along? The cops would see its anisette-white skin and that would be enough; they'd lock him up in the district jail. Maybe they'd throw his child into the hole for idiot kids, that stinking dumping ground of a house he'd seen on the

TV. No. Tano wouldn't have that. He wouldn't give his beautiful weak-headed girl to that hole for idiot kids. He'd rather she met her maker decently, quietly. He'd miss this meek child that huddled her silly head against his shoulder. Her face was more beautiful than brandy. He'd miss her so much. After a kid dies, it goes to the other dead folks, Tano reasoned. And her mother died—Tano had no idea if she passed away a week or a year ago—and the kid would join her. That was all there was to it. He thought of his wife. She was a good woman although she hid the money she made in the Greek's workshop. On the other hand she'd given him fried sausage and brandy after she got money from the truck drivers, she'd paid the bills, they had their electricity restored and they'd watched TV...

The baby squirmed and squealed as if he was cutting its head off. It was a blue-eyed thing and it would grow into a beautiful whore, and it was a pity it was bawling its eyes out. Tano made up his mind: he'd leave the kids be in the room and he'd come check on them in the evening. If he could pilfer a coat or a jacket and sell it, he might buy some food for the children. He needed a drink to set his scattered thoughts in order. Hopefully he'd talk the Greek into buying the blue-eyed baby and the second girl. In fact the second one wasn't that unbearable. It was pretty, too. Her skin was the color of brandy that has stayed years on end in a mulberry barrel, and her eyes were deep and translucent like cognac. He could foist the two brats on some silly old wife and wheedle a fiver or two out of her. That was the best way to make a fast buck. He had made a pledge to buy clothes for his feeble-minded daughter. Are you a man if you can't scrape enough money to feed a softheaded child, Tano thought?

He wrenched his trouser leg from the grip of the halfwit, paused, thought hard, and took off his old coat. Then he dumped the children in a heap on the floor and covered them with the coat. They'll be warm and they won't kick the bucket, he said aloud as he stroked the feeble-minded one on the head and started for the door. A thought crossed his mind: the two bigger ones could crawl to the backyard through the broken door. Somebody could catch them and have them for free. So after Tano left the room, he produced a piece of wire from his pants pocket and tied the door handle to long nail driven to hold the rusty hinges. It was late but he could not tell if it was in the morning, or in the evening. He'd robbed a woman a few days before and got uproariously drunk and lost track of time. He'd better mug another old woman soon. It was freezing cold and the wind bit his face. Women were not stupid. They wouldn't go out in a storm, damn it. Tano cursed under his breath and started for the railway station. I hope the night falls quickly, he muttered. The women that worked in Sofia, the capital city, got down from the night train and hurried home.

He couldn't say how long he'd been waiting at the station, but it was evening for sure: the sky had thickened and grown dark. Then a bright moon shone overhead and that was good for him: he could see which women had money in their purses—the ones that had expensive coats on their backs. Tano robbed three of them. The first two, thick and round, kept mum just like his feeble-minded daughter, and he liked them a lot. Generally speaking, Tano fell for women who didn't talk much, didn't scream and didn't whimper. He took their purses and their bags and let them go. The third one however was different, she hollered and shrieked, and he feared the cops would hear her screams so he kicked her a couple of times to shut her up. Whatever the trouble, the catch was good. First, he sold the coats to a local junk man then he sold him the empty purses of the women he'd robbed, then at last he had a drink. He even poured some brandy on the cement floor in the pub in memory of his wife who'd just died. He hoped that after he croaked he'd find her somewhere up there, and they'd live together again. They had been so happy. They had watched TV together at the time she took cold hard cash from the trubrachesck drivers and there was plenty of food in the fridge. He'd even agree to look for the blue-eyed baby among the clouds—he was sure it had met its maker on the bare cold floor where he'd left it. The thought of death calmed him down. Then he changed his mind. He decided he didn't want to die only because his feeble-minded daughter would remain all alone in the world and they'd throw her into that hole for idiot kids.

The brandy was good and he drank so much that the earth bent and caved in under his weight. He went home and even before he opened the door, he felt something had gone wrong. How come the three kids were all quiet? As for the baby, it was weak and blue-eyed, it could have bitten the dust, but where were the other two?

"Hey! Hey!" Tano shouted. He did not remember what the names of all the children were, and he very often doubted they were his children—how could they possibly be? His eyes were not blue. "Tanya! Tanya!" he roared.

Tanya was the feeble-minded one. She was the only one that had a name.

No kids squealed or whined on the floor. There was no electricity and Tano knew he had to set fire to something so he could look around. There was nothing to burn in the room so he took off his shirt—an old rag his wife had bought him after their first daughter was born. He struck a match and lit the sleeve first, then the collar and then the other sleeve. After it became light enough to see he realized the children had gone.

"Hey! Hey!" Tano thundered, "Hey!"

There was no answer.

"Tanya! Tanya!" he screamed. That was his first daughter, the feeble-minded one. His wife had given her another name—maybe Maria or Anna, or Theodora, he didn't remember clearly. He called her Tanya, and he was Tano, thus he could never forget her name even if he was drunk as a skunk. This half-witted child was the only thing that was his own in the empty house, in the empty pub, and here under the rain.

"Tanya! Where are you, Tanya!" Tano shrieked waving his burning shirt in his hand.

He could not find her. The other naked toddler was gone, even the wailing blue-eyed baby had vanished. Somebody had taken them. Tano knew the guy who wanted to sell them. Yes, the idiot wanted to sell the kids for sure.

2.

I'M BIG AND MY HEAD juts out into the air above the men's heads although I'm a woman. I'm stronger than most men.

"I wonder how come you're so huge," Mother says. "Your father's tiny—a runt of man and, between you and me, his moustache could barely reach my breasts. He was as thin as a spindle. I baked food for him, his stomach gave him big trouble, he groaned and moaned but didn't die. Look here, I'm petite and you're as tall as the belfry of Saint Ivan Rilski Church. So your father's right. He kept having doubts on whether you come from his seed or not. Not that his seed is something to admire and applaud. No, Sir. He was sick all the time. I've run after other men, yes, that's true," Mother admitted. "It's only human! My husband had money to burn. Nonetheless he was a sick man. You grew up as sturdy as a hill and he suspected that somewhere along the line I hadn't let the chances slip by. I wondered why you loved him so much. He lay in his bed wrapped up in loads of blankets all smelling of infusions and you sat on a stool by his head and sang to him. Your voice is as big as you, I tell you.

It's not only huge it clobbers you on the head, that voice you keep in your mouth, so I think you've taken after Hunchback Hristo. He was over six feet tall but the way he stooped made him look shorter. He towered above everybody else in town. Yes, Hristo was almost as tall as the monument of that poet in the middle of the square… I've forgotten his name.

Whatever, Hristo sang beautifully although most of the time he howled on account of drinking too much. Dana, my girl, your father knew there was nothing weak or sick in your blood and he used to love you. I wish his bones burned in his grave. I hope the worms still eat his liver and his stomach gets worse in hell where he belongs. He couldn't stand me and he left me nothing, not a penny to bless myself with. He transferred the house, the fields, and the dairy and the sewing factory to you. Now I watch your hands, perhaps you'll throw a chunk of bread my way, I think. I stare at your table like a hungry dog and I'm your mother.

Although you stick out like a street car among the rest of us, you've taken after me too. A caravan of men is waiting in line for you. And they are not after your good looks, believe me. You are not much of a beauty, Dana, write this down somewhere and read it often, girl. They are after your money. They tell me you paid the guys for their love and it's a shame for a woman to pay for love.

"Listen, Dana," my mother went on. "You change your boyfriends like handkerchiefs, and I don't see anything wrong with this. What I'm driving at is that you don't get in the family way. To put it plainly and more directly you can't conceive a baby. You are a barren woman. So what? I don't know what's better: to be an unfruitful lady or to have a litter of snotty brats that trail after you like whooping cough. You can't get rid of their dirty socks, not even if your life depended on it. Therefore I think it's much better for you to be barren."

Barren Dana—that's what they call me in the town of Radomir

and in even in Pernik which is the capital of the district, but I don't give a hoot. The crystal glass factory went bust, the shoe factory and the all three forge shops went bust and the aspirin plant was forced to drastically cut production. So the men in these parts who don't go to pick olives in Spain or dig ditches and build brothels in Amsterdam don't mind earning big bucks off me. I pay generously and I know how much a man is worth. At times I wanted a guy like the grass in the field-thin and wiry in summer, and full of thorns and snakes, I wanted a small man. Then I sent for Stoichko who used to be a sapper in the army, a guy so little and punk that his own wife was burlier than him. He was agile as a weasel. In winter, he was un-employed like everybody else and in summer he was a construction worker. For a night with me I gave him more money than he earned for a month at the construction sites in Sofia. His wife often met me in the street. She didn't call down black curses on me the way she did after I invited her husband for the first time. She said "God bless you, Miss Dana" instead. Of late she took a step back, bowed before smiling, with a smile so grateful I felt like kicking her ass. I didn't care about her hungry kids. She'd sent them time and again to clean my backyard and I thrust some banknotes into their pockets, or gave them cheap nylon bags full of chocolates. They waved their hands when they saw me in the street, grinned and beamed and shouted, "Thank you, Miss Dana! Love you, Miss Dana!"

Stoichko's wife sent me home-made cakes and pies, and she wrote me great thank you letters. She didn't use commas or pe-riods, capital letters or any other punctuation, and it was evident Bulgarian grammar was not a favorite with her.

"thank yu for the money
stoichko want to come to you again.
say when do u want him
he won't be late"

In the town of Radomir all men were shorter than me. Their ribs protruded in their chest like hammer handles, and they were tough and lean. They ate bean and lentil soup and kept the meat for the children.

At times I sent for Tano who used to work as a backhoe operator for the coal mine in Pernik that went bankrupt a couple of years ago. The guys pilfered everything worth pilfering to the last scrap of coal, and the colliery turned into a muddy crater. The ditches were full of rain water and gradually became vast areas of swamps. I couldn't say where the frogs came from; so many frogs that thieves stepped on them, loud-voiced crews that constantly croaked at the top of their lungs, so the folks in Radomir called the whole mountain The Frog. The hills, all dug and carved by the miners, were now frogs that croaked with their rocks, their drying trees, muddy dirt roads the trucks had made impassable years before.

When Tano was drunk I threw him out directly on the road in front of my front door, or in my backyard. It is a big place encircled by a sturdy seven feet high stone wall. There is an enormous house as white as the month of January with all its whirlwinds, snow-drifts and blizzards. It's mine—I lived in it. Twice a week, a girl from Radomir came to clean the rooms, and my neighbors must have thought about me, 'She's a barren woman and she's big as the hill therefore she positively likes women." I didn't give a damn about women but the girl didn't know that and asked me very politely, "I'll love you more than Tano the drunk and Stoichko who's meager as a dead rat, Miss Dana."

"No, thanks," I said. "Take that," I gave her a fat bundle, "Go home and tell your friends I beat the daylight out of you. Let them wet their pants."

After the kid opened her mouth and told my neighbors what

I'd done to her, I couldn't get rid of women. A line of them as long as the seven feet high wall waited for me to interview them and hire the luckiest one to work for me. One would say Radomir was the town where the most beautiful women in this part of the world were born. The minute I showed my nose in the street—I loved to inspect my lands in the morning, I rode my horse, Giant or I drove my Jeep—the beauties shouted, "Miss Dana, can I work for you as a housekeeper? I speak English and Italian, Miss Dana. I can impress you with home cooked delicious Italian cooking!"

Yesterday I grabbed a loudspeaker and shrieked, "I'll choose one of you and I'll send my jeep for her."

I'd never sent for a lady, ever. I preferred huge Tano instead. He was the only the human being taller by a whole inch than me and it was terrific to have a taller man by your side. His wife died recently. She was among the chicks who queued up at my front door hooting and hollering, "Miss Dana! Look at me!" as she unbuttoned her dress.

I didn't feel like watching her pink swollen belly or her tits. I'd seen milk squirting from them. She'd just given birth to a third daughter and I guessed she didn't know who the father was. Tano, her husband, was hammer drunk most of the time and on the days he wasn't, I sent for him and paid him generously for the fact he was an inch taller than me. So I believed this woman's third daughter wasn't Tano's offspring. One day, she brought the baby to my place. I saw it was as big and blue-eyed as my Angora cat Mikhail, so I sent for her. I wanted to give her something good to eat. She tried to kiss me on the mouth.

"Stop it!" I yelled.

She reached for my arm. Her fingers burned and her eyes were furnaces in which something I couldn't name melted and went dead. I knew this woman would close the earth behind her.

"I don't want anything from you," I said. "Go to that bed over there and get some rest."

The woman couldn't make it to the bed. She collapsed onto my kitchen floor, and I was scared she'd cash in her chips under my roof. I carried her to my jeep and drove her to Doctor Gospod. She was a good doc, Gospod was. She bent over her sick patient and said, "This lady is dead."

Tano's wife had passed away. Her breasts still leaked milk. Who'll suckle her baby now, the one that has blue eyes like my tomcat Mikhail, I thought? Well, that was none of my business. I sent Tano a message; one way or another he was the dead woman's husband. I warned him I wouldn't have a drunken idiot at my door. If he'd drunk, I'd dump him in the gutter—that was what I said. Tano was not drunk. I gave him a pork chop and apple pie to eat and a two glasses of apricot brandy to down then I enjoyed his being taller than me for an hour and a half. At a certain point he burst into tears.

Was it possible for a man who was an inch taller then me to shed tears as heavy as raindrops? He wetted both my sheets and my mattress.

"Why are you blubbering, man?" I asked.

He didn't breathe a word about his problem just broke into tears once again, more powerfully this time. He was as drunk as a lord and unable to stop bawling. No one had wept buckets at my place like this guy.

"My wife's dead and cold. My house's empty. There's nothing more to sell in it," he mumbled. "Even Aggo, the junk man, wouldn't give me twenty levs for the kids. I feel sorry for the half-wit girl… She's mine. She'll die like a dog, the poor thing. Dana, you wanna take the half-wit to live with you? She doesn't eat much. I'll love you every day, Dana. I'll love you long and strong as long as you want and I won't charge you a dime for it. Please, take the halfwit. Take her, Dana.

"Your wife has two other kids," I said. "Where're they?"

"I reckon I'll give them to Aggo, the junk man if he wants them. I'll charge him ten bucks a kid. He can give them away to the Greeks. Or he could find a mother for them, a barren woman like you, Dana."

"You listen, Mister," I said. "If you don't shut up I'll throw you out. I summoned you here to love me, not to turn on the waterworks. Do I make myself clear?"

"My wife's dead," he sobbed. "She died. The blue-eyed brat is to blame! She was born like a dog. I don't know for sure, but I reckon she went and poisoned her mama's blood. She died, you know. I left the three of them on the floor, three kids stark naked. And there's not a thing to sell in the whole house."

"You left the three of them on the floor? All bare-assed! You idiot!"

I wasted no time and called my friend who cleaned my house for me. She was a decent bachelor girl, my classmate. After she scoured a room everything in it sparkled, and her meals were miracles. She put all of Italy on my kitchen table, with her stews and soups. This clever mademoiselle knew the tricks of the trade. My saucepans and my frying pans accommodated Calabria, Rome and Seville every single day. I ate Sicily at breakfast, I sank my teeth into Milan at lunch, and in the evening I had Naples as an appetizer. So I paid the girl to drive the naked kids to my place, not that I cared that much for children, not in the least. Everyone in these parts knew I was as barren as the paving stones in the street, but the third one of them, the puny baby that did the dirty on its mother's blood, had blue eyes just like my tomcat Mikhail. I hadn't seen the second one. They said it was swarthy, and its eyes were pitch-black. Perhaps its mother had got that kid by an Arabian man and that was the reason the neighbors saw desert and heat in its eyes. Whatever the truth, I could not leave a little girl to croak on a bare cement floor. Tano told me he had wrenched the wooden boards from the floor and exchanged them for two glasses of plum brandy. The girl who cleaned for me and brought Italy to my table three times a day came back home and reported, "Tano's cubbyhole's empty. There are no kids there. Shall I tell Sto the cop to go search and rescue them? What do you say, Miss Dana?"

"The feeble-minded one! Where's my feeble-minded one?" Tano squirmed and blubbered at my table.

Well, was I to blame his softheaded daughter had got lost? It was not me who undressed the kid and sold its pants to Aggo, the junk man. I'd never seen a man as tall as Tano snivel and howl like he did.

"Stop it," I said. "Shut up, I tell you. I'll give a cash reward and somebody or other will bring me the girl here. If you don't see the feeble-minded one in half an hour from now, you can kick me in the face."

I couldn't stand watching this guy suffer, his shirt wet with tears, spittle and snot. He was a big man meant to love women as tall as me, so I called my girl who cleaned for me, an honest soul I entrusted with the key to my magnificent wine cellar.

"Isabella," I cried out. "Bring this jellyfish a bottle of brandy. The sight of him makes me sick."

"Shall I bring an expensive bottle, Miss Dana?" she asked as she bowed before me. I didn't know who'd put it into her head she had to curtsy to me. Perhaps she had picked that habit from the guys who came to love me when the nights were too hot and I felt like jumping out of my skin.

The men in these parts were undersized as cats. Perhaps the

reasons for this were the severe droughts, undernourishment and other things I couldn't change. I was as powerful as a hill. God must have made a mistake when He decided to make me a woman rather than a man. He must have been sleepy at that time. One way or another, I was unable to conceive, so I'd rather be a man with that towering height he'd put in my bones. After love was over, the undersized men took the money I'd prepared for them, kissed my hand and bowed. For an hour I gave them more than they made as they toiled and moiled at in Sofia, or as they picked olives among the bushes in Spain. They asked me what type of deodorant they should use the next time and wanted to know when I'd summon them again.

I had no idea. It should be too warm or too rainy, or Tano, the only tall man in town, would be too drunk to catch my drift. At times I shouldered Tano and dropped him into the bathtub. I made Isabella, my chief expert in all things under the sun, undress and wash him with cold tap water for me. She preferred using a garden hose and letting the water run over his clothes, shoes and all. That way, she explained, he'd get sober more rapidly. I didn't need anybody else when Tano was available.

"Miss Dana, can I take the Feeble-minded one with me when I come to your place?" he'd asked me many times. "She'll stay an hour or two, no more. I won't drink if I look at her. That's the only way I can stay sober. I have to look at this kid."

One day I allowed him to bring her.

She was a runt of a child, no bigger than Mikhail, and she kept silent as a roof beam all the time. Her eyes reminded me of that woman's face, the one who had breathed her last, strong milk squirting from her breasts for her blue-eyed baby that had turned her blood into poison. I saw the woman's mouth in the weak-headed child, and her delicate bones too. I wondered how she could give birth to three daughters: she'd been so reedy and frail. How could she accommodate the enormous Tano, the Arabian truck driver who fathered her second child and the blue-eyed bad hat who got her pregnant and gave her a blue-eyed cockroach? Life had been hard on her fine bones and her milk.

"Shall I give him good brandy, Miss Dana?" my chief expert Isabella shouted although she knew I hated it most when she asked me the same question twice. What saved her life was her curtsey. She bent to the ground just like the men did: the undersized ones who came to love me but were scared, because they knew how strong I was. I had to get very much tired before I went to sleep.

"Give him the worst brandy we have," I said. "I like the way you bow before me, Isabella. Good for you!"

I gave her ten levs because she was a good girl. She knew what I needed at all times: Stoichko nimble as a weasel although shorter than his own wife, or Tano sturdy as a poplar, cursing under his breath. Isabella brought me the right person at the right time so I counted on her for my own good. I didn't even think what exactly I wanted, she knew better than me: meatballs in a Seville way, or poached eggs from Venice. I disciplined her in cases when I sent for Tano, but she had been unable to keep him sober. As a punishment for her negligence, she had to lug him to the bathroom by herself, lift him and drop him into the bathtub. I hoped that would knock some sense into her.

Tano drank only the most despicable brandy I stored in my cellar but even that was too good for him. I kept that contemptible swill for the short gentlemen callers I regularly had. Small men are like small change, they're good for nothing, I thought. I wouldn't even let them smell my thunderbolt double distilled brandy. I and my girl and chief expert Isabella drank it in the evening. We poured each other twenty five grams of it, which was enough to fill a thimble, no more, no less. Isabella would sit down across from me. I'd swig my thimbleful, she'd down hers, and then we'd repeat the procedure a couple of times. I wouldn't let her go home for I hated to remain alone in a huge house and swill thimblefuls all by myself. Once in a blue moon, the girl would be itching to tell me about her boyfriends—it was only natural she had a lot of them for she made heaps of money off me—but I wouldn't have that.

"Miss Dana," she said one evening, "Do you want me to love you? You haven't tried it and chances are you might like it."

"No," I said. "Stay where you are. I'm okay the way I am."

I wanted her to keep me company. Loneliness was like jaundice to me and I had to be on a special diet to be able to stand it. When I could hear Isabella breathe by my side my fear of big loneliness hid behind the chimney-piece. The two of us drank our thimblefuls, she made me tomato salads with onions and from time to time I asked her to breathe more loudly. Thus, loneliness vanished into thin air the way mushrooms disappeared in dry summers. I knew these toadstools would come up again with the first raindrops, and Isabella's breathing made the dry summer last longer.

"Do you want me to hold your hand, Miss Dana?" the girl asked me but I didn't want that, I wanted her to fix me a tomato salad with onions, to make my bed and wait for Tano to prove he was an inch taller than me. After that she saw Tano off or walked him home.

Before I went to sleep in the evenings, I made her read fairytales to me. My father was a rich man, that was true, but he had no luck with his marriage. My mother had never read fairytales to me. She was too pretty to waste her time with dragons and golden apples. However, that Isabella girl read to me both newspaper articles and novel excerpts with great enthusiasm. She had a lovely voice and she cooked meatballs that had more Italy in them than the city of

Rome itself. She always knew what I'd like to eat. She bought me tailored suits and shoes since I hated shops and malls. I loved my jeep. I got into it and chased hares in the fields. I didn't shoot at them. One day I killed a hare and he squealed so hard and loud that I ran a temperature for a week and Isabella rubbed vinegar and hot water into my skin. What I loved most was to take Tano with me in my jeep and look at him. I didn't let him drink brandy or wine. He was taller when he wasn't drunk. I could admire him for hours even if he was drunk when his lips had turned blue on account of my hogwash brandy.

Now I was watching him guzzle my worst brandy directly from the bottle weeping uncontrollably.

"Stop it!" I said. "Stop it and blow your nose right now."

He wiped his face with his sleeve but his tears as big as buckshots dripped from his eyes onto my sheet. The man had already wet my mattress through and through.

Then Isabella, my expert in all areas of knowledge, entered my sitting room carrying a naked baby in her arms. I knew this runt, blue-eyed like my tomcat Mikhail, crumpled like a piece of yesterday's newspaper, and as dry as the chunk of bread I'd thrown to the dogs in the morning. Isabella carried one more child, too, one with long, disheveled and dirty black hair. The kid's skin was swarthy, her face as small as a plum her eyes deep and black like dried up wells. She was stark naked too, shriveled like a baked fish. A puny naked toddler staggered a couple of strides behind Isabella. The ribs of the little one were as prominent as the coils of an electric heater and her face was the face of that woman who took her milk to the world beyond instead of giving it to her baby.

"My feeble-minded child! My feeble-minded little treasure!" Tano chucked the bottle of despicable brandy on the ground, jumped from the bare mattress and wet as a catfish flew to the rawboned child. It winced and grabbed the hem of my expert's dress, i.e. the girl who knew just exactly what Italy was and cooked Milan and Sicily for me.

"Daddy," the feeble-minded one blurted out.

I didn't know which way to look: the three kids suddenly started squealing all at once, and I was a normal barren woman that had never taken care of a child in her life. I never seriously doubted the truth of my sterility. Many wives in Radomir blessed me for they renovated their houses on my money, raised their kids and fed their pets and I could not conceive a child. I was as barren as the asphalt in the street so I didn't know what to do with the three naked kids.

"Please, please, Miss Dana, please," Tano whimpered as he pressed the feeble-minded child to his chest so powerfully that I feared he might break her weak ribs. "Take the feeble-minded one to live with you, Miss Dana. If you take her I'll love you all day long for free. You won't give me brandy, not a drop! I'll love you more than God loves you. Take her, please!"

"What about the other two cry-babies?" I asked. "What am I to do with the blue-eyed one and the little Arab?"

"Well," my expert Isabella who knew more about Italy than about her own mother said, "Shall I send for Aggo, the junk man?"

3.

"Girls, where are you, girls?" the woman who shouted at the top of her voice was squat and chunky. Her voice was thick like a ball of yarn, and the words she used were a heap of broken branches someone had just set on fire. She had gone out of the second-hand clothes shop where she had just arranged her merchandise, and she was huffing and puffing, her heart clattering like a drawer of an old chest, her hands resting like two cushions on her enormous breasts. "You're no better than geese," the woman panted. "You pair of geese!"

Two female voices rose in the backyard behind the shop, a wild place thickly overgrow with yellow spiky grass, elder trees and brambles. The first voice wove the melody confidently, majestically, with perfect precision. It clambered above the leaves of the grass, soared higher than the old cherry tree whose branches held half of the sky and a whole flock of angry blackbirds. This voice rocketed up to the blackbirds and climbed higher than the clouds; the other voice hobbled like a fettered horse, rolled and fell into the grass with the lizards and waited there powerless, having no tune or melody in it. But the second voice persisted and squeaked on, thin and helpless like a small shovel unable to deal with a huge heap of sand.

"Binna, Sinna," the plump woman shouted. "Come quickly, girls, you two sleeping saucers! Come, your father's very hungry."

The voices suddenly dried up among the bushes. Two girls wearing identical gray dresses, identical ribbons in their hair and identical sandals showed up on the path that led to a small low house. The two of them were almost the same height, thin as leaves of grass. One of the girls had dark skin, narrow face and perfectly brushed dark hair. Her glowing eyes seemed to be bigger than her whole face. The other girl had blue eyes. The quiet sky of July, its happy clouds and warm winds sparkled in her blue eyes. She looked like a little forgotten snowdrift at the end of spring in the wild garden, so out of place amidst the brambles, nettles, in the dust and the shells of dead snails that covered the path.

"You are so beautiful," the dark haired girl muttered. "If only I looked like you..."

"What would you do?" said the girl who carried the month of July and its cloudless sky in her eyes. Her hair was tousled, her dress was old and plain, and the sandals she wore were covered with dust.

"I'd smooch with all the boys one after another behind the library," the black-haired girl shouted. "I'd make them eat their sneakers and I'd wait and watch them do it if they wanted to kiss me one more time. I'd make them lie in the mud, and I'd walk on their tummies. I wouldn't get mud or dust on my shoes. Or I'd stick a stamp to their asses—no, I'd carve the letter S with a branding iron on them so everybody knows they are my boyfriends—every single one of them. Do you see what I'm driving at? All of them, all! If a boyfriend of mine doesn't obey me! I'll make him drink water from my shoe, do you understand?"

The blue-eyed girl smiled dreamily, scratched her head and said, "Come off it, Sinna," but the swarthy girl, gray and more dangerous than a hail cloud, charged against the other thin child. The dark girl bent down. She was a trifle taller and bigger than Blue Eyes, she pushed her to the trunk of the old cherry tree, its branches heavy with all the blackbirds of the small town. She pressed her mouth to the blue-eyed child's mouth, then her teeth slid down and sank into the skin and cut savagely the neck that was softer than January's snow.

"Ouch!" the blue-eyed girl screamed but then the dark face bent closer over the handful of snow and the teeth sank again this time into Blue Eyes' lips.

"I love you, Binna. I want you to know this. If someone does something bad to you, if a boy bites you like this, or draws blood like this..." the swarthy girl bit her and the cut under her teeth oozed blood. "I'll kill him. You are the prettiest girl I've ever seen. If somebody touches you...I'll kill him!"

In a flash the dark girl broke free from the snowdrift, smoothed the other girl's hair, muttering, "Can you ever forgive me for biting you? Look at you! I injured your pretty neck. Will you forgive me?"

"I will," Blue Eyes whispered. "Let's go. Mom's looking for us."

"If you forgive me so easily, I'll bite you one more time. I'll carve wounds on your back, on your belly and your legs. You mustn't forgive me. You must make me crawl like a caterpillar at your feet. You have to crush me!"

"But I forgive you," said the blue-eyed girl. "You are strange, but it is ok. Let's go home, mom's calling us."

"She's not our mom, that pudgy little turtle. A junk-dealer's wife! She's not *my* mother. She chucks me chunks of bread, but that doesn't make her my mother. An old-clothes shrew! If you say one more time she's my mother, I'll bite and bite you and bite until you die. Take this now!"

The dark girl bent, lifted up the other girl's gray skirt and her teeth vanished digging a red angry wound below the Blue Eyes' knee. Sinna thought the knee was cold and sweet like ice-cream although a nest of lizards had already been hatched, and the summer hissed snapping and sweating under their sharp tails.

"Ouch! Let me go!"

"I'll make you never forgive anyone! Do you understand what I want to make you do? I want you to beat me black and blue for biting you. Is that clear?"

"Yes," the blue-eyed girl muttered under her breath as she touched her thigh where Sinna's teeth had carved black bloody marks.

"Do it then! Make me squirm. Make me stew in my own juice or I'll bite you here and here and even there!"

"Well, squirm then," the blue eyed girl said as she rubbed the bruise on her neck.

"Stop it, Binna!" the dark girl spat on the palm of her hand and massaged the bloody bruise below snow white girl's knee, then spat again and carefully, slowly rubbed the welt on her neck. "I love you, Binna. I won't let anybody badger you. Do you want me to sing for you? Do you want?"

The dark girl did not wait for an answer. She opened her mouth and suddenly out of her teeth that a minute ago slashed gashes in the pearly skin, a quiet gentle melody flowed. Binna's song had no words in it, the tune poured and took the hill, a simple "na-na na" and its sounds ran along a powerful brilliant road as if stars flew from the sky into the dry ditch, moons danced with the lizards, and the crags shook. The blackbirds in the cherry tree stopped pecking at the fruit and rose, a heavy, black flock, hiding the sky from view for a whole long minute. The tune mixed with the birds, a thick black melody that for a split second was meek, then kissed the sun, but most of the time bit and kicked, such a powerful and clear melody in her huge voice that the blue-eyed girl froze in her tracks as if someone had tied her to an invisible post.

"Do you like it?" the dark girl asked.

"Yes," the fair-haired girl said. Now more than ever before she looked out of place in the sun-scorched field full of savage summer and wild heat that ate the wind.

"You mustn't speak like you've been dead for ten years!" the dark girl cut her short. "You have to say: 'It's magnificent! I can't breathe, it is so beautiful. I can hear it creeping under my ribs. I can feel it bite my legs and my face. I can see it drink my blood. I can see it put live embers under my ass and I can fly away from here to kill all nasty blackbirds and mosquitos.'"

"It is magnificent. Your song doesn't bite me. You bite me. The song caresses me," the blue-eyed child said.

"Shut up, you silly girl! I love you and the song drags you to the river. And it will drown you in the pool because you are stupid and you stay in this dead field with the lizards."

"I like lizards," the fair-haired girl objected. "Look at them basking in the sun. They look like stones that come to life when they start running."

"I think you are a stone that will never come to life," Sinna said. "A precious stone... some guy will take you and keep you as a fancy decoration. But I won't let him touch you."

"Girls, hey girls"

"We're coming, Mother."

"We're coming, fatty!" the dark girl shouted. "Why are you looking us for? We swept your junk shop in the morning."

"You shut up," a voice, deep and heavy like a cannon-ball, rose in angry protest. "Your father's waiting. It's time for lunch."

"What! Aggo the junkman is not my father. Barren Dana gave him two donkeys and he agreed to take us," the girl snapped the way she had done many times before. "And you, fatty, turned the beasts into sausages. They're still hanging under the eaves. Even the ravens don't want them. They are hard as concrete, your sausages."

The round short woman growled something unintelligible, grabbed at her walking stick and waved it at the dark girl, but the child wasn't scared. She wriggled herself, swayed her hips, lifting up her skirt so it became evident: she had not put on panties because she didn't feel like washing them. She went about the house naked as a fish under her gray skirt and that was the reason why fat Vancha, Aggo the junkman's wife, more often than not sewed her smocks and dresses, using thick fabric that showed nothing of her meager body to prying eyes. The couple had no luck with Sinna. The real name that Aggo's wife chose for the child was Elsinna, but the girl mumbled "Sinna, Sinna" even before she learned to walk. From a very early age, she bared her teeth to all grownups that came her way, snarling like a wolf. She tore at you biting your leg through your pants or your chest through your shirt, attacking like a shark. If you called her "Elsinna," she'd gnaw on your ankle, responding only if you said, "Sinna, dearest." This Sinna, dark like the lower-case letters in a newspaper, drifted about the house or rushed to the yard like this, no panties under her shapeless gingham frocks in front of her husband Aggo the ancient junkman. Vancha knew that the doddering old man didn't look at that place which the gingham frock shouldn't show him. The worse thing was that Sinna went and kissed the old man goodnight. She squatted in front of his bed her eyes glued to his face, her fingers as dark as leeches pressing the blanket that covered his feet. What will this kid do after I die, Vancha's husband fretted? God, she couldn't survive without me.

Years ago, Vancha became aware Aggo was no longer a man. He was only a junk dealer. He was not that much of a man even when he was young. She wondered vaguely how her son came to be. Surely the Holy Virgin Mary had intervened, and one of the rare outbursts of attention on the part of the junkman occasioned the conception of Naum, Vancha's son. Apart from Aggo, Vancha had known no other man. She was not interested in men because men seldom looked at her in the first place and didn't give a damn about her fat paunch. She, on her part didn't respect them at all. The woman was convinced men in general were second-hand dealers keen on wringing every last bedside lamp, tea table or hot plate from the harebrained folks in Radomir District, and the only thing they wanted from their wives was a pork stew. In Vancha's opinion, the only goal husbands pursued was to fill up their stomachs with pork stew; once a year they formed a pretty good idea it was about time to somehow cram a child in their wives' bellies so no one accused them of being good-for-nothing bad eggs.

Therefore, Vancha knew perfectly Aggo the junkman's net worth. He had wanted nothing from her for years now, they slept in separate corner beds, and it was his loud snoring in the night that reminded her that she had a husband at home. Vancha was out of sorts when Sinna, the dark scapegrace, put on fine tulle dresses. All right, Vancha said to herself, who gives this little rag money to buy tulle? Nobody does, but the rag steals from Vancha's second-hand shop that sold used clothes, second-hand curtains, stoves and knives. Generally speaking, all merchandise in the shop was second, third or ninth hand; most probably Sinna filched tulle from the shelf and sewed skirts she put on right away. Everything was plainly visible under these skirts if one cared to have a look, and it was not *that* bad for numerous boys thronged the place exactly for this reason. It was true they didn't care about second and ninth-hand shirts sold in the shop, but Vancha was cunning enough to beguile them into buying a rag or two—a jacket, which looked like a tortoise, or slacks which five nincompoops like the asinine customer could easily crawl into.

So far, so good, the boneheads bought everything, staring at Sinna's tulle; the worst thing was she knocked about like this in front of old Aggo as well. It was not that he even glanced at the perilous place, the poor soul. One shouldn't call him even a junkman anymore come to think about it. His legs hurt so bad he couldn't go around the houses in search of old clothes. He was too weak to manage the shirts and skirts his son Naum transported in huge trucks was it from Germany or the Netherlands? Vancha didn't give it another thought where her son got all these trucks from. When Naum came back home, he gave Sinna an enormous roll of cloth that was as thin as paper—it was silk from Ceylon he had told his mother without explaining where exactly Ceylon was, perhaps somewhere in Germany. However under Sinna's Ceylon you could see all there was to see as if you looked at the map on the wall in plain daylight. Naum also squinted his eyes, trying to see through Sinna's Ceylon although they said there were many girls wearing Ceylon in Germany, and they loved you dirt cheap, you gave them a few euros and they loved all you had from head to toe.

Vancha hated it when her son stared at Sinna, his mouth gaping as he thrust ten-lev bills into her pocket: Sinna had added a special pocket to all her skirts where she collected the money of the guys that watched her Ceylon. These daft guys didn't know a thing about the dreadful diseases which afflicted Ceylon! One's Ceylon could bleed to death at childbirth. One could die like the neighbor's bitch that whelped in March. She had seven puppies and met her maker, the poor beast. Vancha's Ceylon suffered a lot, too. The doctors removed her ovarian cyst, a polyp, then gave her many pills to swallow on account of what Doc Gospod had said—Vancha's Ceylon had sprouted some sort of fungi which had grown so big and strong that Vancha would rather drive a nail in her own eye then go pee in the bathroom or ask Doc Gospod for help one more time.

Guys didn't have the slightest idea about women's diseases, and jostled each other trying to cram the money they should spend on second-hand shirts into that pocket Sinna had added to her skirt. Naum, too, left a fat bundle for her, and Aggo, her junkman husband, didn't even stir a finger, the idiot! Would a junkman protest? Yes, when pigs learned to fly. But in the evening, crushed by pain, his feet swollen like the pillows on the sofa, Aggo asked Sinna, his voice gentle as it was on the day when his son Naum was born, "Please, little Sinna, sing a song for me."

At this point, even Vancha could not deny—that lazy spendthrift although she loafed about the house naked like a fish, dressed only in Ceylon because she was too lazy to wash decent clothes, or maybe because she thought that God knew what was visible under her Ceylon, this good for nothing deadbeat didn't have a voice in her throat—she had a towering steep mountain and ten thousand mineral springs, a hurricane and an ocean in her voice. It was as if God himself descended and waited in the girl's mouth when Sinna started to sing. Perhaps because her mother, Dora, God bless her soul—Dora was a rag all right and she carried the scalps of all truck drivers along the Greek speedway in her apron, but she was as pretty as a picture. Surely even God had spent a night or two in Dora's apron. It was a good thing that the woman died; otherwise she'd have spread infection throughout Radomir district exterminating all men alive, junkmen or no junkmen, who happened to crawl on the surface of the earth at that particular time. Sinna, her daughter, whose father was probably an African guy, had a voice that was stronger that the voices of ten thousand throats. If she sang at night, dawn broke over the town, if a patch of fog had swooped down on the neighborhood, the sun shone and drove it away. If you had stomach ache, it went away, if you were furious, you didn't knock the poor blighter off, you treated him to a beer instead. If you were merry, you suddenly felt like getting married. That was the sort of voice Sinna had in her lungs. Even Vancha who readily brandished her walking stick above the black leech's back could not deny that it was Sinna who cured her nerve diseases with the volcano of her voice.

In the evening as Aggo and Vancha lay in their separate corner beds, Sinna would start crooning. She sang for no more than three minutes; she couldn't stand a song longer than that since laziness made things difficult for her and she beat it to some friend or other, but it turned out those three minutes were enough. Vancha calmed down and slept happily just like Stormy, their dog that lay prostrate like a roof beam in front of the house. Both Stormy and Vancha slept like logs until early in the morning Sinna shouted at the top of her lungs, "Hey, the fat missus over there! I won't sell all day long in your smelly shop for you!"

Or maybe Vancha's dangerous diseases went away on account of Binna, the blue-eyed daughter of that rag, her mother Dora. Dora that had shacked up with all men born in these parts, junk-men or not, and along the highway she had done a lot of things that made one blush with embarrassment. It was true she was pretty even before she met her maker. Maybe guys forget they're junk-men with women like Dora, old Vancha thought. At times God might have descended into their valley and awarded Dora—she was pretty all over the place—to the men. And maybe at that time even if a guy is a junkman, for a split second he becomes generous like a General. And maybe all men who did things with Dora off the highway left their generosity to this blue eyed girl, Binna. It was Vancha that named the child after her own grandmother, God bless her soul. Grandma Albinna was small and plump, given to uproarious quarrels with neighbors and relatives her shrill voice cursing that damned town of Radomir, but the old woman loved Vancha. She gave her sesame rings she'd hidden from her other grandchildren and told little Vancha her favorite fairytale about the Princess and the golden apple. So Vancha named the blue-eyed girl Albinna. But the dark puppy, Sinna, bit and clawed at all men alive that called the fair-haired child Albinna. The dark one said the baby's name was Binna and if you shouted "Albinna, Albie, Binni," the black whirlwind sank her teeth now into your arm, now into your neck or cheek. She bit you through your clothes never letting go until she drew blood.

Blue-eyed Binna was Vancha's medicine. She was the daughter, the cat, the lamb that God had not given Vancha so far. This girl was the last precious coin in her purse, and she was Vancha's "thank you" to God for taking away her nasty diseases from her. Binna could not sing at all, but she could cook magnificently, and her smile started at Easter, warm like bread, and ended at Christmas. Her face gentle with her quiet smile made Vancha forget that nobody cared about her junk shop, that her diseases weighed her down, that her husband Aggo had never said, "You're a great girl," that her son wouldn't get married and day in, day out dragged different sweethearts, a dollar a piece each, to his room. Apart from that, her son Naum had nailed an enormous photo of the dark cloud Sinna, dressed up all in Ceylon, in his room, above his bed. The only thing one could focus on under that Ceylon was Sinna's dark skin as smooth as an asphalt road that would take you either to a ditch to get your skull smashed or to a knife with which your bosom pals would skin you alive. Parallel to the big photo, Naum's room abounded with Sinna's smaller pictures: Sinna in the junk-shop, Sinna in one of the big trucks with which Naum brought dirt-cheap merchandise from Germany, and Sinna sticking out her cheeky tongue at you as if Vancha hadn't had enough of her insults all this time!

"Come on, girls, it's time for lunch." Vancha hated the thought of the snarls and barks she'd receive in response from dark Sinna who would call her "greasy meatball" and then would rumble, "You think you are my mother? Have a good look at me. Do you think I look like you? If I did look like you a tiniest bit, I'd stand all day long by the highway giving money to the guys to spit in my face for being that podgy!"

However, Vancha was impatient to give the kids food because at lunch the blue-eyed girl sat by her side. Binna took her hand as if the skin of Vancha's fingers were not cracked like dried mud on a scorching hot day, Binna held her tired fingers smiling at Vancha, and Easter, Christmas, Virgin Mary's Day, and All Saints Day came all together and lit her face. Then the smiling girl said, "Sit down, mom. I'll bring you soup in your bowl and some soft bread, too. Take it easy, there'll be no crusts, I know your teeth are not that good."

It was then that Vancha said to herself it was true God lived in the sky above Black Peak. To be honest, she had never believed a smile like this could flicker across a human face. In Radomir, faces did not smile. They cursed and screamed, lied, spat and swore, but Vancha rubbed her eyes—lo and behold!—God above Black Peak had given her this smiling child. He had helped her get rid of her nasty diseases and she lived for these hours at lunch when her adopted girl smiled as she poured thin nettle soup or bean stew into her bowl. The girl chose the best, the softest piece of bread for her, brought her the most expensive gold-rimmed plate, the only one remaining of the dinnerware set Naum had brought from the Netherlands. Vancha had sold the other plates to women from the villages nearby, but she had preserved the best one for the blue-eyed child.

At times, Vancha held Binna wishing she could press the child to her heart for hours listening to her breathe so that she became convinced the girl really lived in her house. She wanted to have a year more to look happily at Binna before God took her beyond Black Peak, but then Sinna, black, fuming and growling like Stormy, the dog, when he smelled a cat, wrenched the girl from her hands, waved her fist at Vancha and shrilled, "Don't touch her!"

They all had lunch together. Naum did not sit at the head of the table for he was a guy that frequently went off to Germany, the Netherlands and other Germanies and Netherlands in the world collecting clothes and microwave ovens people had thrown out in the streets. Aggo, the junkman, did not sit at the head of the table either. He had felt from the very beginning he was an unimportant player in his home, and it was a miracle that a son was born to him. It was only natural Vancha didn't sit at the head of the table either. In the best easy chair, the one Naum had procured from an Italian gambler very advantageously indeed, settled down snugly and proudly like a cock on top of a dunghill, sat Sinna.

Blue Eyes cut the bread, poured soup into Vancha's bowl first, her hundred-year old smile gently touching the old woman, then the same smile, somehow sadder caressed Aggo as the girl gave him soup. Then Naum's turn came. He smiled back at Binna, but his was not a grin a man had for a woman he had planned to take to his room. Naum looked at the fair-haired girl the way a guy glanced at a little child that had just learned to ride a bicycle. At the end, Sinna poured soup into her own bowl. They all ate quietly Vancha unable to take her eyes off the serene fair face from time to time reaching out her hand to touch Binna and give her bread. Unlike Sinna, Blue Eyes covered her pearly skin as much as possible while Sinna's neckline was bigger than her whole dress. It revealed a lot of details which Naum had eternalized in numerous photographs. The blue-eyed girl's dress had no neckline to speak of. It buttoned under her chin yet Vancha thought she'd never seen a more beautiful neck although the whole Radomir District regularly visited her junkshop.

Before finishing off with the dessert, Sinna rose from her chair, cut the best part of the cake and placed it in front of her blue-eyed sister, then sat down and glanced either at Aggo, the junkman, or at his son, Naum. If her eyes dwelt on Aggo, the old man, although his feet were dreadfully swollen, staggered up to Sinna, cut the cake and served its pieces slowly, clumsily like a cow having difficulties calving. As he came up to Sinna, placing the cake in front of her, the dark fox stood up and kissed his bald pate, caressed his head and let his eyes enjoy her pretty, dark skin. Maybe Aggo saw the night there. Maybe he saw all junkshops in the world which sold old shirts, trousers and microwave ovens. His face was calm and quiet, a beautiful face of a junkman, who had just bought the old-fashioned but very well preserved shoes of half the world at a very reasonable price. If it was Naum who served Sinna her cake, she didn't bother to look up, didn't budge even, and the man, disgruntled, grunting, dumped a piece of cake in front of his mother, hardly noticing she was there.

Aggo, on his part, silently thanked God for the day when he accepted to raise the two girls. Then Barren Dana paid him two donkeys plus a meager field in which two gypsies dug a ditch thinking there was a treasure buried under a big stone, and the gaping hole unexpectedly spurted mineral water. It was impossible to tap the sloshing and splashing liquid, so a deep pit teeming with frogs and water snakes appeared in practically no time. Guys suffering from weak kidneys came from all parts of Radomir District, squatted down next to the frogs, sucking mineral water, teeming with tadpoles and water snakes, through straws together. It was scary how many weak kidneys there were in one single district! Each visitor paid Vancha 50 pennies for having sucked her water, and she had already filled a shoebox with clinking coins. Aggo was truly happy as in the evening he took a seat close to the box and watched it enraptured for a long, long time. The coins took destitution from his home, drove away poverty that had dogged him all his life, and he had often sensed its teeth sinking into his bones.

Aggo felt even happier when Sinna, brown like a brick from a crumbling cheap house, kissed him at lunch. Aggo did not want to look at her skin or her small sharp breasts. Those things did not really interest him. He wondered why nothing attracted him in this world; maybe that was the reason why he became an old-clothes man focusing on giving the world tit for tat; he collected its garbage and threw it back into the world's maw. Now, an old man, he came to believe that apart from rubbish and refuse there was beauty in Radomir, too. It was Sinna, the only living thing except for his late tomcat King Marko that came up to Aggo without recoiling in disgust from his tired skin. Years ago, Aggo and the tomcat ate off one plate. Then the old King Marko died, letting out a small, tortured sigh, and Aggo the junkman fell ill. Except for King Marko, no one had loved him in the world overflowing with useless fair-weather friends. His wife Vancha didn't say anything but he saw in her eyes she did not think much of him. Yet he was a lucky man. He had deliberately chosen Vancha—a plain, plump woman—so she wouldn't throw temptation in another man's way. Let her make fun of him, it was ok with Aggo. Let her taunt him, but be faithful to him. Let her quarrel with him, but be faithful to him. As if by magic, his son Naum was born wiping shame off Aggo's face.

Then that girl, Sinna, came to his house. Aggo blessed the day when Barren Dana brought him the two babies wrapped in shabby blankets: the blue-eyed one hardly able to breathe. The other one was still vigorous, brown like clay, both of them naked thrust into simple bags of artificial fertilizers which Aggo sold at 50 cents apiece. Then he protested against accepting the babies but Vancha's mulishness prevailed and he drove them home with his truck.

This Sinna! She grew up to be wonderful!

The only living being except King Marko the tomcat that did not loathe the sweat glistening on his balding pate, nor did she hold in abhorrence his legs swollen like balloons below his knees. Sinna brought him warm tea to drink when he was down with pneumonia, and Aggo thought God would take him to that place beyond Black Peak where all junkmen rotted in hell. Sinna made thick soup for him, rubbed brandy and aspirin on his skin to bring down his fever, and she wiped the sweat from his forehead while his own son Naum went and drunk himself to death in a sleazy pub.

"I don't want you to die," Sinna had said, or maybe Aggo had imagined she had said it. "Only you don't look at that pocket I've added to my skirts to collect the money. You are not my father, Aggo, but I want you to know this: I am your daughter!"

4.

THEN I TOOK HER ON, the dim-witted child. I named her Ana, a short name, very easy to remember. I didn't know if she was short-witted or off her nut, how could I know what was happening in her little head? Ana took to closely following my steps, and I was a barren woman. How should I know why a harebrained child would drag like a tail after me? She looked quite scrawny and undernourished, her hands thinner than the cobwebs hanging from the ceiling in the toolshed, her legs reedy like pencils. If I trudged towards the kitchen on account of my growling stomach and extreme hunger, she staggered after me. If I went to pour myself a glass of wine, she crawled on her hands and knees behind my back. I loved red wine; it was my weakness so I could drink red wine for four consecutive weeks without interruption. Down in my cellar, I had five thousand bottles, and I could drink them all by myself. I usually sat on the floor in the living room. It was covered with a thick carpet bought by my chief expert Isabella. She knew everything there was to know about dresses and carpets, Italian recipes and dishes and guys, but she knew nothing of wine. In the beginning, I made her sit down by my side and drink together with me, but after downing the second glass, Isabella wore a big grin on her face, got blotto within seconds, collapsed on the carpet and went to sleep.

"Isabella, wake up. Come on, wake up. Let's drink another one!"

"Ok, Miss Dana, just as you say. Give me another one," she mouthed, however all she did was pour wine on her hair and drip onto the white carpet. "I love you so much, Miss Dana," she added, dropping asleep right away.

I enjoyed sitting on the carpet by her side, and the wine couldn't get the better of me for I was tall and it could hardly reach my head. I didn't belong to the short, small folks in these parts; I was as big as the hut below Black Peak which jutted out like a crown above Radomir. So I slurped my wine and chewed dried donkey sirloin—I bred a special donkey breed: small and wiry. I personally brought them water, and I fed special feed to them, a mixture of wheat, barley and millet, so I obtained dried sirloin suited exactly to a big lady like me: the meat was both hard and its smell was delicious, warding off inebriation. So I chugged a few glasses slowly, serenely, imbibing my best red wine. I made it from my vineyard on the southern slope of a hill called Pounder—if you climbed to the top and your heart didn't pound hard and loud like a smithy, then you'd live to be a hundred, and God wasn't in a hurry to summon you beyond Black Peak. Therefore I made use of the opportunity since God didn't care about dragging me beyond the peak, downed the red thunder and chewed my donkey sirloin—I had cut the beasts' throats with my own hands, and I prepared the minced meat as well. Isabella slept like a top by my side. The red wine was too strong for her and she pissed in her pants. She made a puddle plump in the middle of my white carpet, but I was not that persnickety in this respect. On the following day she'd clean up her mess and the only thing I was mad at was that I had no company: I didn't have anybody to get drunk with like a normal lady.

These days, as I drank serenely, the little harebrained girl sat by my side, staring at my face. At times, she grabbed at a piece of donkey sirloin and chewed on it. I was scared stiff she might choke on her own tongue; she was a little bit silly and could pronounce one single word, "Daddy." She called Tano "Daddy" after I summoned him when I had the blues again in the scorching heat. The guy kept his promise, and he loved me like a lord free of charge all the time. The harebrained wee lassie called me "Daddy" too as she clutched at my trouser leg. The kiddie was often exhausted, heavy with hours of creeping like a beetle in my wake. Then she hung on my pant leg muttering "Kiss girl, kiss girl." I kissed her cheek once, but her shirt smelled like rot and I could not endure it, so I said to Isabella, "Hey, Bella, give a bath to the half-witted lassie. She stinks like a rubbish bin."

Isabella really botched up the bath. In my opinion, that woman wasn't barren, not by a long shot, but she was no good at giving kids baths. She was expert at selecting guys for me, the only thing she did was glance at my mug, and she knew if I wanted a man as meek and tractable as a heap of sand in front of the Town Hall, or I needed Stoichko—the dude was as small as a hen, but on the other hand he was a high-spirited eagle, I gave him that. Therefore, Isabella gave the toddler one more bath, but she still smelled like a dustbin. Then I made Tano, the father of this unfortunate pumpkin, give her a bath. Tano took his time indeed, spending half a day bathing the kid in a kitchen sink and the little girl shone like the sun, but Tano put the same filthy shirt on the little one's back, so the lassie stank worse than before. Isabella was tasked with buying some kiddie clothes and at long last the little girl stopped stinking of manure and dead swans.

"Look here, Dana," Tano said. "Her mother used to wear dresses, and the kid held onto the hem. Why don't you buy a dress, too?"

"Dana in a dress! Hey, Tano, have you ever seen Black Peak don gloves and dress?"

"I haven't," he admitted. "Look here, woman, it's not important if it's a mountain or a fish. What matters here is that the thing puts on a dress. Ok?"

I was as crazy as March hare, I took Tano's advice and summoned my chief expert Isabella.

"Bella *mia,*" I ordered. "Go buy me a dress from the shop in Radomir."

"Oh! Are you ok, Miss Dana?" she mouthed. "Do you want aspirin or some other medicine?"

Apart from cooking splendid Italian and Spanish pizzas, she cured me from different diseases and scratched my back when my skin was itchy.

"Buy me a dress right away or I'll fire you here and now!" I threatened. "You know how many women are waiting outside? I have to wave my arms and you're cooked."

"You can't wave your arms without me," she pointed out and she was perfectly right.

So far so good. They didn't have dresses for a sturdy woman like me. One way or another, Bella *mia* bought a gown and I tried hard to drive my torso into it, but the damned rag was too short. It stuck like glue to my tits and wouldn't budge. Therefore, I made Isabella cut a curtain into pieces—gorgeous red merchandise from Italy it was, costing five hundred juicy euros, and lo and behold, Isabella sewed me the most magnificent attire!

"You have to treat me to a box of chocolates, Miss Dana!" Isabella said. "This is a lovely evening gown, and you can take my word for it. It will be very becoming on you. You'll be a model, Miss Dana, I tell you."

So I put on the dress, and Tano commented, "Get rid of this tent, woman. You look like a cow in it."

Then the harebrained lassie saw me dolled up in my dress,

stuck herself like a stamp onto the hem, gripped the skirt, shouting, "Mommy! Mommy!" I have never been so happy in my entire life although I was a very happy woman. If I went through all my pockets I found a bundle in each one of them. It was my dairy, my dressmaking and tailoring workshops, my forests and my flocks of sheep that provided peasants and townsfolk with jobs in these parts. Therefore I said to Isabella, "Look here, Bella *mia,* I'll hold a delicious feast for a very good reason indeed: the loopy kid calls me 'mommy'!"

Wasn't that a nice cup of tea! Isabella broiled a young lamb for me. In the beginning, I drank some powerful plumb brandy with Isabella from cups as tiny as thimbles, then I made her drink red wine with me, but after the third glass she was dropping asleep like a sack of turnips. Therefore, I said to myself, if you, barren Dana, fall into a deep sleep and the slowwitted girl goes out of the room? She'll get drowned in the fountain!" And a peculiar child she was: sat all day in her little chair, watching me like frozen in her tracks. I gave her bread to eat and she wouldn't touch it. I threw a piece of meat at her as if she was a dog, and the little one snatched at the food and gobbled it down. I felt drowsy, so I lay down on my bed. The kid had her own little crib. It was Aggo the junkman that gave it to me for free because at that time I wasn't sure if I was going to keep the kid in my house, or foist her on Isabella to bundle her away. After I crawled into bed, the silly thing came up to me, climbed into bed and snuggled close to my feet dressed in her tiny pajamas. She didn't cover herself with the blanket, just hugged my knees and said once more, "Mommy!" Should I make Isabella bring Tano to me, I was wondering at that time, but the kid's little voice changed everything in a flash.

"What is it, Ana?" I asked and the girl, on hearing my words, crept out then snaked her way under the bed.

"Why are you hiding from me, kiddie? Come here. Please!" I said as imploringly as I could. But Ana, being harebrained, didn't budge, and the more I implored her, the deeper under the bed she edged.

Isabella lay prostrate, stone drunk, sleeping like a rusty rail, therefore I kicked her several times, shouting, "Sober up, you, and get the half-wit out from under the bed."

Isabella seemed to sober up as she pushed her head under the bed to extract the kid, then she went to sleep on the spot. She'd got so bent out of shape that another yellow puddle appeared on my white carpet, but I was dreadfully worried: the girl kept mum under the bed. I couldn't see or hear her, so I panicked: she might've choked to death, and she could be pushing up daisies! A one and only harebrained child called you "Mommy", and what did you, barren Dana, do? Let the kid croak, you idiot! No. Over my dead body!

"Little halfwit sweetheart! Silly darling!" I shouted and pleaded with her, but the girl had vanished into thin air. I had sunk into my curtain dress like a bull in mud, so I tried hard to scramble to my feet, but stepped on the hem and reeled back dangerously against the wall. I was sure I wasn't drunk because I'd received special training in this sphere. I'd drunk four bottles of wine all by myself and I made a bet with Stoichko that I could climb the cherry tree and pick cherries and shoot blackbirds. Yes, I'd poured a gallon of red thunder into my belly and sniped at blackbirds like a champion. On the following morning, Stoichko and I counted how many songsters I'd gunned down; he counted four, but maybe there were more, for I had three tomcats, therefore I reckoned that each of my beasts had breakfasted on a birdie or two. I wasn't drunk, yes, I was only furious at the small nitwit for slinking off under my bed, and with Isabella for snoring, three sheets to the wind, under my bed, too.

"Tano! Tano!" I called out.

After I took the harebrained girl to live in my own room, her father Tano moved in with me, settling down in the backyard. I had a heart of gold but I had brains as well so I refused to let Tano set foot in my house. Every cobbler must stick to his last, I thought to myself, and right I was. Let him love you as much as you want, then send him packing. You've provided him with enough space in the storage shed for garden tools so let him stay with the spades, rakes and pickaxes, I said out loud. The shed was as good as any other building for him. It was just under my bedroom window, so I could watch him like a hawk to prevent him from running away. On the other hand if I wanted to have sex, all I had to do was rush to the shed. If it was scorching hot in July or if by chance it rained cats and dogs, I didn't even bother to open the window. I roared, "Tano!" and if the man was not drunk, he ran like stink to me, strapping Tano, the only guy an inch taller than me in southern Bulgaria. In the garden shed, I left more food for him than all workers toiling and moiling on the highway Sofia—Athens had ever dreamed of. I gave him a pail of honey biscuits Isabella had baked especially for him. There was another pail full to the brim with chunks of meat, chicken, veal, pork, and the big wooden bucket was crammed full of fruits like apples, pears, bananas etc. Isabella bought bars of chocolates and stored them in a crate for Tano to eat. And I had only one condition: I wanted him sober whenever I summoned him, and I summoned him because I'd also eaten bars of chocolate, I'd gorged myself on a ton of chocolates and I could jump over the six-foot stone wall surrounding my house and backyard. Well, I guzzled red thunder wine when I felt like sending for Tano. In the morning, the man was a sack of turnips, unable to budge, incapable of waking up and speaking to me. Therefore I said to Isabella, "Throw him out of the room. I want to sleep, too."

Isabella pushed him, kicked him, put a wet shirt on his forehead, but Tano neither stirred nor twitched a muscle. I made up my mind it was much more convenient to put an old mattress in the garden shed. Therefore, I told Aggo the junkman, "Take twenty levs, man, and give me a mattress. It can be a torn one for all I care." Then I inquired after the two babies I had sent him.

"The babies are doing fine, God bless you, Miss Dana," the junkman said. "Especially the plainer one, you remember her, the darker one. She's like medicine to me. Yes, it is true, Miss Dana, this girl rescues me from death every day."

"You see, Aggo, your mattress interests me much more than your death. Well, I wish you good health. Bring the thing here and leave it in front of the shed. Here, I give you ten levs more. Buy the babies a box of biscuits each."

Therefore, I kept not only rakes, pickaxes and hoes in the shed; I had a mattress there as well, so instead of bawling for Tano, I ran to the building as fast as I could. We reached an agreement for the tall man not to get pickled on Wednesdays, Thursdays, Fridays and Saturdays. I had filled his crate with chocolates and his pails with superb food, so I descended to the mattress on Wednesday to check on him, and lo and behold, the gentleman had unwrapped seven chocolate bars, had bitten into seven apples, and two empty brandy bottles lay at his feet. After two bottles of my cheap brandy even an iron casket would get looped, and would stay drunk for a fortnight.

"You, lousy nit, I told you not to get blotto on Wednesdays, Thursdays, Fridays and Saturdays!" I yelled while he lay stretched out face downwards, incapable of registering my presence. Well, he was not to blame in this case. Isabella was to blame. Isabella was the guilty party, Isabella, the total scumbag, had given him brandy and let him swill two bottles like an eel.

"Isabella! Guilty Isabella, you are guilty all over the place!" I hissed. "Pour a pail of water over this idiot's head. Today is Wednesday, you clucking hen! Why did you give him brandy? Wake the moron up, spruce him up for me, or you'll take his place on the mattress. Do I make myself clear?"

Isabella's head however was a block of wood on account of the wine. She remained stuck under my bed. As for the harebrained little pumpkin, I could neither see her nor hear her breathing. So I waited as mad as an erupting volcano in my red curtain dress, Isabella's yellow puddles gleaming at my feet, the tiny halfwit darling had vanished under my bed, and nobody called me "mommy, mommy" anymore. What should I do? Well, I had also quaffed half a gallon of the red thunderclap from the southern slope, gorgeous wine I sold only to Brits and Fritzes from Munich or Dusseldorf. I'd like to make a point here that I still hadn't sold *all* the red thunder from the southern slope to Brits and Fritzes therefore some wine boiled and bubbled most radically in my head. I felt like flying as much as my red curtain dress would allow me, and parallel to that I was raging mad with that near seven-foot tall mule Tano that lay flat, drained and looped in the garden shed. Therefore I ran to the shed, collapsed on top of him, and got no response. Then I stepped on his back and walked along it: no response again.

"Hello there! Today is Wednesday, Wednesday, you filthy bull," I shouted, but he couldn't care less as he snored on the concrete floor.

What should I do? What?

"Isabella, dirty and guilty Isabella!" I bawled, hardly able to stir a finger in that abominable dress which had coiled itself up into a ball on my bellybutton: a venomous snake of a dress it was.

"Is today Wednesday, guilty Isabella?" I asked, but she didn't know if today was Wednesday. She had thrust her chest under the bed and slept like a bump on a log.

I made efforts to open the front door, a huge iron affair embedded in the stone wall, surrounding my house. It was unbearably difficult for me to walk in this darned dress; now the hem hit my tits, now I stepped on it. Donning a dress was a proof my stupidity knew no bounds. I could not breathe, the thing closed in on all sides. Why did I put it on in the first place? I did it for the hare-brained sweetheart. It could hold on to the skirt and then call me "Mommy!" Wasn't I nuts?!

Stoichko's house was just a stone's throw from mine. I ran towards his front door, pounded, kicked and attacked it, all to no avail. The family slept like moles, but they didn't know me. I grabbed a stone and hit the door with it. At a certain point, Stoichko's wife, like a fat rat, trudged up to me. Then Stoichko, in his pajamas, slipped out of the house, a guy as short as a criminal. In my opinion, all short men should be imprisoned, however in this case I was lucky they had not put Stoichko in prison, for it was Wednesday, and I needed his assistance.

"Miss Dana, do you want me to give you aspirin or anti-diarrheal drug?" the wife asked. Her voice had difficulty creeping out of her cheap nightgown. "Miss Dana, do you want me to make camp bed for you? You can lie down on it while we wait for Doc Gospod. It's well past midnight, and she's probably sound asleep, the poor old Doc she is. Wait a sec, Miss Dana, just wait a sec." and the woman bent forward and you could see she was about to kiss my hand.

"Stoichko!" I shouted at the top of my strong lungs. "Get up, man. We have to tug on a little child that got stuck under my bed."

He set out for my backyard in only his pajamas bottoms, creased gray pajamas the cheapest I made in my dressmaking establishment on the top of the hill. It was at that moment that I felt the red assassin wine I sold to Fritzes and English dudes, the explosion I made from the vines on the southern slope, had sneaked into my brain and pulled me towards the dust on the path. Perhaps I had not eaten enough meat at dinner for I could walk no more. I must have tumbled to the ground plumb in the middle of Stoicho's backyard, and the small man got lucky I didn't collapse on him for the only trace he'd have left would be a yellow puddle like the ones Isabella produced on my white carpet. Although Stoichko was smaller than his wife, he was a tough guy. That particular Wednesday, Stoicho's power was more enormous than the wine I sold to the Fritzes, greater than his gray cheap pajamas, and much bigger than the man. It turned out he'd dragged me from his backyard to my house, and put me to bed. I couldn't tell you how long I'd slept. At noon, I woke up in my bed, feeling happy I wasn't wet with the morning dew. Stoichko had vanished into thin air. Somebody had covered me with two thick blankets, and the harebrained toddler slept tucked up in her crib. Isabella must have sobered up earlier than me.

5.

"THE COFFEE YOU GAVE ME is no good," the dark woman said as she pushed her cup aside. "Give me coffee the way I like it. Come on."

The man, tall and thin, his face like a heated heap of scrambled eggs, did not budge in his bed.

"Ok," the woman said. Her dark skin suddenly flowed all over him, her wild black hair splashed her shoulders. She pressed her body against the man, bit into his lower lip and after a couple of seconds droplets of blood dripped from her teeth. He groaned, but the woman wouldn't let go of him, her teeth climbed down his chin, his neck sinking into his flesh that was as white as curds. The man whimpered and she wouldn't let him go. Her teeth played for a while with his skin, then got drowned in his stomach, soft, whitish, with lots of thick yellow hairs around his belly button.

He moaned quietly, happily, relaxing in her arms. She bit his nipples, then his armpits, working out the reddish-blue route of her teeth all over his body, transforming the dimple above his knee into her last stop.

"Don't make a move," she said. "Keep quiet."

The man, obedient, meek, tried to hold his previous pose, but she pushed him back, weighing him down under her dark body as if she wanted to creep under the yellow hairs on his chest.

"You know the coffee I like," she said.

The man didn't respond. She pressed against him one more time, as his head obediently turned in the direction she had chosen.

"Come on," she said.

The room was white everywhere: white walls, white ceiling, white marble floor, white frame of the enormous mirror, even the night above her dark body was white. The man sank back into his bed, his hand freezing on the smooth, swarthy patch of her stomach as she hissed, "Coffee!"

The man scrambled to his feet, transparently white, lost in the white flowing contours of the walls, a white shadow of a man on his way to brewing coffee.

"Come back," the woman summoned him back to her pillow. "Now I want something else."

He hesitated then obeyed her, bending down to touch her body. She punched his chest, pushed him onto the thick white carpet on the floor and her teeth carved a shallow bluish-red pathway through his obedient skin.

"Now you can bring me some coffee," she said after a short while. "Remember this for the next time: when I want something from you, make it the way I want it. You have to know that."

"I love you," the man blurted out. "Sinna, Sinna, Sinna…" His mouth was paralyzed as his lips repeated her name throwing the sounds into the groove of his weakness.

"Our son's screaming," she cut him sort. "Go check what he wants."

"His nanny is in his room," the man muttered. "I'm afraid I might disturb his sleep."

She did not look at him as she reached out her hand towards his pearly white skin. This time her nails landed on his stomach, but did not claw him, her fingers declaring a state of readiness, as taut as the spring of a mouse trap.

"Make sure the baby's all right, or I'll tie you to a kitchen chair," she whispered. "Then I'll bite until you stop breathing. Now run."

"Tie me," he breathed. "I love you. I'm crazy about you. Sinna, Sinna..." his voice landed again in the furrow her name had dug in his mind.

"I thought you were in love with my sister," she said. "Haven't you written a poem about her blue eyes? As far as I remember you wanted to marry her. You married me instead."

"But then I didn't know you."

She grabbed his hand and dragged him out of the room. The house was as big as a hill, startlingly white outlined against the blackboard of the night. The white verandas, the eccentric outlines of intermediate floors, bizarre turrets jutting out above well-lit rooms made the place look both magnificent and unreal.

"Where are we going?"

She gave him no answer as she tugged at his shirt, making up her mind, then she pushed him onto the concrete alley which ended out of sight in front of the garbage can.

"I'll do it here," she said. "Next time brew coffee for me when I tell you. Does it hurt like this?"

"Yes," he said. "It hurts."

"Does it hurt worse now?"

"Yes," he said.

"This is because you wrote a poem about Binna's blue eyes. Now you know why I hurt you so bad. You didn't write a word about my eyes." Then she kissed his jutting, gasping ribs, kissed all of them in turn, her teeth sinking into his whitish goose skin. "You are as white as a worm," she said as she pressed his back against the paving blocks. "Does it hurt now? Tell me."

"It hurts a lot."

"You jilted her and you married me. I'm punishing you. I love her. I love her a million times more than I love you. Do I make myself clear?"

"You do."

She suddenly jumped to her feet leaving him prostrate in the alley that went no further than the black dustbin. Behind it, night began and the black hill devoured its moon. He tried to sit up.

"Don't move," she said.

"Again?" he said, broken-hearted.

"Again," she said. "You should have made coffee for me when I wanted it."

"I'll make you some coffee now," the man scrambled to his feet. He was much stronger than she as he caught up with her not far from the house that was empty like a crater of a dead volcano in the avalanche of the pine forests surrounding it.

"Don't go," said the man. "Our son will wake up. He'll cry for you."

She ran along the alley, stark naked like a silverfish, endless like the night, menacing like that hill that one day would collapse burying the white verandas and turrets of the house.

"Think of the boy," he implored. She said nothing. "He'll throw you out. He will, I tell you, like it happened last year. I'll give you a ride, if you want... and I will wait for you..."

"Your coffee was no good," she said, not turning back.

"When will you come back?" the man asked, but the night kept silent. "Naum won't let you see the child," the man said and the dark wind devoured his words. "If he does something bad to you... if he calls you names... I'll kill him. I'll pay and they'll kill him for me. They'll cut his belly into pieces! I'll pay them!"

6.

"WHAT!" THE SHORT GRAY-HAIRED WOMAN froze in her tracks spluttering, saliva flying from her mouth, her kerchief loose around her neck, her neck rumpled like an old shoe, bloodshot, looking reddish-black.

"Stop hissing, you fat lump," the dark-haired girl said. "If you don't shut up, I'll tell everybody in the neighborhood that Aggo's his father."

"Goodness!" the old plump woman panted as she suddenly stopped spluttering, sweat and anxiety spewing from all her pores. Her face seemed to drip together with her sweat, soaking into her faded cheap dress.

"So you think Aggo can't do it, eh? He can't do it with you. Everybody can do it with me, even a dead man. Is it clear? A cripple can too."

"Wait, please wait, Sinna. Listen to me," Vancha gasped and pressed her hands against her heart, then clutched at her dress and tore it open on her chest. Her skin at places swollen and bumpy with lumps of lard, at others sunken and sagging, glistened with sweat. "Wait! Can't you abort this baby? I'll pay, I will. I'll call Doc

Gospod right now. She'll cut it like a pear in no time and you... you'll get rid of it. You'll be free."

"You want me to abort the kid, eh?" the dark girl stuck out her tongue at Vancha. "Do you want me to kick your ass or bite it for a change? Look at your neck! Isn't it gorgeous? I'll bite it in half then I'll call Doc Gospod to stitch it up. What do you say?"

The old woman winced and took a couple of steps back. Sinna guffawed and patted her stomach.

"Scared, are you, old bag? You can feel how it kicks."

Frowning, Vancha tried to withdraw from the battlefield as the dark shadow grabbed her shoulder.

"If you don't put your fat hand on my stomach now," she growled, "I'll bite and I'll chew you until you look like that pelt," the dark one pointed at the pear tree where a bloody sheepskin of a recently slaughtered ewe was left to dry in the sun. "Give me your hand. Now."

"Okay, Okay, let the baby kick," the short plump woman mumbled.

"I said 'Give me your hand'" the dark one pulled Vancha's wrist that was as thick as a blood pudding, then lifted her skirt made of fine red tulle. Her skin gleamed like wet asphalt, and her stomach wobbled like a small molehill in which a little mole pushed and kicked in a dark prison.

"Shame on you! All neighbors are looking. Pull your skirt down!" the old woman lisped out.

The dark molehill turned with the speed of lightning to the neighbors' backyard her naked bellybutton pointed at the sky. She had no fear the little mole inside her might be cold.

"Okay, Okay," the old woman said. "Let me feel how it kicks." Her swollen hand crawled like a rat and stopped on the protruding belly. "So it can be our neighbor's child?" she asked her voice full of hope. "Tell me honestly, Sinna. Look at God and tell me," she turned her eyes towards the Black Peak. Everybody in Radomir believed God came there from time to time to have a look at their valley. "It's not Naum's child... it's not my son's child, is it?"

"Feel how it kicks," the dark molehill smiled. "This kid is as strong as an ox."

"Yes, it will be a strong baby," the old one said. "Please tell me it's not Naum's child."

"Why not?" Sinna smirked as she let fall the red tulle on the baby that was as strong as an ox, and patted it with her hand, satisfied. "Have no doubts about Aggo, Vancha. All I can say now is that the mite is not Aggo's son."

"Aggo's sick, the pour soul. He sleeps like a stone by my side. His legs are no good...he can't even get out of bed without me. You sing to him every evening... but he never talked to you in private..."

"Hey, Vancha, tell me why you summoned the police officer, and told him to put me under arrest? Make a full confession why you sent for Sto, the policeman."

At the end of March, the grass was still brown and there was nothing the sheep could graze. If you hadn't bought enough fodder from Barren Dana, you'd have to skin many a sheep pelts and let them dry on your pear trees. Even if you did buy fodder from Barren Dana you couldn't pay the vet. Sheep suffered from some horrible disease so all farmers turned to Barren Dana for help. She gave you a loan and you paid the vet to save your cattle from the axe, and you'd even have a buck or two to buy your toddlers cough medicine. It was always the same smelly syrup Doc Gospod prescribed. The flu was poison, six days it sucked you wry and dry, and if you didn't ask Barren Dana for a loan to buy Zinat, that damned drug, you never knew: it was a question of your kid or his grave.

At this point Vancha blessed Barren Dana's soul on account of the loan; Vancha was grateful she managed to drive away the grave from Aggo's swollen feet. If she had buried her junkman of a husband where would old Vancha find a shoulder to cry on, whom could she tell about Sinna, this big-headed fish, and about the mole in her belly? She couldn't talk to a stranger about it. Whose child was the little mole? Was it Naum's? On the other hand, many women died during childbirth. Sinna had turned her tulle into an inn: if you paid, you entered any time you pleased. Vancha felt her heart like stale bread inside her chest. Even if Sinna didn't kick the bucket during childbirth, you could leave the newborn mole in a room with open windows. A day or two of open windows and there would be no more mole to speak about. No! Dark thoughts seared her mind. Shut up, Vancha, stupid woman! This is a sin, you old hag! Don't you dare do this! A newborn baby is the most important thing in the world. You can't leave a baby in a room and open the window. No matter if it's Sinna's child. It has a soul too, doesn't it?

What if it was his her son's baby? What if it wasn't? At that point Vancha remembered her neighbor, the baker's wife. The woman had gone to Spain to pick olives there. Her husband, the baker, sold their car, and spent all the money he took from the deal in Vancha's second-hand shop. Indeed, he came every day and bought rags left and right. The old wives said the baker burned the second-hand clothes he bought in his stove so they didn't smell of carrion and old geezers from Europe in his house. The big-headed fish, Sinna, who now carried her big pregnant belly like a banner, went to clean his living room for him. Vancha wished God had cleaned up this baker from the world. Then perhaps He could deal with Sinna, the impudent frog. She cleaned many other living rooms in town; she struck roots in the backyards of those men whose wives were in Italy, Spain or UK, taking care of old ladies and gentlemen. Sinna burst into bloom for the blockheads that had come back home to Radomir from Rome, Paris or Vancouver with pockets full of dough, after they had shoveled tons of manure into trucks all over the world to earn it. Sinna cleaned the living rooms of all city bigwigs that had villas in Radomir; the cheeky tart struck the high-standing folks speechless, and their wives, accompanied by a police officer, trudged through snow and mud to collect their erring husbands. A banker from Sofia, the capital of Bulgaria, who like Aggo was more of a junkman than a husband, had said to Sinna, "You've got talent!"

At that point Vancha had speculated as to whether "talent" was her ability to clean men's living rooms: on the one hand she took all their money, one on the other she made them sell their furniture to buy her red tulle. The bigwigs from Sofia wept for Sinna's cuckoo's nest—"Don't go, Sinna. Please. I cannot breathe without you. I cannot smoke without you." Vancha had heard her husband Aggo speak to Sinna, "Sinna, only you and my tomcat Marko the Magnificent, God bless his soul over the Black Peak, are decent folks for me. I can live without my medicines, Sinna, but I cannot live if you don't kiss me Good night. I cannot take a deep breath if you don't sing to me. I cannot take the pills for my swollen legs. I'll ask God to take me away from my bed if you go away and I couldn't hear your songs under my roof, Sinna."

That was what the old grouch babbled. However it was not the reason why Vancha had sent for Sto the policeman, asking him to put the swollen-headed pest under arrest. It was not even the fact that Sinna had cleaned for Vancha's son Naum when he brought the trucks full of second-hand merchandise to Radomir. Poor Naum was a dunce as well. He spent his hard-earned euros on red tulle and transparent Ceylon for the frog with her dirty mouth.

"I want you to know that Police Officer Sto did not drive to the police station after he put me under arrest," Sinna explained to the old woman. "He took me to his house, and I took care of his guestroom."

"He doesn't have a guestroom, you liar," said Vancha, outraged.

"Well, I cleaned it all the same. Now Police Officer Sto has a sparkling clean house." Sinna laughed and reached out her hand to the junkman's wife. "This gold ring here, on my middle finger, can you see it Vancha? It belongs to Sto's mother. Are you interested to learn more about that?"

"No!" the old woman breathed.

"Isn't it beautiful!" the dark girl smirked. "It's the last thing of value they have in the family, that was what Sto told me. Well, Police Officer Sto is as poor as the dry hawthorn bush over there. Can you see the dry hawthorn tree, fat woman? That's how dirt poor Sto is. No other woman would be talked into cleaning Sto's guestroom. That's why he gave me the ring. Would you care to know what he said? He said, 'Please, Sinna, come twice a day to clean my guestroom. Come three times!' I think, however, he can't do it three times a day, he's a weakling. 'I'll apply for leave,' he said. 'Tell me when you'll come, and I'll go on leave for you.' Do you like the ring, little lump, police officer Sto's ring?"

"Listen..." the old woman said as she stared at the Black Peak.

"Now explain to me why you wanted Sto to put me under arrest? Be careful. If I catch you in a lie I'll bite your neck in a way Aggo had never bitten you."

"But..." the old woman muttered under her breath, crashing down onto the bench. She could not stand for a long time. Her feet hurt several months after she gave birth to her son Naum, now something was wrong with her heart and she was drawn to benches and chairs most of the time.

"No buts! You cackle your 'buts' to you dim-witted friends. Tell me why you sent for police officer Sto. Now."

"Binna," the old woman said under her breath. "I did it for her sake. I sent for Sto to put a curb on you. You let no boy come close to Binna. You shoot Aggo's shotgun at any man that's talking to her. Then you go to Binna and you…"

"What?" the dark girl bristled as she gripped Vancha's swollen hand that was as sticky as cheesecake.

"I…" the old woman hesitated. "You know what."

Vancha felt sorry for blue-eyed Binna. She had lived too long and all these years had taught her to love her more then she loved her son Naum, a grown-up man who was no more her own blood. While he was in Bulgaria, Naum constantly arranged cut-price deals selling his merchandise: threadbare suits, shabby pullovers and old shoes which feet of German grandmas and grandpas had sweated in before God took them to Black Peak. The pullovers belonged to well-fed Spanish old-age pensioners who looked very much like Vancha. Her son tried to find a place where he could cheaply kill lice, fungi and other vermin by pouring chemicals over his second-hand or 22nd–hand clothes. Doc Gospod has said that fungi had sprouted exuberantly in the worst place of her body; the doctors had removed her cyst and the polyp from that same dangerous place. Naum had seen the light of day as he squirmed out from that place, and a bucket of her blood had poured out of her from that place after she gave birth to him. Yes, Naum was her son, but he also was the son of the second-hand merchandise, which used to belong to the plump Spanish and Italian old women and retired ladies. He was the son of the old shoes which he sold complete with the fungi that throve in their soles. Vancha's child was Binna, the blue-eyed girl. She combed the old woman's hair and she rubbed her aching back when she came down with a bad attack of the flu, a nasty disease that quickly turned into pneumonia.

Binna learned to give her insulin injections after Vancha contracted diabetes. Binna gave her these injections in the morning and in the evening telling the old woman about the big book she had read in the library. Her blue eyes were as quiet as the road to Radomir in January, soft and serene like the clouds in summer. Vancha prayed she could look into those good eyes as many days as God had made up his mind to let her toil and moil, and suffer from diabetes and flus that hurled her down onto benches and couches as if she were a sheaf of straw.

"Good night, Mom," that girl said to her in the evening. No voice had sounded like a warm cup of tea for Vancha before. She listened for this voice day and night. Binna was so pretty, as pretty as a picture! Vancha knew the city folks said any picture on the wall was a *landscape*, but the old woman was convinced no painter and no artist in the world—even the ones she'd seen on the TV—could put on paper or on a blank canvas Binna's beauty, *landscape* or not. Boys came to the library on account of Binna, and it was a narrow dank place which smelled of mice.

Vancha was worried sick that poisonous flu would strike her girl. Boys put up with the mice in the library, hoping to have a word with Binna. Sinna, the black dust devil, ambushed the guy who had talked to the pretty librarian, and opened fire on him with Aggo's shotgun. Sinna had already put all Aggo's buck-shots in in the guys' backsides, and Vancha knew it was not the musty smell of books and mice that attracted the boys to the cold narrow room. No, Vancha didn't begrudge Sinna the buck-shots. The old woman was scared stiff that those young men on coming back from Spain where they'd picked all the olives they could get their hands on, and still smelled of the lousy shacks and beds they'd slept in, would deceive and hurt her blue-eyed daughter. She didn't want an olive picker for her girl. But who else would set foot in that icy morgue where even the books suffered from whooping cough in the humid darkness?

On the other hand, Vancha knew that time passed, and any woman, no matter how old she was should have an Aggo by her side. Her Aggo wasn't much of a guy—he was a rag-and-bone man—but he gave her a son. Vancha knew that her blue-eyed daughter should have an Aggo of her own, so she prayed for a kind-hearted guy. "Make a good man visit the library, God! Then send him again packing, but let him first make Binna a little son. Then let the wind throw the bastard out to the prickly bushes in Spain." Vancha hoped there were wolves in the Spanish bushes, and those beasts in her prayers were hungry so they willingly gnawed at the bastard's bones, while blue-eyed Binna cooked for her wonderful son. In her dreams, Vancha saw a little boy, a kind soul that listened, enchanted, spell-bound, to the fairytales she told him.

She had to face reality, alas. A mole kicked and stirred in Sinna's black belly. So her grandchild was a mole and Vancha would tell fairytales to a mole. The old woman tried hard to calm down thinking to herself that the mole could be their neighbor's child who had just come from Spain, and Sinna cleaned his living room for months as long as the money he got for his car lasted.

Their neighbor sold his Opel so he could buy Sinna tulle, then the crazy bugger, naked as a slug, crawled with his tail between his legs to his wife, asking for a piece of bread and a bowl of soup. Or perhaps the mole under Sinna's transparent tulle was the police officer Sto's son? She had cleaned his tumbledown house, the rotter. She had cleaned his living room so painstakingly that now the only gold ring in the policeman's family shone on her finger, and that was Sto's late mother's ring! Vancha's own flesh and blood, her son Naum who thought he was so smart and shrewd, had also fallen like a ton of bricks for Sinna. Naum on whose account Vancha lost a gallon of her blood after she gave birth to him, as much as the huge bottle of brandy which Vancha kept in the cellar and used in winter to rub Aggo's chest and back, steering him clear of flu and pneumonia. Vancha recalled Doc Gospod had wrenched Naum— choking and blue—out of her, his navel string wound around his neck like a halter. That very same Naum came back from Germany, and after he parked two huge trucks full of clothes in their yard, he said to Vancha, "Mom, I want you to know that Sinna and I are waiting for our baby. Take good care of her. Look after her like she's a truck full of jewels because I want that baby more than I care about a truck full of jewels. I labor and plod and slog in Germany for that baby alone!"

At that point, Vancha opened her mouth and was about to scream, "Are you crazy? Are your eyes in your stomach, son? Can't you see Sinna's as filthy as the clothes you drag in here from Sweden? Anybody could be this baby's father: police officer Sto, our neighbor, too, and many other neighbors whose wives look after old ladies at places you buy your rotten rags from. Sinna goes and cleans the guys' living rooms."

"I can't sleep a wink without Sinna. I can't curse if she's not around, and I can't walk. I can't even put on my shirt. Sinna's on my mind even when I've got no money. Can you understand what she and our baby mean to me?"

Vancha tried hard to explain his position to him, "Are you blind, Naum? Can't you see you haven't brought a dirtier rag than this Sinna of yours although you look for rags in Sweden and Germany?"

After a while she gave up trying. He *was* blind. He was unable to button up his shirt without her, and he imagined the mole in her paunch was pure gold. The idiot! And Vancha was to tell this little frog fairytales. She could live with that, but that dark toxin Sinna shot at the guys who talked to her blue-eyed girl. The wounded victims consulted Doc Gospod who extracted the buck-shots from their buttocks and rubbed antiseptic solutions on their skins. Vancha could live with that, too. There was one thing she couldn't stomach: in the evening, a week ago, she had set Warrior, the dog, free and just after she had fed the chickens she saw Sinna, the black vulture. The black vulture's breath smelled of carrion as one could expect, and the black vulture Sinna—in her belly their neighbor's son writhed like a snake!—pressed the blue-eyed girl against the trunk of the old cherry tree.

Vancha could not discern if the black vulture bit her or hit her, however she could clearly hear the vulture's voice, "I'll kill them all, you fool. If he touches you, I'll shoot him dead."

Vancha believed she had more sugar in her blood than in a sugar factory, so Doc Gospod advised her not to worry a bit about things if she wanted to live. How could old Vancha keep calm after she heard those venomous words? Her heart was about to burst! She raised her walking stick hoping with all the deathly sugar in her diabetic blood she'd hit the vulture's cheek and crack her skull. Sinna clutched at the walking stick then chucked the thing into the lime-pit. The loss of a walking-stick was nothing compared to what Vancha saw a minute later.

Her girl's neck had been bitten black and blue as if Warrior the dog before he was too old and his teeth fallen out had torn at her chin. It was as if Aggo, with his infirm hands, had tried to slaughter a lamb—that was how her Binna had been bitten, stung and chewed, as if a carpenter had whittled at her neck with a plane. On Binna's chest and breasts white and fragrant as Easter bread, Vancha noticed other traces of Sinna's teeth, smaller, shallower ones, like traces of a sled in hard snow. Then Vancha's blood sugar level soared and touched Black Peak, and the old woman was about to step over the other side of the ridge. As good luck would have it, Doc Gospod was nearby, the ambulance arrived in time and the Doc brought old Vancha back home. What will happen to Binna if I leave Binna here and fly to God on Black Peak, Vancha thought. They'll tear her to pieces, if I go. She's quiet, my poor soul.

Doc Gospod pumped two thousand chemical compounds into Vancha, and her sugar level vanished somewhere. I have to put an end to all this, Vancha thought as she called police officer Sto, asking him to put the vulture under arrest, or, if possible, throw her into prison. Let her deliver as many babies there as she pleased. Vancha signed some thick documents, heaved a sigh, thinking she'd done a good thing for the whole town of Radomir: for the women who looked after old ladies in Italy, Spain, Greece and Sweden. Vancha knew very well who cleaned their houses and who swept the floor in the living rooms when the husbands came back home to sell their ancient cars, to repair the roof or just to call on their mothers if the horrible flu had not already sent the old darlings beyond Black Peak. It was Sinna who took care of all men's living rooms and guest rooms in Radomir.

"It was wrong to send for police officer Sto and ask him to put me under arrest," Sinna said quietly. The old woman looked around, startled. What was the dark pest up to? When she lifted her tulle up towards their neighbors' houses, Vancha was not scared. But she shuddered every time Sinna droned as quietly as she did now. Years ago, Vancha and Aggo had a dog named Murat. The beast used to howl like death then suddenly shut up as he threw himself against you sinking his teeth into your calf. They were big, his ugly teeth! The wound wouldn't heal for months. You went to Doc Gospod to stitch it up, and the more the Doc stitched, the more pus it oozed. Vancha poisoned that Murat with her own hands and thought to herself, "I did something good for the whole town of

Radomir." Murat had bitten three kids and a young woman; however her son Naum wouldn't allow her to kill the mongrel because his sharp teeth guarded his trucks against robbers and muggers. No matter what, Vancha bought ten levs' worth of poison, and she didn't regret it a bit. She was willing to fork out a hundred levs to bump off the beast. What was Sinna up to now? The dark mud's voice, just like Murat, was getting ready to snap at her leg.

"What do you want?" Vancha asked alert enough to use her walking stick if worse came to worst. It was a pity her best and heaviest cane had remained in the lime-pit. Naum extracted it after he came back from Spain, and smashed the thing to smithereens, storming mad.

"I don't want anything," the black berry declared as she proudly thrust forward her belly in which her baby as strong as an ox kicked just as strongly.

"Then I'll go feed the chickens," Vancha said. "You'd better go and clean police officer Sto's living room."

"I'll clean whoever's living room I please," the dark pest said. "You can issue orders until you are blue in the face, I don't obey you. I want you to know I love Binna. I swear I do. Let Naum's truck run over me if I lie. Let me catch cancer if I lie. I love no one more than her. Do I make myself clear, fatty?"

"Then why did you bite her?"

"I wasn't biting her. I was kissing her."

"A man should kiss her," Vancha snapped, her voice strong, unwavering, that came as a surprise. She was sorry she didn't have a thicker club in her hand. She could clout the vulture on the head. She could even smash her nose in if she was lucky. Let's see then how the dark scavenger would clean the guys' living rooms, all those poor souls that had just come from Spain where they picked olives in the thorns. Vancha's walking stick was a weak thing, just an old dry branch from her cherry tree. What could a dry cherry branch do? "If only Naum hadn't chopped up my thick walking stick!" Vancha added. "I'd have shown you."

"So you think a man should kiss her?" the black-haired girl grinned, tapped on her protruding belly trying perhaps to scare the little mole that kicked inside it, then burst out laughing.

7.

I don't know if Radomir will be a desert one day soon. Many women work for me in my dressmaking workshop, most of them old, their missing teeth turning their mouths into gaping caves. Younger men work in my butcher's shop. I had a dream that my land was deserted. Wolves had eaten up the men. Spain ate them up. Women rarely gave birth although they were not barren like me. Well, could they choose a decent man for a father of their children? Not by a long shot! A driver was their best option. The man got out of his truck, paid a girl, then picked up his bag and baggage, and beat it. No girl is that crazy as to give birth to a runaway driver's son. Why should she take care of his seed, nursing the little bastard at her breast and making mashed potatoes for him? No way! Before dumping the trucker, a working girl from Radomir relieved him of his money then scampered across Europe, landing in Spain. She'd look after old sick Donnas there, which was a lucrative job no matter what. She'd nurse Spanish babies through illnesses as well, and if she caught a Spanish husband, she'd willingly take charge of his seed. It was true she'd give birth to a kid in Galicia, Spain, not in Radomir, Bulgaria, and nothing in Spain was as marvelous as we had in Radomir. The girls knew this, none of them were stupid—you could print out this statement and put it in a prominent place on your desk. The Spanish husband didn't clear off as a Bulgarian hubby would; the hidalgo earned enough dough for his bride and kiddie to bring the little one up in a most considerate manner.

I knew the Sahara was a desert with a lot of sand in it. There was no sand in Radomir. There were some folks still clinging to their houses. My Isabella who cooked Italian dishes for me knew which men were in town, but this was not necessary any longer. Tano, the tallest guy in Bulgaria, had moved in with me for good. I had locked him in the garden storage shed. He drank there, very often indeed, then puked. However I was vigilant—I made sure he didn't get tight on Wednesday, Thursdays, Fridays and Saturdays. I came to guess at how Tano's late wife felt. I remembered her: she came asking me for a job just before she breathed her last, her boobs swollen with poisoned milk. It became clear to me why she, a professional who had handled an endless line of truckers, put up with Tano for free, Tano with his tattered pants, filthy sweater, and muddy shoes—because his soul was big. So big that the guy made me, a huge, barren lady, feel no different from the other women in Radomir who had a tail of smiling snotty kids clinging to their skirts. I was scared when Tano was not in that garden storage shed. I thought Radomir was desolate as the Sahara and my white house gradually turned gray, jutting out like a bad tooth on the hilltop.

Stray dogs would sniff at the concrete fencing on which I forked out a wagon train full of dough. Finally the weakest mongrels would bite the big one; the dumbest folks would beat it to Spain to pick olives and if there were no people in town, dogs, like ravens, vanished searching for a better place to live. Then wolves would turn up to piss on my fence and it would collapse. There would be no robbers to ransack the house looking for gold rings, for they'd be out thieving in Madrid. I'd stay at home with Isabella, my best friend and chief expert that cooked and cleaned for me, had ideas of cropping my hair, ironed my trousers, and time and again sang me a lullaby in case Tano was drunk like a skunk, or he felt drained of energy on account of my love to an extent that he was unable to speak let alone climb off his mattress. I used his love intensively, I granted him that.

"I can't do it again, Dana," he groaned. "You'd better kill me. I can't. Marry somebody else. Stoichko is your guy."

No way. How could I send for Stoichko if you were on my mind all the time? I didn't care a fig about Stoichko.

So I sat at Tano's side, feeding him with a little spoon. I was a normal barren lady. I had no children, and I was as un-reproductive as the hide of the ewe that had tapeworms—Isabella skinned the poor devil and stretched the pelt to get it dry on the pear tree. I was as fertile as that hide: I could procreate a tapeworm at best. I had never fed kids and kids had never slobbered all over me, however I fed Tano a healthy diet. First, I gave him butter and broiled meat, then chocolate. I made him gobble up a fat bar of chocolate together with a glass of my brandy, my best liquor I sold the German Fritzes. My German clients were as powerful as dead cows. The poor gents downed a glass or two, lay flat, sprawling out on the floor, sleeping like old sneakers for three days in a row in my hotel on the outskirts of Radomir. Therefore, I gave Tano my best brandy otherwise he wouldn't eat chocolate which gave him more energy. Then I took his love and kissed him, and kissed him until he went to sleep. He lay numb and immobile as if I'd soaked him in boiling vinegar for ten days without a break, incapable of lifting a finger, raising his eyebrows, as limp as the ewe that had tapeworms, his eyes closed. Perhaps he was sick and tired of looking at me, but

I couldn't take my eyes off him. Where the sun had not touched his skin, he was white, even translucent, but if you glanced at his face you'd infer: this guy's mother or father were surely brought into the world amidst African sands. However the truth was that the sun beat down on Tano as he drank in the pubs or slept in the field.

He worked as a lumberjack before I locked him in the garden storage shed: he illegally felled trees in my forest.

"Stop felling my oaks or I'll break your head, man." I said. "Tell me if you want to live like a king."

God on Black Peak was my eyewitness: I collected all Tano's things and brought them into my room, but then I set them on fire for I have never seen a thing as filthy as his shirt. I bought him everything he needed—beginning with socks, ending with a fashionable cap. Tano gambled away all his garments or drank the money he got as he sold them to Aggo the rag-and-bone man. On that very same evening, Tano came back to my room, a tattered tablecloth wrapped around his nude body—the barman gave the thing to him in *Motherland*, a pub I owned in Radomir.

"Where's your business suit, where's your shirt, socks and pants?" I asked. He was totally plastered and had no idea what I was talking about. His love hung like a wet scarf as he waved the tattered tablecloth in the air. I forgave him right away and ordered Isabella to carefully wash all of him. After that she cut his hair and nails very short as he was sprawling on the couch blind drunk. Then she took his measure and brought everything the big guy needed: brand new items each one of them, starting from his socks and finishing with Panama hat which crowned it all. After that, Isabella and I lifted Tano and had a hard time doing it. I took hold of his head, Isabella clutched his legs, then with a lot of effort we heaved him up and dumped him on my bed.

Isabella had chosen my sheets: all of them white silk, so she was just putting on Italian airs and graces with me. My pants, my jeans, and my toothbrush: she'd bought all these from Milan, Italy. All she cared about was Italy. After Tano sobered up, I fully grasped why his wedded wife let him drink her pay checks away: a whale could swim in the ocean of Tano's soul, it was as big as that. A horse could gallop in it for a year, and would not reach its end. All Italian sheets and nightgowns, even the ones neatly folded up and arranged in the chests were worth nothing compared to one single nail of Tano's. Therefore I thought to myself, let all my seamstresses leave me and go pick olives in Spain. I'll stay here, in my room, looking at him. I won't make him cut old trees, ruining his shoes up the rocky hillsides. I'll have him where he's now, by my side.

Therefore, I had Isabella run some errands for me, the first of which was to buy me some bars of chocolate. I was away no more than ten minutes i.e. the time I needed to shake Isabella awake. She had had assumed the solid shape and pattern of a drunken rat, I had treated her to the wine I sold to my German jewels, the Fritzes. Isabella had tumbled down over all three stools arranged like a bridge one next to the other, sleeping like a bear in January. I had to stir her into action, so I waited for her to clear her throat and sober up. When I opened the door to my room, I froze in my tracks: Tano was not in my bed. He had vanished, leaving no trail behind; my white silk sheets from Milan were gone. The mattress had disappeared, my clothes, my new shoes—all made in Italy—were gone as well. I thought to myself, now I'll send Isabella to shoot him dead. I'll order her to shoot at all nitwits he drinks brandy with. And if he's speaking to a hot babe, Isabella, put a bullet through her head too. Without delay!

Isabella started her Ford—I'd bought her a good sturdy car. Why? For example, if I wanted some lettuce salad, Isabella was to jump into the Ford, drive to the field, pick the most delicate lettuces she could lay her hands on, and I wanted my salad ready before spittle dried up on my lips. If I was dog tired, Isabella spoon-fed me. I felt lazy in cases when, for example, I had driven my Jeep trying to jump over the Matta River. The Matta River was full of mud all the time, more frogs than river, which was all there was to it, but it did my heart good to sink the Jeep into the mud and wrench the tires free with my own bare hands. Other times I exhausted myself as I rode Giant Adriano, my Italian stallion. I sent Isabella on a business trip to Italy; she was tasked with choosing a charger for me, and she did a perfect job: old Bella bought me a stud as huge as a mammoth. I had even called him Mammoth for a month, but he, being Italian, wanted high culture, so we renamed him Giant Adriano.

Other times, I felt exhausted after I won fist fights over a guy from Radomir, Toncho by name. I assigned Isabella the job of bringing this fighter to me if I felt like beating somebody up, or when I had fears Radomir would turn into a desert wasteland. Toncho was an ex-boxer; and in winter he was an electrician, while in summer he became a mumbling Spanish waiter. If it was pouring with rain, and I couldn't jump over the Mutter River with my Jeep, I sent for the guy, and we fought fiercely. I boxed him hours on end; I clouted him around the head, and he buffeted me like I was the muddy brink of the Mutta River, at times I won the game fair and square, or he did. I often went for a swim in the Pear Lake. The water was so cold you thought the waves sawed your chest in halves, but I plunged into the whirlpool and swam, cutting it, thrashing it, drinking it. I shouted to Isabella, "Come on, Bella, jump. Let's swim together."

"I can't, Miss Dana," she said. "You know last time I swam with you I got a cramp in my brain and you had a hard time pulling me onto dry land."

"Cramp my foot!" I cut her short.

Isabella was in charge of my towel, and the second I got out of the water she threw it on my head then I made her light a roaring fire for me, but it frequently happened that I jogged around the lake bare-assed. I swam in the buff, no suit, without a stitch on me, punishing my barren place by soaking it in the ice cold water. I could feel the poor thing freeze up, turning into a packet of frozen raisins. In the meantime, Isabella stoked up the fire to a blaze and read dirty novels about lovers and mistresses by Italian authors.

"Don't read filthy books. Come run with me." I tried hard to convince her, but she shook her head.

"I can't run as fast as you, Miss Dana, my immune system gets drained and tired," she said, so I let her and her immune system drag slowly forward for appearance's sake. One night, I made Isabella read to me about the lovers and mistresses in her books. The horror! She had chosen the foulest writers in Italy. I asked her, "Is that the reason why you kiss my forehead every night, Isabella?"

"Not in the least," she said. "Tano's made himself scarce. I kiss your crazy head so you can sleep well."

Running naked around the lake shattered me, and in the evening I made Isabella feed me. She cut the hair of my head, she picked and chose my clothes for me, so I paid for her sewing classes, and the clever girl learned all sewing techniques under the sun. I sent her to study with an Italian seamstress in Sofia, and I squandered a load of money on that blessed program. Now, Isabella was repairing my only dress, the one I bought on account of the silly little gourd that called me "Daddy" if I wore pants, but if she saw me in my red dress, a big smile gleamed on her face and she said, "Mommy"! Even if I was in my nightgown the little pitcher still called me "mommy" and came up running like lightning to me. She was scared to creep under the blanket and the silk sheet, though;

the tiny bonehead snuggled up against my feet, or ate the chunk of meat I'd thrown on the floor beforehand. I asked her, "What's your name, kiddie?"

On hearing my voice, the first thing she did was thrust her head and shoulders under the bedside table, then sobbed as powerfully as her tiny throat would go, and I pulled her out trembling and jittery from her hiding place. She shook like the little cat my jeep ran over last year. The cat died. Before she clambered up the Black Peak, the poor ameba heaved a soft sigh that still gave me the creeps. It was on the following day that I bought a tomcat, and I saw to it he was well fed like a prince at all times. He became a large, strong-built fellow, this tomcat, like an ambassador extraordinary and plenipotentiary: I gave him two sausages and a fish every day hoping to forget how that little ameba-cat shook and writhed before she crept to Black Peak. Therefore, I said to the little girl, "Don't shiver, kiddie. My jeep won't run over you, I promise," but the little one pissed in my palms as I carefully held her close to my chest. Isabella took her from my hands, washed her and put new tiny pants on her.

"Hey, what's your name?" I asked, and the toddler bawled again, but after I gave her a bar of chocolate she mouthed, "Mumma."

"How come your name is Mumma, kiddie? It's impossible. We'll give you a strong, beautiful name. You aren't Mumma."

The little one shook and pissed in her pants again; therefore we called her Mumma the way she wanted. It was on account of Mumma that I made Isabella sew two more dresses for me. And because her little head was as dumb as a goose's, she opened the wardrobe, stood in front of it, and addressed my dresses as "mommy". A wonderful, silly kid, you see. The minute Tano glanced at the little thing, he babbled happily, "My precious baby. Daddy's tiny harebrained pumpkin!"

It was not that interesting to watch a man as big as a garden shed weep like a damsel in distress. You'd think the Matta River poured out of Tano's eyes, complete with its frogs, frog-spittle and duckweed. Well, I didn't mind his tears. Let him sob his heart out as long as he didn't make yellow puddles on my white carpet from Genoa, a precious thing to be prized above all else, which Isabella managed to procure at a very advantageous price. Let the guy weep until it grew dark. However there was a detail I'd like to focus on: if tears gleamed in Tano's eyes, his love was no good. He just sat there, waterworks on, tears rolling down his nose. He said no sad words as I had heard women mumble before they left for Spain to take care of old crones and grumpy geezers there, the grandmas and grandpas in Radomir in charge of the small children. Tano used not a single syllable as he sobbed, his red-rimmed eyes shedding and shedding gallons of tears, and he was unable to love me. Therefore, I told Isabella, "Go wipe his eyes and help him blow his nose."

Then I turned to Tano. "Tano, I won't have it like this. You can't just sit slobbering on my white carpet. You do nothing substantial or essential. If you go on whimpering, I'll dump the dim-witted kid, I warn you. I don't like your lamentations at all, man."

Of course, I was only putting pressure on him; I liked to browbeat the big man. I loved the way the silly darling called me "mommy" and snuggled up against my knees in my bed. I was very happy if somebody breathed by my side when I went to sleep otherwise it seemed to me Radomir had become a desert, and I was all alone in my big white house, and wolves and bitch-wolves peed on my seven feet high stone wall encircling it. I was scared that the hill, the forest and the lake would become a grim wasteland. I asked Isabella to stay in my room and breathe as hard as she could until she dropped asleep. Then in the morning I asked her to breathe until

I became fully awake and put on my clothes. These days, Isabella breathed on my left, and the tiny darling breathed gently and easily on my right, very close to my head, and my fears that the desert would assault Radomir vanished into thin air.

Well, it was true Tano slept in the garden shed just a sigh away from my bed. It was also true Isabella bought him everything the hunk could dream of, starting from his socks, then going as far as his panama, all of them Italian items from start to finish. The worst of all evils was that while I waited for Isabella to clear her throat and sober up, Tano went missing complete with my mattress, my nightgowns all of them Italian down to the last stitch.

"Isabella," I said. "Go find the idiot and kick him… well, you know where. Then bring him to me."

"What if he's caught a plane? Shall I provide Stoichko for you, or you want me to kill and fry three chickens for your lunch, Miss Dana?" Isabella asked, so it became evident she was still blind drunk. She should have known that after Tano any other guy would feel like a sack of manure compared to a sack of emeralds.

"If you don't bring Tano to me, I'll either fire you on the spot, or… I don't even know what I'll do."

Then I remembered what happened last year when I still hadn't met Tano. Stoichko had come down with flu, so I asked Isabella to find another gentleman for me. She had a guilty look on her face, keeping her head bent down, her eyes glued to her Italian pantyhose.

"There aren't any other gentlemen, Miss Dana," she said. "Today is the 6th of May—the Day of Courage, and everybody is sloshed."

"I'm fed up with the Day of Courage," I said, thinking out loud. "What shall we do? Go bring a plastered guy to me, I wouldn't mind."

"I did, Miss Dana," my chief expert reported. "I brought three sloshed guys to you: the first is a construction worker from the speedway Sofia—Athens; the second is a cement mason, and the third is a plasterer. They all snore like lions in my truck. I admit I could not awaken them to a sense of duty, Miss Dana."

"Then tell me what you think: shall we go for a swim, Bella *mia,* or would you prefer sniping at hawks?" Of late years, Radomir teemed with hawks. The darned feathered robbers hung like rags in the branches of the oaks, and you could hear them chewing the pullets they had snatched from my hen-houses an hour before. I could read their filthy hawk minds: they planned to loot my poultry farm, divesting me of my prize-winning, egg-laying chickens. There were more hawks then air above my head. I knew very well hawks caught mice, but the fuckers learned to eat cats along with rats, and my chickens were their idea of a special delicacy. So I said to Isabella, "Bring me my gun. I'll go shoot the disgusting beasts dead."

"But it's not the same thing, Miss Dana," Isabella objected. "You can't compare love to exterminating hawks."

"Then what, shall I go chop down an oak tree? Will this calm me down?"

I often cut down trees so Stoichko could get some rest from time to time although he was agile as a weasel. At a certain point, he even wanted to ditch his wife and marry me. Wasn't that man crazy! When he got dog tired, I asked him, "Now what?"

He said, "I'll find a big oak tree for you, Miss Dana. You go cut it down, and I'll get some sleep."

He was sharpening the axe while I flung my pants and blouse on, then I got into my jeep and drove it like mad to the forest, clutching the axe in my right hand. Once in the wood, I attacked an oak, I scratched, pushed and slashed it, I nicked and kicked the bark, and I sank the blade deep into the tree. Isabella was always by my side, making a fire, as she watched me closely. The minute I broke a sweat, she gave me fresh clothes to put on, or rubbed my wet back, belly, legs, and buttocks with a towel. Apart from that, she kept two flasks for me: red thunder wine and brandy. But after I was with Tano, I never happened to think about felling oaks or hewing logs. When I was with Tano the only thing I did was to summon Isabella and ask for my towel.

"No, Miss Dana, don't fell oaks today."

"Do you have a better idea?"

"Who cuts your hair every two months?" she asked.

"You do."

"Who trims your toenails, and who wishes you Good Night every evening?"

"You do, Isabella."

"Who sews your dresses, who buys you panties and who washes them?"

"You do," I said, utterly unable to see what she was driving at.

"Who cooks for you, who makes your bed for you, and who changes the dirty sheets?"

"You do."

"Who removes all splinters that get under your skin when you shoot at hawks? And who plucks the hair on your legs with tweezers?"

"Okay, Okay, you do. Cut it out!"

"Who do you drink your thunderbolt with, the roaring wine you only sell to Brits and Fritzes? Who breathes for you until you drop asleep every evening and in the morning when you come to your senses after drinking so much?"

"You do, peanut Isabella. You're beating about the bush, girl. What's eating you? My poor ears are getting sick and tired of listening to your yarns."

"Miss Dana, Tano's gone, Okay? Stoicko came down with the flu yesterday. So you can try with me while the gentlemen in my truck get sober again."

"What do you want me to try with you?"

"The same thing you do with Tano and Stoichko. It shouldn't be much different with me. Folks in Italy do it willingly, and this procedure is widespread, and very popular. Then you won't fret: Tano will never again pilfer your mattress and nightgowns, and your things won't smell of his dirty socks."

"Shut up, Isabella."

"Don't I kiss your head every evening as I wish you Good Night?" Isabella pointed out. "Don't I breathe most diligently, ensuring sweet dreams for you?"

Therefore I let her kiss me, but her tongue tasted like rubber boots.

"It's no good, Isabella. Don't you ever tell me what procedures are widely spread and popular in Italy, girl. Tano is popular with me in the garden shed. Go bring him to me." I thought hard for a while, then I added, "If you can't find him, grab a towel and give it to me. I'm going to take a swim in the lake. I'll take the axe with me in case I feel like cutting down an oak tree. You, Bella *mia*, build a big fire. Be careful to quickly wipe the sweat off my back and ass, for this flu drains you dry like a drying furnace. Although I'm a barren lady, I wouldn't like to meet my maker in my youthful days."

Therefore, I swam for three hours in the lake. It was embedded in the open north mountain slope, and there still were chunks of ice in the water. My hair froze solid as I chugged across the wide bay. That was why I crept out of the mud and ran three laps around the freezing blue surface, my glowing posterior a lighthouse flashing its lights all over the place. My teeth chattered, so I was felling a dry beech tree when Isabella arrived in her Ford truck, my chief expert in everything under the sun. Tano sat behind the driver, naked as a garden slug, no gray woolen suit, no new tank top, no mattress, and not a stich of my stolen nightgowns were anywhere in sight.

"He'd boozed away everything he had, Miss Dana," Isabella

groaned. "He was shouting he'd pawn a kidney for a bottle of brandy when I found him. Oh, Miss Dana, the hard time I had catching him! He'd reached the Greek border and was preparing to run away to Athens!"

Although he was naked as a slug and shivering, and I was freezing, I could hear clearly what he said.

"I'm a man, Dana. Men want to travel around the world," he declared. "I want to travel around the world, too. Forgive me quick-I'm fresh like a cucumber, and I haven't drunk a drop for five hours now."

I forgave him in a flash.

And I had been forgiving him for a week although he hid a bottle somewhere—I couldn't find it even if my life depended on it—and the imbecile got drunk as a rusty Ford truck, so Isabella and I dragged him from my room to the garden shed.

I fed him properly, forcing him eat two bars of chocolate. On Sundays I let him sleep in until 4 p.m. and he slept so soundly he couldn't even snore. He used to snore so powerfully that the roof of the garden shed shook, and now he sprawled on the mattress motionless like the monument of the poet in the middle of the town square. I left him alone and hurried to shoot at the hawks. The loathsome stinkers had eaten fourteen of my pullets and six egg-laying chickens so I paid two levs for any killed hawk. The citizens of Radomir, both young and all, rushed to bump the winged leeches off: children, grandmas and grandpas came on Wednesdays. My working hours started at 7 am, and I closed my shop at 9 pm. In the beginning I paid the exterminators, then Isabella took charge of all payments and remunerations. It was true almost all grown-up men and women from Radomir picked turnips and olives in Spain; it was the street urchins that learned to bash the feathered sharks' heads in. The kids aimed at bloodthirsty birds with their slings and did away with them. Dexterous kids, I give them that.

I'd been swimming in the lake for almost a day, yet I felt as strong as if I still hadn't taken my pants off. I was keen on breaking a sweat, so I clutched a pickaxe intent on tearing out donkey willows by their roots. The donkey willow is a plant that has long and tough roots. If men's love in Radomir had such roots, our neighborhood would be teeming with population, and Radomir would not become a desert, on the contrary, it would be crawling with faces like Shanghai, China. So I caught hold of the pickaxe and cut off donkey willows root and branch. I brought the little girl with me and wore one of my disgusting dresses. The half-baked little one shuffled her feet in my wake like a turtle, clutching at the hem of my skirt so I walked as slowly as an ant, both physically and mentally alert not to tread on her tiny foot. She called me "Mommy, mommy", and for the first time my dress was not tight at all, and I liked it, and my heart felt as big as the sky that in September began on the Greek border with all its stars and the moon, and reached as far as our Black Peak. I was as happy as a lark so I rushed to the garden shed.

Although I'd been uprooting donkey willows for six hours, I kissed Tano as powerfully as if I hadn't found the pickaxe. There was immense strength in me. I gave him a gallon of milk to drink first, then I gave him a chunk of herb-roasted lamb: Isabella roasted it using special dry heat, an open flame, she said, as she spread exceptional Italian butter on it. I added two glasses of my thunderbolt, and Isabella brought him a bucket of hot chocolate, the best combination of vitamins to take on a daily basis, plus a glass of apple juice and carrots, which she had prepared three minutes before. Tano ate serenely, I watched him, my soul swimming in pure bliss. I didn't think Radomir would become a desert; on the contrary, the town was swarming with tourists and young folks in the main street were more numerous than in Brussels. The three of us would live happily ever after, I, Tano and Isabella who'd cook, squeeze, and bottle homemade apple juice for us all. I'd make Tano stand up after he finished his meal. I'd never tire of checking that he was a whole inch taller than me. Those were the happiest minutes in my life, and I didn't need anyone to breathe by my side while I slept. I didn't need Italian silk sheets.

On Sundays, I uprooted donkey willows, shot at hawks, swam in the lake or ran in the woods. In spring, I didn't want Isabella to make fires for me or hold towels in her hands to rub my sweaty back. She waited for me, a sun screen tube in hand, plus a bowl of tuna fish. At times, after I'd run three laps around the lake, feeling totally bushed, she fed me the way I fed Tano: milk, roasted lamb and Italian butter spread on it, hot chocolate and Vitamin C, plus all the other vitamins under the sun. The harebrained kiddie padded in Isabella's wake like a trailer. The little gourd called me "Mommy" even if I wore pants, and she learned to hold my hand. It was the strangest thing: the pumpkin's hand was soiled all the time. I wondered how it was possible to make her tiny fingers that filthy or spread mud, strawberry juice and grease all over the place. But I held her little precious hand tight. I'd never touched a more beautiful thing in my life.

"Miss Dana, why do you grin like a pumpkin at this dim-witted child?" Isabella asked. "She doesn't grin back at you most of the time."

"It does me good to look at her," I said, and that was the honest truth.

The girl often went to Tano, sat close to his head and stroked his hair, then kissed his forehead, but Tano lay spread-eagled on the floor, snoring like a volcano, and dead to the world. The garden shed was too narrow for him, the mattress was thin and frayed, but I wouldn't let him set foot in my room, not if my life depended on it. A fortnight ago, I provided him with access to my bed, but the son of a gun ran away one more time: he jumped out the second floor window. He flew in the air in his baggy boxers as he took off from the windowsill, clutching the casket in which I kept the money for bullets and buck-shot. Isabella and her posse caught him near the town of Dupni: throwing tantrums and drowning his fury in good booze in a pub called "The Dusty Counter". He had already pawned one of his kidneys. So I kept him locked up in the garden shed as if he were a hoe. I visited him as often as I pleased and the silly girl trotted along at my skirt, stopped in front of the garden shed, shouting like a church bell, "Daddy, daddy!", working her small way toward the mattress. I didn't allow her to stay, the kiddie squatted on her tiny haunches and cried.

"Isabella," I said. "This baby's bawling and squalling like a rhino. Take her to the swing in the backyard or play with her."

Isabella took the small thing off my hands. Suddenly the toddler started crying, sobbing her heart out, and I could hear her tears trickle down—they dripped right into my heart, her little tears, and I imagined her teeny chest all shaking and heaving.

Then I left a huge bowl of popcorn in front of the shed. I visited Tano while the harebrained pumpkin made for the bowl, no sobs, no hiccups, and after a while I could hear her chew and munch. Then Isabella collected her and probably the two watched Cartoon Network. I never knew what exactly was so interesting. I didn't go out before Tano dropped off to sleep. I didn't go out even when he did. I slept by his side, our bodies packed together like sardines, not enough space to drop a shirt button on the floor—the damned shed was as cramped as that. I knew Isabella was waiting for me, a clean towel in hand on account of the nasty flu that baked you for three days in its oven, but I didn't leave Tano alone until the little gourd sobbed, "Mommy, Mommy!"

I didn't know how her sobs found their way to me. I couldn't hear what Isabella said though she had a reputation for her shrill, ringing voice. I listened to the soft "Mommy, Mommy", and rushed like a torch out of the shed in my bikini, the harebrained thing rushed to me, her face a happy smile. She hugged me close as if I were God that had clambered over Black Peak to say 'Good night'. Her hands were greasy with popcorn, and I could feel her fingers getting stuck on my back or meddling with my hair, but I was the happiest woman in Radomir, in the Sahara desert, and all over Bulgaria.

"Do you want me to give you something, kiddie?" I babbled into the child's neck, pressing her against my chest, hoping I could make all her tears dry up.

8.

MR. MARKO SHOT A GLANCE at his wife's pale, terrified face, then rushed to her, a cup of tea in hand—heal-all hawthorn, rose hip and valerian. Mr. Marko, a renowned lawyer, known as Mr. Equanimity among his colleagues at the Bulgarian National Bar Association, was a prudent man capable of keeping a cool head in tense and embarrassing situations. Whenever their son Samuel rang him up at midnight, a sure sign something had gone wrong, Mr. Marko woke up Greta, the family's housekeeper, ordering her in a soft, low voice to brew heal-all hawthorn, rose hip tea. His wife, Antoinette Marko, had naturally glowing skin, but her face acquired a frightening shade of green every time the telephone rang after 11 p.m. Greta, the housekeeper, was accustomed to remedying potentially explosive situations. She'd become a consummate expert with heal-all hawthorn, rose hip tea, and Mrs. Marko's bosom friends, distinguished ladies all, hired Greta on her days off, and drank pails of her miraculous pacifying concoction. They saw themselves as clear and playful as mountain brooks, and felt perfectly rejuvenated. They secretly hoped that Mrs. Marko would fall ill; ideally, she'd be admitted to hospital and they could make use of Greta's invaluable skills.

Greta was a very good house-keeper, no, she was a perfect one. She knew everything one could know about Mr. Marko's bone spurs. Week in, week out she wrote down the cholesterol levels in his blood in a specially procured notebook; every morning the housekeeper took the gentleman's blood pressure, and twice a day his wife's, then she drew complex diagrams reflecting the fluctuation of the couple's pulse-rates during the four seasons of the years, and was particularly alert to dark spots on the Sun, for they fired off strong solar storms as a result of which Mrs. Marko became very irritable indeed. Greta also measured Mrs. Marko's weight twice a day, in the morning before breakfast, and in the evening after dinner. She brewed green Chinese tea for weight loss, boiled bran that eliminated wrinkles and massaged the fair lady's forehead, restoring her spiritual balance. Greta restored Attorney Marko's spiritual balance as well by offering him a *Mystery* cocktail in the rare cases when idiots at the Lawyers' Association or somewhere else had made efforts to disturb the peace in his heart. It was Greta who knew where Mr. Marko was so she could take him back home in case danger threatened the lawyer's precious health. In fact, Greta knew the very same Mystery, an ambitious solicitor, a Miss Boeva, who worked for an Austrian company of good repute in Sofia. The young solicitor made it easier for Mr. Marko to endure the unpleasant legal issues. Greta brewed heal-all hawthorn tea for Miss Boeva as well, who in her heart of hearts hoped she would become Mrs. Bern in the nearest future, Mr. Bern being the legal advisor to the reputed Austrian company. Alas, the nearest future never came, and Greta was urgently sent for to make a gallon of pacifying tea for the prospective Frau Bern.

"Greta, take care of Mrs. Marko," Mr. Marko said as he slipped a Wedgewood bathrobe over his shoulders. He waited a minute as Greta carefully massaged his wife's face, and his quiet, well-meaning voice insisted everything would be all right. "Greta," the lawyer turned to the housekeeper after his wife heaved a painful sigh, although she had drunk a cup of heal-all hawthorn tea. "Greta, take a bathrobe for the boy, too. I'm sure Samuel had forgotten it. The two of them must be freezing. Grab a towel, the little one is probably drenched to the bone. Take a jacket. Samuel must have gone out in a T-shirt."

Greta selected a bathrobe, a towel, an old Yves Saint Laurent jacket and left the well-lit apartment. Mr. Marko sank into his easychair, thinking of his *Mystery*, which was a sure sign that the situation had deteriorated. His face looked composed, even impassive the way a lawyer's countenance should be no matter what, so the man sipped brandy as he turned his back on his wife. Her expression spoiled the pleasure the beverage gave him. He regretted not having earplugs at the moment; quite often his wife's controlled breathing exasperated him and that was the reason he bought German earplugs, produced by Jürgen and Sons GmbH, Nordrein Westfalen. He thought that their family pet's growls—and he was powerful German shepherd, Cannibal by name—sounded much more attractive than Antoinette's dramatic sighs. Now she breathed fast and hard.

"Stop choking, Antoinette, damn it," Mr. Marko spoke quietly yet categorically.

"You stop being so cruel to me," she said bitingly as she reached out to Cannibal looking for support.

It was at that moment that Greta entered carrying a little boy in her arms. The child was in a dressing-gown under which the trouser legs of his pajamas told the tale of expensive fabric and impeccable taste. The child looked absorbed as it thrust his fingers into Greta's hair and pulled energetically at her ears. A young man followed Greta and the child into the room; he too was in flawless pajamas, his hands pressing a towel to his heart.

"Again?" Mrs. Marko asked.

The young man did not answer. His handsome face, which reminded one of Mrs. Marko's exquisite cheekbones and Mr. Marko's thick, bushy eyebrows, broke as he turned his red-rimmed eyes to the floor.

"Have you been crying?" Mr. Marko asked.

The young man did not say a word. He slumped into the easy chair, and the towel he held fell onto the French carpet.

"Greta, I want David's nanny here in ten minutes," Mr. Marko ordered, and Greta hurried to the telephone as she kissed the little boy who happily played on with her graying hair.

"Did the sour one go away again?" Mrs. Marko, hidden behind her pale face said, heaving another of her sighs.

He should know for the next time: earplugs! Mr. Marko thought. It was only natural the Sour one had beat it, and stupid Samuel brought his grandson to their house as if Mr. Marko was to blame. The child, as always, was in his pajamas, damn it. Was his wife Antoinette mentally retarded? She was too slow on the uptake; her friends called her *"Ah, toilet"* behind her back and rightly so: Antoinette spent the prevailing part of her adult life at her toilet or with her seamstress indulging in fashionable alternations and creations so disgusting he could hardly stand her new dresses. Mr. Marko was disgusted by his son's folly as well: to lose a bundle and appetite over a woman who was his own wife!

Well, his daughter-in-law Sinna could make a railway lose all its marbles, he'd grant her that. Mr. Marko stared at his son's yellow-grayish cheekbones and wondered how it was possible that Sinna agreed to marry a jellyfish like Samuel? Yes, Sam was his only son, but why should Sinna choose him? *Tarde venientibus ossae*, Mr. Marko muttered, feeling sorry for himself. The Romans came up with this unshakable truth: he who is late eats bones. Mr.

Marko had to gnaw at dry bones; Samuel had chanced on Sinna first, otherwise Sinna could have been the girl Mr. Marko could share his *Mystery* cocktail with on Wednesdays.

The experienced lawyer was quick to grasp the truth that his son's marriage would fall apart the minute he set eyes on Sinna. His prospective daughter-in-law exuded power that few of the wedding guests could perceive. She said little. But the way she looked in Mr. Marko's eyes as she shook his hand when they first met made the lawyer shake. He had noticed her tongue carving hot trajectories along her lips, and her eyes expected much more than the trivial "*Welcome to our family*" greeting. Yes, Mr. Marko doubted from the very first day that his son's marriage would last. He could arrange for Samuel's divorce within twenty-four hours, but... the lawyer glanced at his wife's greenish face as she let out a huge sigh. Then Mr. Equanimity took a squint at the easy-chair where his son's dropping head rested on Cannibal the dog.

Samuel was a ruin. His pajamas were hideously crumpled, the sagging skin of his cheeks was a mess, and his hair looked as tousled as if the whole mankind had spat on it and Samuel had never, in his tortuous life, used a comb. Bruises on his neck were clearly visible so Mr. Marko studied them and discovered traces of love bites under his chin.

"I can arrange for your divorce within twenty-four hours," Mr. Marko pointed out, trying to ignore his wife's next avalanche of sighs. "She had other men before you, and she has another child."

"Dad, please."

"Gregory!" his wife groaned.

"I can arrange..." started the lawyer, but his son's eyes were suddenly bright with large tears.

"Greta, take care of him," Mr. Marko said. "Bring me my grandchild first."

Greta padded to the lawyer and rapidly handed over the boy who was quick to whine and snivel. The little fellow grabbed at the housekeeper's hair and refused to let it go.

"I want Gretchen, I want my Gretchen," the child whimpered.

"Where is his nanny, damn it," Mrs. Marko exploded between two sighs. "She's not worth the money we pay her. How outrageous! How irresponsible!"

"David, come to Grandpa," the lawyer said as he clutched the boy's hand and pulled at it." Grandpa will give you a golden ball."

"I don't want it," the child said. "I want Gretchen."

"Grandpa will buy you a Ferrari toy car if you stop sniveling," Mr. Marko said. "Pay attention to what I say. You'll get a toy car if you stop blubbering. That's my condition. Stop blubbering. Now."

"I want Gretchen!" the child screamed. "Gretchen! Gretchen!"

"Greta, make him shut up," Mr. Marko said.

"You know how to do it," Mrs. Marko chimed in from the comfortable easy-chair into which her despair had driven her. "Take my *Morning Dew* balm. It will alleviate the love bites under his chin. As for the bruises, well, maybe *Scar Lotion* or *Scar Cure* will do the job. Of course, you know what to do."

Greta approached the chair in which the young man was prostrate with grief, and carefully touched his shoulder.

"Come on, handsome boy. Let's go."

"Perhaps *Sensitive Skin* Lotion," Mrs. Marko suggested. "Or rosemary ointment. You know what's best, Greta."

"I want my Gretchen," the boy sobbed as he hit Mr. Marko's eye with his fist. "I want Gretchen."

"If you want a new toy car or a new computer shut up," Mr. Marko ordered his grandson.

It was evident the boy wanted neither a toy car nor a laptop.

He hit his grandfather's other eye, spat on the floor and screamed, "I want Gretchen."

The lawyer let him go.

"Go to Gretchen then. You misbehaved, David. You are a bad boy. There will be no toys and no laptop for you because you misbehaved."

"Come to Mommy," Mrs. Marko said as she rose from her easy-chair.

The boy rushed to her, bit her knee, threw himself to the floor, kicked his legs, spat in the air then muttered through his clenched teeth, "I want Gretchen."

Another woman, a small one, her faced dark and narrow as a shoe, entered the room panting, rushed to the child that was sobbing on the floor.

"David, dearest little David, tell nanny who's made her dear boy so angry."

"Idiot nanny, nanny is an idiot," the child shouted. "Nanny, out! Out! Out!"

"Why should I go out, David? Nanny loves David, Nanny loves David so much. Give Nanny a kiss, please."

"Nanny's nasty, Nanny sucks!" the child yelled from the floor as his anger gradually subsided.

"Nanny loves David," repeated the flat old shoe in the woman's face. "Come, let's play *Slap-slap*.

"Slap-slap," the child yelled delighted. "David loves *slap-slap*. Let's play slap Nanny in the face."

The small dark woman bent over the boy, embraced him warmly as she tried to lift him off the floor but she failed at her first attempt. She made another try which flopped miserably, so she lay on the floor by his side, smiling sweetly at him. The boy bit her neck. The woman didn't flinch. She let him slap her face then stood up and managed to lift the child whom she pressed against her chest like a big suitcase. She staggered, took a couple of unsteady steps as she tried to restore her balance.

"Slap-slap," the child cried out full of enthusiasm as he held up his hand with his fingers extended. In a flash, he jabbed his nails at the woman's nose. "David loves Nanny," said the child and slapped his nanny's sweaty, scarlet cheeks.

"Let's not make *slap-slap cheeks* any more, David," she said, making desperate efforts to smile under the vigorous thrashing her charge gave her. "Let's play something else."

"I want *slap-slap*," the boy shrieked happily, slapping her on the head.

"Go kiss Gretchen good night," the nanny said. "Go kiss Gretchen, please, then I will read you the fairytale about the ugly duckling."

"The ugly duckling's stupid. The ugly duckling's nasty," the boy said. "David wants to fight. David wants *slap-slap, bang-bang*. Thud! Bang! Bam! Bam!"

"Ok, ok, my heart," the nanny agreed. "We'll watch movies. Please say *goodbye* to grandpa, Antoinette and Gretchen."

"Grandpa's stupid. Grandpa's nasty. Antoinette's stupid," the boy said. "Gretchen's cute. David loves Gretchen."

The kid wrenched himself free of the nanny's arms, rushed to the housekeeper who was rubbing his father's forehead with an aromatic napkin.

"Gretchen, give Dave a kiss, give Dave a kiss quick."

Greta bent down and the child pressed his head against her face. After the housekeeper stood up, the wounds the boy's teeth had carved shone scarlet under her chin.

"David loves Gretchen so much. David loves Gretchen so much! Gretchen, give Dave a kiss! Gretchen's a little cutie."

The boy's head, virtually a jungle of thick auburn hair, plunged toward the woman's cheek. After the avalanche of curly wisps shifted to her shoulder, the deep and cheerful marks of the boy's teeth glowed on Gretchen's skin.

"David loves Gretchen."

"Gretchen loves David so much," the housekeeper said, beaming a smile, although the bloody traces of the little one's love were hell on her nerves.

"David wants to play with Gretchen!" the child screamed.

"Gretchen has to play with your daddy," the housekeeper said the bright smile on her face unaltered.

"Daddy's foolish," the boy shouted. "Daddy's nasty. Davie loves Gretchen."

"Davie loves Nanny, too," the small dark woman said, the old shoe of her face alive with apprehension. "Come on, little sugar, come with your nanny. We'll shoot at beer bottles with your little gun. We still have some wasps buzzing in that big jar. Do you remember it?

"Wasps! Buzzing wasps, still alive!" the child shouted, ran to his nanny and pressed his head against her legs. "David is lazy. You carry Davie to the wasps. David wants the buzzing wasps in the jar."

The boy and his nanny left the room, Mr. and Mrs. Marko reclined back in their easy-chairs.

"It's your wife that spoils him," Mrs. Marko muttered under her breath. "I told you that from the very beginning, Samuel. She will be the death of you."

"Mother!" the young man groaned under Greta's fragrant towel in his deep armchair.

"She ruins your nerves, she pampers David and as a result of her arrogance the child becomes wild and unruly," Mr. Marko remarked. "Son, I want you to know that I can make arrangements for your divorce. You will be a free man within hours if you want. Trust me."

"If she goes away, I'll commit suicide," the young man whispered as he pushed his face towards Greta's hand. "If you and mother chase her away from me, I'll commit suicide."

"We have not chased her away," Mrs. Marko said in an even business-like tone of voice, although her face still looked yellowish-green.

Greta looked up at Mr. Marko who nodded to her.

"Come here, my dearest boy," the housekeeper said softly as she took a step to the young man slumped disconsolately in his armchair. "Greta will take good care of you. A hot bath with lavender oil and Epsom salts... Greta knows best what Samuel needs. Please, come."

The young man scrambled to his feet, leant against the housekeeper's plump, rich body, covered with clean white dressing-gown. She took hold of his limp hand and the two of them trudged out of the living room.

"We'll go to your room," the housekeeper's voice sounded warm and encouraging. "I've prepared your favorite dark-blue sheets. I've embroidered your name on them. I used black thread in the corners and scarlet in the center of the sheet just as you'd asked me, dearest Sammy. I paid that artist—was his name Tafro? He is great, Sammy, congratulations on choosing this man of genius! He's painted your wife so exquisitely that if you look at the picture, you'd say she was in the room by your side. Oh, the picture is huge—three yards by two—the way you ordered it."

"O, Gretchen!" the man groaned. "Gretchen!" he flopped down into the chair, his head sinking into the housekeeper's plump round shoulder. His red-rimmed eyes wetted her immaculately clean white robe. "She left me, Gretchen."

"There's nothing new under the sun. She's done that a couple of times before. We'll go to your room, and you'll feel better. Come on, my heart, we'll cry together."

The man stood up, searching for support on her shoulder as the two of them got the better of the maze of corridors lined with pure white wood panels. Greta led the way to a flawless blue room: the floor was covered with thick light blue carpet that looked like a patch of July sky. Indeed, the sun cheerfully shone in its left hand corner. The walls were sky as well and the stars in it encouraged one to fly away to clean, serene places, and ultimately to the horizon that went to sleep the minute Greta's feet touched it. The ceiling was the impossible blur of dreams. The name *Sinna* was embossed on its four corners: Sinna to the East, Sinna to the West, Sinna to the North, and Sinna to the South. The blue sheets were exquisitely embroidered with her name; however nothing could compare to the portrait of a dark lady with enormous black eyes that stared from the wall at the newcomer amidst the blue infinity of dreams. The portrait knew it owned the sky, the summer and the infinity.

Gretchen sat on the edge of the bed. The man caressed the name printed in purple sewing thread in the center of the coverlet, his hand impatient, his fingers tracing the outlines of the letters that seemed to exude a soft glow. He took a deep breath as if the name radiated heat and aroma, sobbed and collapsed on the bed. His head sank into the housekeeper's lap, his shoulders shaking, a bag of disconsolate bones, as he wept. The woman cautiously let fall her fleshy hand onto the man's head and massaged his temples, as lightly, as caringly as if his life depended on it.

"Gretchen!" the man sobbed.

The housekeeper had been working for the Markos for fifteen years. It was her job to take note of everything taking place in their home and she, true to her duty, noticed that thinning hair had afflicted an area above Samuel's forehead. Mr. Marko, his father, had a big bald patch on his head that made him look like an ancient, honorable sage. Most probably the son, too, would take the path to hair loss. For now, Samuel's hair was wet, unruly, the color of ripe wheat. Greta admired its amazing glossy abundance at the back of his head. She had cut it, combed it, fortified it with extracts of chamomile and mango, she had dyed it and she had even arranged his hair in a way that it looked as if Samuel had it permed.

"Gretchen," the man sobbed, pressing his forehead against her knees.

"You'll be all right," whispered the housekeeper. Her strong hand left his hair, glided down his neck then pulled lightly the pure silk collar pajamas, after a heartbeat the woman let her palm rest on his back. The man gave a start then his shoulders slumped.

"Gretchen," he breathed.

"It's all right," the plump middle-aged woman said. She knew his shoulders, his back, his arms, and everything there was to know about Samuel: she had taken care of the boy when his parents visited relatives abroad, when they played tennis or spent the night in a bar at the seaside. She had done her best not to let the fair skin on his shoulders get burned as Samuel soaked up in the sun. She had spread suntan lotion a thousand times on Samuel's chest, back, cheeks, forehead and legs. She had squeezed his pimples and had treated his oily skin giving him various pore minimizing treatments. She chose his shirts for him, she typed his poems on his computer, she washed and ironed his linen, she wrote his letters to his girl-friends, and she took him to the doctor concealing from his parents, at his most earnest request, Samuel's complaints of pain and discomfort when peeing. It transpired he'd got the clap. Years ago Samuel went on his own initiative to Color me Wild Tattoo Studio, and the tattoo artist printed in flaming ink her name **GRETA** on his lower abdominal area. The man tattooed a female face next to the name and Sam insisted it looked like Gretchen's, however the housekeeper disagreed with him on this issue. Her hand slalomed down his back; she knew the small freckles on every square inch of his skin. When Sammy was involved in a car accident with his new Jeep Wrangler she extracted the shards of glass from his wound with a pair of tweezers; she had removed a bee sting from his ear-lobe, and she had rubbed his naked body with a vinegar-soaked rag when the young man lay weak and delirious with the flu, mumbling, *"Sinna, Sinna."*

"Greta," Sam whispered in a soft voice she knew well.

His tears had already wet her immaculately clean apron, a constant presence in their home since Mr. Marko had been a speaker at a conference in Lausanne, Switzerland, and had availed himself of the opportunity to buy several lengths of sparkling white silk fabric. The lawyer hired a fashion designer and had 19 perfect aprons sewn by hand for Greta, the family's housekeeper. Mr. Marko provided Greta with various sports appliances: an exercise bike, a rowing machine, a treadmill etc. It was his desire that Greta be in good shape, and wearing her magnificent aprons for years to come. She had been working for the Markos for fifteen years now.

This time Samuel wetted not only Gretchen's white silk apron, but also the housekeeper's intimate apparel and her legs. She knew how warm his tears were; she had wiped them from his eyes when Sam got poor marks for his essays or his homework in mathematics, chemistry or physics. She talked to his teachers at William Shake-speare private school where Samuel received first-class education together with the sons and daughters of other leading lawyers and judges. Greta had blotted his tears with a soft handkerchief after Sam was with a girl for the first time, and unable to control himself had finished too rapidly. She had taken care of his tears when in the beginning Sinna had refused to marry him, and also at a later stage, after she left him a couple of times.

"Greta! Gretchen!" tears gathered in his voice, but there were live coals there as well, a situation she was familiar with.

"It's okay," she whispered.

The man stood up. He was much younger than the housekeeper. She removed her hair clip—Greta had dyed her hair red—and his mouth landed on her shoulder. Then his hand hidden under the elegant sleeve of his crumpled silk pajamas slowly crawled to the buttons of her clean apron. His eyes, not yet entirely dry, calmed down and waited near her welcoming, smiling lips.

"Greta, Greta, Greta," he whispered as he sank into her soft freckled skin. He felt warm and comfortable there; her lap was a place where no one abandoned him. Perhaps the woman with the powerful black eyes on the picture did not approve of what was happening in the sky, the sky being the light-blue carpet on the floor, and the yellow face of the sun woven in one of the corners.

"Greta," the young man breathed happily forgetting his distress as he relaxed in the easy hot nest of her soft flesh that felt simple and round like a loaf of bread. It accepted him in his gentle, soothing rhythm.

"It's okay," the woman said, smiling encouragingly.

It meant peace for him or at least two hours of sound sleep.

The young man relaxed, his smile sinking into her freckled warmth. His hand stroked her, taking its time, carefully, gently, enjoying her beautiful rotund fullness, the wonderful curves, a result of her love for Vienna strawberry rolls. Greta's wonderful softness was the reason he was full of respect for Viennese baked goods. Her freckled dampness had never misled him. Her skin did not criticize him; it accepted him with joy and gratitude. It was so reassuring.

"Greta..." the young man whispered going to sleep on her shoulder. "Don't go."

"Would you like me to draw a lavender bath for you, Sammy?" she asked as she let her fingers trail down his back. He was sweating profusely and Greta had to swab his chest with eau-de-Cologne.

"You are magnificent," he said, half-awake.

The housekeeper cautiously detached herself from the blue warmth of the carpet. She thought of the soft blue towels; she, as a rule, prepared them well in advance, smoothing the inviting fabric with care and sprinkling aromatic lavender elixir over it. Patiently and skilfully, taking her time, the housekeeper wiped the sweat from his skin, buttoned up his pajama bottom, then thrust a pillow under his sleeping cheekbones, under the auburn hair she'd made up her mind to wash after Samuel awoke. She studied his face for a long time. It's time to shave that beard, she thought; Sammy loved the touch of the safety razor on his cheeks. After it she applied aftershave, enjoying the anxious twitch of his startled muscles. For the exercise with the aftershave, Greta put on one of the special white bathrobes that Mr. Marko had given her. Sammy adored playing with its belt. The housekeeper covered the young man with the blue sheets on which she had embroidered *SINNA* with black thread in the four corners. Sinna's name was emblazoned in the middle of the sheet as well. Greta was sure that a name faded from memory quickly. It won't be necessary to draw a lavender bath for him, the housekeeper thought. She took a step to the door, opened it quietly and left the room.

9.

SHE LIKED THE HILLS AND their shadows that towered over their house. In the evening, their tops looked like children waking up after a day of tests at school. There were no paths or springs on them, they were wild mountains overgrown with prickly trees that pressed and pushed each other fighting with their spines and thorns to grab as much as possible of the sky. The hawks built their nests amidst the thick branches, and foxes dug their lairs under the sharp roots. In winter, wolves rushed out of the woods, one, two or three, their black shadows spreading panic in the valley. Like a blizzard, the wolf pack raided houses and backyards. One day Binna saw a wolf in Vancha's barn; the beast, his muzzle dripping blood, was tearing the young donkey into pieces. In summer, the hills hissed, shivering under the agile weight of the snakes and the thin claws of the lizards. In June, the old women, all of them herb-gatherers willy-nilly, scurried around the meadows and woods to pick goose-grass, chamomile blossoms and yarrow leaves. Judging by the heaps of herbs they gathered one might infer that there were no healthy or fit men in the whole valley.

The hills were still state property. However rumors had it that a bigwig from the capital was going to buy them the way he'd put in his pocket the whole Barren Ridge, the Muddy Creek, coming complete with its source, its fish and the leeches in the mud. No matter what, the hills were common lands and no one bothered to guard them with the exception of Space, the forest ranger, a loner and a drunk. Two years ago, he buried his mother, an old crone who had dragged a hoe, a rusty tail in her wake, bent to the ground, and had dug her meager garden years on end. Space's father had gone to pick olives and oranges in Italy; he didn't call his family and never came back home. Space's mother believed he had died. There were no olives, no oranges, they all were green; obviously he had left too early for Rome. He and the men from his group had to pick cones from some very big Italian pine trees. These were unnatural cones as big as brandy bottles, full to the brim with seeds. Those seeds were reputed to cure the sick: if a man was no longer a man with his woman, they gave him back his manliness, and if a lady ate too many of these Italian seeds she grew a thin moustache. And if a pregnant woman happened to consume a tiny bag of these, she gave birth to an infant with shoulder-length hair and teeth in his mouth. Those miraculous cones gave men back their youth and that was why Space's father picked them although he was on the wrong side of seventy. Just his luck—a cone as big as a grenade crashed into his head. He plummeted to the ground, a stone hit him in the small of the back and the only thing he could do was to crawl a couple of yards and breathe his last. He had not even got the money he'd earned. The poor devil was saving up for Space's wedding. Not that Space was itching to get married. Was there any woman for Space to marry apart from barren Dana and the herb-gathering crones? Not at all: any girl able to conceive a child ran to give birth to it in Greece. Then the girl gave her baby to a childless Greek belle, collected the dough she'd bargained for and came back with the fat bundle to the Bulgarian Black Sea coast to enjoy life as much as she pleased and as long as the bundle allowed. Perhaps her son Space would have children one day the old woman hoped, months before she met her maker.

Mother and son lived far from the center of the town, under the hill; an unlucky place that gave rise to torrents of mud and sand in rainy autumns and springs.

The floods had carved a long broad cut into the red stone in their backyard. Space's mother, rapidly getting on in years, threw the garbage into this *pit* which proved to be a wrong move. Rats as fat as piglets infested the area; they attracted homeless dogs and creatures unknown so far in these parts. When Space killed a strange beast the biology teacher said it was either a jackal or a Greek wolf, he was not exactly sure which, for he had never visited Greece. These monsters were arrogant and had no shame: they stalked the fields, sneaked into Space's kitchen and filched bread from the table. After Space's mother died the beasts had nothing to steal because no matter if they were jackals or Greek wolves, none of them drank brandy—the only item Space's house was well-provided with.

One day Binna found him prostrate on the bottom of the stone groove, his gun abandoned on the edge at the top, his empty canteen at his feet, and a couple of jackals, their ears pricked up, spreading stink in the air. Binna approached the deep cut in the stone. No one feared jackals now; the beasts were dangerous in winter, in summer they kept their distance, wearing their grayish-black coats like foul-smelling flags of insolence throughout the valley. Binna shook the forest guard, but he didn't budge. The smell of the jackals had disappeared; the place was filled with the appalling stench of dirty clothes and cheap brandy that had cemented the air enveloping the body like a concrete fence.

"Hey," Binna called out. He didn't stir. "Hey."

She bent toward him. He was breathing slowly and deeply. The bag in which he carried his food was torn with only an onion left in it. The jackals must have eaten everything else and now they were waiting for him to die, then an onion, tattered clothes, a pair of old plimsolls which Space put on his bare feet, and the empty canteen would be all that would remain of his life.

Binna wiped the dirt from his cheek, stroked her fingers over his hair and left him. On her way back home she'd probably find him again sound asleep in the thick air of his smell. If Space came to his senses, he'd disappear in the forest. Could he really guard the trees? The big oaks had been all cut, young and old used them as fire wood in the savage winter when the snow had covered the kennels. In the dead of night some villagers cut the plum trees in the backyard of their neighbors who had gone to pick olives in Spain. People burned the old chairs and tables of their relatives who were in England or Italy hoping to survive on the money they earned by taking care of invalids. No benches, boards or old shoes remained in the town of Radomir, men had burned everything that could burn. It was so cold that the spiders in Binna's library froze to death.

Children from the primary school came, wrapped in thick knitted shawls, to return their copies of *Wild Stories* and borrow *If They Could Speak*, a thin book of short stories by Yovkov, Binna's favorites, for the test in Bulgarian literature on Tuesday. Black and empty, the library hall gaped at Binna. The central heating had been turned off, and Binna sat close to a tiny electric heater, although it was expressly forbidden to use heating appliances in the library. She read over and over Talev's *The Iron Lamp,* trying to commit to memory a passage she particularly liked, hoping she'd somehow get warm. Her hands had gone numb with cold. Then a fierce blizzard broke the electrical wiring, it was impossible to switch on the heater, so the mayor informed Binna she had to close the library for a week or two.

She had no other job; perhaps Barren Dana would send for her. Binna could read that excerpt from *The Iron Lamp* to her. Rumor had it that Barren Dana went in for sobbing while she perused a sad book; she was said to drink red wine, her tears dripping into her glass as if her eyes were a watering pot. On Wednesdays, Barren Dana dedicated two hours of her time—from 2 pm to 4 pm—to commiserating with her fellow-townsmen's woes. She let folks enter her house encircled by a ten-foot-high wall and talked to them. She wanted to know who suffered from high blood pressure; who had died, so she could give some money to the family and help with the funeral costs; who was sick, so that she could give him a hand with procuring medicines that were difficult to find, or she just hired a man to clean her stables, shoe Giant, her horse, or recruited a woman to embroider something for her or bring her herbs which would help Dana conceive a child.

The truth was Dana had given up drinking fertility herbal drinks, and had taken to guzzling natural immune-system boosters instead, predominantly red wine, as well as herbal infusions against warts and moles, occasionally downing a glass or two of new concoctions reputed to help ladies lose weight. Dana was not fat, not at all; she was simply as big as the clock tower of the Town Hall, and although the clock stopped twenty years ago, the locals believed it brought them good luck. As it was, the old women who roamed the woods and fields in these parts could find any herbs their clients wanted: herbs that gave you love and ones that helped you get rid of love; thyme that cured you of your spots and thyme that made pimples grow on your forehead and burn like candles there. They could find such grasses for you that could force the donkey to harness himself and start pulling your cart. Those old women from Radomir were great herb-gatherers indeed.

Vancha was a skilled herb-gatherer, too, but she was only interested in grasses that killed lice that bred in the second-hand clothes her son brought in heavy-weight trucks from Spain, hiding in the heaps of tattered jackets olives in barrels. At times, Vancha's son imported rusty bone-shakers, too.

Binna remembered. This happened many years ago, perhaps she was fifteen at that time. Vancha had spoken in great detail to Barren Dana about her tractable adopted daughter that loved reading books most of everything else in the world. Her nose was buried in dusty pages all the time. Dana had snapped, "Okay, bring Binna to my house; I want her to read something to me. The book must be sad. I want to shed two jars of tears. I am sick at heart," Barren Dana complained. "I tell you, Vancha Auntie, I love all children in Radomir as if they were all mine, every single one of them."

On the following day, Binna took *The Iron Lamp* and was honored to read to Ms. Dana. Isabella, Dana's trusted expert, was in the reading room too. Dana lay in bed and listened, all the time grunting and snorting; the fact that she couldn't fill two jars with her tears no matter how hard she tried obviously displeased her. On the other hand, Isabella couldn't take her eyes off Binna. Was the expert afraid the teenage girl was going to pinch something, or had she just loved *The Iron Lamp*? Binna was unable to decide. She was just about to go when Barren Dana remembered something and said, "Binna, sit down. I'd like to talk to you, and I don't feel like getting up. I chopped up a dry oak in the morning, my girl, and I shot three hawks and I want you to know this. I like the way you read. You put commas in your voice and pause too often, but that's fine with me, Binna. Something else is eating me, girl. I can hear those vile hawks chewing my chickens in their beaks, the brazen bastards."

"What about jackals, Miss Dana? They are brash too, aren't they?" Binna said. "A week ago Donni, our donkey, disappeared. We found hooves and bones in the field. The pack must have killed Donni and dragged him to the river."

"O, my!" Dana brightened up, sitting up in her bed. "Binna, come back and let me know everything you know about the brazen bastards."

Binna told her about the jackals in minute detail, described their shadows weaving thin, piercing howls into the dusk. The beasts had surrounded Aggo, the old-clothes man; the poor darling was not dead, Binna said, he had just collapsed on the path on his way back home, and the beasts waited for him to die so they could gnaw at his bones. The man shouted at the top of his lungs, and luckily at that time a car slowed down then stopped, and the driver saved his life.

"Good!" Barren Dana laughed delightedly. "Awesome! Now I know what I'll shoot at. I'll ambush the bastards first thing in the morning. What do you say, Isabella? I wonder... guess what! I want to catch a jackal and strangle him with my own hands."

"I don't think this will be possible, Miss Dana," Isabella, Miss Dana's business assistant, said. "The jackal is a strong and dirty pest. They assemble in small nasty packs and scavenge for food in the trash and..."

"Binna, don't you know what I did to that big wolf? How come you haven't heard! He was a huge son of a bitch. The whole town got into panic when the freak ate a calf and slit a stallion's throat. Todor, my shepherd, nearly went off his nut over this loss. Haven't you caught a whiff of this problem, Binna?"

"No, I haven't, Miss Dana."

"It's all right. Your mom says you're an oddball at times, staying at home like they've thrown you into the dungeon and reading like an idiot. There's no money in books, my girl. Money gives you forests and lakes, fish and fields heavy with tomatoes, onions and peppers. Money gives you men that are taller than you. Money gives you herbs to get pregnant. Money gives *me* learned people like you, Binna, and now you're sweating over that *Iron Lamp* to sadden my heart and make me cry. I can pay for learned men from Sofia, but to tell you the truth, I have no faith in their cackling lectures. I am not sad at all these days, Binna. What do you think—am I a normal woman? Choose the most heartbreaking words in the book. I want to sob with sorrow. I haven't sobbed for two years now. Do you think red wine can cause permanent brain damage, Binna?"

"I don't know, Miss Dana," Binna said. "It's not a bad thing that you are not sad."

"Shut up, Binna," Barren Dana cut her short. "Bring me a sadder book tomorrow. I want something about love and jealousy to let my tears loose. You told me about the fucking jackals, thank you. I'll catch a son of a bitch, I'll fatten him like a pig, I'll smother him with a pillow and I'll bring you here to watch and describe what I'm doing. Your mom tells me you're constantly writing something. You hide from the guys and scribble like a son of a bitch hermit all the time, don't go out on dates. How come! You're a pretty girl. Well, tell me what sort of tales do you write—perhaps sad ones?" Dana's voice slowed down, full of hope.

"Unfortunately they are not, Miss Dana. I'm not sure my tales are any good."

"Shame on you, girl, it's you who writes them, isn't? If you aren't sure they're good who else will be? Me? Pull yourself together. I'll tell you about my life and you'll write everything down. Men and women should learn what they don't know about me. Do I make myself clear? Hey, Isabella, tell Binna here about the wolf that was as big as a horse. Tell her how I cut the son of a bitch's throat."

Isabella's eyes crawled to Binna's face first, then hurried to Binna's eyes the way a hungry man rushed to a loaf of bread and held it like a clothes-hanger held a coat on its hook. Was Isabella scared Binna might oust her from the stone house and the lake, from the fields and the acacia trees surrounded by a ten-foot wall?

"I like reading," Binna said. "I think that Ms. Isabella is the best qualified person to work for you, Miss Dana. I will not be able to stay with you for a long time."

"Come off it, Binna. Who presses you to stay with me? You'll come on Tuesdays and you'll read to me for an hour or so. That's all there is to it. You'll benefit from your visits in many ways: a free bath in a warm bathroom, free ham and cheese. It's Isabella who offered to prepare the bathroom for you. It's not too much trouble for her. She'll iron two additional towels and she'll bake a dozen jam rolls more than usual. I and Isabella love these jam rolls! Come on, Isabella. Tell the girl here about the freaking wolf."

It was pleasant in the room. The sun shone through the window, touching the fleecy rugs, the wraps, even the Persian carpet put on view in the middle of the room. There were rag carpets, too, all made in Radomir, spread on the parquet floor made by several outstanding Italian furniture makers. Japanese mahogany chests of drawers jutted out next to big crate-like boxes, rough boards hammered together, looking quite unstable.

"Speak, Isabella," Dana impatiently encouraged her expert as she grabbed a chunk of warm steaming bread and sank her teeth into its crust.

"Miss Dana, why don't you let me rub your back in the first place, and she'll see what you did to the bastard. Every time I massage your back you howl and growl like that wolf. The beast tossed and turned as hard as if he was your brother."

"Don't be a smartass and tell us about the wolf," Miss Dana advised her expert. Then, in a sudden flash of inspiration, she added, "You can simultaneously massage my back and speak about the bastard. So we won't waste precious time."

"Well, the wolf… he…" Isabella started as she took hold of Dana's arm and squeezed is as hard as she could. "Look here, Miss Dana, your muscles sag like an old mattress. I'll spread some quail liver oil on them and they'll glitter as hard as a gold necklace. Well, I say. That wolf was as big as a bull. Miss Dana and I got into the jeep, and the son of a bitch gaped at us as big as a church. I tell her, 'Quick! Let's beat it, Miss Dana. Let's make ourselves scarce, I tell you! This idiot here looks hungry!' Miss Dana says, 'He's not hungry, Isabella. You drive the jeep and I'll put a bullet through his fat ass.' Miss Dana, let me rub your feet now. Your muscles droop like a calf's. That's the honest truth. I'll spread some quail liver oil on them and they'll shine like the sun and the moon."

"Tell her about the wolf,"

"Well, the motherfucker was bigger than our jeep."

"Tell us more about him! You're driving me crazy, Isabella. Stop humming and hawing or I'll kick your ass. Is it clear? Tell Binna what happened to the wolf, and massage me hard, woman. No wonder my muscles droop like a calf's! You're not massaging, you're sleeping and snoring. Push me, press me. If you can't press hard enough then take the steak hammer, and hit my back. These are legs, woman, they aren't pats of butter. Tell her about the wolf or I'll strangle you with my own hands."

"The wolf was huge… I was driving and I wanted to pee. I thought to myself, this son of a bitch will get at my throat, he'll chew my poor head like popcorn and I'll croak. I was about to wet my pants. I wasn't scared, mind you, I didn't stop driving. 'If you stop driving I'll shoot you dead, you louse,' Miss Dana told me very openly. So I drove on feeling the wolf's eyes on my throat all the time."

"On your throat my foot! What happened after that? Speak up or I'll order Doc Gospod to give you an enema," Miss Dana shouted. "Press harder! Those are legs, Isabella, not eggs. Harder I tell you. If you are not strong enough step on my back and run on it, but wash your feet first."

"Okay. Well, the wolf took to his heels. He galloped to the river and Miss Dana raised her gun—bang! Bang! Bang or no bang, the son of a bitch wasn't impressed. Ran on like a sprint champion and didn't give a damn she was shooting at him."

"Okay, Okay, leave that bullshit in the past and tell her what happened at a later stage," Miss Dana growled.

"Well, at a later stage… Miss Dana, shall I massage your stomach now? You ate a ton of that rotten veal. Honestly, Miss Dana, you gorged yourself on steaks and they were as good as ropes. You're full like a leech now. I'm afraid you'll get cramps and make me sing and dance for you. Even if I sing and dance for you the pain won't go away, believe me. Let me rub quail liver oil into your belly and it'll shine like a shield. O, my, it will glow like the roof of the Town Hall! You won't ever suffer from stomach ache or gut ache, you can take my word for it, Miss Dana. You'll be so happy that you'll sing and dance for me. I'll applaud you of my own free will, it won't be necessary for you to force me to constantly give you standing ovations."

"Speak about the wolf, woman."

"Ok, ok. Well, at a certain point, Miss Dana got into a huff. 'The freaking bastard,' she shouted. 'I'll crush his freaking skull like a nut.' 'Excuse me, how will you catch him?' I asked. 'The son of a bitch races like a Ferrari through the fallow fields, so you can't put a bullet through his brain.' And that was the honest truth. You couldn't even put a bullet through his tail, Miss Dana, so I couldn't conceive as to how you were going to crush the bastard's skull like a nut."

"It's true I didn't shoot him. You don't have to rub it in," Barren Dana warned her manager. "Press my stomach harder, woman, once you took to massaging it. It's full to the brim of beefsteaks, and they all were stringy like reinforcement of concrete work. Why did I gobble a ton of veal, why, Isabella? I slaughtered the calf myself, and I skinned it. And its meat was strings and ropes all over the place."

"You should've let the calf alone, Miss Dana. The poor thing would've died of its own accord if only it had looked at you," Isabella pointed out. "Then I could've soaked the meat overnight in apple vinegar then your steaks would've been as gentle as candy floss."

"Tell us about the wolf, Isabella!"

"Well… the bastard was a very particular son of a bitch. I'd say he was a dinosaur, not a wolf, no sir. At a certain point, Miss Dana tied huge chunks of meat around her waist. A couple of hours ago, a couple of jackals were tearing a cow into pieces, but they couldn't tear the poor animal to the end for the following reason: Miss Dana opened fire against them. The beasts couldn't even squeal their last, rotten stinkers they sure were. We cut the meat of the dead cow into massive *segments* and we set ourselves an ambitious goal: to lure the wolf with the meat. I didn't go in for lures or wolves, not in the least, but Miss Dana tied the chunks of meat around her waist, around her ass and thighs and I told her, 'Don't tie cow's carrion to your legs, Miss Dana, for you cannot run fast enough when the wolf chases you.' She said, 'I'll teach the motherfucker a big lesson.' So Miss Dana got out of the jeep single handed, no gun or knife on her, and ordered me, 'Isabella, you'll come with me. Take this piece of rope. We'll tie the motherfucker with it.' I was walking by her side, but I passed out and…"

"You didn't pass out. You faked a heart attack," Barren Dana corrected her chief experts, outraged. "Now rub my back hard. Your whopping lies make every single bone in my body hurt. The stringy steaks are not to blame. You are the guilty party, Isabella."

"I did lose consciousness, the rope and I both collapsed on the ground as the wolf rushed and attacked Miss Dana." The chief expert swallowed hard then made up her mind and said firmly, "Miss Dana produced her gun and bang! Bang! At that point I came to."

"I thought she didn't have a gun," blue-eyed Binna said.

"She did!" Isabella exclaimed. "I gave it to her before I swooned. The wolf lay like a worm, sprawling all over the place and spitting blood."

"He was not spitting blood," Barren Dana corrected her. "He lay peacefully on the grass. You were unconscious at that time and you couldn't see what he was doing."

"The wolf lay peacefully and spat blood, and Miss Dana said to me, 'Drive Kamen, the vet, here without delay.' 'Are you crazy or what, Miss Dana,' I tried hard to give her food for thought. 'Kamen, the vet, is having a kidney fit, and he's treating his kidneys with elderberry and chamomile infusions.' 'He'd better not treat his kidneys with elderberry and chamomile infusions. I want him here to immediately examine the wolf,' Miss Dana categorically instructed me. The beast was as big as a hill, I tell you the truth. Miss Dana tied his legs, took off her blouse and cut it into strips. It turned out the piece of rope was too short, so she tied the son of a bitch's muzzle with strips of her blouse and other rags. I went to Kamen the vet's place. The poor bugger lay in bed, treating his condition: a big electric iron hissed, glued to his left kidney, another iron, a smaller piece, was pressed against his right kidney. 'I cannot cure this wolf. He's lost gallons of blood,' the vet declared, rapidly establishing the diagnosis, but after Miss Dana gave him a fat bundle, the guy's kidneys healed within an hour.

Kamen, the vet, patched up the wolf and made his pierced coat as good as new.

We imprisoned the beast in the tool shed. Tano's mattress lay on the floor; we'd forgotten to remove it from the shed. I don't know what ideas coursed through the son of a bitch's mind. Has a wolf got any mind, in the first place? The idiot tore the mattress into tiny bits and filled the shed with cotton tatters and foam. You can't imagine, Binna, how hard it is to collect the foam of a mattress! It was on that day that I busted my immune system. I ruined the darling system of mine while I cleaned the damned cotton tatters and the foam. And a motherfucker virus knocked me down."

"Yes, it knocked her down all right," said Barren Dana. "She couldn't stir a finger and I rubbed her back the way she's rubbing mine now. But I pressed her bones hard; I didn't put on airs like she's doing now. I forked out three grand to bring a decent doctor to Radomir—the guy was a luminary from Sofia, from the Medical Academy, and he did Isa's measly virus in. Well, let bygones be bygones. She got well on the following day."

"O, stop it, Miss Dana! The stinking virus made a frail mouse of me. My immune system is a shambles now."

"Doc Gospod says your immune system is as strong as the crags on the hill," Dana chided. "Go on about the wolf now."

Binna glanced at her watch. It was high time she went home; in the evenings, it was she that fed the animals and cooked dinner. Vancha could walk very slowly and Binna's father, Aggo the junkman, lay in bed most of the time.

"No matter how often you look at your watch I won't let you go. You have to learn what happened to the wolf at the end. You haven't cooked dinner for Aggo and Vancha, you say? No problem. I'll send old Vancha a chunk of the meat from the calf I had just skinned. I had to wait a day for its muscles to truly die. It goes without saying I didn't wait, so the meat's as stringy as a truck tire. So your mom and your dad will boil it for a couple of hours. I'll send someone to feed your cow and give the hens some corn. You listen to what I tell you about the wolf. Tomorrow, you'll have to describe everything in details. Isabella, speak. Now."

"I'm sick and tired of that beast, don't you understand this?" the expert got in a fret, but the air in the room shook as Dana's nervous hand waved her words off. The expert heaved a deep sigh then went on. "Well, the damned son of a bitch, I mean the wolf… Kamen, the vet, worked here every single day of the week, in this very room, treating the freaking beast. Poor Kamen spread quail's tallow on his ass, and the wolf glittered like a silver baking dish. He shone more brightly than the stars and that was bizarre. Every time I passed by the shanty in which we had penned up the monster, the damned wolfish idiot threw himself on me—jumped to the left, bounded to the right—to the ceiling did the bastard leap, and I—since my bladder is no good, you know—gradually pissed in my pants. Miss Dana didn't show any understanding for my plight and told me very rudely indeed, 'Your bladder is no excuse, you shifty Isabella. Go feed the wolf.' I fed the bastard; this freak of nature gobbled down two calves and grew as tall as Miss Dana. She realized how stupid she'd been and said, 'He'll pay through his nose, the son of a bitch.'"

"You forgot something," Barren Dana dangerously shifted in her bed. "You didn't mention a very important thing: we weighed the bastard as he sprawled on the scale. I shackled his legs together, tied his muzzle, his poor buttocks sprayed with my bullets. The animal weighed 260 pounds."

"Yes, that's true. Miss Dana ordered me, 'Go weigh the bastard, Isabella.' But my miserable bladder, you know, did the thing again… so a team of vets from Sofia was sent for. They weighed the freak of nature. Five big guys they were, each one more learned than the next one. They toiled and moiled, and tossed and turned, and ran and cussed. At long last, the vets measured how long the wolf was. All their bladders were so weak that... you know what I mean. Why don't you ask me how I felt all this time with my poor... you know what I mean. Then Miss Dana slaughtered him."

"Pull yourself together, faint-hearted Isabella! Tell the girl what exactly I did. Stop beating about the bush and don't focus on your bloody bladder. Put it plainly and more directly what measures I undertook to bust the bastard. Or I'll send for Doc Gospod, and you'll undergo medical treatment."

"I don't need a doctor. I've fully recovered my health," the expert reassured her boss.

"Explain to the girl how I shaped him up," Miss Dana urged her manager. "Sorry Binna. I don't usually shout this much; I have to push her on, you see. Isabella leads us out of the story all the time. She's a white-livered lady that's why she can't concentrate."

"White-livered my foot! Miss Dana, let's keep it at that. If I start insulting *you*, I can talk for days. And I'll speak no lies, mind you. Ok, let's get down to brass tacks. Miss Dana entered the shanty with knife in hand. I shouted at her, 'Don't do that. This crazy specimen will eat you up.' But the specimen didn't eat her up, she cut his throat instead. I was waiting by her side with a rifle in my trembling hands. If the specimen had half a mind to guzzle her, I'd instantaneously put a dumdum bullet into his big fat head. He'd be dead meat all over the place. But I didn't have to stir a finger, no Ma'am. Miss Dana grabbed the mutant's muzzle, squeezed it hard then slashed his throat with the kitchen knife."

"I'll slit a jackal's throat as well, but we have to catch the bastard first. I hate it if young and old in these parts complain about them... I am furious over jackals. If I catch one, I'll cut his ears and I'll have Isabella nail them to the wall above my bed."

"Not above your bed, Miss Dana. They'll stink," Isabella pointed out.

"You'll kill the stink," Barren Dana said. "Isabella, I've had enough of your massaging efforts. Binna, did you commit to memory everything Isa said? Describe precisely what I'd done to the wolf, namely: how I sank a dagger into his fat throat. Don't mention I didn't hit the bastard when I shot at him. Folks don't want to know that. If you're no good at verbs, adverbs and other grammar stuff don't worry. Tell me i-mmediately. I'll pay a professor from Sofia, and the chap will fix things after you."

"Of course, Miss Dana, I'll write about you. Can I go now?"

"Why don't you take a bath first?" Isabella suggested. "I've prepared the bathroom for you. It's as hot as a flat iron in there. I bought Graciella body lotion and the best hydrating face cream, Venice Dawn," Isabella's eyes fastened on Binna although it was hardly possible for the girl to pilfer anything.

"Look, I hear curious tales about you, Binna," Barren Dana said pointedly. "They tell me you roam the forest all by yourself. That's stupid of you. You don't belong in the wilderness."

"You mustn't wander from your course like a moon-struck lunatic," Isabella commented.

"There's nothing else I can do," Binna said. "One day I saw a drunk on the road. Dogs were licking his face. I chased them away and cleaned his cheeks. A man should be neat and tidy."

"Come and tidy my room, then. Rooms should be clean, too."

"Stop it, Isabella. You'll tidy your room yourself."

Binna walked into the bathroom. Everything in it was white: big, dazzlingly white tiles from Sibari, Italy, showerheads from Naples, shampoos and cakes of soap from Milan, and a towel from Rome.

"Do you want me to rub your back?" Isabella turned to Binna.

"I know perfectly well which body lotion will be the best choice for your skin."

"You are very kind but no, thank you."

"I can dye your hair for you if you want. I've got a magnificent dip dye hair kit from Italy."

"It will not be necessary, thank you."

"Then let me take a bath with you. It's so cozy in the bathroom. The walls are warm now. We won't go to all the expenses of warming them up one more time."

"You take a bath first, Isabella. I'll wait."

"Why? Look, folks speak about head lice infestation in town," Isabella took a step to the girl, reached out and touched her face. "Do you have lice? Let me see. Magnificent skin! Magnificent! I know which moisturizer is best for you."

Binna took a step to the door and Isabella followed her.

"Go away," Binna said.

"I will," Isabella's hand returned to the pocket of her apron. "But I'll check if you have lice first and I'll give you the best moisturizing day cream."

"I don't have lice," Binna said, but Isabella had turned on the Italian faucets, and the girl's words drowned in the warm water.

"Don't be afraid."

"I am not afraid. Go, Isabella."

"Ok, ok, I'll go. See? I'm getting out of here. Take your time."

Isabella withdrew towards the corner and was gone. The girl hesitated and locked the door, then bolted it and checked if the narrow window on the wall was properly closed. The two latches were in place. Then Binna took her clothes off. She had never seen such splendor in her life. Naum, Vancha's son, maintained that bathrooms in Italy looked much worse than Barren Dana's full bath. The whole town spoke of Barren Dana's bathroom with admiration. Naum had procured the tiles from Naples, the faucets and the showerheads from Milan, the shampoo and body lotion bottles and the cakes of soaps from Rome. He was firmly convinced that baths in Italy were of a much poorer quality than Miss Dana's bath, but no one in Italy believed what he said.

Binna turned the faucet on, and magnificent hot water, plenty of it, enveloped her body. At home, the faint trickle of lukewarm drops ran dry after five minutes of pathetic dripping and gurgling. Vancha saved every drop at home every single day. The bathtub here smelled so good, her shampoo was soft and gentle, and the towel was so fragrant that Binna kissed it.

On the other side of the wall, Isabella watched intently, her eyes glued to the windowpane. She'd frozen in her tracks, her breath babbling, rasping in her throat, dangerous, edgy, iridescent like the hot water, gushing from the faucets.

Half an hour later, after Binna left the Italian tiles and the showerheads from Milan, she saw something that frightened her.

"Isabella, are you ok? Your face is as red as embers."

"Oh… well, I remembered the way the wolf snarled when I fed him," Isabella muttered. "Look here, you can come here on Mondays and Thursdays. You can take a bath in this house every day if you want. Give me a call, and I'll prepare the bathtub for you: shampoo, body lotion, salts, you'll have everything. And you can describe Miss Dana's life as long as you please."

"Your face is red," Binna said as she rushed to the courtyard where the ten-foot high wall merged with the horizon and ate the brown winter branches of the trees.

"Mondays and Thursdays, ok? The bathtub will be waiting for you. Find something deathly sad for Miss Dana. She's itching to sob. She hasn't sobbed for two years now."

"Good bye," the blue-eyed girl said.

She didn't describe any events that had unfolded in Miss Dana's life.

Although the day was sunny, a stiff wind cut through the valley. She had showered at home and her hair was wet; it turned out the thick shawl she'd put in her bag was a good idea. Binna walked along the deserted street. In front of the houses, on rough wooden benches, the old women sat, dreaming of herbs able to kill any pain under the sun. They could find elderberries for you if you told them you wanted your cheek tooth to grow again, although the young dentist pulled it out a week ago; they sold herbs that gave you a lover, and other herbs that drove your lover away; they had dry grasses helping you to conceive a child, but in these parts few women showed interest in remedies of this sort. The girls in these parts got pregnant without resorting to thyme or sage. Folks bought herbs against pissing too often, against bad blood pressure and heart palpitations. Barren Dana wanted a baby, looked for thyme and sage too, but none of the old women offered herbs to solve her problem.

Students from a dozen villages studied at the school in Radomir and dropped in the library to take short story collections, poems, or fairytales. Most of the boys didn't care for books; they just stared at her.

"You are very pretty, Binna," a boy from the high school nature class said one day. "My brother says he hasn't seen a prettier woman then you. He's picked olives in every square yard of Italy, Cypress, Greece and Spain, and he knows everything worth knowing."

Sometimes girls touched the sleeve of her sweater; Milena in the biology class said that after she fingered the blue-eyed librarian's dress, a guy she enormously liked finally asked her on a date. She touched Binna's dress one more time: on the following day they became a couple and made a decision to beat it together for Spain.

The hidalgos in Barcelona would hopefully hire them at some hotel or other. There was another detail to the story: Binna had lost her blouse, a cheap thing from Vancha's second-hand shop. Milena in the biology class found it, put it on and couldn't believe what happened! The guy asked her to become his wife! Another girl in the biology class, Simona, had an idea: she cut a piece of cloth from the blouse and put it in her coat pocket. She didn't reveal who had asked her out on a date, but on the following day the girls in the biology class clutched at one another's hair. Everyone wanted a piece of Binna's blouse although it was nothing to brag about: a handful of wrinkled fabric. Binna's second-hand shawl vanished as well.

The guys in the biology, Bulgarian literature, mathematics and chemistry classes visited the school library very often in winter, it had not been closed down, although even the spiders croaked in the cold. Mice too decamped for warmer mouse-holes, but the place still smelled of rats. The smarter boys like, for example Nikolay, gave Binna artificial flowers on account of the fact that there were no blooms on the roses in the school garden.

"Here, Binna," Nikolay said. "This is for you." And he gave her tulips made of plastic spoons. She gave him a piece of her cheese pie she'd brought for lunch, but the young man shook his head. "I've got something better than your pie," and he produced a small bottle of Sun brandy from his pocket. "Take a swig. You'll drop dead if you don't. Brandy will warm you up."

"I've got an electric heater," Binna pointed to the thing that glimmered like a firefly in the frosty air, its feeble light making the room colder. A week ago, Nikolay brought her a thick woolen cardigan that weighed five pounds.

"It's my mom's," he had said. "My mom's in Spain. It's summer all the time in Madrid. They've got winter too, but it lasts three days, and they can't collect three pounds of snow three winters in a row. It rains sometimes, but the roofs aren't leaky like yours here."

"Thank you, Nicky," Binna had said. "I've got thick sweaters too. I've put on two of them today and I'm not cold."

"I'll graduate from school and I'll leave for Spain. My mom's already found a job for me at a parking lot, and I'll have a second job, a vampire's assistant for a small circus," the boy explained. "I'll roll in money, but..."

At that point, Binna offered him more of her cheese pie.

"Have a quick bite to eat. Thank you for the cardigan and the brandy, but I don't feel like drinking now."

The boy took a swig from the bottle.

"Brandy makes you plucky," he blurted out. "I don't want to go to Spain."

Binna smiled and touched his hand. Suddenly Nikolay grabbed her fingers.

"I don't want to go to Spain, Binna. I want to stay in the library. I'll read all the books if you want me to. I'll read the musty newspapers too. I'll paint the walls. No one will read the dirty inscriptions saying what they'll do if they can catch you."

Nikolay was six years her junior. Boys from tenth natural sciences class came to the library plastic flowers in hand. They took Ivan Vazov's selected short stories and returned the book on the following day. One boy, very keen on mathematics—his mother worked as a housekeeper for two elderly sisters in Toscana, Italy, and had given her son the most expensive mobile phone the town had seen—that boy took photos of Binna with his ungodly expensive machine. The clever guy stopped paying attention to what his math teacher said, gawking at Binna's pictures instead. But his mother got a whiff of this problem and took her son to Italy, complete with mobile telephone and Binna's pictures in it.

Nikolay collected the cardigan Binna didn't want, and took to drawing her portrait. He skipped contemporary Bulgarian literature class, bought a paper pad; bit the metal tip of the pencil then drew her face. Curved lines and circles glared in his picture; there was no face there. The truth was Nikolay couldn't draw a straight line without a ruler. At times he ceased painting altogether, staring at the library, hating the fact he was six years younger than the librarian. Although he knew he'd work at that parking lot in Spain and be a vampire's assistant in his spare time, he bought more of the brandy that made you a courageous man. The bottle failed him; it didn't give Nikolay much courage. He acted audaciously one single time: kissed Binna's hand. It was as cold as the frozen carp Grandma Nada sold in her small grocery store.

"I don't want Spain," Nikolay had said to the frozen carp of a hand. "I hate Spain. Sixteen days more and I'll graduate from school. The month of May will begin and school will be over. I hate the month of May. May spring never come! Binna, can we… before the month of May begins…" his courage ran dry in spite of the Sun brandy he'd downed. He kissed her fingers, not her cheek, the way he had planned. If his friends had seen that they'd have named him the dunce of town. But Nikolay knew: in Spain, he'd miss her cold fingers, her smile, the library full of Ivan Vazov and Bulgarian fairy tales arranged in severe rows on the shelves above her blue eyes.

Binna walked shivering with cold. There was a fierce wind blowing, and she ran to the scree that cut Space's backyard into halves. These gray hard stones fathered bad winters in these parts. At times the wind was so evil it wrenched out the stakes in Space's garden i.e. from his late mother's garden; the poor woman had grown three hundred tomato plants before she died. Space had not collected the stakes and they rotted in the mud. Perhaps he planned to use them as firewood, but the previous year the snow was so deep the stakes remained buried under it.

Binna wondered what Space was doing in the freezing cold. Did he have food, did he have a stove?

10.

WINTER WAS QUITE DIFFERENT FOR SINNA. Young men came back to the town of Radomir to check if the fences around their houses were still steady, if their mothers had survived the blizzards or pneumonia and flu had sent them to Black Peak. The guys painted the town red for a week in Barren Dana's pub, guzzling down Dana's cheap hogwash brandy. When they sobered up, Sinna cleaned their kitchens and swept their guest rooms as long as Euros rustled in their pockets. Before the poor devils returned to the olive groves and parking lots in Spain, they came to say good bye, thundering and shouting below Sinna's window. Binna and Sinna slept in one and the same room and the man whose house had been recently cleaned roared *Take me to an old country pub,* Sinna's favorite disco hit. Could the poor pub seat all fellows who itched to take Sinna there? The guys screamed this line only—no one remembered anything else of this song—and persisted until Sinna climbed out of her bed to clean for the last time the most desperate man's house.

They gave her gold rings and gold necklaces, these fools, nailed their photographs to Vancha's fence—every picture wrapped with thin nylon sheet, protecting it from snow and storms. Vancha's fence, separating her second-hand realm from the churchyard was coated with guys' photos. Time and harsh climate deleted eyes and beards, but the names of the towns printed in indelible purple ink under the guy's blurred face stayed on: Granada, Seville; many men —one could only conjecture if they were fair-haired or not—had written **MADRID** under their chins. Sinna crammed gold necklaces in two fruit jars as the old grandmas complained that guys shrieked at the top of their drunken lungs, cawing, gaggling and imploring Sinna to kiss them good night to which she answered, "Kiss my ass."

Worried sick, the old ladies called Sto, the policeman, and right they were: health was an important issue, their nerves jumped like frogs, and each one of them felt like a potential candidate for Black Peak. Sto promised that yes, he'd take care and settle this problem, but even in the same afternoon Sinna went and cleaned his living room.

She didn't stop cleaning it for two days, then went on polishing the pieces of old furniture and at the end of the event came back home ten silver spoons in her pocket: Sto's grandfather had taken them as a trophy from a deserted house in Vetra, Hungary. The man he had fought in the World War II and was awarded a silver medal for his courage. Sinna didn't know what to do with the archaic silverware, so she made Binna cook various soups every day—potatoes today, rice on the following day etc.—and she slurped her soup using a gorgeous different spoon every day.

Men went to the olive trees in the long run, and it was Space, the forest ranger, who stayed on to guard the timberland above Barren Dana's house, or perhaps the forest guarded him: when the poor soul got drunk, he collapsed onto the dry autumn leaves and the trees shook with his explosive snoring. Snakes heard it and ran away; probably the jackals already knew Space well enough for they ignored him totally when he lay prostrate on their path in the thicket.

At times, Naum, Vancha's son, showed up in Radomir. Huge trucks wallowed like buffalos in the mud behind her house. It was only natural that Naum distributed most of his merchandise to the stores that sold designer second-hand clothes at bargain prices in Sofia, but he left some rags in Radomir, too, in his mother's shop. Every time his trucks dropped anchor at Vancha's place, Sinna disappeared into thin air. No one saw her at breakfast, lunch or dinner. She made a short personal appearance, a minute or two, just enough to kiss Aggo, the junkman, goodnight and sing to him. She assured the old shirt he wouldn't kick the bucket in the night. Her kiss drove death twenty-two thousand miles away from Radomir, Sinna told him. But after Naum returned from Europe, she stopped using her silver spoons. She said she had more important issues at hand: teach Naum a couple of new tricks.

Naum's room was four walls of photographs: Naum a naked baby; Naum, a proud teenager with his silver medal from swimming; Naum at 14, 15, 16 and 17; Naum and his girlfriends; Naum a sergeant major in the Bulgarian armed forces; Naum, Vancha and Aggo on the day they opened the second-hand designer clothes store. This winter, Naum brought a heap of crumpled designer clothes, Sinna marched into his room, and he followed her, shouting, "Do not disturb me." Binna brought them food once every three hours, and at regular intervals loads of dirty dishes, gnawed bones and apple peels materialized in the corridor. Vancha gave these items to her poorer neighbors to help them keep body and soul together.

After Sinna's baby was born, Vancha carefully studied the runt: a boy, thin legs, thin neck, and extremely scraggy arms.

For years after the puny thing was born, on coming back from the olive trees, all men from Radomir, no exception to the rule, dropped in to see him. The boy was as quiet as the dust under the table, his transparent fingers twitching when guys from Spain, Cyprus, Malta, Brussels, Calabria patted him on the scrawny shoulder and asked, "How are you, son?" Sto, the policeman, also came to see the little one and, having asked Vancha's permission first, took him in the police car for a short drive.

Binna took care of the boy her sister had named Aggo after the junkman. She led him by the hand to Space's place, hoping they'd find him sober. Binna and the kid carried a bag of his linen and socks that Binna had washed. They brought meatballs in a metal box for him. His house smelled of brandy and cheap cigarettes, of dust and dirty shirts. If Space was sober, he sat silently at the table, tense, edgy, his chin propped on his fists. Binna tried hard to overcome the smell as she cleaned the room, and he stared at the torn tablecloth, silent like a stuffed toy. His eyes somehow managed to follow her steps, his body leaning towards her.

"Eat, "Binna said as she gave him the iron box with the food she'd brought. Vancha was a generous soul, within reasonable limits, of course. If she had a piece of meat or a bone, she'd prefer to offer it to her dog, not to the drunkard, although he was the only man Binna cared about; the only one too that didn't go pick olives, strawberries of raspberries in Italy, Greece, England or a dozen of other places in the wind.

"You are in the soup, baby," Sinna grinned at her blue-eyed sister. "He's a pair of dirty pants, and you are a pair of old-fashioned boots."

Binna didn't say anything; she fed little Aggo, Sinna sat on a stool opposite them, staring, unblinking, her black eyes pools of black fire.

11.

The month of April was cold and windy, and angry with Radomir. The herb-gathering ladies waited for the crocuses to blossom, but it snowed instead, then the snowdrifts melted, turning the streets into lakes. Not a soul stirred in the open as if all houses were dead under their low roofs. Even the stray dogs had vanished; perhaps some had beaten it for another, thicker forest, others trawled the wasteland nearby Space's house, looking for something to gnaw at among the odds and ends the villagers tossed there. Dogs, cats, rats scavenged for food in the trash. But folks in these parts didn't throw out even their gallstones, so the waifs and strays were as meager as ghosts.

The rats in well-to-do towns (where many women could cook) were big and lustrous like zinc buckets, while their brethren in Radomir behaved like cockroaches: cowardly shadows, permanently on the run, scared for their lives. Mongrels hunted them; cats lay in wait for them, and villagers, especially the herb-gathering women, crushed the rats with their walking sticks, hurled stones at them, or treated the pests to poison they concocted themselves, using noxious leaves of grass. Often dead mice filled the narrow streets, their bodies purple with the old ladies' poison. Although starving and able to eat a horse, the stray dogs stoically ignored them.

Mice returned to Binna's library. Crouching by the firefly electric heater, in two pullovers and the woolen cardigan Nikolay had given her, Binna read *The Brothers Karamazov*. Nikolay had just left. He had brought her a pine tree branch and had made a paper flower that looked more like an airplane.

"I'll drive Grandma Raina's car today. You know her old crate of a Ford vehicle she transports flour and stuff for her grocery store with." Binna and everyone in Radomir knew the crate well. "I'll buy cabbage from the market in Sofia for her," Nikolay blurted out. Then he lifted *The Sun*, the flat bottle he hid in his coat pocket, to his lips and took a long swig. His white face gradually reddened which meant that *The Sun*'s courage was pouring into his head. "I'll drive Grandma Raina's car today," Nikolay repeated. "The rusty engine starts first time. I can take you for a ride if you want. We won't be snowed in by the blizzard; you can take my word for it."

The blue-eyed librarian asked, "Where will we go for a ride?" although what she wanted to say was, "Does your grandma know, won't she mind?"

She didn't know how to tell him she didn't want to go for a ride with him. Was it a good idea to say she had to take one of Vancha's lambs to the vet? Or she was scared of fierce blizzards and snow? Grandma Raina was a queer fish. She wouldn't let anyone lay a finger on her decrepit Ford. Binna knew Nikolay had changed the oil in the car and had spray painted it, and Raina permitted him to drive it.

"I'll take you to Krakra Fortress in Pernik," Nick said as he took another swig from *The Sun*. Courage ran away from the flat bottle and flowed into his red cheeks. "I'll pick you up in the afternoon, after work," he muttered. He passed her the pine tree branch and the paper flower that looked like an airplane. "Take these," he said. "I'd have picked real flowers for you, but the crocuses are covered with snow."

"Does your grandmother know about the ride?" Binna finally asked. The boy blushed scarlet; evidently *The Sun*'s audacity had turned his head.

"Well... yes," Nikolay said.

A week ago, old Raina, a tall, gray-haired woman, the most dexterous herb-gatherer in Radomir, and that meant the best in Bulgaria, visited the library. Her face looked smooth in spite of her seventy-eight years that had curved her fingers into an eagle's claw. It was the moisture, eating her bones, while she raked her nails through the grass, searching for Portobello mushrooms she sold to the Greek merchants. Old Raina was well respected in town; she had cured a young man from Turkey, Mustafa Ismail by name, who couldn't walk. Even Doctor Gospod, after she studied the ultrasound image of the guy's belly, said that his internal organs—starting from his heart and ending in his guts—were enlarged and swollen more than a doctor could either imagine or explain. The guy had to undergo complex medical treatment in the capital otherwise his mother would have to put on mourning garments. Honestly, Doc Gospod who had cured dozens of times all grandmothers and little tots from Radomir and the neighboring villages strongly doubted that the Turkish lad would survive.

Old Raina, Nikolay's grandmother, got the guy on his feet and slowly restored him to health. Mustafa and his mother moved into her house and occupied Nikolay's room, so Nikolay slept in the kitchen. After three months, Mustafa learned to run again, and after six months Doc Gospod declared, "Your internal organs are neither enlarged nor swollen. You can go marry a pretty girl tomorrow, young man."

At the end of that autumn, the old ladies made way for Raina when she turned up in a queue at the bakery, all glancing at her admiringly, "Hi, Raina, how are you, dear friend? God bless you, Raina, treasure."

So old Raina her rosy cheeks glowing, her wrinkles too tiny to see in the dim light, entered the library. It was now snowing, now raining, a blizzard blew and the old lady's kerchief was sopping wet.

"Good afternoon, Raina," Binna said smiling. "Hasn't the postman brought you *My Garden Weekly?* Tell me which issue of the magazine you need, and I'll find it for you."

Old Raina sat down on the chair Binna had quickly brought for her, reached out to the hardly visible electric heater then said, "I don't care for *My Garden Weekly*. I've come to talk to you about Nikolay."

"Are you... I hope you're not in a hurry," Binna said, embarrassed. "Wait, I'll go and buy some cheesecake for you from Stanka's bakery. I saw her open the shop in the morning."

"I don't want cheesecake," the old woman said. "Listen, I want you to share the pillow with Nikolay at night."

"What..." Binna blurted out. "I... I am not..."

"He's already been with Sinna, your sister," old Raina went on. "Who hasn't been with Sinna? Only a man who wasn't born under the sun! Now the boy knows there isn't anything special to this sort of thing. I hoped he'd get over you, but he couldn't, the young fool."

"Raina, I ... I haven't promised Nikolay anything."

"He didn't get over you," the old one went on evenly, stonily, her blue eyes crushing Binna's. "It's getting worse. He draws your face. The lines he puts on paper don't look like you, but he says they do. He sleeps with your face under his head at night. He talks to it, calls it *Binna*."

"Raina, if you want..." the librarian's voice was weak autumn grass. "Shall I move to another town for a month? But I don't know where I'll go."

"I gathered herbs and believed they were strong enough to lure him away from you," Raina went on. "I climbed the hills above Radomir and plucked powerful grasses. They didn't work. It became worse."

"I'll ask Miss Dana to take me on. I can read to her at her place. I won't go out and Nikolay won't run into me."

"Share a pillow with him," Raina said. "He'll see you are like all the others, like Sinna. The queen has the same thing as the jenny-ass, her serving maid."

Rain was lashing the windows, but it was so quiet inside the room that one could hear the dust gathering on the bookshelves.

"Nikolay will see you're like everybody else," Raina's white voice drummed on, a smooth voice, not a single wrinkle in it. "This will help him to get rid of you."

"I..." the librarian started, faltering. "I still haven't met anybody."

The dusk in the library thickened and sharpened. The electric heater threw its feeble light against the two women, making the room darker.

"Are you lying to me?" Raina asked.

Binna didn't answer. A pine tree branch and a paper flower that looked like an airplane lay on the desk in front of her.

"Then why do you trudge up the hill to Space's house day in day out?" the old one snapped.

The rain turned into snow. The wind, bent double like a sick man in the cold, hit the wall and the windowpanes clinked.

"Space looks at me," Binna muttered.

"Nikolay looks at you too," the old woman said, her eyes sharp. "You've had no one before him, so what."

For a while, Binna's breath plowed the hushed darkness: as if a child scooped up sand with his toy shovel and dispersed it at his feet. Binna was a splinter lodged in an old heel. Raina's breath pushed the gray afternoon, a deep, murky tunnel, leading to the opposite slope of a dark mountain. The gray-haired woman dug her fingers deep into her bosom; after a second, she produced a handkerchief folded four times and put it on the table next to the pine tree branch. A yellow coin as thin as rolling paper glittered on the white handkerchief.

"It's gold," Raina said. "It's an ancient gypsy penny. An old man from Pernik gave it to me. I cured his grandson of a bad cough. Take the coin. I want you to share your pillow with Nikolay."

"But…"

"I leave the gold penny here. How old are you: twenty three, twenty four? What are you waiting for? It's ridiculous to wait."

Binna glanced at the coin. Bizarre curved letters—she had seen no symbols remotely resembling these anywhere in the moldy books on the shelves—were carved in the thin circle of glittering metal. Somebody had pierced the coin; she noticed a tiny hole near its rim.

"Nikolay is very strong," the old woman said her voice a frozen lake. Every single word she uttered was hard and firm like the tiles on the sidewalk. "He knows how to do it. Your sister Sinna taught him."

The old herb-gatherer stood up, taking her time, a tall beautiful old woman, her hair thick and gray, her face a freezing cold day, blue eyes that saw nothing much without glasses, yet it felt as though they'd already read the thoughts racing through your mind.

"Raina, take back your gold coin," Binna rose from the chair and wrapped the gold penny in the handkerchief. "I don't want it."

"You're twenty-four. Soon you'll be twenty-five. You can't stay on like this." She paused sinking her dark blue gaze into Binna's frightened eyes, coughed then went on, firm and unbending like the asphalt street which led to Sofia. "You mustn't hang around in this fleabag library. You drive boys to distraction. Move in with Space, the lousy forest ranger. Marry him. Give birth to three tots then come back to this hole and read as many books as you please."

"Take your gold coin," Binna said. Her cold fingers brushed Raina's warm skin one more time.

Old Raina, the best herb-gatherer in Radomir, which meant she was unsurpassed throughout Bulgaria, did not say another word. She smoothed the handkerchief with the gold coin in return of which she'd cured the Gypsy's grandson and turned to go. At a certain point, she remembered something, came back to Binna's desk, took the pine tree branch, then grabbed the paper flower, which looked like an airplane, and left the library.

... At the end of the work day, Nikolay wanted to give Binna a ride to Krakra Fortress in Raina's shabby car. Binna did not lie to the boy that the cold wind scared her. She knew Nikolay had changed the oil in the old Ford and had spray painted it. Binna knew all this, but she said, "I will not come with you to the fortress, Nikolay."

He was silent like the poplar tree that the flood had wrenched from the field, and now its roots faced the sky. She caught hold of his hand—a big boy's hand with protruding veins and thick hairs, piercing the skin, a warm hand that didn't depend on the heat of the firefly electric heater. Binna held his wrist, lifted it to her lips and kissed the palm of his hand. She could tell him nothing more.

"I'll go," Nikolay muttered.

Binna remained in the library. There, the blizzard could not touch her. The rain had painted the air of April with its gray pieces of chalk. In the room, the smell of the mice back home from worse places had mixed with another odor: that of a snapped pine tree branch. Yet another scent lingered above the old shelves, one that only Binna could capture. It was the smell of the strange paper flower that looked more like an airplane.

12.

"Isabella, you must immediately take me to Doc Gospod! Come here. Smell me. Do I stink?"

"Yes, Miss Dana. You stink. You rode your best horse, Ogre. Now you smell both of Ogre and of his saddle."

"Warm up the bathroom for me and immediately come to rub my back."

"Why do you want us to go to Doc Gospod, Miss Dana? Are you ill? Yesterday you cut that huge oak tree for less than two hours and you rendered me speechless. The other day Tano couldn't get up after your session. The poor bugger slept two days in a row as if they'd had him skinned alive. I went and washed him, Miss Dana. You'd ordered me to launder his dirty pants and then I was supposed to give him a bath. But I couldn't lift the idiot. He slept in my hands, and he didn't wake up when I poured cold water on his head and ass. You exhaust him dry and dead. You aren't ill, Miss Dana. Believe me. Why should you want me to warm up the bath? I guess you want me to breathe deeply by your side until you go to sleep. What do you say?"

"If you sat near me, I'd kick your head, that's what I say. When I tell you 'Rub my back,' you'll rub my back. And when I tell you to take me to Doc Gospod, you take me to Doc Gospod, you stupid Italian wiseacre."

"I'll take you to the Doc, Miss Dana, why shouldn't I?" Isabella reasoned on. "You are as strong as the cobble stones on the road to Pernik. In my honest opinion, you're healthier than Ogre, your stallion. Yesterday you squeezed three pails of sweat out of the poor beast, God bless his tail."

"I'm filled with doubt," Barren Dana said. "Honestly, what I feel leaves little room for doubt."

"Cancer?" Isabella froze in her tracks as if a gunman had shot her dead. "If it's cancer, Doc Gospod won't cure you of it. I'd better take you to old Raina. Quick, woman! It won't be necessary to give you a bath or rub your back. With old Raina you can stink as much as you want."

"I have moments of huge doubts," Dana said. "Look at me closely and thoroughly. Can you see a change in me?"

Isabella took a couple of steps back, and half-closing her eyes, studied intently the tall strong woman whose chubby cheeks shone like an advertisement of a healthy lifestyle, which Doctor Gospod supported with all her heart.

"Well, yesterday night we drank that wine you sell to German Fritzes, I got blotto and perhaps you hit your head against the wall, and now it hurts," Isabella suggested, quite uncertain. "You always give yourself a bump on your head when I'm not near you to fluff up your pillow for you. I'm sure you've got at an immense bump and now you want me to see to it."

"No," Barren Dana cut her short. "Have a look at the lower parts of me."

"Tano bit your neck, and his teeth have left purple patch there. The idiot! Now your skin itches, and you want me to spread whiskey and iodine on it."

"You're totally slow on the uptake, Isabella. You drive me crazy, I tell you. It's a pity I spent a fortune on your education. Didn't I pay that balmy Italian guy a wagon of money to teach you the tricks of the housekeeping trade? I did! Either look carefully, or come closer to me so I can hit you on the head."

"Well, you rode Ogre and you bruised your backside. You'll kick your pants off and you'll want me to put your hip joint into place and spread whiskey and iodine on it?" Isabella made another logical suggestion.

At that point Barren Dana unbuttoned the blouse she'd thrust in her pants and lifted it in the air, so that her stunned assistant faced a flat, white belly. Barren Dana had commissioned a local printer to produce one thousand business cards for Isabella all printed in golden ink: *Isabella Ileva, Chief Expert; Business Advisor.* The card didn't make clear whose Business Advisor Isabella was, but young and old beyond the left bank of the Struma River knew Isabella advised Barren Dana. Therefore, Dana's flawless white skin flashed like lighthouse in front of her advisor's nose: not a trace of blubber, not a wrinkle or flab in it; muscles all over the place, tough and powerful like laminated iron, with one and only exception: the belly button. Once in a blue moon, when Dana remembered she had a belly button, she made efforts to clean it with Italian body lotion "Felicia", but at the very beginning of the procedure she lost patience and seethed, thoroughly enraged, "Sleeping saucer Isabella, where are you! Run! Come clean my belly button!"

Isabella carefully used the Italian cosmetic wonder "Felicia", then spread Italian lotion "Libertà" on the belly button, and finally dried it with Italian cotton "Roma".

"Miss Dana, I cleaned your navel three days ago, and I don't think you've again filled it with mud," the business advisor was silent for a while, thinking hard. "If one lies on that mattress with

Tano, one can fill one's navel not only with mud but also with nits," she said at the end.

"Watch attentively my stomach," Barren Dana said. "Do you find it any different?"

Isabella bent over the white skin as taut as a bow string, smelled the belly, touched the navel, making sure Tano had not filled it with nits and mud then answered, "You ate too many beefsteaks from the platter I gave you in the morning. I told you, '*Don't be guzzling down underdone meat*', but you went and gorged on four steaks! Now you feel wretched," Isabella nodded understandingly as she suggested, "Let me rub your belly button and you'll recuperate as fast as a bitten mongrel."

"Look here, Isa, my monthly period is late: ten or twelve days. You know I don't take the curse that seriously, but..."

"Oh, come off it," Isabella exclaimed. "Your period will be late when the pigs start to fly."

"Go bring me the calendar. It's you that marks my monthlies on it."

"Starting the nonsense again?" sour Isabella inquired, pulling a long face. "You and I have managed to keep the peace for months. Why don't you go on cutting oak and beech trees like a normal woman? Why don't you swim in the lake? I'll let the two bitches Blizzard and Rage plunge and flounder through the mud with you so you won't be lonely. The two beasts will breathe by your head while you're freezing in the water."

"You mark my monthlies on the calendar, don't you?" Barren Dana insisted.

"I do. I mark everything the way Doc Gospod told me to," Isabella said. "Wait, I'll show you the calendar in a sec," Isabella rummaged through her numerous pockets, which were most obviously Italian, and finally produced a crumpled sheet of paper.

"Let me see," her boss grumbled.

"Don't interrupt me, Miss Dana."

"Speak up! Don't drive me mad! Speak up," Barren Dana cawed.

"Your last period started on 6 February, and now … let me see. What's the date today? Let me check. April 3rd. O, come off it. You've forgotten to tell me, Miss Dana."

"I haven't forgotten. My period is late. That's why I made you study my belly."

"Don't cherish moronic hopes, Miss Dana. You remember what happened when you cherished moronic hopes last year. You said your period was late; Doc Gospod opened your eyes, pointing out you were not pregnant, and you hit the roof. You smashed a cupboard full of saucers to smithereens, shattered the TV set, swore and used language at me for six days in a row. Don't start this shit again."

"But my period is late," Barren Dana declared obstinately. "And do you know why? Tano is the only man in Bulgaria who's taller than me, that's why."

"Don't you imagine things," Isabella warned her. "It's no good warming up the bath, rubbing your back and running to Doc Gospod for nothing at all. Let's drink some wine instead. If your period is really late, then you'll feel like puking. You won't be able to even glance at the wine we sell to Fritzes and Brits. Let me put you to the test now."

Isabella rushed out of the room; after two minutes she rushed back three dusty bottles in hand, which she held as tenderly as if they were three newborn princesses.

"Miss Dana, you need to concentrate. Look at these bottles. Intently and fixedly look at them. Do you feel like throwing up while you're staring at them?"

"Not in the least," Dana answered, watching the bottles

intently indeed. "I feel very much like drinking these, the three of them altogether."

"Then let's face the facts: your period is not late. It's no good trudging through the flood to Doc Gospod."

"It's late, I tell you."

"Ok. Don't waste time then. Try the wine. If its smell makes you retch, you'll immediately pile into the car. I won't stop it anywhere along the road, I assure you. I'll kill the engine in front of Doc Godpod's waiting room."

Isabella handled the two bottles adroitly. The business advisor didn't bother to go look for glasses. She raised her bottle, clicked it against Dana's and said, "Cheers, Miss Dana."

"Cheers!" Dana responded, and the two women sucked on their respective bottles. They didn't pause and needed no rest; they had systematic training and drank peacefully and with ease. From time to time, one of the women dropped her bottle onto the carpet and hiccupped, muttering, "Cheers."

"Cheers," responded the other then the two went on boozing.

"Have some homemade beef sausage, Miss Dana," the chief expert and business advisor said to her boss as she extracted a piece of dried convoluted bratwurst from a bottomless pocket in her Italian jeans. Pieces of thread and small balls of dust—Italian pockets abounded in these items—stuck out of the sausage, but Isabella didn't bother her head with these issues right now. She broke the sausage into two unequal parts, sank her teeth into the bigger piece and gave the other one to her employer.

"For appetizer, have some of this lousy bratwurst, Miss Dana," she said.

The two ladies had some sausage for appetizer then again raised the bottles to their lips. At a certain point, Miss Dana said, "Give me a song with a strong melody."

"I don't want to sing now," Isabella objected, but Miss Dana dragged her over the coals. "Give me a song, or I'll kick your ass."

Isabella belched and pleaded for forgiveness, "Let me swallow the damned bratwurst first," she said.

After a while Miss Dana sang the song *Fairyland* in such a formidable voice that the canary who so far had lived peacefully in his cell went into total panic, crashing his head into the wires, throwing its wings against the roof then against the floor of its prison, but Dana sang powerfully on, ignoring the poor darling altogether. At a certain point, she jabbed Isabella in the ribs, "Isabella, sing!"

"I hate *Fairyland*. It sucks."

"Then come closer, and I'll kick your ass. Sing!"

The two women sang together, "Fairyland, you're magnificent" roared the one; "Fairyland, you are rotten" thundered the other, music erupted from their volcano throats with tremendous force, the canary's terrified chirrups chiming in.

"Isabella, come and dance with me," Miss Dana said.

"Ok, I'm coming," the assistant and chief business expert said delighted.

"I'll lead," declared Dana. "You pay attention I don't step on your toes."

"Ok, you lead, I'll pay attention," Isabella agreed.

"Sing. Now!" Dana said as she decisively tangoed, holding onto her chief expert. The two women sang together, spittle spraying from their mouths and sticking to their faces mixed with spurts of wine as they plowed on through the song. Tiny pieces of sausage they had not yet swallowed got stuck to their cheeks and chins. After a while, the two dancers forgot all about *Fairyland*, venturing on *Love and Passion,* rumbled and bellowed on, clinging to each other until Isabella dropped her head to her boss's shoulder, hiccupping loudly. A squirt of wine spurted out of her lips and slowly soaked into Miss Dana's new Italian sweatshirt.

"No sleeping now, girl," Miss Dana grumbled. "Come on, move it, or come closer. I'll kick your ass," while the tall woman was uttering the last word, she felt like turning in, so she lifted her snoring wine-bathed assistant high in the air, took a couple of clumsy shaking steps toward the sofa and dropped Isabella onto it under the panicky canary's cage. Then Dana looked over her shoulder, saw no other bed, made efforts to recline in the easy chair, but missed her target and sprawled on the floor covered with a thick carpet.

"Fairyla—a—and… fairyla—a—a—nd," she wailed half-awake then she slept like a log.

… True to life story registered by Isabella Ileva, chief expert, business advisor and agent, working for Miss Dana Dancheva known far and wide as Miss Barren Dana. *However, Miss Barren Dana is not barren anymore. The goal of this story is to help the community of honest citizens from Radomir to get acquainted with some significant episodes in Dana Dancheva's life, CEO Dana Ltd.*

Honorable Vancha and Aggo, fellow-citizens and members of Radomir's elite, in particular the elite from Arch Neighborhood, checked my story for fundamental errors. Vancha is a decent and trustworthy woman, although at times she is not decent at all. The story was ruined by a filthy, good-for-nothing Professor from the Bulgarian Academy of Sciences; in the beginning, I refused to pronounce his son of a bitch's name. The son of a bitch distorted every single sentence I had written and added commas all over the place, the filthy academic scumbag. He poisoned half of my significant episodes and I was often about to clout him one. "One should not write things like these," he said. He knows nothing about the way we write, the fathead. He was chewing learned words all the time, so one couldn't make out if he wanted to use the loo or he wanted a glass of beer. Therefore, I signed this text with reservation on the oddball scholar, who was obviously off his onion, but at a later stage, I had a change of heart.

*This is the reason I pronounce his name now: Professor Michal Bilov. I saw him as an abomination while he deleted words and verbs in my story. Professor Bilov was fundamental garbage before he drank the wine we sold only to Fritzes and Brits. After the scholarly fellow downed half a bottle of our red lightning, he made a decent person of himself. It was with great difficulty that the Prof drank the whole bottle, and then he imbibed one more bottle with great ease. He and I sang together **Fairyland**. Afterwards, the guy felt like caroling and he caroled so hard, I could not prevent him from caroling. It was at that particular phase when it dawned upon me that I had been terribly wrong about this highly civilized man! Great scholar; refined and cultured all over the place! He knew all the stanzas of **Love and Passion** as well. We had sung together for more than three hours. We tangoed several times, and we woke up in each other's arms. The scholar earned 6000 (six thousand) levs for his expertise, and told me he was extremely content both with the wine and with me. I let him add as many commas as he pleased, and I allowed him to patch up all the subject-verb agreements in my text. Honestly, I am more than brilliant with respect to subject-verb agreement, and I am perfectly able to piece them together; however I said to myself I didn't have a bone to pick with this sophisticated guy. He made money digging like a mole in grammar; obviously, he had to delete some of my sentences to justify the fat bundle he pocketed. Ok, it's my treat. He asked me to his place on 20 December to try his wines in Sofia; he could add some more commas if I wanted to, he said. What have we done during the night? I wondered. Why don't I pack my things and leave for Sofia?*

Doctor Gopod examined Miss Dana Dancheva, using ultrasound imaging, a non-invasive diagnostic technique. Doc Gospod is convinced that what she has seen leaves no trace of doubt: Miss Dana is pregnant. The baby will be born in December. Doctor Gospod established this happy diagnosis and signed it! And the lady is a magnificent doc who has cured young and old in these parts for thirty years—the guys, who are now picking strawberries, olives and oranges all over the world, were born in her hands, their sons and daughters were born in her hands too, and thanks to her clever head they all got rid of bad bouts of flu, pneumonias, heart attacks, the clap and other diseases.

Forthwith, Doc Gospod stated she harbored no doubts about Miss Dana Dancheva's pregnancy; her diagnosis was confirmed by Professor Dionis from the National Health Academy, Sofia, Bulgaria. Three days and three nights, the entire population of Radomir reeled and staggered drunk to the bone after the party that Miss Dana threw for the citizens. Every herb-gathering lady received financial encouragement amounting to five times her monthly pension plus five pounds of beans. Miss Dana gave each household from Radomir and nearby villages two bottles of virgin olive oil. Mr. Tano from Radomir received three thousand levs for his remarkable skills, and hundreds of citizens thanked him from the bottom of their hearts. The mayor registered him as the father of Miss Dana's baby, as a result of which the guy was allowed to leave the toolshed for two weeks, and the shed was where Mr. Tano lived for now. He was allowed to spend his leave of absence, fourteen calendar days, in the town of Pernik, at Perun Restaurant, in parentheses *Frog Bar*. In case of necessity, Mr. Tano Tanov would be sent for, and urgently transported to Radomir where he'd be expected to lend assistance to Miss Dana Dancheva.

It was only the honest writer who put down the story in writing i.e. I am Ms. Isabella Ileva, from Radomir, Bulgaria, a lady who remained as sober as a dry stone—until 2 am—at the party thrown by Miss Dana; after 2 am Miss Isabella Ileva could remember nothing at all. The intention behind Miss Isabella Ileva's sobriety was for her to describe in honest writing the momentous event in the interest of the present and future generations' intellectual development. However, Miss Isabella Ileva overdid her duty. She continued writing even after she got very slightly drunk, penning twenty-one pages altogether. She described everything for the townsfolk in minute details. Henceforth, let young and old read, admire, and learn. The ulterior motive in doing this essay was her passionate attachment to truth.

Truth is a universal language. One has to speak it or leave it even after three bottles of the wine we sell only to Fritzes and Brits.

24 July 2016   Radomir, Bulgaria.

I, Isabella Ileva, Chief Expert and Business Advisor, certify the veracity and accuracy of the information above with my signature that I put of my own free will to this document.

...Meanwhile, Albinna Aggova, known as Binna, remained sober like a judge and alone at this all-night party. If one asked Raina, the best herb-gatherer, who Albinna Aggova from Radomir was, the old lady would snap, "I don't know her." If the same person asked the other herb-gatherers, they'd say, "Well, she's a pretty woman, as thin as the wind, blue eyes, smiling most of the time at no one in particular, perhaps at the sky."

"You don't say," old Raina objected. "No one smiles in these parts."

... But if you asked a student from the biology or mathematics class who Binna was, he'd say, "She's the prettiest girl in Radomir," and that meant *the prettiest girl in Bulgaria.* It was only Binna that the students addressed as "My God, how beautiful you are, Lady." According to a retired teacher in Bulgarian literature who read a lot, some obscure poet wrote this line a century ago, but the boys had no faith in his knowledge. Some secretly believed the poet was still alive; he must have glimpsed Binna through the window of the library. Positively, this poetic guy was not born in these parts. Here, folks addressed God only when someone breathed his last at the hospital and hastily left for Black Peak. His friends whispered, "God rest his soul,", but they also remembered God when they spoke of Binna.

"My God, how pretty you are, lady," said a student from the biology class. Binna blushed to the bones and went to old Olga, the hairdresser. Olga cut the librarian's hair short like the grass in a meadow Vancha had mown. Binna hoped she'd look homely, and no one would tell her, "My God!" She'd love it if the student said, "Hi, Binna, give me a copy of Vazov's short story collection, I have to write an essay again. I'm afraid I'll flunk my literature exam."

13.

This happened years ago, but Binna remembered as vividly as if was yesterday.

…"Let's catch Mumma and beat her black and blue," whispers a little girl in a dirty pink frock, pink socks and old pink sandals. The girl's skin is dark and smooth. Her eyes glisten like the puddles in the street that reflect the enormous dazzling heat. The girl turns to another thin, small girl who has clear fair skin in which the month of June waits and smiles in her blue eyes.

"I don't want to beat Mumma," the blue-eyed kid says, plucks a leaf from the maple tree and lets it swim in a big puddle.

"You're afraid to do it," the dark girl sneers. "You dumb scaredy cat!" Coward! We'll catch Mumma when Barren Dana takes her bitch Hurricane for a walk, and thickheaded Mumma loiters around Dana's skirt. We'll say, 'Miss Dana, can we touch the doggie? What a great evil doggie she is, a sweet big darling! Can I play with Mumma for a while?' 'Of course you can, sweetheart,' Barren Dana will say smiling like a wolf. 'Here, take fifty cents, and go buy a bar of chocolate.' I'll tell her, 'Your Hurricane, Miss Dana, is the toughest bitch in Radomir and she's the spitting image of you, so intelligent and powerful.' It's your turn now, Binna. You'll say, 'Hurricane is the cutest creature in the world.' Dana will rummage in her bag; finally she'll produce one lev, or maybe a fiver, if we are lucky. You know she's not all there. 'Pretty girls, go buy ice-cream, run, waste no time!' she'll instruct us. Ice-cream my foot! We'll buy ten bottles of make-up, Binna. We'll paint our faces down to our throats. I'll put a mile thick make-up on you, then you and I will go pick up boys."

"I don't want to pick up boys," the blue-eyed girl says. Her dress is pink and perfectly clean. Her socks and sandals are pink, clean, her pinafore is meticulously ironed, but she notices a tiny crease above the seam and smoothes it out. The girl's hair is tidily combed.

"Why shouldn't we pick up boys? We'll pick up boys! We'll kiss them, and they'll buy us waffles. Well, you know what? Petar has been saving up for weeks. He doesn't eat honey-buns for breakfast, he drinks no milk. He stashes away cents and dimes to buy me lemonade and cherry cake. If you don't know how to kiss a guy, I'll teach you."

The dark-haired weasel of a kid grabs at the other child's meticulously ironed pinafore; presses the thin fair skin against her boney chest, her mouth swoops down and catches the translucent lips of the blue-eyed tot. The dark-haired kid's teeth do not let go. The clean pink socks wriggle, the dark kiss is so tight that the other child can hardly breathe.

"Ouch!" the short squeal quickly dies.

The dark girl lets go of the clean dress, saying, "You must hold the boy like this while you're kissing him, and he can't escape from you. You put your left hand here like this."

"Ouch!" the clean pinafore moans. "You're clawing my back."

"Ok, you don't want to pick up boys and you don't care about giving Mumma a thrashing. Then let's go to Isabella's place. You know the signora—it's the one who buys Italian dresses from our second-hand shop. We'll pinch a fiver from her. I'll talk to her, you listen and learn. I'll check if you've made any progress. I'll tell her, 'Beautiful Isabella, I've torn the strap of my sandal, and she'll say, 'Little girl, how pretty you are. Let Isabella repair your sandal.' She'll be meddling with the thing, and I'll say, 'Isabella, you are as beautiful as an Italian lady, and I feel like drinking a glass of orange juice.' She's as dumb as a duck, so she'll believe she's really beautiful and she'll put fifty cents in every pocket I have. 'Buy orange juice, honey," she'll mumble. While Isabella's fooling with the cents, you'll bring Mumma. She's not afraid of you, so you take her hand and lead her to me. The kid's as stupid as a worm, she'll go everywhere with you."

"She is not a worm and is not stupid at all. Mumma is a very good child. I play backgammon with her."

"Oh, cut it out. You can't play backgammon with thickheaded Mumma. Or you are crazy, too, but it's Ok. Tell her, 'Mumma, my treasure, let's play backgammon.' Meanwhile Isabella the sheep will give me a fiver, and I'll ask her, 'Can we play with Mumma in your backyard, it's cool in there.' She'll say, "Play as long as you please, little princesses.' We'll take Mumma behind the house, among the hawthorns and briers, and nobody will see. We'll give her a whipping, pinch her cheeks, kick her ass, we'll steal her blouse and shoes and we'll let her go. 'If you sob or squall, Mumma' I'll warn her, 'I'll graft a hump on your stomach, and you'll become a boy. Snivel or whimper, and I'll do it. You know me.' She's as fainthearted as a hen. A week ago, I put a dry branch from the apple tree on her belly and told her, "This piece of wood will grow into a bulge, and you'll be a lad in the afternoon.' She blubbered so hard that cracks opened at the side of her mouth! We'll steal her pants and we'll watch her crawling naked like a caterpillar in the grass. Then we'll sell her things and we'll earn a fortune. We'll be the richest kids in Radomir and we'll show them all."

"I don't want to give Mumma a whipping," the girl in the clean pinafore said. "I want to play backgammon with her. Little Mumma is a clever kid."

"Who will we beat black and blue then? Whose frock shall we steal and sell? All children in town wear dresses from Vancha's rag shop. Their clothes stink of sprays for head lice, pants, skirts and shirts alike."

"We won't steal anything."

"Then how shall we become the richest kids in Radomir? You are a wimp and a chicken. If I had a pair of eyes like yours, every boy alive in Radomir would buy me chocolates and orange juice. No one would eat breakfast; he'd be saving up his pennies for me. I'd make any lad take me from Vancha's house and carry me on his meager back to my desk in the schoolroom. At the end of the day, he'll carry me back home. The idiot would be as happy as a king. I tell you. Well, he can carry me on his bicycle if he has one. He can carry you, too, but you are quite stupid, Binna."

The girl in the clean clothes said nothing. She collected some stones from the ground, sat down and carefully arranged them in a straight line. Slowly, the stones began to resemble a wall. The dark girl approached, kicked the dust up, paused then grabbed a handful of stones from Binna's construction and hurled them at the sky.

"Take that! You too! Take that!" she shouted, flinging her dangerous projectiles. "I'll break Vancha's windows. Now! I'll smash her head. Take that!"

All stones were gone. The dark child clutched the hand of the pink pinafore and shrieked. "Let's play the husband and wife game. I'll be the man. You'll make soup for me. I won't like the soup and I'll beat you black and blue. Let's play."

"I don't want to play this game," the clean pink socks said. The blue-eyed kid found more stones and started building another toy house.

"Do you want to be the man? I'll be the wife. You'll come back home from work. I'll send you to the convenience store to buy rice and sugar for me, but you won't bring me any sugar or rice. 'Husband,' I'll say to you. 'Why didn't you bring me sugar? You are stupid, that's why you didn't buy any sugar or rice!' I'm the wife, and I have been cooking all day long like Vancha does. I'll get mad at you. I'll throw a fit, I'll fly off the handle and I'll beat you black and blue."

"I don't want to fight," the clean pink socks insisted. "I want to sing my doll a lullaby."

"Your doll! It's stupid to play with dolls. You don't want to pick up boys, you don't want to play husband and wife games, and you don't agree to give Mumma a thrashing! All blue-eyed girls are such blockheads. Stand up. Now. I want to see something."

The fair-haired girl left the stone wall she'd been building. The dark one examined it from all sides then said, "Your dress is too clean, Binna. So are your socks and sandals. Let me do something for you," the dark child bent to the puddle, scooped up mud, chucked it at the smaller girl's chest then spread it all over the pink pinafore. She did the same to the little one's socks and treaded on her sandals. "Ok, now you are dirtier than me, Binna. Build your stupid wall. Go on."

The small kid sobbed, "Mommy."

"Don't whimper, Binna. If you don't stop sniveling here and now, I'll graft a hump on your belly and you'll become a boy."

The smaller one shut up, but her eyes didn't; tears ran down her cheeks. The taller child scooped up more mud from the puddle, spread it on her own chest as well then bent and kissed the smaller kid, on the left cheek first, then on the right one, but the kiss lasted only a second, not like the way one picked up a boy.

"Ok, Ok, don't cry, Binna. Ok, I'll take you home and I'll give you a bath, sweetheart. I'll wash your pinafore, I promise you. Don't cry, little darling. I'll buy you a chocolate. Please don't cry. I'll never ever hurt you again. You're my little sister. I love Dad Aggo and you more than everybody else in the world."

14.

"YOU KNOW WHAT, ISABELLA? MY God, it's nasty to be pregnant! O how I feel like rushing to the lake! And what's all I can do? Open my mouth and snivel. I'm itching for a swim, woman! Do you want to come with me? When I get out of the water, you'll stick a blanket to my big stomach, so the tot inside won't catch a cold. I'll make all docs in the region eat their damned diplomas, the learned idiots! 'She can't carry a child,' they shouted. She can't my foot! Well, they didn't know Tano. Oh, Isabella, my shoulder blade's itching. Scratch me hard and long. O, shit! You are unable to scratch my back properly after I got pregnant. You could scratch me like thunder earlier."

"Miss Dana, doc Gospod emphasized you must not exert your strength in the lake. The baby might get dirty or become inflamed inside you. Water will infiltrate your stomach from below, a bacterium or two will wriggle their way, too. These bastards can bust your little angel."

"I'll not swim naked. Listen what, I'll put on thick pants, and we'll stop all sons of bitches bacteriums."

"You must not go swimming, Miss Dana. Let's go shoot the damned hawks instead."

"I shot at hawks yesterday and I shot at hawks the day before yesterday. If you drop another hint about hawks, I don't know... You're too far from me to give you a good kick in the ass."

"Oh, you can go kick the dog, Miss Dana, but oh, not Giant! Not him, poor dear Giant. We won't kick Blizzard, Rage and Beast, not them; let them bark as loud as they please. You can kick the stray mutt I bought you for one Lev from Kamen, the vet. The mutt is the perfect target to punt and hack: he's spiteful like a snake and wicked like you."

"But I kicked the mutt the other day. I put the boot in his ass twice and, later on, he licked my shoes, the lousy quitter. I don't want to kick him anymore. Warm up a blanket for me, quick. I'm sick and tired of being pregnant."

"You must not swim in that freaking lake, Miss Dana."

"If I mustn't swim in that freaking lake, then you'll sit in that chair all day long. Isabella, you will sing to the baby. You heard what dotty doc Gospod said the other day. Ok, ok, I know she's not dotty, but now and then she blows a fuse. She said, 'Let the baby listen to music.' Therefore, stop shillyshallying, Isabella. Sing! My child mustn't be a low-brow dolt who knows nothing about music."

"How should I sing to the baby, Miss Dana? The little one is in your belly. Your belly has no ears, it can't hear me."

"Shut up and sing," Miss Dana pulled her shirt out of her wide jeans, and her stomach, big and round like a drum, shone in the sun.

"Start, Isabella. Come on. I want *Fairyland.*"

"I don't feel like singing, Miss Dana."

"Come off this shit, girl. Start. I'll give you the pitch. Listen to me, *Fai—i—iryl—a—and, Fai—i—iryland.* Ok, *Love and passion* as a last resort."

Isabella, barren Dana's chief expert and business advisor, coughed and hiccoughed, coughed again and bawled, *Fairyland, my Fairyland* then abruptly lapsed into silence.

"You're very far from my belly," Miss Dana said. "The baby cannot hear you. Bend forward to the belly-button and sing. On your mark, get set, go!"

Isabella bent down, coughed again, and sighed.

"Look here! I haven't hired you to teach the baby to cough. If you don't start singing in five seconds, I'll kick your ass."

Isabella instantly stopped coughing, hamming and hawing and roared at the top of her great lungs about poor *Fairyland,* but something in her throat went horribly wrong. She was unable to strike the right note, and her song plummeted downhill.

"I haven't hired you to teach the baby to bark," Miss Dana said deep in thought. "Listen, girl. Drink a glass of wine, then hopefully the tune will come back to your mouth."

"Ok," agreed the chief expert and business advisor.

After a short while, the two women ended up clutching a dusty cobwebby bottle each. The business advisor took a sip and momentarily choked because the wine was sharp and strong like a machine gun, then she took a swill from her bottle and said, "Miss Dana, you must not drink. If you do, the baby will become a drunkard in your stomach. Doc Gospod said you shouldn't even think about alcohol."

"From time to time, Doc Gospod is not all there. She's getting on in years and has a bee in her bonnet about spirits and spiritual things," Miss Dana assured her business advisor. "A bottle of this wine will make the little one as strong as granite."

"It will make him drunk."

"Don't you remember Dora, Tano's wife? She's the one who died after she gave birth to Binna. You know her. She drank like an eel. Do you mind the way Binna looks now? The child's prettier than the sun! She's more beautiful than twenty suns put together, if you ask me. Dora must have drunk a lake of brandy with the truck drivers while Binna was kicking in her stomach. Think of the truck-drives the woman serviced, more drivers than cobblestones in the street. Eh, what's wrong with Binna? She's the most magnificent kid in Radomir, therefore the most magnificent one all over Europe."

"Magnificent, but daft as a dozen of brushes," Isabella pointed out. "First, she does not let me talk to her, second, the kid runs away the minute she catches a glimpse of me. I give her small change, I bought her a doll, but she wouldn't listen. Her sister's a sweet child, perfectly adorable. She's noticed I'm pretty no matter how young she is. She addresses me like, 'Cute Isabella, lovely Isabella!'".

"Sing," Barren Dana cut her short.

"Ok," the chief expert said as she raised the cobwebby bottle to her lips, hoping she'd feel the urge to burst into song. She hiccupped, raised the bottle one more time and unexpectedly suggested, "All right, let's go for a swim. I hate the thought of singing, and that's the truth, pure and simple. The baby in your stomach is not at all drawn to songs or *cantatas*. I openly share this insight with you, although I've kept it to myself so far. If the little sweetheart fell for music, I'd be itching for a tune. Follow closely my every move now. Do I look like a woman dying for a carol? I drank the bottle almost dry, and look! I still bitterly loathe *Fairyland,* every sound of it, and I am an artistic soul, aren't I? You know me."

"The child is surely thirsty," Dana pointed out. "Let's give him a sip. If he doesn't want this precious wine, then I carry a fool under my heart."

"Oh, he's not a fool, believe me," Isabella objected. "Let's put him to test. Doc Gospod hasn't mentioned anything against one tiny sip."

"Let me drink a drop before you do. I don't feel like drinking by myself," Barren Dana said. "I almost forgot. Isabella, run to the florist and buy me a rose or two. Doc Gospod said I should look at flowers and the baby will be very beautiful."

"Shall I pluck some grass for you, Miss Dana? Roses and grass don't make any difference to you, it's all just flora and fauna, you know," the business advisor suggested. "If the little one watches grass now, he'll learn to mow quickly when he grows up."

"Doc Gospod expressly and expli… explicitedly said flowers," Miss Dana objected.

"Now and again, Doc Gospod has a screw loose, I tell you. Ok, ok, no offence meant here. She's a magnificent doc. If you say she hasn't a screw loose then she hasn't. Do you want me to pick some irises from the backyard? Irises are as good as any other flora and fauna. Why should I trudge up hills to Pernik, huffing and puffing? To buy a pail of freaking roses! You know what? Why don't I spread pig's lard on your stomach? It will do the baby good: I spread lard on your belly and that means I spread lard on his belly, too. Meanwhile your skin won't crack and peel and you won't get stretch marks. That's what Doc Gospod instructed me to do: 'Spread lard on her huge belly and thighs, Isabella, and her skin will be as smooth as a windowpane.' What do you say?"

"Go ahead," Barren Dana agreed. "But you'll be drinking while you're spreading that lard. After you sober up, you go buy a pail of roses from Pernik. Well, buy three pails at a time. We'll put the roses in the fridge. Now I remember, we haven't asked Doc Gospod what color the flowers must be, red or white."

"Don't be stupid, Miss Dana. White is cows' color. We won't fork out three hundred bucks on trash. Red roses or orchids! Go the whole hog. I'll bring you three pails of them. Let the baby look at some Italian flora and fauna, damn it. He mustn't trifle with cheap nosegays, roses or no roses. I'll bring you some lard now. I'll just be a minute."

Miss Dana's chief assistant and business advisor was spreading lard on her employer's belly, a thick layer with no grain of salt in it.

"This child is quite wild. I can feel him kicking like a horse,"

Isabella remarked. "I think he likes lard. Look! He kicked again. A very active infant, I'd say. He'll be shooting at hawks when he grows up. Let me spread lard on your thighs."

"You forgot you had to sing," Barren Dana said.

"*Fai—i—iryla—a—and,*" Isabella went off like a gun, losing no time to cough discreetly by way of preparation.

"*Fai—i—iryl—a—and, Fai—i—iryland,*" Barren Dana chimed in, but at a certain point she stopped singing and declared, "You rubbed me so hard that now I want Tano."

"I haven't finished rubbing you, "Isabella objected. "And we haven't sung our song to the end. We're still dealing with the first verse, and there're four of them. I'll have enough time to spread lard all over the place."

"Bring Tano here. Tano must be in this room before the spittle gets dry on my mouth."

"What if he's drunk?"

"Didn't I tell you he mustn't be drunk while I'm big with child?! Why don't you pay attention?"

"O, I pay so much attention that you could kill a whale with it," the business advisor stated energetically. "It's the only thing I pay! But what if he's drunk? Although I pay undivided and close attention! Shall I send for Stoichko? You know what, it would be best if I didn't send for anybody. Let me spread lard on your chest, too."

"Go bring Tano here before I kick you in the head!" Barren Dana shouted. "Bring an armful of grass. I don't have flowers and I'll look at grass. Grass, flowers, it's all leaves, flora and fauna. Goats graze on these with equal appetite. You're right; perhaps the tot will learn to mow quickly."

The day was brown and boring. Neither cherries nor strawberries were ripe enough, and it was cold. Miss Dana could not ride Giant nor could she wrestle with that stocky guy, the boxer who had won silver medal at the national boxing championship. In the past few days, she went for a swim then sent for Doc Gospod who auscultated the baby. The doctor said the little one was ok, and recommended that Barren Dana listen to music and stare at flowers; she reminded Miss Dana to have cold cream spread on her stomach and breasts, and go for a walk every day. Even if it rained, she'd have to walk three miles a day.

It rained most of the time, alas. Instead of summer bloom and purity, clouds as black chimneys seized the town. The sky went away and hailstorms swooped down, instead of cherries, wasps and gadflies showed black in the trees, and Miss Dana went for dozens upon dozens of walks a day. She woke up at 6 am, her strong blood impatient to see the dawn's clear light. Then she shook snoring Isabella on the sofa in the same room: the business advisor was obliged to breathe reassuringly, give her employer water to drink and be on the alert for signs of distress on the part of the baby. If Isabella sensed something was wrong, her task was to call both Doc Gospod and Professor Dionis from the National Health Academy in Sofia, but the baby was as strong as iron and kicked enthusiastically all the time. On the other hand, Isabella didn't breathe reassuringly the way she was supposed to; she snored instead, but Miss Dana snored too, therefore the snuffling sounds the business advisor produced soothed her employer.

Mumma, the feeble-minded girl, slept in the same room, but now nobody described her as "feeble-minded" because it turned out she was a perfectly normal and very smart child. It was only Tano who at times mumbled, blind with fatherly love, "My dearest feeble-minded pumpkin!"

The skinny runt stopped sniffing and sneaking like a dog; she took food only from the table and spoke in a sweet voice, the words like pearls on her lips. The small thing had her own spoon which she proudly used and kept it under her pinafore next to her heart. In the evenings, Mumma went to sleep, her face pressed against Dana's shoulder.

"Mommy, mommy, I'm thirsty," she half said half whispered, and Dana, dizzy with happiness, scrambled to her feet her belly big like a church bell.

"Do you want to have a little brother, Mumma, sweetheart?" Dana asked and the girl jumped with joy.

"Yes, I do! I do!"

"Now your brother is in my stomach, do you understand?" Miss Dana explained to the kid. "Give me your hand. Feel the way he kicks. Your brother is very strong."

"Yes, he's very strong!" the child exclaimed happily. "He is constantly fidgeting like our cat Stoyan the Robber!"

All family pets in this house had big and heavy names like "Mace", "Giant" or were called after a famous politician. The horse, the dog and the tomcat were huge indeed. Isabella had written hundreds of letters and emails all over the world, declaring her employer's willingness to buy the biggest animals the livestock traders could lay their hands on. Giant, the stallion, was bigger than three ordinary horses in these parts, the bitches Blizzard, Rage and Ogress looked like oxen, and Stoyan the Robber, the tomcat, weighed four pounds more than Mumma, and ate one fried chicken a day.

"Mommy, why is my brother in your stomach? Have you eaten him up?"

"Not at all, sweetheart Mumma. It is the stork that has left it there," Dana explained in a business-like manner. "The baby has to kick inside my belly for a while. Your brother has to learn to kick as well as a soccer star and after he's learned the tricks of the trade, the stork will bring him to our house."

"Where was I when the stork put my brother in your belly?"
Mumma asked.

"You were sleeping," Barren Dana said.

"What a pity!" the child breathed. "I've wanted all the time to
see the stork's long beak. Why didn't you ask him to give me one
of his feathers?"

"Do you want me to catch a stork for you?" Miss Dana suggested eagerly.

"Oh, no, mommy! Let him fly in the sky," Mumma said. "He's
already left my brother in your stomach, hasn't he? If he brings one
more brother, there won't be enough room for the two of them."

In the night, the girl slept by her side and the sounds of her
childish breathing calmed Dana down. Isabella snored on the sofa
bed, and her explosive snores pacified Dana even more. If, by
chance, she got restless, which happened fairly often—and that
was perfectly logical: Tano was still an inch taller than her—Dana
knew where she could find him. He slept in the toolshed where the
business advisor Isabella had brought an electric heater for him.
Barren Dana still felt very strongly he was the only man bigger
than her in Radomir, Pernik, Kyustendil and all other towns in
southern Bulgaria. The tall woman softly and carefully kissed the
child and put her head on the little pillow. Sometimes the little one
woke up.

"Mommy, where are you going?" she asked.

"I'll be back in a minute, tiny Mumma, sweetheart," Dana said,
kissed the girl on the forehead, tucked her in, then tiptoed by snoring Isabella. Barren Dana was sure she wouldn't rouse her assistant.
It was true Isabella suffered from insomnia, but it was also true
the business advisor tried to cure her condition with the wine for
Fritzes, so within three minutes she stopped suffering from insomnia. On the contrary, she suffered from such deep sleep that when

at 6 am Dana shouted, "Isabella!" Isabella could not recognize her own first name and slept as soundly as the frozen Arctic Ocean.

Dana screamed one more time, "Isabella!" but Isabella went on suffering from insomnia in a very peculiar way, snoring thunderously on. "Come on, Isabella!" Dana screamed a dozen times at the top of her powerful lungs, lost patience, made coffee and sandwiches for herself and her advisor, put the mug of coffee on a chair near Isabella's head, and made no further efforts to shrill or shriek, correctly assuming that the wine had comforted her chief expert's tormented soul. She energetically grabbed her business advisor's blankets, chucked them onto the floor and showing no trace of tenderness, pushed and prodded Isabella. When even these measures proved fruitless, she clutched at the business advisor's shoulders and shook them the way she shook the mutt Isabella had bought her from Kamen the vet, or the way she kicked her horse Giant before she rode him in the meadows.

"Get up and eat these sandwiches. They are next to your left ear, you sleeping sack of zucchinis! Drink your coffee. The mug is by your left ear too. If you don't drink it in five minutes, I'll kick you hard. I want you in spick and span pants and blouse. We're going for a walk."

"U—h, U—h," Isalella mooed. At long last she ceased to snore and very rapidly learned not to spew her "u—h", for Dana gripped her shoulders again, pulled and pushed her assistant much more expressively than before. She even lightly slapped her business advisor's face as a result of which Isabella's mouth bled and Dana sent for doc Gospod. Wasting no time, the doctor examined the advisor and stitched up her injured lips. Dana paid the doc's fee amounting to five hundred levs, so after these five hundred levs Isabella stopped mooing and learned to swiftly get up from the sofa bed. She put on her jeans and blouse, meanwhile chewing her sandwiches, slurping her coffee and cursing, and after ten minutes was perfectly ready to go for a walk. Isabella was a model chief expert, business advisor and private secretary in this house. In spite of the above, she was unable to deduce what she was supposed to do so early in the morning. She declared she needed to use the bathroom, took a couple of faltering steps, lay down in the corridor in front of the bathroom, and succumbing to the strong influence of the wine for Fritzes, went to sleep again.

"Isabella!" Dana shouted over her head as she sat down on the floor by her side. The advisor reluctantly sat up, slowly and gradually stood up and at long last lugged a bucket of orchids to Miss Dana, huffing and puffing all the way.

"These bastard orchids! They are not flowers, believe me. They are poison, every single inch of them, rotten flora and fauna!" Isabella concluded.

Miss Dana watched the bucket for a minute the way doc Gospod had recommended, all the time muttering under her breath, "The old doc is positively off her rocker! The flora and fauna is not all there! Freaking orchids, every single inch of them! They are not flowers. They are a bucket of sawdust!" The business advisor was manicuring her boss's nails, taking a nap every now and then.

"A son of a bitch manicure," Miss Dana muttered under her breath. "Doc Gospod is nuts all over the place. Why should this crazy medicinal woman meddle with my health and fat ass? Why should she press Isabella to polish my toenails with almond oil? Why check my teeth for tooth decay? Isabella, let's give medicine the slip today, eh?"

But this particular day, Isabella was a staunch supporter of the medical doctrine, a tower of strength who dripped twice the usual amount of almond oil now onto her employer's nails, now onto her own or directly onto the white Italian carpet. Miss Dana, not fastidious at all, found no fault with her expert. Isabella, a neat and dirt-free expert, would wipe the floor spotlessly clean on the following day.

After painting her employer's nails dauntingly red, the business advisor, now wide awake, took to checking Barren Dana's tooth enamel. She thrust a fork in her boss's mouth, illuminated her oral cavity with a flashlight and after a long while announced, "No caries, not even the smallest hole! Your teeth are stronger than the fangs of our bitches Blizzard, Fury and Ogress. You can take my word for it." Then Isabella carefully studied Dana from all sides, making sure if her dress was immaculately ironed and her shoes perfectly polished.

"To tell you the truth, Miss Dana, your dress is like a pancake fried in deep oil, especially the segment of it on which you sit," the chief assistant said. "How could you turn gorgeous raiment into a garbage dump for such a short time? It beats me. If I paid you a million bucks to crumple up your dress, you wouldn't be able to make it look so ugly. Let me iron the wrinkles out of the poor thing."

"What! Can't you remove the wrinkles as I stand, without making me take off the rag? If you can't, then forget about it," Miss Dana declared, fairly annoyed. "No ironing now. I hate dresses and skirts, do I make myself clear? We're going for a walk."

"You look messy like a crushed pickup truck after a car accident, and that is if one looks at you from behind."

"Then don't look at me from behind," Miss Dana instructed her.

"If I am in front of you, Miss Dana, you look like a pickup truck after a much worse car accident, but the pickup truck has a big protruding hood," the chief assistant informed her boss. Her words produced no effect whatsoever, so the two women headed for a five-mile walk through the fields.

It was cold; no one was in sight apart from a couple of old-wives, the shorter one hugging to her heart a hoe much bigger than she, the taller one digging like a mole in her tiny garden. Time and again, an old boneshaker hissed and coughed along the street, the driver honked his horn in polite salute, the ancient vehicle came to a screeching halt, and the old codger suggested most courteously, "Miss Dana, I can give you and Isabella a lift anywhere you want."

"No, thank you, grandpa Gogo, we don't need a lift. Isabella and I love to walk for the sake of the fresh air. We love nature very much, you know."

"Fresh air is a son of a bitch," the business assistant grumbled. She sincerely hated both nature and fresh air. For her, nature was a glass of the wine Barren Dana kept for the Fritzes.

Soon Miss Dana got sick and tired of walking along the road so she took a shortcut through the woods, another shortcut across sopping wet fields, the grass drowned in cold nasty dew. Barren Dana made great headway, striding energetically across puddles and clumps of nettles, her dress soggy all over the place. Slowly the creases and folds in her attire straightened out of their own accord, and she told her business assistant, "Look here, Isabella, I did you a big favor. Tomorrow you won't have to iron my dress. The thing looks like as if you brought it to me from the fashion shop ten minutes ago."

Isabella didn't bother to inspect the dress. She moaned instead, "I'm as wet as a fish with this bastard dew. There's not a dry square inch on me from my heels as high as my bellybutton. It's your long freaking walks I loathe, Miss Dana. I hate their guts. Can't we go for a walk in the living room? You can rush from the living room to the kitchen, breathe hard and loud, then bustle around the kitchen table, swearing at me. That's what I call a magnificent walk."

"Shut up," Isabella's employer roared, "Or come here. I must kick your smart head." Then she happily patted Isabella on the back. "Look at the air! It's as clean as a glass of white wine."

"The air is a bitch," Isabella commented. "Why should we, two intelligent ladies, trudge through this nasty clean air? Can't you lie in bed where the freaking air is clean, too, and I'll stretch and fold your legs for you? The baby will like this much more than if we went trekking in the hills like two idiots in the foul dew. The old wives will laugh their heads off the minute they catch a glimpse of us. The old men will make fun of us, the high school students will say we're not all there and rightly so! Listen what. You lie in bed. I'll stretch and fold your legs for you, all the time sprinkling icy water on your stomach, if you are so keen on that son of a bitch dew. What do you say? Our cellar is full to the brim of impressive white wine. Drink a glass and you'll forget the clean air. And the kid will learn to acknowledge good wine even before he sees the wide world. On the other hand, you and I won't have to wade one morass of muck after another like two crazy mallards."

"No way, Isabella, Doctor Gospod said I should go for a walk twice a day. I'll walk and I won't put on too much weight."

"Is that what's eating you, Miss Dana! You should have let me know months ago. If you feel like losing weight, I'll cook meager meals for you. You'll sure weigh ten pound less within five days, and we won't have to go for bastard walks twice a day. Or if you want to put on a pound or two, now's the time to tell me! I'll cook square meals so that both you and the baby will be as strong as iron bridges. Why should you and I writhe in anguish like two wet cuckoos in the fields?"

"Doc Gospod says I must spend as much energy as I can. That is why."

"Then why do we keep Tano in the tool shed, I ask you? Why did I buy an electric heater for this jerk? Why do I fry a chicken, bake pies and cook veal stew every day for him? He's become as strong as a bull. A couple of months ago, he got drunk on one bottle of plum brandy, nowadays he downs three big bottles and nothing happens. The idiot dances! His backside swells at a frightening rate. I feel sick to my stomach every time I look at him. Listen, Miss Dana. I have a suggestion. You can spend a lot of your energy with my help. I'll lie down on the floor and you'll run in circles around me, swearing at the orchids. If you don't agree, I'll just sit on the floor, you'll glower at the orchids, and we will swear at the sons of bitches together. What do you think? Tell me."

"No way, woman! We tried this a week ago and I was bored stiff. If the bastards were hawks, I'd shoot at them, but the bastards are orchids, just freaking flora and fauna. Tano is a piece of cake. I wake up when? Let's say 4:30 or 5 am. At that time Grandpa Dobri drives the herd of cows to Crossroads Hill. I rub my eyes to pull myself together and I rush to the tool shed like the wind."

"Shame on you, Miss Dana. It's a barefaced lie you are throwing in my honest face now. I suffer from insomnia, Miss Dana, and my ears are as subtle as a pair of radars. I can hear your cheek sinking into your pillow. Therefore, it is impossible for you to plod through the room without waking me up. It's the most absurd tale I've heard in my honest life."

"Absurd or not, it's true," Miss Dana objected vehemently.

At 5 am, when Grandpa Dobri drove the herd of cattle to Crossroads Hill—the old man had just one cow, but collected all other beasts from the houses, lining the main street—Barren Dana planted a big kiss on little Mumma's forehead, tucked the kid in her bed and tiptoed to the tool shed. Tano used to sleep under a shabby blanket and looked like a heap of edges and recesses. His shoulder jutted out like old eaves, his knees protruded dangerously, acute angles of bones, under his tattered blanket. But when it became known far and wide that Barren Dana was pregnant, Isabella designed a new schedule for him. Three times a day, she brought the big man huge meals, breakfasts, lunches and dinners plus a bottle of the wine for the Fritzes.

Tano gobbled the food, throwing nothing away, leaving empty saucers in his wake. In the beginning, he even sucked the marrow out of the chicken bones, and his neck was a hammer handle on account of going hungry for long days and weeks. Then gradually he started forgetting a bone or two he'd been gnawing, and grew bigger. The heap under the shabby blanket lost all its angles, turning into a mess of round bulges as if Tano was a horse's rump and not a drinker of flesh and bones. It looked as though he had used blubber to pad his shoulders, his paunch a flabby knoll in front of him. The trouser legs of his, too wide for him a month ago, now the two of them sewn together could hardly hold one of his thick calves. Once in a while, Tano rushed out of the toolshed, grabbed a spade and furiously dug burrows in the lawn, shouting at the top of his powerful lungs, "A—a—a! O—o—o—o!"

He didn't bother to ask Isabella's permission, a very wrong move on his part, and set free the three bitches, Blizzard, Fury and Ogress. The big man tried to wrestle with them, but the dogs refused to fight him. They loved the sight of his big shoes, licked his hands, sniffed at his cheeks and nose. Whenever he ate a chicken Isabella had fried for him, the hulk of a man tossed the bones and chunks of meat to them. He shared the broiled veal, lamb and pork steaks with the three beasts, and Blizzard, Fury and Ogress did not lash out at him; they wagged their tails and yapped happily instead. Exasperated by their lack of mettle, Tano mounted Giant, the tremendous stallion, and rode him within the confined space of the backyard.

It was true the lawn behind Miss Dana's white mansion surrounded with ten-foot stone walls was vast, practicably interminable. Tano and Giant, the huge horse, could not cross it for a day, but the tall guy had already familiarized himself with every pebble and speck of dust on the property. He got into the habit of imitating the dogs: pissed under the elm tree and howled at the moon. With the passage of time, the colossus pissed everywhere and knew everything, holes, stones even lizards in the meadow in minute detail. He had a big itch for a ride to Pernik, for Isabella had said once with utmost disgust, "Tano, Miss Dana allows you to go to Pernik and stay at *Blue Waves* for two days."

Blue Waves was a cheap restaurant built in the vicinity of an empty swimming pool. Rains had filled the pool with mud and slimy water that was rapidly infested with hundreds of frogs, tough, die-hard fauna, so instead of *Blue Waves* the locals called the place *The Frog*. Tano was allowed to spend his day off at The Frog. Dana's sweetheart had a day off every two weeks. He ran to The Frog, produced a fat bundle of 20-lev banknotes Isabella had given him and ordered everything he could see at the bar: whisky, vodka, gin, French cognac, all of the above fake and glittering like the moon. Workers paid by Dana produced the French cognac in her counterfeit alcohol factory. Four geezers and a mentally re-tarded boy worked at the workshop. The boy had gone to Spain to pick olives like everybody else, but was so weak-headed that couldn't distinguish between an olive and a cucumber. He had come back to Radomir, Bulgaria, in the neighborhood known far and wide as the Arch. Tano treated all the patrons of *The Frog*, including the weak-headed kid, to anything the guests had taken a fancy to.

Tano's day off was usually Wednesday, and on Wednesdays the big man drank so much counterfeit alcohol that the proprietor of the establishment commissioned a local artist, a haughty bigwig, to paint Tano's portrait. Truthfully, the owner most solemnly hung Tano's picture on the wall next to the icon of Saint George the Victorious: once a fortnight, on Wednesday, Tano bought all booze, both from the shelves and from the cellar of *The Frog*.

"Cheers! Cheers!" men shouted at him from all sides. They drank like sharks, in the beginning only the workers from the slaughterhouse, then the employers of Sanitation Ltd in charge of emptying the waste containers in town. *The Frog* was a drinking establishment of standards plummeting below the bottom of all possible standards, but gradually men of the world shone like guest artists on tour in the Frog's paradise: teachers, technicians from the Opel car service accompanied by their girlfriends, surveyors and their wives etc. Young ladies and gentlemen reserved tables at *The Frog* for Tano's renowned Wednesdays after midnight on the following Thursday. Strangers kissed on the dance floor, and everybody was itching to kiss Tano who footed the bill, drank more than everybody and rumbled every now and then, "I'm not scared!"

He drank and hugged guys and girls, swilling down brandy, making efforts to sing, but managing to produce a deafening thunder, "A—a—a! O—o—o!" The rest of the guests chimed in, their gurgling wails a 'thunderstorm against the wind', and that was what they contributed to the song. The crowd was thoroughly canned and so happy they could hardly open their mouth to roar on.

Late into the night, Isabella arrived with her Ford truck to take Tano back home. She threw a fiver at the owner, also pretty mellow, ordered him to lug blind and bombed Tano to the truck and load the colossus into the freight section. Tano whose portrait adorned not only the Frog bar, but also the façade and the WC of the establishment, slept like a heap of dust. The Frog's proprietor had proclaimed him a benefactor to his food and drink business.

"Did you see women with him in the Frog Bar, Isabella?" Miss Dana often asked. "Did a tart sink her teeth into him? Men are daft and fall in love like horse-flies."

"I saw no tarts with him, Miss Dana. I saw men, all drinking, their faces green and blue. At a certain point, everybody prostrated themselves under the tables. No nanny goats in Frog Bar, believe me."Apart from her Tano-related duties on Wednesdays, Isabella was a liberal and merciful woman. The business advisor took Mumma by the hand, lead her to the middle of the lawn and read *Bulgarian Folktales, Volume II,* to the little girl. She often stopped reading, wrathfully exclaiming "Bastard fairytales!" but the kid asked, her eyes glowing, "What happened later? Please, read to me, Isabella. Please." Grudgingly, the business assistant slogged through the problems of the lazy old tsar and his wife, thinking there were two hundred more fairytales, bastards all of them, especially the one about the apple of gold.

"Isabella!" the toolshed shouted at a certain point.

Isabella happily dropped the apple of gold, grabbed an enormous pink towel she had prepared well in advance and sprinted to the toolshed. Miss Dana emerged from the darkness, blushing and exhausted. Isabella had prepared a blanket she constantly kept warm by an electric heater. She immediately put the pleasantly soft, and of course Italian, fabric on her employer's protruding stomach.Doc Gospod assured Dana she would give birth to a baby boy.

"And this is ok with me. If the little one was a girl, she might be as big as me. How could I find a husband for her?"

After the blanket warmed her perspiring stomach, Miss Dana turned to Isabella, "Bella, his beard is stubbly like a broom. If he refuses to shave himself, you shave him. Make him take a bath. If he refuses, wash him with the garden hose. Last Wednesday, he cut his foot, stepped on a shattered beer bottle. It's a festering wound. Cure him. Stitch the wound. I need to get some rest. You feed Mumma and read ten pages of fairytales to her. If you don't,

I'll kick you hard and tough, and you won't remember what time your TV series *The Woman in Red* begins."

"I'll read to her fifteen pages, Miss Dana. But that's not the point. You look too red in the face to me. Obviously, you carry it too far with Tano. Remember what Doc Gospod warned you against it."

"Doc Gospod is being odd. I think she plays the dummy too often lately," Miss Dana said. "Not carry it too far with him, eh? And wait for a brassy piece of tart to steal Tano from me under my nose in the Frog Bar? Is that what Doc Gospod advises me to do? You won't find a tall guy like Tano in Radomir, Pernik or throughout Bulgaria."

"You won't find a guy as fat as Tano, Miss Dana. He's plump as a camel, believe me. Look at Giant, the poor horse! I feel like weeping bitter tears for the beast. Every time Tano mounts him, the unfortunate stallion bends and sags like a willow sprig under the tosspot's weight. It makes my heart bleed for Giant!"

"Leave the horse alone. I worry about you, girl," Miss Dana said. "Do you want me to marry you off to a decent guy? I'll rub quail's grease into your skin for you after you get pregnant. I'll give you freshly squeezed apple and carrot juice four times a day. You'll be the apple of my eye, Isabella. Tell me the name of the guy you want and you'll have him in a week."

"Let me be, Miss Dana," Isabella said. "I'm an isolated case."

"I know your case very well, Isa. You must have a child."

"I'm doing all right," Isabella said. "Don't make it hard on you for my sake. I perfectly maintain my physical and mental health."

"Don't give me that bullshit. Here, take this money. Go look for somebody. I haven't heard of a girl like you here in Radomir, but you might find one in Pernik."

"I won't go anywhere, Miss Dana."

Isabella had saved up a lot of money. Isabella ate the best meals among the townsfolk in Radomir, Arch Neighborhood. Isabella and Miss Dana got along pretty well. The business assistant was fond of the feeble-minded kid who, after all, turned out perfectly normal and healthy. A cute, quiet darling, despite being too keen on that son of a bitch apple of gold! Little Mumma was willing to listen to two hundred pages of Bulgarian Folktales at a time! But the kid was so sweet.

Once in a blue moon, for no reason at all, Isabella thought that her bedroom, the most luxurious one in Radomir, was too narrow for her. She felt her food, very expensive and healthy though it was, didn't taste good, and that something had gone wrong with the sun. It shone brightly, but didn't give her warmth. She so much wanted to meet that small blue-eyed girl, as beautiful as the first warm day after a month of snow and blizzards, wonderful like an Italian picture, and kind like an Italian child. She wished she could somehow be that girl's mother. She wished she had given birth to the tiny tot and raised her. It wouldn't have been hard for Isabella. She waited for the blue-eyed kid in the street, but the little one ran away. From that day on, Binna, the wonderful kid, rushed to the convenience store, the bakery, even to Grandma Simeona hairdresser's shop every time she saw the business assistant. Isabella had never seen a more beautiful child than Binna. Binna's sister, dark, scraggy, silent, noiseless as a cat, was a horse of a different color. Isabella gave her small change, pennies and dimes, bought her ice cream, gave her kid ball gowns, asking, "What do you want me to buy you, Sinna?"

"A chocolate bar," the kid said looking calm and confident. "I want the biggest chocolate bar. It costs five levs." The kid's smile was bigger than her head. "You're very pretty, Isabella."

The smile was too syrupy, but Isabella didn't mind. She liked the dark secret in the dark kid's eyes, she put on socks and sandals on the dark little feet, or the bright T-shirt she'd bought for her. She wished the skinny little runt was her daughter as well. At times Isabella dreamed of two loving daughters in her expensive Italian living room, but those moments were very rare indeed.

15.

ALTHOUGH THE SUN WAS A speck of gold amidst the tree tops, it was cold in the library. The windows to the north were tapestries of cobwebs, silver and heavy with hoarfrost. Binna cleaned the windows yesterday, but now the thin threads of rime and cobweb held the sun in its net of gold. The ceiling of the smaller room of the library, breathing out damp dusk, was the kingdom of the spiders. Binna rarely turned on the light; in the small room were the books printed before 1940 that obeyed different grammar rules, and nobody wanted them. The Mayor of Radomir, a middle aged lady, brilliant mathematician, had tried to sell these tomes to the Bulgarian National Library and repair the town square, but the National Library said, "No, thank you." The books remained on the shelves and the Mayor suggested she sell fiction, poetry and non-fiction to anyone who wanted it dirt cheap. No man had money to burn on old moldy paper. The spiders on the ceiling above the ancient tomes were more numerous than the Gothic letters in which the texts were printed. While the lights were on and Binna searched for *Village of Studena* by V. Varadinov, the spiders in the dusk panicked. The space was not enough for their cobwebs. The grown-up spiders looked bigger than

Binna's hand as they hung on a thread swinging above the books as if they were desperate to read *Village of Studena* by V. Varadinov. The caravans of the numerous offspring explored the walls, reminding Binna of the cockroaches in Vancha's second hand shop where the designer clothes were entangled in thick cobwebs. Vancha cursed the spiders dryly, in a matter-of-fact tone of voice. The old woman was often enraged because the disgusting insects frightened her clients away. It went without saying the old herb gathering ladies bought used skirts and didn't give a damn, spiders or no spiders. It was their grandchildren who got in trouble in summer despite the clean air; the kids were scared stiff of the spiders as big as swallows and talked in their sleep when their parents took them back to the olives in Spain.

The tots shrieked, "Spider! Spider," and absconded from the shop, rendering their grandmas speechless, unable to buy a second-hand designer dress from Denmark at a symbolic price.

"The spider is a meek animal," Vancha said to her herb-gathering audience. "He catches flies and doesn't meddle with things that don't concern him."

At times, these hairy beasts were really annoying. A couple of months ago they multiplied into a million little spiders, outnumbering by far the city folk. A huge spider had drowned in Aggo the junkman's, teacup. Aggo's eyes were not that sharp anymore, and the old man gulped down the huge creature. Binna knew Aggo's legs and feet hurt, and the old man could hardly walk. Doc Gospod told him his kidneys were no good. She thought he suffered from gout as well.

"I'd be surprised if you didn't suffer, man," Vancha told him one evening. "You gorge yourself on beef suet, pork cracklings and bread. You eat junk food in the morning, at noon and in the evening. Don't complain of your gout. Stop guzzling brandy. What can Doc Gospod and I do with you?"

Aggo's feet hurt so much that a couple of times he passed out. His face told Vancha he suffered, but the poor devil didn't complain. Was his gout so bad, or did the suet poison his liver? He spread pig's grease on bread and ate it, drank hogwash brandy and didn't whine even when the blue circles under his eyes dropped down to his chin, and the man looked gray and almost black. The minute before he passed out the blue bags were yellow.

"Watch him," Doc Gospod said. "If his face turns yellow, give him two of these pills. Or we might lose him. But if you give him the pills, he'll be ok."

Vancha fed the pig, the geese, the hens and the donkey, then ran to the kitchen and studied the circles under his eyes. If they were blue she heaved a sigh of relief and kept the pills in the pocket of her apron. If the circles were yellow, she gave him the pills, a glass of water touching his mouth as if Aggo was a baby, too weak to hold anything in his hands. One day the bags under his eyes were so bright yellow that Binna stopped dead in her tracks.

"Dad's going!"

"No!"Vancha said evenly. "He's not going anywhere. He's staying with us."

As always, their son Naum was somewhere with the fashion brands, waiting for a European old lady to croak, so he could take her designer clothes and sell them at symbolic prices in Vancha's second-hand shop in Radomir, Arch neighborhood. As always, someone had asked Sinna on a date, a bigwig from Pernik or from Sofia. Anyway, when in Radomir a posh car came to a halt in the town square, it was obvious big wheels had turned full circle dying to meet Sinna. "A posh car" was any vehicle different for old jalopies, Opel 1995, Renault 2000 that the herb-gathering community drove in these parts of the world.

Space, the forest ranger, had no car at all. Years ago, he was in possession of a bicycle, but one evening he got drunk, fell off his vehicle and went to sleep. Some non-resident Roma guys stole the bike and that was the reason why Space, the forest ranger, walked the length and breadth of the woods all alone.

Sometimes Binna followed him, and if occasionally the man turned around, she took some nervous steps towards him, keeping silent. Space said nothing. They looked at each other, both of them blue-eyed. Binna was the prettiest girl in Radomir, Arch neighborhood, and that meant in the whole of Bulgaria. She had made her peace with the spiders and their nets, reading books that obeyed the old rules of grammar and punctuation of the Bulgarian language. Space, the forest ranger, was a queer fish. No one had ever said he was attractive; the guy walked ten miles a day in his filthy green uniform, a dozen or so patches sewn on it with white, red, black or blue threads, depending on the color of the spool he stumbled across first.

In the cold evening, Binna and Space stared at each other, dwarf spiky shrubs surrounding them. The beeches had been cut years ago and used as firewood, but the trees were of no consequence. The evening wasn't either. The wind was unimportant. The forest ranger told her, "You're beautiful", but she already knew that. Every time someone told Binna she was pretty she hurried to old Olga, the hairdresser, and had her hair cut, so she wouldn't lure the students from the only high school out of their classrooms. Binna wasn't scared when Space said she was beautiful. She took a tiny step to him, he raised his hand, but didn't dare touch her, and she thought of Nikolay from the high school.

The boy would never let her go if she didn't have a man her age at home. How could Binna find a man her age in Radomir, Arch neighborhood? The only man there was Space the forest ranger.

Space had lifted up his hand to her cheek, but let it hang in the air, like cobwebs, an inch away from her skin. Binna came up to his fingers. Space the forest ranger asked her, "What do you want with me?"

It was the first time she'd heard his voice. It was hoarse with too much brandy and cheap cigarettes.

"Nothing," Sinna said.

She did not explain she needed to find somebody his age so that Nikolay would stop thinking about her. The best thing was he went peacefully to his mom's place in Spain. The woman had arranged for him to work as a security guard for St. Vicente Circus. Binna had to convince him to go; the boy shouldn't waste his life, loitering in Radomir. In this small town, one saw old geezers suffering from gout, books obeying old grammar rules, goats and cows. At the high school, the students learned to speak Spanish and pick olives. In the library, Binna had a puny electric heater that gave off as much warmth as a glowworm.

Binna caught the forest ranger's hand. He jerked it free and dashed across the clearing, sinking into the thicket of dense thorny shrubs through which even goats could not squeeze their way. Space did. He ran as if his shirt was on fire, prickles and barbs gripping his green uniform sewn with threads of all colors. Rags from his sleeves and trouser legs hung like garlands on the branches of the shrubs in his wake.

Sinna was a different kettle of fish. Big guns from Pernik, Sofia and Plovdiv arrived in chauffeur driven cars to "have a word with her". The dark jug of poison had a small place where she took them all: an old roadman's lodge nearby the village of Rudar where ruins of an old salt mine could be seen. The locals had stolen the salt, leaving the narrow road to the mercy of nettles and briars. The villagers had plundered the house as well. The more enterprising ones had lifted the wooden window frames and the roof tiles, but no matter how enterprising they were, the men grew old. They could no longer climb to the roof to steal the remaining roof beams. A courageous geezer had tried, and afterwards Doc Gosod had a hard time stitching him up. It was in this roadman's hut that Sinna accepted the limos, the Toyotas, and the Mercedes. In the beginning, the big shots' vehicles carved a dirt road to the shabby building. Then a big cheese from Pernik stole heaps of rubble and built a safe road to the lodge. Every time Sinna had a day off and was free to get away from Barren Dana's pub, she had fun with her gentleman callers at the roadman's hut.

The gentlemen made a contribution, now substantial, now meager to improving the ramshackle building, and it had acquired exquisite rosewood sashes, a brand new armored door, glittering marble slabs on the roof, an ebony table, an ivory vase and mahogany easy chairs. A very necessary item attracted the visitor's attention, a four poster oak bed with a lace canopy and matching bedspread. Cobwebs abounded under the canopy but neither Sinna nor her admirers minded the spiders' efforts. The spider, as Vancha said, was a meek animal. He wove his nets and didn't poke his nose into your four-poster bed.

16.

It is imperative to cancel my appointment with my hairstylist Davidov, Mrs. Marko thought bitterly. Hairstylist Davidov had been in charge of her hair for seven years now. He dyed it, brushed it, shampooed it, cut it, trimmed it, curled and permed it. He made it glossy and thick, using Chinese herbal infusions, he spent hours in meditation with Mrs. Marko, attempting to impart additional strength to her hair roots; he followed complex procedures to regain its full volume, translated specialized articles from French, English, Spanish and Italian, doing his utmost best to explain to Mrs. Marko that her good will and good faith were indispensable to her hair's resistance and survivability.

A renowned beautician, Mr. Chirpan, took care of her skin, emphasizing the significance Mrs. Marko should attach to the corners of her eyes. Of course, she should under no circumstances underestimate the corners of her mouth, although the beautician made it a point that both the honorable lady's lips and eyes belonged to the best preserved face in Sofia, the capital of Bulgaria. A famous masseur gave her massages, and a philosopher, holder of PhD earned at University of Heidelberg, Germany, was responsible for Mrs. Marko's spiritual balance.

Mrs. Marko worked for a ministry of crucial importance for the country as a translator/interpreter from the French. She never uttered the name of this important institution, bearing in mind the confidential information she processed there. Lady Marko was convinced that apart from her, the other employees at this organization were dark and dull provincial types, all of them. She was a representative of the fourth generation of an illustrious family established in the capital of Bulgaria 270 years ago.

Mr. Marko, a prominent public figure and official at an agency of crucial importance for the country, had made it a point that his wife was to be treated with respect both by the elite and her colleagues coming from backwater provincial towns. The working hours at the institution were as follows: 9 am – 5:30 pm, lunch break, 12:00 – 12:30. Mrs. Marko arrived at 11 am, went out to grab a sandwich at 11:30; came back at 2:30 pm, explaining she had to inform her son of a major development in the country's trade policy. She informed her son of crucial developments in the country's trade policy twice a day, so it was imperative that she see the boy. No one had seen her translations from Bulgarian into French. The position *translator/interpreter from the French* was specially established for Mrs. Marko, so the lady could enjoy appropriate spiritual working environment, but she wholeheartedly disapproved of this position.

We are hundreds of light years away from the developed western countries, Lady Marko sighed bitterly. The experts there are honorable and civilized. Look at the vulgar types who rule us! Nasty wild country! Regret ate at Mrs. Marko's soul every time she thought she had to live in this brutal land. She even more deeply regretted she had to cancel her appointment with her beautician Mr. Chirpan. Her heart bled, she felt that her hair badly needed nourishing lotion, and the skin at the corners of her eyes was inexorably traumatized.

Last week she was obliged to translate a business letter; it was true the letter was not more than a half page long, but the text was riddled with technical terms, so Mrs. Marko telephoned 17 experts, explaining to them what the ignorant bumpkin, author of the pitiable document, meant. The letter consisted of 12 lines, for Christ's sake, but the so-called "experts", yokels every single one of them, dared ask her, "You've been working for this ministry (on account of the confidential nature of the processed information Mrs. Marko never used the name of the institution) twelve years now. How come you don't know the meaning of this term?"

Mrs. Marko was terribly sorry she lived in this despairingly parochial region of the world where instead of heads, men wore softwood on their shoulders. No matter what, she was a champion of justice i.e. each cell of her perfectly kept body was a champion in itself.

"My husband, Mr. Marko," she addressed the expert, a typical country hawbuck, brazen-faced enough to ask her provocative questions. "Mr. Marko," she repeated clearly and loudly, "That is my husband, will be disappointed if he learns that you are wasting my time, attempting to satisfy your idle curiosity."

Put to the blush, the "expert" shut up his mouth, turning ashen and swallowing the rivulets of his own sweat that ran towards his mouth.

"Mr. Marko is your husband, Ma'am? Oh, Ma'am…I am deeply impressed… more than deeply impressed. Please convey my deep respect, warm regards, and best wishes to him."

Then the same clodhopping "expert" asked Mrs. Marko to the cafeteria at the ministry (Mrs. Marko would not reveal the name of the institution on account of the confidential nature of her work!) where the imbecile explained the essence of the term to impatient Mrs. Marko. Then the sod complemented her on the elasticity and softness of her skin, on the perfection of the corners of her eyes and the impressive quality of her three-piece suit.

"It's Giorgio Armani," Mrs. Marko said modestly. "Mr. Marko bought it for me from London. Oh, no, forgive my forgetful brain, I suppose the city was either Paris, or Milan or Shanghai. Could you send me in writing the explanation you provided me with, Mr... What was your name? Yes, at my e-mail address."

The "expert" burped like a horse and clumsily kissed then shook her hand. His mouth was full of saliva, a significant part of which remained on Mrs. Marko's pearly skin. Mr. Chirpan, the beautician, had put in a great deal of sustained effort in order to keep Mrs. Marko's hands in perfect condition: ethereally soft and sweet-scented, the hands of a genteel and stylish European lady, but the ill-mannered boor slobbered on her fingers, drowning the fair lady in the flood of his provincial smiles.

Oh, how Mrs. Marko detested bootlickers! They were worms, sucking the country dry. That was why the backwater territory Mrs. Marko called her motherland made no progress at all, because of brownnosing apple-polishers, currying favor with their superiors. The "expert" plunged into the fawning pool of his own voice, all grease and compliments, wishing her a wonderful holiday season. And the idiot most probably thought he'd paid the price for his sins by planting a fat kiss on her hand, the lamebrain. At the very end, the bumpkin concluded, his tone of voice all honey and butter, "Let me again express my very best wishes and give heartfelt greetings to Mr. Marko! Please tell him I do deeply respect him. Please! Please!"

Look here, imbecile, I'll tell Marko about what you've been blabbering about after the bones of the dead men burst into bloom, Mrs. Marko thought, but she was a civilized, well-educated European lady, so she said out loud, "Of course I will, Mr.... What was your name?"

"Petar Petrov," the imbecile said.

Today Mrs. Marko was outraged.

She cancelled her appointment with her beautician, Mr. Chirpan, and deep inside her heart she hesitated—for the third day in a row—to have her hair cut or simply nourish her poor hair roots. She consulted her personal astrologer, a brilliantly educated man, who declared that on the one hand it was advisable to have her hair cut thus tapping the powerful influence of Venus, which translated into intimate conquests, splendid innermost emotions and love confession, a romantic guy etc. On the other hand, if Mrs. Marko applied root nourishing oil, she'd attract Mars's positive influence; this would promote career success and glamorous events in the sphere of learning and culture. She suffered hours of mental torment.

What should she choose: cultural glitz or an intimate conquest? Mrs. Marko's top priority had always been the intimate sphere i.e. Mr. Marko. He would knock at the door of her room, clean, perfectly groomed, smelling of sexy manly cologne, a flower in hand. Mrs. Marko had given him a list of flowers that exacerbated her allergy. She had provided his secretary with the same list because it was Elvira, Mr. Marko's personal assistant—an old lady eligible for private pension benefits—who bought the flower bouquets for Mrs. Marko. Elvira's face was more of a net of wrinkles than a human physiognomy. The crow's feet around the old crone's eyes were the most disgusting picture in the ministry. Mrs. Marko had selected her with utmost care, and was sure her husband would not give in to any temptations of sexual nature. So, on Wednesdays, wrinkle-faced Elvira bought a bouquet from Heavenly Aromas Boutique, and Mr. Marko, dazzlingly stylish in his silk pajamas, willing to fulfill his duty of a loving husband, knocked at Mrs. Marko's door, a bunch of tulips in hand. His gallantry lasted but a minute, a fact Mrs. Marko welcomed. She, as Mr. Marko's wife, was tolerant of her obligations, which she met with becoming patience of a civilized European lady, but would prefer, if possible and if this would not ruin the harmony of their marriage, not to waste her precious time, engaging in carnal activities.

She hoped a day would come soon she wouldn't be obliged to honor the above. If her husband could make do with only a kiss in the morning, she'd interpret his understanding and reticence as an expression of a European gentleman's free spirit. What if she found a lover? She might like one. Mrs. Marko had heard of agencies offering this type of service. Why not hire a lover? A new man in her life might prove a fruitful experience. Mr. Marko, faultlessly groomed, kissed her every morning as behooved a caring European husband, wished her a wonderful day and while Gretchen, their loyal housekeeper, poured tea into their cups and served them a traditional British breakfast on the mahogany table Mr. Marko had bought from Morocco, Mrs. Marko smiled radiantly and encouragingly at her husband. At a certain point Gretchen said, "You look magnificent today, Ma'am," a convincing expression the housekeeper had been using every day for seventeen years now.

"You have selected your necktie with care, Sir. It accentuates your individuality and jovial mood," that was another statement Gretchen had not changed in the course of seventeen years.

At breakfast today, Gretchen did something she had never done since the Markos had employed her as a domestic worker in their household.

"Mrs. Marko, Mr. Marko," Gretchen began, blushing, her eyes on her feet, "Your son Samuel asked me to inform you that today, at 3 pm, he would have the pleasure of introducing his future wife to you. Please allow me to ask you on his behalf to be available at home today, at 2:30 pm. He has given me the menu, providing me with detailed description of the dishes and drinks I'll have to prepare in advance. All ingredients shall be acquired in due time, I will see to it and I will have the meals ready to your taste Madam Marko, Mr. Marko, Sir."

Mr. and Mrs. Marko froze dead in their tracks. Even Mr. Marko, the epitome of self-control, stood up, staring at the housekeeper. Both Mr. Marko and his wife were dropping hints that they would like to have a grandchild and it was time a young lady crossed the threshold of their honest home.

It went without saying no one had hasty marriage in mind or marriage at all. Couldn't the young people live together for a while, getting to know each other first? As a matter of fact, their son Samuel had gained an intimate knowledge, multiple times already, of young Mademoiselles. He took his girls to the family mansion in Boyana, the most prestigious neighborhood of the Bulgarian capital; Mr. Marko gave the place to his son as a present for his twenty-first birthday in an attempt to transform Sam into an independent young professional. In practical terms, the young Mademoiselles and Sam got to know each other very well very quickly and lost interest soon after that.

The young ladies were influential men's daughters; they had already received luxury villas as presents for their seventeenth birthdays, so they felt they were independent, and didn't care to stay with Samuel in his mansion in the pinewood forest. They said it felt like a hole in a desert where geography ended and wilderness began, a provincial den, dull and isolated, far away from Europe. So the young folks' intimate knowledge lasted no more than a fortnight, and their son's heat was free like the wind. Samuel had often informed his parents, with the kind assistance of Gretchen, the housekeeper, that today he'd introduce his girlfriend to them, but he had never so far used the evocative phrase "my future wife". It sounded too categorical even to a pair of parents of liberal and democratic upbringing.

"Greta," It was Mr. Marko who pulled himself together first. "Could you repeat our son's message?"

Greta repeated Mr. Samuel Marko's message, resorting again to the phrase "my future wife".

"Did he mean his… his helpmate?"

"Mr. Marko, the exact words Mr. Samuel used were, 'I will introduce my future wife to my parents'. I do not think he mention anything about a helpmate."

So Mrs. Marko had sufficient reason to cancel her appointment with Mr. Chirpan the beautician and now she was unable to let him take care of her hair roots or concentrate on her upset skin. Samuel and his *future wife*! What had gone wrong with her wonderful boy? So far, he had not alluded to a possible marriage. He was being secretive, and that she didn't like. Even Greta, old loyal Greta, had not heard a thing about marriage or another alternative form of a long-term commitment to a woman on Samuel's part.

Greta spent Mondays and Thursdays at their son's mansion in Boyana. Mrs. Marko didn't know what exactly Gretchen did there, perhaps she talked to Sam. Mrs. Marko had hired a charwoman who cleaned the rooms, a gardener to take care of Sam's trees and flowers, and a cook, an old decent lady, in charge of Sam's and Greta's meals. Good old Greta went and communed with Samuel, did it four hours in the afternoon on Mondays and Thursdays, damned it, and if in the wide world a human being knew *everything* about Samuel Marko, it was good old Greta. Sam had confessed to Mrs. Marko that he could cry only in Greta's presence. She was his confidante, his nanny, his personal advisor, tower of strength and his beloved shrink: all the above was loyal Greta to Sam. But even she did not have information relevant to his planned marriage.

"Greta, has Sammy disclosed any details, no matter how insignificant they might seem, about his future wife in your presence?"

"He has not spoken a word about her, Mr. Marko. I am sure of that. He met her four days ago."

"Four days! And he will marry her!" Mrs. Marko exclaimed, terrified. "He has not consulted the marriage counselor of our family! He has not let us know!" she breathed, completely shaken. At that moment she remembered that the unrestrained gestures and facial expressions would inflict irreparable damage to the skin around her eyes and mouth, and immediately her passions cooled.

"Did he tell you where he'd met her?" Mr. Marko said his voice a block of ice.

"Yes, Sir, he did. He met her in a library in Radomir."

"What was Sammy doing in Radomir?" Mrs. Marko would have used stronger and more expressive words like 'It was none of his damned business to loiter in that backwater provincial hole,' but she decided she shouldn't let her ignorance show. Probably Radomir was a well-known Sofia suburb. She knew, for sure, all arrondissements of Paris, had visited all 26 major squares in Brussels, the heart of Europe, and had gone shopping along 5th Avenue in New York City. But she didn't know—and didn't care—where Radomir was. Most probably this hamlet was situated in a mountain or in some narrow valley. Mrs. Marko hated useless or irrelevant information; it caused wrinkles on neck and forehead, and upset hair roots. Facts, bearing no relation to skin rejuvenation treatment, seaside and ski resorts, fashion boutiques, beauty studios were redundant, spiritual waste and provincial boredom.

"Sammy had to search for toponyms typical of the Sofia District," Greta explained.

Mrs. Marko doubted she knew the exact meaning of 'toponym'. Unwilling to expose her ignorance to her housekeeper, she abruptly turned to Greta, "Gretchen, didn't we send you two weeks ago to find the toponyms Sammy wanted? We expected hard work from you. You were supposed to accompany him during his trips to shanty provincial…" at this point Mrs. Marko once again refrained from blurting out 'provincial towns'.

"I did accompany him, Madam. We travelled together every-where. I can assure you I took good care of your son. I let him go to work only after he was well-fed, gave him the vitamins his doctor had recommended, closely inspected his clothes and shoes with re-spect to cleanliness and high quality."

"We do not doubt your judgment," Mr. Marko cut her short. "Were you with Sammy when he established contact with this… this person?"

"With this Radomir person," Mrs. Marko added.

"Unfortunately, on that particular day Samuel assigned me a job to do, Madam. His printer broke down, and we could not print the materials Samuel needed. He called me a taxi and sent me to our authorized support provider in Sofia. Sam remained alone in his car. I worried over his health. Of course, we called each other every hour, but I could not set my mind at ease. I had checked if there were good restaurants near Radomir. There were none to Samuel's taste, so I telephoned Globe Restaurant Network in Sofia, and they brought Samuel food of his liking to his car. I cooked for him in the house we had rented after I consulted four real-estate brokers. The atmosphere of the property we rented seemed to raise Sam's spirits: three bedrooms, designer furniture, well equipped modern kitchen, two spacious, well-fitted bathrooms. British and German tourists rented the house before us, Mrs. Marko. I can assure you Samuel wholeheartedly approved of it."

"And he met the person in question when you were in Sofia with the broken printer?" Mr. Marko asked, summarizing the situation.

"Yes, Sir," he did."

"Did Sammy introduce you to the person in question?" Mrs. Marko asked impatiently.

"He did, Madam."

"What does she look like?" at that moment, Mrs. Marko forgot that she had cancelled her appointment with her beautician and her hair stylist. She didn't even think of her hair, although at the back of her mind she was aware that lack of care placed her hair roots in serious jeopardy.

"She looks good," the housekeeper said.

"Describe her," Mr. Marko ordered in a tone of voice that instilled awe and fear in his subordinates.

"Slim and tall, blue eyes, white skin and auburn hair. The idiomatic expressions she uses do her credit, her vocabulary is impressive, and her sentences are well-constructed unlike the dialect spoken by the locals," the housekeeper had mastered the art of speaking to the point, putting into practice what she'd learned from her daily reports for Mr. Marko. "I cannot say how old she is. She may be twenty-two or thirty. She may be twenty. Sammy has not asked her."

"What's her name?" Mr. Marko asked.

"Albinna, but she asked me to call her Binna."

"Binna?" Mrs. Marko repeated her voice a bag of thorns. "Binna? I think I sense an attempt at concealing her double0dealing nature. Ok. No, it's not ok. I have to call my masseur. I am in urgent need of my massage therapist. I need my hair stylist. Now! I can't meet my future... my... um... um... my future daughter-in-law looking as exhausted as a doormat. Greta, call Chirpan. I can't go to his studio. He must come here. Now! Call Mr. Marko's masseuse as well. Gregory," she turned imperially to Mr. Marko. "Go. Shave yourself and take a shower. You need a facial massage. You can't possibly meet your future daughter-in-law in your bathrobe. How horrible! Daughter-in-law! Here am I, saying it. Can you imagine: a *daughter in-law!* I am still young. Daughter-in-law! How horrible! When will they be here? At 3 pm… She comes from a provincial dunghill. Oh, my God, she sure is a rural gold-digging bitch."

The sun shone, the grass was golden-green, luxuriant in the shadows of the marvelous park, appearing bluish-greens at places. Perhaps the gardener had applied greater amounts of organic fertilizers there. The Markos family mansion was built in the most prestigious and green suburban area of the capital. Only genteel, civilized and very cultivated families lived there, all of them having proved their social value was high and awe-inspiring. Their offspring, well-educated and brilliant, resembled Samuel in a number of respects, although none was as bright as he was. Oh, my God, so many girls, ravishing, smart, civilized, fighting like tigers for Sam's attention, and he went and fell for a provincial wench! Greta let him slip out of her control for a day and he walked into the trap, grabbing the first slut in the village that crossed his path.

If one assumed Samuel lacked experience, he'd be wrong. Sam had a girlfriend as early as when he was in the ninth grade, then he lived with two successive charming girlfriends, heiresses of wealthy old-established families. At that time, his father made a major step that, in Mrs. Marko's opinion, was unreasonable and reckless: he allowed Sammy to move into the huge Boyana mansion and live by himself there. Of course, Mr. Marko gave him the place after Samuel turned twenty-one. It goes without saying that Greta was constantly with their boy, and good old Greta did a wonderful job. She went shopping with Sam, chose trendy clothes and sensible shoes for him, bought his food from trustworthy licensed retail food establishments and cooked with greatest pleasure for their son, doing her utmost to satisfy his sophisticated taste for healthy and wholesome food.

Several times already, Sammy had confessed to Mrs. Marko that he awoke good old Greta at 2 am, 3 am, 4 am; he so much wanted to drink Golden Chrysanthemum chocolate milk, and loyal marvelous Greta got up with pleasure, boiled raw milk for him and let him drink, looking at his happy countenance, a soft smile on her lips. Samuel suffered the pangs of remorse that he roused her in the dead of night, but what else could he do? Hunger, in his opinion, was the worst negotiator, and good old Greta was so kind! Samuel studied at Sofia University and Greta took care of him all the time, of course. He was an excellent student and his mother was very proud of him.

Sam had a number of girlfriends, and Greta had not made errors in her judgment: the girls were all refined and intelligent. Samuel had been in Köln, Germany, earning his Master's Degree in the course of three long years, and naturally, Greta stayed with him all the time. At this stage, Mr. Marko raised certain objections: it was very expensive to pay another person in Germany, but on the other hand, Gretchen bought wisely and spent thriftily, ate little, although looking at her abundant backside, one wouldn't say so. Sammy declared he didn't care about his master's degree if Greta didn't accompany him to Köln. He needed her. This argument crushed Mr. Marko's resistance, and now he was exceptionally content that he made the right decision at that time.

Sammy earned his master's degree, and would have probably found a job and remained in Köln, but Greta's mother met her maker, God bless her soul, so Greta flew out for the funeral and cleared the air about the inheritance issue. Samuel refused to stay in Germany even a day without Greta, so he returned to Bulgaria ten hours after her. He was a brilliant young man, her son! Of course, his father pulled stings, contacted old friends and found a top paying management job for his offspring. Sam insisted that

Greta should stay with him in his Boyana mansion, but this time Mr. Marko was adamant. Mrs. Marko supported her husband's negative vote.

The husband and wife regularly had breakfast together, personally served by Greta; she was in charge of the family-cooked dinner as well. Late in the evening, the housekeeper came back to Sammy, so 'If there is a will, there's a way' Mr. Marko pointed out, proud that he had come up with a good compromise. The Markos waited for Greta to be served at dinner, she was their loyal, well-mannered housekeeper. Twice, often three times a week, the family chauffeur drove Greta to Boyana mansion, if Samuel needed her, and she stayed there for three to four hours. Needless to say, Sammy employed a charwoman and a cook, so what did Greta do in Boyana? On Mondays, Thursdays, Saturdays and Sundays, often on Wednesdays as well, she visited Samuel and talked to him. The two of them were birds of a feather and got on really well.

Yes, the family had a house built in the quietest, cleanest, and greenest neighborhood of the Bulgarian capital, Mrs. Marko repeated in her mind while her masseur worked on the elasticity, firmness and appeal of her chest muscles. He worked on her athletic legs, too, paying special attention to the calves, showing great diligence and explaining to her what his goal was: to put a stop to her cellulite by circular movements in anticlockwise direction. He simply refreshed her skin by improving her blood circulation through elements, postures, and some good moves of Tai Chi fighting techniques. Last Wednesday, her masseur started clarifying exactly what he was doing to her pelvic floor muscles, but Mrs. Marko asked him to say nothing more. She was lost in her thoughts. Would her make-up artist, Maestro Betev, come in time to take care of her face? Was it advisable to have a lover? Would a young male presence in her life rejuvenate the skin of her thighs and improve her understanding of the world? The sun was too bright, damn it, which *fond de teint* was she supposed to choose? What eye-shadow would look best on her big green eyes, discrete soft pink or soft light blue? No matter how discrete pink looked, she suddenly felt it was vulgar. Yes, she'd like dove gray-blue and why not silver? Silver was the color of aristocratism and intellectualism. She'd have to make a decision on something of crucial importance: what type of perfume should she wear-soft and enticing jojoba magic or the mystic touch of *River Legends?* She could not choose. It was a good idea to consult her astrologist.

When at 3 p.m. Samuel Marko entered the reception room of the family mansion, 7 Moon Lillie Street, accompanied by a young woman, both Mr. Marko and Mrs. Marko stopped breathing. Their son's girl was unbelievably beautiful. Her clear white face seemed lit up by a soft glow, coming from within her, perhaps a side effect of the sunrays, giving gold to the walls, but the girls blue eyes glowed too, softly, warmly, so serenely that for a minute Mrs. Marko forgot the girl came from a backwater region at the back of beyond, a place where geography was powerless. Mr. Marko stood motionless, quiet, looking at her, a tiny smile on his face, very different from the practiced grin he wore on his face when he met VIPs, all of them his superiors, supercilious fat cows. Nor was it the sneer of disgust he kept for his subordinates, giving them nightmares. It was a smile that had not touched his lips for forty years. A century ago, he smiled at his favorite cousin, a girl in a yellow pinafore, and he smiled at his grandma, too. Mr. Marko stood motionless, beaming at his son's girl. A whole minute passed before Mrs. Marko noticed that her future daughter-in=law's dress was desperately far away from the cutting=edge selection of fashion *haute=couture,* a shapeless, high-necked abomination a middle-aged housewife would have put on, listening to funeral sermon in North Rhine Westphalia, Germany, thirty years ago. But even in this dress her son's girl looked stunning. Mrs. Marko had rarely seen such a beautiful young lady.

"Antoinette Marko," Mrs. Marko said, shaking the girl's hand. The newcomer's skin was warm, her fingernails very short, no nail polish, a blunder that, on another occasion, would have disgusted Mrs. Marko. Her son's future wife wore too cheap makeup; Mrs. Marko could catch the smell of the tasteless eyeliner the newcomer had used so sparingly and poorly she could well do without it. Under different circumstances, Mrs. Marko would drop a broad hint the young provincial tart was probably slow on the uptake. But Sammy's girl was impossibly pretty.

"Call me Anni," Mrs. Marko said.

Extremely rarely did Antoinette Marco allow anybody to call her *Anni*. The only human beings who had her express permission were the Prime Minister's wife and the President's mother.

"Greg Marko, Sammy's father," Mr. Marko said unwilling and unable to take his eyes off Sam's girl. The famous lawyer's face still held traces of that century-old smile. One way or another, Mr. Marko took his exhilaration in hand. "Please allow me to say, young lady, that you are exceptionally beautiful. It is my honor and pleasure to welcome you."

"My name is Albinna Aggova," the girl said and Mrs. Marko thought that her voice was as pleasant as the impression her future daughter-in=law's eyes conveyed. "Please call me Binna. I am Binna for all my friends."

17.

ON THE DAY WHEN THE blue bags under Aggo's eyes grew almost entirely yellow, Binna stiffened with fear. Space, the forest ranger, had run away from her, racing for safety as if his bones had burst, tearing to pieces his green uniform in the hawthorn bushes. Now Aggo's yellow cheeks smoldered like wet autumn leaves.

"Mom, dad is very ill," Binna shouted.

Vancha was working in the backyard. When her blood sugar was ok and Doc Gospod told her, "You're doing just fine, my dear old friend," Vancha went out and inspected her garden. This Tuesday, digging up the flower beds of her sword-lilies, she heard Binna's shriek and ran, her heart in her mouth, to the bed in the kitchen, where Aggo was dying.

"Dad won't go away on us, Binna. No, he won't. Bring me cold water. I'll give him his pills. Run bring lots of water, Binna."

"Vancha…" Aggo the junkman breathed. "Is that you, Vancha? I can't see if it is you or Binna."

"It's me, Aggo," Vancha said. "You'll be ok. Here, take these pills. Swallow them. Tomorrow you'll be alive and kicking, as strong as a willow tree."

He was so weak he couldn't open his mouth, but this had happened many times before. Vancha knew what she should do, Doc Gospod had taught her. The old woman thrust her finger between the yellow lips, pushed the pink pills into Aggo's mouth then rapidly—as rapidly as a woman of seventy five suffering from diabetes and high blood pressure could manage—lifted his head and put it on her lap. Then Vancha grabbed a deep spoon, the one she used to cook brown sauces for her potato and leek soups, and slowly poured water, drop by drop, into his mouth. Aggo choked, reddish salvoes of pain hit his cheeks, but this was a thing Vancha had seen many times. Bracing up, she lifted his body and let his head rest on her elbow. She stroked his chin then slowly, gently let water drip into his mouth.

"Did you swallow the pills?" she asked.

He did not answer, but his breath was even.

"You swallowed them," Vancha said. "Good boy. Get some sleep now. I'll be at your side. Tomorrow you'll be in fine fettle. You can take my word for it," she carefully lifted him and let his head lie on the pillow. Their son Naum had bought the pillowcase in Sweden, and only God knew which Swedish grandpa had breathed his last on it. A magnificent pillow case it was, with two big green rabbits embroidered on it. One of the rabbits was wet with Aggo's spittle. Vancha put a handkerchief on it, so Aggo's cheek was comfortably dry. The old woman slumped down onto the chair by his bed, her hands dropping on her lap.

"Vancha," Aggo's yellow cheeks whispered.

"What?" she said. "Speak louder, I can't hear you."

But he couldn't speak louder. Vancha put her ear to his lips.

"I loved no other woman like I loved you, Vancha."

"Shut up, man," Vancha snapped. She knew Aggo was telling the truth. His love was so small and rare that it wasn't enough for her, let alone another woman.

"You are my only woman, Vancha. I didn't care for anybody else."

"Don't speak," Vancha scolded. "Get some sleep. Take your medicines. Tomorrow you'll be as fit as a fiddle."

"In the jacket you've prepared for my deathbed… in the breast pocket…I've got a fifty-lev bill and two fivers," whispered Aggo the junkman, who all his life had been collecting old odd-come shorts and rubbish thrown out by his neighbors. "I was thinking… I wanted to buy you a shawl, a brand new one."

"What would I do with a shawl?" She whispered. "No, Aggo, I don't need a shawl."

"You take the fifty-lev bill. Give each girl a fiver. Give Sinna and Binna fivers, please. I've got a military cross. You know it, it's from the war, Aggo Aggov's military cross of courage. Give our son Naum my military cross. He'll keep it for me."

"Ok, ok, I will," Vancha said. "Calm down. You took the medicines. Tomorrow you'll be alive and kicking."

"You're the prettiest woman I've ever seen. I didn't have time to tell you that you… I haven't told you that you…"

The words of the yellow lips merged into a long, black sigh. Vancha reached out her hand to the glass of water, but Aggo's sigh was no more. The bags under his eyes were yellow, as bright yellow as sunflowers in bloom, and no breath escaped his lips.

"Aggo!" Vancha cried out. "Aggo! Here, drink some water. Take this pill… Please. Drink some water, just one drop. Please. You'll be ok, dear…"

Aggo didn't have time again to tell her something very important. A tiny cloud, no bigger than a baby's towel, wafted softly up to Black Peak, a thin light cloud. Probably Aggo the Junkman from Radomir, Arch neighborhood, travelled with it to God.

Vancha touched his yellow face.

"Aggo, Aggo, don't go," she breathed, but the cloud had already reached Black Peak.

18.

THE DUSK IN THE LIBRARY thickened, the two 7th grade boys had already left and Binna thought that no other reader would visit the library until the end of the working hours. She loved the dark, quiet minutes when she was alone with the books and the light of the small electric heater, the room's good orange eye. Even if the weather was not good, boys from the high school visited the library in late afternoons, skipping classes, asking Binna what her plans for the evening were. She had no plans.

After Aggo had died, she hurried home and sat by the window across from Vancha. The old woman knitted pullovers all the time, and when Binna tried to stand up Vancha rested her hand on the girl's shoulder, and the two of them waited silently together in the deep night, the sky invisible, the moon a pool of faraway silver, until Vancha felt very cold. She thought she saw Aggo too, a tiny gasp behind the clouds, and wondered how she'd live on. The two of them peeled potatoes, then had dinner: bread, potatoes, cheese and onions. After that Vancha turned in, Binna washed the dishes, checked if Vancha needed extra blankets and left some food in the oven just in case. No one knew when Sinna would come back home.

Very often she didn't show up for weeks, but when she did, the snake pounced on the food, ravenous, voracious, exasperated, no time to sit down, guzzling bread, jam, cheese, onion all at once, stuffing handfuls of crumbs and sugar cubes into her mouth, her heavy boots, woolen coat and shawl on, then without warning she threw away the loaf of bread she was biting and chewing a minute ago, and tumbled into bed, her head almost crashing onto Binna's neck.

"Are you sleeping?" Sinna asked.

Even if the blue-eyed girl was, Sinna violently shook her sister and woke her up.

"Do you have money, Binna?" the swarthy one asked and refusing to wait for an answer, threw a hundred Lev note onto her sister's bed. "That's for you. What happened to that kid Nikolay?"

Binna said he'd brought her a paper flower and an iris he'd picked from the flowerbeds in the schoolyard, or from his grandma's garden.

"How come he brings me nothing?" Sinna wondered. "You can't even start imagining what I've been doing to your Nikolay for months now, in his house, under his grandmother's nose. That's Raina, the fucking hag, the old jenny ass that passes for a fucking herb-gathering magician. 'Can you find a cure for me if I catch the clap, old Raina?' I asked her and she went and hissed, 'If you give Nikolay the clap I'll poison you. Your ugly mug will start to swell like a frog's. Even Vancha won't know it's you she's looking at.' 'Raina,' I hissed back. 'Do you want to learn where Nikolay kisses me?' The old bitch barked, 'If you show me where you make him kiss you, I'll give you a cup of tea and that spot on you down there won't stop bleeding for months. Do I make myself clear?'"

"Raina is a dangerous woman," Binna said.

"She's dangerous for you. Binna, no man or woman can scare

me. You'd better remember this. I am afraid of no one, don't forget that. I can gnaw a hole in any guy's belly and the idiot will love me for it. I can slash his throat. I bit Nikolay thousand times and nasty Raina watched the biting. I bit him so hard he screamed in the dead of night. The hag got out of her bed and boiled something to stop the bleeding from my bites. 'Why don't you kick me out of your house? Can't you see where I'm biting him? It's your home. Why do you let me chomp on him, crumpling the sheets you bought a century ago for your own marriage bed?' 'Because I want him to forget Binna,' the old owl said. 'Nikolay won't remember you an hour after you've gone. You are,' the hag barked on, 'you are crab grass, the worst weed. It grows fast, takes and plagues the whole garden, but bears no fruit. That's what you are.' 'O, yea?' I said to her. 'You think I'm crab grass? Then look at this,' and I showed her a gold piece as thin as cigarette rolling paper with a little hole drilled in it. 'This is your gold piece, Raina, the one that the gypsy old man gave you because you'd cured his grandson.'

'Yes, it's mine,' Raina said.

'It's no longer yours,' I corrected her. 'Nikolay gave it to me because he loved the way I bit him. He appreciated my kisses too, so you, Raina dear, be careful which poison you cook for me. If I bleed down there, what will your grandson do?' Hey, Binna, I wonder why Nikolay still plods up the stairs to this stinking library of yours. He brings you irises. He's never given me a flower, the idiot. Binna, go fix me something to drink. I want linden tea today. Come on, move it. Tell me about Space the forest ranger. The herb-gathering hags, freaking old harriers all of them, laugh at you. They tell me the guy runs away like thunder the second he spots you. Why do you go to his house?"

"I like the woods," Binna muttered. "I like looking at the slope of loose stone debris behind his house."

Binna didn't say anything more, stood motionless by the cooking stove, her eyes on the dried linden blossoms.

"If you want to pick him up, buy him a bottle of cornel berry brandy. Here, take a fiver. Yesterday I gave you a fiver too, but you didn't buy brandy, did you? What did you buy—chicken breast sausages for Vancha?"

"Yes," Binna said.

"Go buy brandy. Now! Tomorrow I'll come back home early. If you haven't bought brandy, I'll bite you black and blue. You know where I bite. Your belly button will swell up, and I'll bite and bite you until you're as deep purple as a plum. You don't go out with guys one way or another. So it won't make any difference if you are blue, purple, bitten or not. And you know Isabella, Barren Dana's gal pal?"

Binna nodded, let the linden tea brew long enough, then removed it from the stove and asked, "Would you like some sugar?"

"Do you have to make me tea for thirty years before you grasp the fact I love sugar. I want sugar! I want a ton of sugar in my tea. I want it so sweet that when you, sleeping saucepan, taste it, tears will roll down your cheeks. You know Isabella, don't you? I bit her as well. I bit her long and hard everywhere. Her skin turned black and blue like an eggplant. Look," the dark weasel raised her arm. A heavy bracelet glittered on her wrist under the faint light of the lamp on the table. "It's gold. I checked, consulted a goldsmith in Pernik. Good bracelet, isn't it? You wouldn't believe this Isabella girl has a ton of gold bracelets."

"Sinna, I need some sleep. I have to go to work tomorrow."

"Work? O, give me a break. Work! You take a nap every afternoon on that moldy desk of yours. When you're not dozing, you give the snotty spotty teenagers Yovkov's short story collection twice a year. That's what you call work. You trot behind Space the drunk's ass like a dog. And you can't pick him up. A sheep would! I'm ashamed of you! Give him brandy then sit down by his side. Just sit down and let things take their own natural course. I thought he was no good, but you're my sister, so I went and checked. When the bloke's drunk, he's as good as dead: you shouldn't waste your spittle on him. But if you happen to catch him in the morning when he puts barley in the trough feeders for deer, Space is all muscles and fire, even if you don't give him a drop to drink. Then he's a man 100 percent."

"I won't buy brandy for him," Binna said.

"Fix me some tea. If it's not sweet enough, I'll drown you in the teapot. Do I make myself clear?"

...Binna loved the dark minutes at the end of the working hours when she was alone with the books in the dim light of the electric heater. She could stay with a short story as long as she pleased, turning the pages, going back to paragraphs she loved. Her father died, Vancha's arms grew weaker every day. Binna's arms grew weaker too, and her eyes were burning away in the thick twilight. Days flew away, leaving no trace in her life, nothing but paper that Binna collected in a big cardboard box. So many paper-flowers had Nikolay brought her that she could make a fire and keep the library warm for a month.

No, Binna could make a paper garden; it would cover the land from Radomir up to the end of Bulgaria, to the Black Sea. She'd have a paper flower for every child at school. She'd give the paper tulips and roses to the little ones, the first and second graders, who came for *Pippi Longstocking* and the books of fairytales. So she did. Every child took a small paper flower that looked like an airplane and happily pressed it to his heart. The kid could smell the aroma of the flower and see the enormous garden that stretched for miles to the very end of Bulgaria. Who knew where the end of Bulgaria was? It must be beautiful, if Binna's flowers grew there. Binna had grown to anticipate Nikolay's visits. His paper tulips made the library light and warm.

But now she knew that Old Raina's gold piece, the one with the hole drilled near the rim belonged to Sinna. Sinna had taught Nikolay how to love Spanish women. He was so grateful that he had given her Raina's drilled gold piece; the same one the old Roma man had offered the best herb-gatherer to heal his sick grandson. When Nikolay came to Binna with irises he had plucked from the flower-beds in the school yard or from an old woman's garden, Binna's library no longer became light and warm. Nikolay's hands trembled like before, and a month ago it seemed they were hands of a good man who made paper airplanes. The first-graders were snowdrop blossoms when Binna gave them flowers made of old newspapers. Now Nikolay's hands were like everybody else's; they'd betrayed old Raina's gold piece. They were hands Sinna had bitten or kissed, which was exactly the same thing.

Nikolay would no longer stay among the books where Binna roamed free, thirsty, and impatient. Nikolay no longer made her library happy. Now Binna had the quiet minutes before the end of the working hours when no one dropped in, the warm glow of the books on the shelves her trusty friend. A day ago, Space the forest ranger ran away from her. But nobody knew—even the most vigilant herb-gathering ladies—that after Binna started for her house, darting across the clearing, Space followed her. No path led to the forest ranger's place, a man living alone does not build a road, the old ladies said; if he had a dog, there was hope. But the forest ranger didn't have a dog. The poor beast had starved to death. A pack of homeless dogs followed Space, even jackals hung around his place, but neither the mongrels nor the jackals could beat a path to his door.

Binna usually hurried across the large meadow to Vancha's

backyard. She walked, staring at the grass that merged with the sky, and in a flash she thought that the clouds were sprouting grass, not green and luxuriant, like a meadow in May. Yellow autumn grass, like Vancha's sorrow for Aggo, grew on the clouds.

"You are pretty!" someone shouted one afternoon behind Binna's back. She turned around and saw him: Space, the forest ranger, was within a stone's throw of her.

His uniform was tattered. Under the torn jacket, the man's skin looked pale like a white flag. Binna had seen only his tanned face, brown like clay, his beard so yellow that looked white and if one hadn't noticed that the forest ranger's teeth were in his mouth, one would think that this was one of the old men from Arch neighborhood. If he was a young man what did he do in Radomir? Why hadn't he gone to Spain to pick olives like everybody else?

"You're pretty," Space said, but it seemed he muttered the words to the grass that had sprouted on the clouds. He was not looking at Binna; he was staring at the air and told the air, slowly, urgently, "You're pretty! You're pretty!"

And Binna believed Space, the forest ranger, could get along well with her books. Her thoughts would lead him to their old pages. She knew she could not live alone in the dark library.

Time was dark at the end of the working day. Binna thought of Vancha, of Aggo who had climbed Black Peak, of the air that spoke in the forest ranger's voice, "You're pretty!" and trees listened to him. Then the dark damp minutes were happy.

... "Good afternoon, I was..." the front door of the library opened, creaking sharply.

Binna had not noticed it was raining behind the windowpanes. She looked up. The man who had entered the library gasped and coughed. He took a step forward and dropped the bag he carried tucked under his arm.

"What are you doing here?" he exclaimed, finding his voice.

"I work here," Binna said. She didn't know the man. Perhaps he was the new vice president for culture at the municipality of Radomir. "Did they send you to our library from Pernik?"

"No. I lost my way. I thought I could find a restroom here."

"It's the other door, the small one on the left."

The man stood motionless, staring at her. For a long while he couldn't take his eyes off her, took a step towards Binna, then another one. Binna retreated to the shadow of the shelf where she had arranged *Pippi Longstocking*, *Emil i Lonneberga* and *The Brothers Lionheart*. The man produced a box of matches from his coat pocket, lit one and lifted its flame to her face. He looked at her until the match burned down and singed his fingers.

"My God," he whispered.

"What?" Binna asked.

"My God…" he lit another match.

"Please don't do that. It's an old library," Binna said, but the man let the match burn, gazing intently into her eyes.

He did not move, silent then coughed and blurted out, "Will you marry me?" He spoke so quietly that the words merged into one low sound, dust that descended on the bookshelves.

"Will you marry me?" he repeated. He was looking at her the way Space, the forest ranger, had. Nikolay looked at her like that too, although he had given Sinna the gold piece with the tiny hole in it. The stranger came up to Binna, touched the sleeve of her dress first—an ordinary calico thing, then touched *Emil I Lonnenberga* behind Binna's back, then touched Binna—her face—and Binna shivered. She shook so badly in her calico dress. No one had seen her tremble like that, and no one had touched her face. One day Nikolay touched her hand and she thought a long time about that. The warmth she had for Nikolay still stayed in her fingers. It didn't go away even after she learned Nikolay had given her dark sister the gold piece.

The stranger touched her shoulders and said, "Don't be afraid. You are very pretty. I won't hurt you. You are so pretty... very, very, very... Marry me."

Her lips twitched, her arms, her legs waited, numb, stunned. She noticed the light of the electric heater, a tiny glowworm. It waited too, scared, irresolute. Then she saw *Pippi Longstocking* fall to the floor. *The Brothers Lionheart* fell too. She could not get control of her trembling fingers.

"Don't. Don't. Don't be afraid. I won't hurt you... I won't hurt you. I promise you. I'll be very careful. I won't hurt you."

The bookshelves danced in her eyes. Her feet were cold. She knew the cement floor in the library was hard with frost, and she'd brought one of Vancha's old rag-carpets here. Binna didn't know how it happened. Vancha's rag-carpet stuck to her back and was freezing cold.

"O, my God," he whispered, his hands trembling like hers. "You're pretty... pretty...pretty..." All the books kept silent. The dusk ran away from the ceiling and flowed into her hands, the spiders sank into the black corners, and it felt as if all the books that had lived in her blood so far had left her. All these novels and short story collections she loved almost as much as she loved Vancha, their front covers warm under her skin, abandoned her.

"O, my God," he groaned. "You haven't had anybody before me," his frightened words did let the books come back to their places on the shelf. "My God... You haven't..." his voice drowned in her mouth, his whisper and his kiss mixed and soaked in her breasts. "How can you.... be so pretty..."

Outside the rain turned into a torrent, darker and blacker than before.

"Wait. Wait," he stopped her as Binna tried to stand up. "Wait. I won't hurt you!" He told her again how pretty she was. It lasted so long that Binna closed her eyes and waited. She was ashamed and didn't want to look at the library. Her breasts and lips were ashamed and unable to hide in the dark rain outside. "Wait a little longer, just a little."

Finally, he buried his head in her shoulder, blurting out, "Marry me."

Vancha's rag-carpet didn't help. Binna was cold. Her dress had frozen.

"My name is Samuel, but you don't call me Samuel. Call me Sammy," the man said, looking up at her once again.

"Samuel," she repeated.

"Sammy," he corrected her.

"Sammy."

"What's your name?" he asked.

"Binna," she said.

"O, my God," the man whispered. "How beautiful your name is. Binna…"

His hand reached for her then he gently helped her to smooth her dress over her legs, softly, carefully as if he was touching a new-born baby. Then he carried her to the window, closer to the heavy clouds that threw out the rain which turned into thudding of angry hooves in the street. The pools were a cavalry squadron of wild rain drops. He carried her closer to the window, her face almost touching the windowpane as he said, "Binna, Binna."

His words sank into her lips. Slowly, he kissed her shoulders, still trembling, panicked, he kissed her back, frozen stiff with the cold of Vancha's rag-carpet, kissed her hair that was the color of the rain and the sky beyond the window, kissed her hands, cold in the old dark library which didn't know anything about the last days of August. He kissed the snowdrops on her calico dress and said, "Don't be afraid. I didn't hurt you. You see? I'll never hurt you."

Binna was not scared, but couldn't stop trembling. Perhaps that was the cement floor, or maybe because the man's hands were white and strong like snow. They were completely different from Space, the forest ranger's, paws. She had seen them clutch the axe or caress homeless dogs, give bread to jackals, the cracked huge forest ranger's hands.

"I'll marry you, believe me," he hurried to say as softly as he could, tossing his impatient words onto her breasts. "I'll never harm you. I won't. Look. Wait. Wait a little longer. It's good, see? I love you."

Was it possible for a man to love you, if he saw you an hour ago when it started to rain, Binna wondered. Was it possible for a stranger to love you because his back was cold with yours on Vancha's carpet-rag on the cement floor?

"You're pretty," the man's voice faded into whisper. "Very pretty!"

Now it hurt less, almost didn't hurt at all. That's what to be pretty means, Binna thought. That's what happens when a woman is pretty.

"Marry me," the man said as his head dropped, hot, sweaty, heavy onto her shoulder. "Marry me tomorrow."

Binna didn't dare to budge. His head might slip off her shoulder and crash into the cement floor, the wall or into a bookshelf.

"Please tap me on the back," the man asked her, touching her lips as lightly as a breeze. Binna couldn't say if he was kissing her or simply happened to be too close to her face. She choked on his breath. "Please tap me gently on the back and tell me 'It's okay."

Binna tapped his back and said, "It's okay."

"I love you," the man said.

That's what 'I love you' means, Binna thought. She remembered the yellow grass in front of Space's house, the slope of loose stone debris, cutting the place that had been his mother's backyard. Now people threw garbage, odds and ends, broken jugs and bottles there. In the evening stray dogs and jackals scuffled in the dust, rummaging for food, ravaging and howling. Lost in these dark minutes at the end of the working hours, sometimes Binna imagined Space was a lizard's length away from her, his tattered uniform touching her floral dress. She saw him now, too, his uniform torn among the hawthorn bushes and briar thickets, under his shabby shirt his pale skin, so fair she could not believe her eyes for Space's face had been scorched and baked by the sun, his cheeks the color of the asphalt.

Sometimes Binna imagined she touched his fair skin under the tattered uniform. In the dark minutes before the end of the working time, she wished the forest ranger wouldn't dash off, hitting thorns and prickly shrubs. Endless hours Binna hoped Space wouldn't run away. He'd let her hold his hand. She didn't want more than that. She dreamed of his skin as beautiful as a cloud. She hoped they'd climb the slope of loose stones and reach the top. The hill was long and steep, the old women didn't go to gather herbs there, and no one would see they were holding hands. Perhaps he'd tell her again, "How pretty you are." He should have allowed her to touch his pale skin under his frayed uniform, should have smiled at her, could have asked if she was cold and why she was trembling. He could have even told her not to be ashamed that her dress was no good. Even then it would be too early for Space to say "Marry me."

But Binna was twenty-four and Vancha told her, "You'll go off your head because of the books, girl."

The books had driven her crazy. Space had to make "you are pretty" to her, and not talk to the white air in her wake after Binna walked away from the loose stones in his backyard. Space had to catch up with her, even if she'd already reached Vancha's house and the old herb-gatherers, plodding their way across the field, would see them. Herbs grew in the meadows near the slope of loose stones, wild, strong, luxuriant, thick herbs enough to fill a huge long train, aromatic plants that cured all diseases under the clouds.

"I love you," the stranger said. "I can't believe it. I can't believe the most beautiful girl in the word is sitting by my side. Please tap me on the back and say, 'It's okay. It's okay."

Binna said once again "It's okay" to his back, and he showed her again how pretty she was. The man still could not believe it was possible for a woman to be that beautiful. He could not believe he had found her, he did it himself, using no advice, no assistance. He left her on the floor, jumped and kissed the door through which he had entered the dark large room.

"Thank you, God. Thank you for leading me. Thank you for taking me to her," then the man turned to Binna. "I love you," he said.

Space the forest ranger would not say so. He wouldn't think of it. Binna had watched him give bread to the homeless dogs and jackals, muttering under his breath, "Eat, boy. Eat." His voice knew they were not dirty mongrels and stinky thieves as the old herb-gatherers called them. They were Space's pals. The beasts licked his face when he lay asleep and drunk in front of his house. Space, the forest ranger, had never killed a stray mutt. He loved them.

He'd give Binna a chunk of his bread and tell her, "That's for you." And she would wash his face and eyes if he lay prostrate, drunk, and dead to the world, on the earth near the slope of loose stone debris.

The stranger helped Binna to stand up. He was quite strong although his body was very thin and long.

"I'll carry you in my arms all the way to my place," he said.

"Greta and I rent a house in the center of the town. You'll see how nice it is. I will feed you and I will wash your feet and hands, and tomorrow I'll marry you."

Binna shivered. Who would sit next to Vancha, silent and brooding, by Aggo's empty bed? Who'd peel potatoes for her in the evening?

"Don't worry. We'll send Greta to tell your parents about us. I'll protect you. Please don't be afraid of anything.

The man let her lock the library door, then lifted her up and said, "I'll carry you to the car. I don't want your shoes to get wet in the rain. You're light as a grain of sand. It feels good carrying you. You are magnificent."

Binna thought he'd again do "you are so pretty" to her, there, in the corridor, the horrified spiders watching, by the old white-washed storeroom. She knew that if she brushed the wall, her dress would be spoiled and would never be clean no matter how hard she washed it. But the man who had looked for the bathroom, his name unnatural and unpopular in Radomir—the man whose name she could not remember at the moment, held her to him, rocking her slowly as if she was a little child, kissed her cheek and said, "I'm so grateful to God I met you."

His lips softly touched hers. Perhaps it was the way it should be, although Space wouldn't kiss her, only his breath would brush her cheek. The man, who had stumbled upon the library, asked her, "Please, pat me on the back. Tell me that everything will be okay."

Binna whispered okay to his back.

"I'll wash you and I'll feed you," he repeated quietly. "Don't be afraid. I'll be very careful."

For the first time in her life, this night Binna didn't return to Vancha's house.

19.

"Miss Dana, did you let him go out?" the financial expert and barren Dana's business assistant cried out. "He's not in the toolshed."

"You are out of your mind, Isabella. I haven't thought of letting him go out."

"Then where's he?" Isabella shrieked. "If you didn't let him go, where should the moron be? I checked: Giant is in the stable. I've tied the dogs myself. Tano is gone. I can't believe the blockhead went to have a bath in the lake. You'd have to bludgeon him with a hammer first before you'd give him a bath. He swears at me so hard that the cobblestones under his feet shake and change places," Isabella commented.

"Hey, Isabella, today is Wednesday, isn't it? On Wednesdays he boozes it up at the Frog Bar."

"Have you been drinking without me, Miss Dana? It's not Wednesday. It's Friday. It's the next episode of CSI tonight, so pull yourself together."

"O, come off it, Bella. Before dawn, I spent so much energy on him."

"O, shucks, Miss Dana. You don't tighten discipline in the tool-shed and let Tano victoriously wave his flag above your head! You go out, and he goes and rides Giant, your own Italian stallion. I wouldn't be surprised if a soft-spoken hen perches on Tano's lap at the Frog Bar."

"Shut up!" Dana shouted.

"I'll shut up, Miss Dana, but Tano's gone. Tell me honestly: did you communicate your point to him in the morning? No, you didn't! "

"Stop chewing on my bones, Isabella. How could I be energetic in the morning?"

"Miss Dana, I have to tell you one thing. You became weak in the head after you got pregnant. Tano is a bacillus. You can't break his pigheadedness by intelligent conversations like the ones you and I carry on. I communicate my point to Tano through the garden hose. Miss Dana," the expert heated up to her subject. "Take into account one more motive.

Tano is a mean nit. I repeat the above in your face. You should leave him on his mattress the way you did a month ago: as yellow as the fleece of a dead sheep. I washed him with the garden hose, and he didn't have enough strength to swear at me. What's the situation now? I don't even have to wash him. He grabs the hose and washes himself! He's energetic therefore you didn't communicate anything to the thickhead. You've become slothful, Miss Dana, honestly. Two months ago, most wonderful communication flourished between the two of you! You got pregnant with Kalcho and astonished the wide world!

The professors in Sofia, luminaries all of them, hit their heads with their fists. How come Barren Dana got pregnant? Didn't I say this was impossible? Even Doc Gospod was about to chew her own boots. I heard her say, 'If Dana conceives a child I'll boil my boots and chew their heels.' You went and gave birth to Kalcho, and he is as healthy and strong as a calf, God bless his soul. But at that time you communicated, and now you are so sluggish you can hardly keep your eyes open. You prefer swimming with me in the lake to…"

"You don't swim in the lake. You only carry my blanket and keep an eye on Mumma and Kalcho."

"Honestly, Miss Dana, you've grown weak in the head. I don't keep an eye on Mumma and Kalcho. They wade in the water of their own accord. I am a liberal lady, but kids, splashing the water of a son of a bitch lake are in for whooping cough."

"Let them splash at each other as much as they want."

"The water is freezing cold."

"Your brain is freezing cold, Isabella. The water is warm like pea soup. And if you refuse to swim with me one more time, I personally will take off all your clothes. I will throw you into the lake with my own hands. You won't learn to swim, I know, but you'll keep your mouth shut. And you don't allow the kids to bathe in the lake. They are my kids. They must swim every day."

"The water is cold." Dana's business assistant stood her ground. "You didn't get my point. There's something else I want to tell you. I didn't want to put it bluntly, I am a delicate person, you know me, but you swear a lot, Miss Dana. Not that I care, you know how much I love you, but it hurts me."

"Stop beating about the bush, what is it? Don't mince words. Speak right away! Is Kalcho wailing somewhere, or is it Ogress that's barking?"

"Kalcho is not wailing. He and Mumma are under the walnut tree, sitting on a rug, and Mumma is reading to him."

"Come off it, girl. Mumma can't read."

"She can't, it's true, but she's reading to him. She's learned by heart *The Golden Apple, The Three Little Pigs* and all other sons of bitches fairytales you made me read to her. I read fifteen pages every single day until I was blue in the mouth and my neck hurt... the little darling committed every word to memory, poor soul, and now she's reading to Kalcho."

"Kalcho can't make heads or tails of fairytales," Miss Dana said. "He takes in as much *The Golden Apple* as a mare would grasp algebra. This kid had a hard time learning to speak. He looks at you, understands everything, but it's so difficult to call me Mommy."

"It's better to have a hard time blubbering than to chatter like Tano, especially when the thickhead is drunk," the business assistant objected. "Haven't you heard what he's babbling after a bottle of hogwash wine?"

"Why should I listen to Tano's drunken prattle? A drunkard is a torn sack."

"Drunkard or no drunkard, I'd listen to what he's jabbering if I were you. The words he throws in the air! Gets drunk and cries his eyes out."

"He doesn't cry, Isa."

"O, Miss Dana. He cries out loud and remembers Dora, his first wife. I don't know if the two of them ever got married. Well, I mean the woman who gave birth to Mumma, Sinna and Binna. They brought the woman to your place half alive, don't you remember? She couldn't suckle the little tadpole she'd given birth an hour before. The woman's milk was wasted. She communicated her point to truckers and all sorts of idiots on the highway to Greece. It's not that I criticize her, mind you, but in all probability Sinna is not a local guy's daughter. Her father must come from some sand desert or other. Binna's father, on the other hand, is a Scandinavian or even someone from farther north. As for Mumma, even she invites suspicion; look at her, as small as a bead, while Tano is bigger than Giant the stallion and his saddle rolled into one."

"Can you repeat some of Tano's weeping words?" Miss Dana cut short her business assistant.

"He doesn't say anything. He wails, repeating, "Dora, Dora", tears like a hailstorm in his eyes, snot all over his face, stains of brandy on his shirt. That's the motive why, Miss Dana, I don't give him good brandy like you've instructed me. I let him swill down pear schnapps with which we clean the cows' wounds on the farm."

"So he wails 'Dora, Dora' and weeps?"

"That's right. I let him cry his heart out. A week ago, I tried to wash him with the hose while he was sobbing. He jumped and swooped down on me. 'You bitch,' he hollered. 'You keep me in this shitty shed like I'm a prisoner in a concentration camp.' You know I hate it when a moron screams at me, Miss Dana, and calls me bitch. I raised the shotgun and aimed it at him. You know the thing, that old Romanian shotgun; you gave it to me to kill hawks and polecats with. So to say, I pointed the piece at him and said peacefully, 'You can be as big as an Italian mule, but I'll shoot you in the head, and the next time you see me, you'll kiss with gratitude the ground I'm walking on.' But the airhead had got blotto and could not figure I'd made up my mind to put a bullet in his head. Miss Dana, on that day you asked me, 'Isa, you have a bluish mark on your neck. Perhaps some fellow gave you a big smooch?' I told you, 'No one gave me a smooch or bit me.' And you pushed on because you lack delicacy and tact, 'Has some dunce beaten you? Tell me who he is, and he is dead meat.' Do you remember?"

"Yes, I do," Barren Dana said. "You had a bad bruise on your neck. Tano hit you. Why didn't you tell me? As punishment, we wouldn't have given him wine for a week."

"There's a reason: I shot at him with the shotgun, Miss Dana. I shot at his large posterior. I expressly ordered Tano to turn his back to me, so the buckshot hit what it should i.e. his ass, and not the component you care about. Miss Dana, I don't know what sort of sounds you'd heard, but you asked me, 'Why is Ogress howling like mad?' It wasn't Ogress howling. The bitch was entirely all right, licking her puppies most tenderly. Tano was growling as I was extracting the buckshot from his bottom. You know what buckshot is like; it sinks like a stiletto into butter, so I cut his blubber first, then I sewed him up. He grumbled, 'Don't pour brandy on the wound, you dirty bitch,' and swore at me. "Give me the brandy, I'll drink it. Cut me as hard as you can and cut quickly. Don't waste the brandy, bitch!' he added. You know, Miss Dana, I hate it when an idiot calls me 'bitch'. He compares me to Ogress: the poor bitch came into her mating season, gnawed through her leash and brought a pack of homeless mutts to our backyard. The beasts trampled down the rye-grass. And I had ordered the seeds from Rome! Ogress and the mongrels wallowed all over the place, and I found the poor grass in a mess. So Tano equates me with a bitch that wags her tail to any mutt! He called me 'bitch' two more times, so I raised the shotgun and fired again. Don't be afraid, I didn't shoot his component. I hit his posterior and had one more job to do, cutting his blubber again and extracting more buckshot. I don't know if you've noticed that Tano keeps the buckshot in a little jar. This is the buckshot I fired into his buttocks; after that I removed it with the tweezers I pluck your leg hairs with. Since that day, he has never called me 'bitch'. He shouts at me 'Dirty snake!' but I don't hate snakes. On the contrary, I respect them. They bask in the sun. It's your problem if you step on their tails. But let me cut a long story short, Tano ran away from the toolshed."

"Why are you so sure he's run away?" Dana turned to her assistant. "Maybe he got drunk as usual and fell into a ditch or some-where in the forest. We'll set Fury, Ogress and Blizzard on him, and they will find him in a flash."

"They won't find him this time."

"Why not?"

"Look what I found on his mattress," the business assistant handed Miss Dana a page torn off *Bulgarian Folk Tales, Tome II*. The page belonged to the fairytale *King Trojan Has Goat Ears*, and on the top margin a sentence was printed in big block letters, "Tano runs away."

Miss Dana fingered the crumpled sheet of paper and heaved a big sigh, then a bigger one.

"Shall I call Sto, the policeman? I'll order Stoichko to come and comfort you just in case."

Miss Dana kept silent.

"What is it, Miss Dana? Are you shedding tears? Oh, my good-ness! It's true he's an inch taller than you, but after he eats soup from a bowl, even the bowl exudes a foul smell. Are you crying, girl? Why, tell me."

"He loves me," Miss Dana whispered. "Isa, come and check. A moth got into my eye."

"You'd better sit down, Miss Dana. You are big and your eyes seem to be as far away as though you are on the moon. Don't fidget. You are not a worm. Listen, Tano doesn't love you. He gets stoned and he calls *Dora, Dora*, and not your name. And I've heard she did it for a bowl of lentil soup. She worked miracles for a four-wheeler driver and took his leather jacket—the guy didn't have enough money. I tell you that Tano still presses this leather jacket to his heart. 'You get hammered, and you throw up. The jacket will be no good soon,' I told him once and he put the rag in a big plastic bag. 'Dora gave in to me,' he muttered and turned on the waterworks. I ask you Miss Dana: how many coats have you bought him so far? Her name is on his lips like lipstick, and you? What are you doing now, Miss Dana: crying your heart out! Brace up. Pull yourself together. Kick his fat ass. I'll be honest with you: Tano doesn't care. You have to be happy he made himself scarce. We'll find another tall guy for you, one two inches taller than you!"

"You don't understand, Isa."

"O, I do, Miss Dana. Things are crystal clear in my mind. I'll bring wine. We'll get drunk and we will cry together. What do you say to that? I'll take Kalcho and Mumma to the kindergarten for a couple of hours. The teachers have one thousand books there. The kids will watch pictures until they drop asleep. I'll buy them hotdogs for lunch. Shall I go bring wine? We'll weep, Miss Dana. It'll be fun. I'll give you handkerchiefs, so can blow your nose and wipe off your tears."

"Who will you cry for?" Miss Dana asked. "Does Tano's absence sadden your heart?"

"Oh, no. No way!"

"Who will you weep for then?"

"Can't you guess?"

Barren Dana thought for a moment and said, "You will weep because you love me and you don't want me to weep all by myself. You are a good woman, Isabella. I'd weep with you, too, if you didn't have company."

"I love you, Miss Dana, that's true. I'd give my life for you. If doc Gospod says, 'Barren Dana must receive blood transfusion,' I'll give you half of my blood, even more than half! You know, when you were about to give birth to Kalcho, I waited in front of the maternity ward. If crazy Professor Dionis had said, 'I need strong blood for Miss Dana's baby,' I'd prostrate myself in a bed and let him draw as much of my powerful blood as necessary. But now,

Miss Dana, I won't cry because of my love for you or for Tano the moron's absence. He ran away on us like that calf you and I bought for Easter; the beast raised his ugly head and decamped to the wasteland. We were lucky the jackals didn't tear him to pieces. I'll weep for another individual."

"And who is that individual? Is it the Gypsy woman? But now she's in Spain, taking care of two elderly spinsters."

"Yes, Miss Dana, I'll cry for her. Don't call her 'the Gypsy woman'. Her name is Anna."

For a while Miss Dana kept silent then heaved a sigh and said, "I saw you with the Gypsy woman, Isabella. I was on my way to Sto the policeman, about to give him a piece of my mind. He did nothing for these homeless dogs! And I saw you and the Gypsy woman behind her house. I didn't feel good after that."

Isabella didn't say anything, lifted the bottle to her lips and suddenly her eyes wetted.

"The kids, Mumma and Kalcho were looking at you," Dana went on. "They were eating and watching you and the Gypsy. And the Gypsy woman's little girl was looking, too. I don't know if she was her first, second or third child. Her mite of a daughter sat on a car tire, three yards from you. It didn't feel good watching you, Isabella. Why don't we marry you off to some decent guy? Just tell me his name, and I will..."

"I didn't notice you were there, Miss Dana," Isabella said. "And it hadn't crossed my mind that the kids would be watching. I left them at the sweetshop with the shop assistant," Isabella said quietly. "I'd never leave them hungry, bought them cream buns to eat, but they, the silly tots, took only a few bites," Isabella sighed. "I didn't do anything wrong. I didn't hurt anybody."

"You didn't," Miss Dana said quietly too.

"Anna's in Spain," Isabella muttered. "I give her children

bread, the chunks we can't eat. I don't give stale bread to the hens and ducks; I bring it to her children instead. Perhaps Anna will visit me for a day or two at Easter. My God, she must be roughing it in Madrid."

Tears welled up in the business assistant's eyes.

It was gloomy and cold. Miss Dana hopelessly wondered if Tano was cold too. She worried that he hadn't taken any clothes, beat it in his old sweatshirt. He'd run away from her three times so far. Had no penny to bless himself with, and came back no coat, no shoes, no shirt, in tattered briefs, a flag wrapped around his shoulders, *Long Live Bulgarian Youth* embroidered on its green artificial silk. Tano had lifted it from a pillar by the highway to drape over his bare legs.

"I'll weep for Anna," Isabella said sadly. "I might have helped her and the kids. I could have given her a ring and earrings if only she had agreed to stay. I'd have taken care of her youngest tot, Miss Dana. I'd have taken care of all her kids if only she'd stayed. But she said, 'I'll go, Bella. It's true I like the gold ring you've given me, but I like Spain more than gold. It is a free country, not a trash can like Arch neighborhood, Radomir. Good bye. Men in Radomir are dunghills, always complaining.' And she kissed me goodbye."

Dana said slowly. "I got scared stiff when I saw the two of you behind her shack," Dana said slowly. "When many guys in Radomir break out in a rash, Doc Gospod glues your girlfriend's photograph on the door of the health center. The doc told me the high school students complained to her of the same itchy rash. Poor Doc Gospod, I was sorry for her."

"I had a bad skin rash, too, Miss Dana. I didn't sleep in your room for a week. Do you remember? We paid the kindergarten teacher to take care of Mumma and Kalcho. I told you I'd visit my brother."

"I remember, Isa. You said your brother had a car accident near the Black Sea coast."

"My foot! My brother washes dishes at Sole Mio Restaurant in Julia Nova, Italy. It was true I stayed in his apartment, but I was receiving treatment for that bastard, the rash. I didn't want the kids and you to get the infection from me, Miss Dana. You are in no danger of catching anything. You spend your days glued to Tano like a poster to a wall, you fool! You ditched Stoichko. You don't look at other men. Why are you as old-fashioned as a calf? Look at me. I take a bath twice a day. Well, what do you think of Mumma and Kalcho? I love the little mites. I adore them. I've read a billion fairytales—son of a bitch every single one of them—to Mumma, and the little gourd listens to me so sweetly and learns every son of a bitch tale by heart. I've grown to love her. Think about Kalcho now: I feel as though I'd given birth to him. We could say that I gave halfway birth to him, couldn't we? I spread sow's grease on your stomach: twice in the morning and once in the evening every day! You shone like sheet iron, every inch of you! Didn't I check the way Kalcho kicked, tossed and turned inside you? I did. I love Kalcho more than you do. I cook delicious soups for him. And what do you do for him? You shove the poor louse into the rotten lake, or make him shoot at jackals, Miss Dana. The kid doesn't want to shoot at the beasts. He wants to play with Mumma. Can't you see he follows in Mumma's steps and snuggles close to her every time he gets the chance?"

"Then your brother didn't have a car accident and you lied to me on account of the son of a bitch rash? We won't lie to each other, that's what you promised me and I promised you. How long have you been my friend? We were in the cradle together, in kindergarten together, and we sat at the same table from the first grade to high school. We used to wear the same clothes."

"Yes, but you grew up too rapidly and became very big," Isabella reminded her. "Your clothes were too loose-fitting for me, and you stretched and tore mine."

"We used the same cake of soap in the bathroom."

"That guy, what was his name, Gosho? The one who now works as a cook in Switzerland?" Isabella said thoughtfully. "He was keen on kissing me, but his mouth stank, and I told him, 'Go kiss Dana.' He didn't want you, so finally I asked him, 'Gosho, will you go to Dana if I let you kiss me?'"

"I didn't know you sent him to me," Miss Dana heaved a deep sigh. "I thought he came for my sake."

"Your mom, may she rest in peace, Miss Dana, asked me to stay at your place and play with you. She fried delicious sausages for me and even gave me your gorgeous dresses. You, Miss Dana, were a very dumb kid: couldn't memorize the multiplication table. The problems about ships meeting on the river, one going upstream the other downstream were the death of you. You were slow on the uptake, and that's why your mom gave me four of your pinafores. But I didn't come for the pinafores and your mom's meals. God bless her smart soul."

"Then why did you come?" Miss Dana asked surprised.

"I came because of you."

"O, come off it, Isa. One day we had a quarrel, do you remember? You snitched to my mom that I refused to play with dolls; I looked for the sharpest knife instead. You squealed on me that I had put a dead jackdaw on Mrs. Daykova's desk, our biology teacher. She gave me bad grades all the time. After we had a quarrel, you told everybody in school that I gave you a fiver for the simplest algebra problem you solved for me. You blared out tales that I carried you on my back so you didn't wet your feet in the puddles."

"But that was true," the business assistant said, cutting short her employer.

"Yes, it was," Miss Dana admitted and went on, swallowing

hard. "At that time I felt like drinking a glass of cockroach poison. You were my only friend. I didn't have anybody else to talk to."

"I didn't come to collect the fiver you gave me for every problem I solved for you. I didn't care for your mom's fried sausages. After we quarreled, I was about to die of a broken heart. I'm not kidding."

"You didn't look it," Miss Dana said quietly. "The best looking boys thronged around you. A dozen dudes a day asked you to accompany them to the park. No one asked me so I paid Kiro, the gypsy, to date me. And he was looking at you. He told me you chose the guy whose dice rolled the highest numbers."

"They all stank, these little ninnies, every one of them did. They were brash. I felt like puking at the sight of them. I tried to establish if they all were the same. I thought to myself, 'Perhaps it's only Stamen that makes me retch. Let me try with somebody else." So I chose Damian and gave it a go. Damian is a big wig's chauffeur in Sofia now. He made me throw up."

"I was ready to pay Stamen fifty cents a kiss," Miss Dana reminisced about the past. "But he refused."

"When you went sparrow hunting with slingshot or grabbed the ax, rushing to chop down a wild briar in the backyard, and after that lay stark naked under the cold water tap, your mom took great pains to put you to bed. She wanted you to be very healthy."

"I've always hated taking a nap in the afternoon, I hate it now, and I hated it when I was pregnant. You waste your time like a fool," Miss Dana said as she took a big gulp of wine directly from the bottle. It was gorgeous, a treasure they sold only to Fritzes.

"Your mom made me lie in your cot next to you, do you remember?" Isabella asked. "You didn't want me there, said it was too narrow for the two of us, but I calmed you. 'There, there, I'm quite small. 'Isabella is such a wonderful child,' your mom said and read fairytales to us. I hate their guts, the sons of bitches tales: balls of yarn, you unwind and unwind and your brains turn into porridge. You, Miss Dana, tossed and turned like a mangy cat, asking, 'What happens later on?'"

"You slept like a rusty rail. Fell off the branch like a pear with a worm in it at the very beginning of the fairytale," Miss Dana laughed.

"Slept like a rail my foot! I pretended so you could fall asleep too."

"I had a hard time falling asleep," Miss Dana heaved a sigh.

"You dropped all right," Isabella said. "I watched you sleeping."

"What!" Miss Dana gave a cry.

"That's true, Miss Dana. You slept and I watched you. You didn't let any boor at school thrash me. You gave them hell, so I made a pledge to give you half of my blood if you wanted it. I'll give you my blood now too, although I haven't wanted to watch you sleep for twenty years. I have to tell you that you snore like a bear."

The roar of a powerful engine tore the afternoon into shreds. The huge police pickup truck stopped in front of Miss Dana's white house. Sto the policeman, a pale, thin man, got out of the vehicle and shouted, "Miss Dana! Miss Dana!"

The business assistant left her bottle of wine on the floor. She had drunk everything to the last drop, but the wine, intended for export to Germany, was meek and noble, and if one wasn't a Bavarian or a Fritz, could hardly get drunk on it. Dana and her business advisor had to down at least two bottles each in order to be able to grow sad and start sobbing as a consequence. They had already tried multiple times. The wine for Bavarians was too polite and quiet for ladies of their stature.

"What does this flea want?" the business assistant said angrily. "Sto, why are you woofing like a dog gone loose? This is a decent home here, so take yourself in hand and behave appropriately. If your arrogance irritates me, I'll set Ogress, Blizzard and Fury on you. Then I wouldn't want to be in your shoes."

"I am so sorry, Miss Isabella. It's my fault. I will not speak loudly," the policeman's tone was soft and friendly.

He was a quiet, mild-tempered man. The old herb-gathering community and the feisty codgers wondered how it was possible for a weak-chested man like Sto to work as a policeman in this wolfish part of the country. The poor little bugger had an overripe peach inside his chest instead of a heart! The teachers commuting to work every day by train from Pernik and Sofia dashed to the railway station to take a seat before night fell and the jackals went berserk. Hobos and drunken scapegraces expelled from the local school ambled through the fields before they beat it for the olive groves in Andalusia, Spain. It was a minor miracle that a gentle, peaceful guy like Sto had stayed in Radomir, Arch neighborhood, for three years now. Perhaps he turned out well because he cared for the folks who remained in these parts. He often said, "I am sorry," then added, "It's my fault"; otherwise the jackals would have eaten up both him and his pistol long ago.

"What do you want?" This time Miss Dana's assistant spoke in a milder tone of voice.

"Please forgive me, Miss Isabella. Two hours ago you called me, asking to look for Mr. Tano. You declared you'd give a 60-Lev award to the person who provides you with information on the gentleman. Three ladies, herb-gatherers all of them, Grandma Tinka, Grandma Migla and Grandma Krema saw the man under the bridge of the Struma River. I drove Mr. Tano and the three providers of information to your place, Miss Isabella; now the ladies expect that you will give the award to one of them. Each of the three claims she was the first that had seen Tano, and each one wants the award."

"Each herb-gatherer will get twenty levs," the business assistant declared. "Tell them that if they oppose my proposal, I'd sue them for damages. Now the three of them are trespassing on Miss Dana's land. I have not asked or invited them to come here. Hello, Grandmas, did you hear me?"

The herb-gatherers, short, chunky and rebellious, jabbered angrily in the Jeep, but were scared to get out of it. Then they grumbled aggressively, "Isabella is a pig, isn't she?" but when the business assistant gave twenty levs and a bag of walnuts to everyone, the grandmas shut up momentarily then muttered, grinding their teeth, "Thank you, Miss Isabella."

Hardly had the herb-gatherers pocketed their awards when Tano crawled out of the vehicle—a tattered undervest, goose bumps and no socks. The man wore good pants, though. He had probably given away his other clothes. Although impressively big, Tano looked down and out, scrubby; in the morning Isabella had forcibly shaved him. Clean-shaven, his hair shaggy and tousled, Tano made efforts to stand up and failed. Probably much of the brandy from the local pub had taken up its firm position in his head.

"Herb-gathering old wives in the Jeep, shut up all of you!" the business assistant ordered briskly. "Make no further comments."

All the time, the herb gatherers had not left their bags unobserved. On the contrary, they managed to notice and mark a dozen herbs for stomach ulcers in barren Dana's yard.

"Sto," the business assistant turned to the policeman. "Grab Tano's legs and try to lug him to the toolshed. The moron is heavy, mind you. Okay, follow me."

The business assistant made her way to the backyard, her steps not particularly steady, largely deviating from the straight line the lady obviously planned to adhere to. Although intended for the tender Fritzes, a bottle of wine still exerted some influence over her.

The business assistant held in high repute the place she had worked for so many years, so she pulled herself together. Within half a minute, her awkward gait became easy and determined; her voice was suddenly a dangerous double-edged sword.

"Sto, drag him out of the way and throw him in the toolshed," she instructed the policeman who, already at the end of his rope, was lugging Mr. Tano to the aforementioned flimsy building. Tano did not look fat maybe because being tall as a pine tree, his blubber was distributed in an even layer on his frame, so even drunk like a catfish, mud from the river all over his face, undervest and pants, Mr. Tano looked good.

"Lock the door of the shed, Sto," Isabella added in a milder tone of voice. "Put your hand in here," she showed the policeman the pocket of her apron, unable to find the darned thing herself on account of her loyalty towards Fritzes' wine which she had meticulously put to the test an hour or so before. Her critical thinking, however, had remained as sharp as a razor. In fact, her critical thinking was sharper than a razor now as a result of which no herb-gatherer dared challenge her decision.

"I locked the shed, Miss Isabella," Sto the policeman reported.

"Then go home. I'll take care of the mess," Isabella said. "So long, Grandmas," she turned to the three herb-gathering ladies who had identified Tano.

Miss Dana watched from the first-floor porch. Deep inside her heart, she knew that her business assistant could gain the upper hand in any stressful situation. Squeezing a bottle of Fritz's wine in her hand, Barren Dana asked herself if her business assistant and expert in all sciences really loved her so much. Maybe this weak wine had left Miss Dana completely befuddled and she was imagining the things she'd just heard. No way. It was impossible for Dana to get stewed as an owl on meek, tractable wine sold to women Fritzes. Was the wine quiet and soft? What if she had drunk herself blotto? Maybe Doc Gospod should be sent for. Just imagine: Miss Dana drunk on her own wine! Die of shame. That's what she should do!

Under the enormous apple tree that each year yielded a truck-load of the best apples in Radomir, Arch neighborhood—and that meant the best apples in Bulgaria—two kids sat quietly, Mumma and Kalcho. The girl was saying something about the sun princess and the moon prince. She held the little boy's hand, and the boy stared admiringly at her, open-mouthed, breathing softly and carefully. That way he could hear the fairytale much better and Mumma would hold his hand until night fell. Kalcho would feel like the poorest boy in Radomir—and that meant in the world—without Mumma's thin, weak hand.

20.

"You're not old, Grandma Vancha," the child said. "You are young. You are. Look at me. I've behaved myself for two hours already."

"Aggo Junior, sonny," Vancha said. "You're a treasure. Run to the library. Tell Binna to bring Doc Gospod to me."

"But why Doc Gospod, Grandma? You are ok. I can see you're ok!" the child repeated. "I'll give you the medicines. Two pink pills, one blue pill, and a bowl of yogurt. Here you are. Here is a glass of water. Drink the pills."

"I'm ok, sonny. Run to the library. Tell Binna to bring Doc Gospod."

The boy held out his hand for Vancha.

"Ok. I'll run to Doc Gospod. I know where her office is."

"Tell Binna, please."

The child looked up and asked, "Why are you crying, Grandma? You're ok. You took your pills."

For a while the old woman kept silent.

"I'm not crying, Aggo Junior. A little fly got into my eye," then she kissed the kid's forehead and ruffled his hair. "Go tell Binna."

"Ok, Grandma."

The boy left the room and rushed to the library. It was cold, the alley was caked with mud, but he ran with all his might. He was a short lad, very thin, sprinted with ease, at times stopped to get his wind back, but it was only a very short pause. Then off he dashed. Grandpa Simeon, who used to be a bread baker, had just collected the goats of the neighborhood. Their bells clambered up the steep hill, above Space the forest ranger's house. The air rang and hopped with their reverberating sounds as the boy ran down the deserted street, the puddles huddled under a thin ice crust bursting under his feet. Why should a puddle freeze in April? It should be warm, and a boy shouldn't be forced to put on a pullover.

He had to find dearest Binna in the library, find her as soon as possible, but why? Didn't Grandma Vancha take her medicines? The poplar trees still had no leaves; birds have perched on the branches, innumerable black wings that had made a sky of ravens above the houses. They were in the boy's dream last night. Perhaps the ravens were bewitched lads like little Aggo Junior, and if he found a glass of magic water for them, they all would turn into boys, itching to play with him. Aggo Junior didn't know any other kids his age. He played with Sissy, the cat, and Purring Cloud, the tomcat, but one day Sissy scratched his arm from his index finger to the elbow, and Grandma Vancha cleaned the wound with brandy. It hurt a lot. Aggo Junior played with Barky, the dog. They ran in a race every day, and Barky always won. Above all else, Aggo Junior enjoyed sitting in his chair and watching his grandma cooking lunch. Her hands knew everything: how much salt to sprinkle on the nettle soup, how to cut the carrots or where to find sunflower oil and vinegar. Her hands also knew to tuck him in.

"Tell me a fairytale, grandma Vancha," Aggo Junior asked her every evening.

Vancha knew only one fairytale: about a boy who loved his granny so much, and she made a corncake for him. Aggo Junior loved this tale. He had listened to it twenty-eight times, and twenty-eight is such a huge number. Little Aggo could count to 6, sometimes even to 7, and every time he succeeded, Grandma Vancha gave him a piece of sweet. On Sundays, when his grandma wasn't too tired, the two of them baked a corn cake. They kneaded the dough, added some yeast and waited until Lena's—Lena was their ill-disciplined goat—milk boiled. Then they put the cake into the oven, and Grandma Vancha told him her tale one more time. In the evenings, Aggo Junior and Binna played *Beggar My Neighbor;* once in a blue moon the boy got scared of the shadow the curtain cast on his bed, wriggled out of his blankets, crept to Binna and told her, "Somebody's hiding under my bed."

"There's no one under your bed, sweetheart, don't be afraid. Look," Binna turned on the lights. "There's no one, see?" she stroked his hair, and he relaxed a little because he liked her warm fingers.

"He's hiding in the cupboard. Let me stay with you and he won't pounce on me," and Aggo Junior snuggled close to Binna. In the morning, he saw her get up to go to work in her black library. There were 28 million books in this cold place! A house full of books, and all of them knew fairytales about 28 million corn cakes, so there would be enough for all children in Radomir, and perhaps the youngest tots would get two cakes each! Aggo Junior so much wanted to play with these kids.

The puddle in front of the library was a lake. Aggo Junior carefully worked his way around it, doing his best to combat the mud and keep his gym-shoes clean. Binna had bought him the pair— strong shoes with round orange laces, just like Spiderman's. Aggo Junior loved these gym-shoes! They knew where he wanted to go.

Parallel to that, they could fly, and Aggo Junior didn't doubt that one day very soon, perhaps even on Sunday—Grandma Vancha planned to bake another corn cake, Aggo would eat a lot of it and become very strong—perhaps his gym-shoes would teach him to fly. In the beginning, he won't fly high, he'd be very careful like Vasko, their drake. Every time a half-baked idea crossed the bird's mind, the volcano of feathers hurled himself forward, a blind horrible shell, and flew. Vasko hurtled past the garden bench and dropped to the mud like an overripe pear.

Aggo Junior accidentally kicked his ball a couple of times, and the ball had, even more accidentally, hit Vasko the drake. This time the volcano of feathers flew like a brick, uproariously fluttering his wings. The ducks watched him, and this time they were not happy, on the contrary, they worried about their leader, the drake. At a later stage, the gym-shoes would positively teach Aggo Junior to fly like a hawk, although of late the herb-gathering grannies hated the hawks' guts. They exterminated the fierce birds with rat poison and shot them with shotguns. Aggo Junior was not afraid to fly like a hawk, it was only the shadow of the curtain that frightened him. The boy believed this shadow looked like a bad man.

Little Aggo entered the black library and hardly had he opened the door than he shouted, "Binna, Grandma Vancha says you must bring Doc Gospod to our place!"

That tall and strong boy Nikolay, who was to go to Spain after two weeks, was talking to Binna. Fifteen days is such a long time, Aggo Junior thought. He could count to six, sometimes even to seven. The lad was friends with Nikolay. Strong Nikolay often passed by Vancha's house. Yesterday, Aggo Junior was drawing the bad man's dreadful shadow under the curtain when Nikolay showed up.

"Give my love to Binna," strong Nikolay said. He always gave

Aggo Junior something very interesting indeed: a little glass ball with a tear in its center, a willow bow and two arrows, or an aircraft made of paper that could fly much higher than Vasko, the drake.

"Don't forget to give my love to Binna," strong Nikolay asked him, but this was unnecessary. The boy never forgot. Aggo Junior though that strong Nikolay was his second best friend after Grandma Vancha and Binna. The lad couldn't explain how it came to be, but he was sure Binna and Grandma Vancha were his best friend at one and the same time.

"Hi, strong Nikolay," the boy had said. "I know you've given Binna a paper airplane exactly like mine. It's great!"

"What's wrong with grandma Vancha?" Binna asked and produced her telephone without delay. "Aggo, run back to Grandma. Doc Gospod doesn't answer. I'll go to her office and bring her to Grandma."

"I gave granny two pink pills and one blue pill," the boy said. "And she ate a lot of yogurt," Aggo Junior wanted to stay a little longer with his second best friend strong Nikolay. Perhaps strong Nick would tell him something very interesting like where the Struma River went, or how the boys in Africa made bows and arrows. Aggo Junior wasn't exactly sure what Africa was, it was probably a place with a lot of willow trees in it, and even the babies knew that one made the best bows out of willow branches. Then Aggo Junior remembered that his grandma had cried in the morning. Maybe it was true that a little fly got into her eye, the boy thought, trying to calm down, yet he knew that there were no flies in the room. The flies were not yet born in this cold month of April.

Aggo Junior left the library and carefully tried to work his way around the puddle. He was aware that if mud stuck to his flying gym-shoes, it would pull his feet to the earth while he was learning to fly. Then he rushed back home. He was surely running faster than those ravens that had built a new sky with their wings above the houses, gluing together their huge feathers. It was so cold because of the ravens, and there could be no doubt about it.

He took no notice of Barky, the dog that was whining quietly, so quietly as if he was digging the ground with his voice. Aggo Junior took no notice of the open door. The boy had forgotten to close it when he went out, and now the wind that flew behind the boy's back played with it, pushing it back and forth. Aggo Junior knew he had to close the front door because the warmth from Grandma Vancha's tile stove squeezed its way into the yard, to the ravens, and the cold month of April with its biting wind would settle in the kitchen.

"Grandma, I'm back!" Aggo Junior called out. "Binna will bring Doc Gospod in a minute."

Grandma Vancha didn't say anything.

"I'm home!" Little Aggo called out one more time.

He darted to the kitchen where the wind had hauled in frost and rime through the open door. The boy looked around. Grandma Vancha lay on the couch, her hands limp on the blanket. Had she put the milk their goat Lena gave them up to boil?

"Grandma, I can help you to boil Lena's milk," the boy offered.

Grandma Vancha didn't answer. She lay on the couch, saying nothing, her eyes closed. The boy had expected she would praise his rapid gym-shoes that had run so quickly to the library.

"Grandma! Grandma!" Aggo Junior dashed to the couch. "Grandma Vancha!"

Doc Gospod and Binna came to the kitchen and found Aggo Junior, one of the most tractable kids in Radomir, Arch neighborhood, his head resting on the old woman's shoulder. Her threadbare cardigan looked darker under his cheek; the kid must have cried.

Doc Gospod was a brave woman and a very good doctor.

A white cloud, as light as one of Vasko the drake's feathers, tried to break free from the sky and fly away to Black Peak. Perhaps Grandma Vancha wanted to accompany it in order to bake a corncake for Grandpa Aggo in heaven. Perhaps God himself waited for her at the foot of Black Peak. He surely knew it was very difficult for an old woman to climb a mountain ridge without her walking stick.

"Hey, Doc Gospod came on time!" little Aggo shouted to the cloud. "Cloud, listen to me! Doc Gospod has six yellow and seven pink pills in her bag!"

The Doc had a big syringe as well and she used it, plunging the needle into his granny's arm.

Grandma Vancha heaved a sigh. Her face very slowly grew a little bit lighter. Aggo Junior watched and yes! The gray patches on Grandma Vancha's cheeks turned yellowish-white, then a tiny bit pink. Then his grandma's beautiful cheeks twitched.

The boy pressed his chest against the doctor's white coat and gently, careful not to give her a fright, stroked the white fabric with his fingers. Then he waved his hand to the little cloud.

Cloud, take a bowl of Lena's milk and bring it to Grandpa Aggo, the boy said in his mind. Tell him I listen to Grandma. Good for Doc Gospod's pills! If only the plum tree in the backyard was strong enough to give the young green plums its powerful juice! If only the plums grew as big as my glass balls! Listen what, Doc Gospod! I'll climb to the top of the tree. I'll pick the best fruit for you. I'll pick a whole handful of plums for you. The best handful of plums will be for you, Doc Gospod! I promise you. And I love you.

21.

Binna remembered it all. It hurt.

Her life was like that.

It hurt a lot.

…"So he introduced you to his family," the dark young woman said. "He carried you to his big car in his arms and took you to Sofia to meet the swell-headed turkeys in their nest. Let me see your engagement ring. O, move it, Binna. Remove the ring off your finger. Come on, I won't eat it."

"Leave the girl alone. Let her be happy for a minute," Grandpa Aggo said from his corner. He hadn't been able to get out of bed for months now, and Doc Gospod said she had to do something for him, send him to the biggest hospital in Pernik to help prevent complications.

Binna could not forget that hour.

Aggo went on breathing for her sake.

That young man from Sofia had turned up in the library like a bolt out of the blue, and like a veritable prince among men gave an engagement ring to Aggo's daughter Binna. Happiness had at last knocked at her door.

"Go suckle your baby, woman," Vancha hotly chimed in as she put the nettle soup in the pot and stirred it. "You gave birth to this boy less than a month ago. He'll tear up his throat wailing, and he's bawling his eyes out. You don't give a damn."

"This runt has a father," Sinna snapped. "Your son Naum is the runt's daddy. Where's Naum now—in Sweden, Germany or on the moon? Why isn't he at home? Why doesn't he care of the worm he has produced? The midget howls his lungs out and doesn't leave me alone for a sec."

Binna trembled as she relived the gray minutes.

"Don't speak of your child like this," Aggo had said softly from his bed. "He is a very handsome lad."

"So what? He screams and shits and he's good for nothing else."

"If you didn't want him then why did you give birth to him?" Vancha snapped back. "Didn't I tell you to get rid of the worm? You didn't want Doc Gospod to scrape it off you. I saved up some money and gave it to you. Go to Sofia to Professor Dionis, I told you. You went and did what—nothing at all!"

"Oh, you're wrong," Sinna turned around to face Vancha. "In Sofia, I bought booze on your money and drank it. The dough you've been saving up for three months! I drank expensive drinks, ate expensive meals and met big expensive guys. It hurt down there on account of the big guys. That's what I did on your money days on end. I tell you everything fair and square. Are you happy now?"

'Don't speak to her like that, Sinna. She is your mother... I am so happy you brought the lad to the world," Aggo said. "I'm grateful to you that you named him after me. I had no luck in life. Let him be lucky for me... He bleats like a lamb. Sinna, please, girl, go see what the lad wants."

"The lad has a grandmother," Sinna said curtly. "Let me see

the ring the blockhead gave you, meek lamb," the dark girl said to Binna. "Why doesn't a dude give me a ring? Why doesn't the fool want to marry me?"

"Well, it's only the mules in the fields that haven't mounted you," Vancha snarled, her lips a tight dangerous line." You and that bitch, Isabella, Barren Dana's stooge, got drunk together on Friday at Jonny bar. You shouted and you sang with the bitch in front of the premises. Shame on you! Gypsy Anna was the first to get drunk with Isabella, the shrew. You're the second one. O, my God," Vancha was whispering now. "Your son cries his heart out, you gave birth to him a week ago, and what you do? You go get blasted, scream and roar and swear like a trooper."

"Eh? Who told you I got drunk with that bitch Isabella? Who squeaked this info to you? Who tells you tales about Isabella the shrew?"

Binna had blushed and tried to hide her face.

Vancha didn't say anything. A steaming bowl of nettle soup waited on the table, and in the near corner the baby wailed again in his new and clean crib.

"Binna, please go check what the little one wants," Aggo said feebly. "Stop fighting, please stop fighting" he gasped to the women who stood bristling with animosity, glowering at each other. It was dark, the trees were blue and the grass black in the night that swooped down and hit Radomir. No one talked about Binna's ring anymore. Binna stood up, bent over the crib and gave some water to the little one. He muttered something under his tiny nose, smacked his lips and went to sleep.

Binna loved this baby more than the whole world.

"Yesterday Sto the policeman came to see the child," Vancha said. "He left one hundred levs by his pillow. 'I'll come the day after tomorrow, and I'll have something more for the little one, Mrs.

Vancha,' he said. 'Why do you bring him so much money, Sto?' I asked him. 'Because... well, just glance at him, Mrs. Vancha. He looks like me... Please excuse my silly words. Maybe I'm wrong... but ... he's the spitting image of me, I think."

"What difference does it make if the midget looks like Sto or not? He wails like a mongrel nonetheless, and shits no less than usual. And he's scraggy, a fretting bundle of nerves, weak like a flea, can't suck my milk. So I go to Gypsy Anna. Her baby rids me of my milk. Otherwise I'll catch mastitis like Steffa, our best bitch."

"Your friend Isabella often visits Gypsy Anna after the pickpocket came back from Spain. They kicked her out of Madrid because she lifted everything she saw like a vacuum cleaner. You and Isabella are constantly dropping in on the thieving Gypsy. Taking care of her latest Spanish baby perhaps? You are very close indeed: Gypsy Anna, you and daft Isabella, bosom friends."

"Yes, we are very, very close. So you can go hang yourself."

"Please. Don't quarrel, please," Aggo whispered from his corner. His bad heart had kept him bedridden for months. If the baby didn't cry, Vancha talked to him. Binna gave him water to drink and cooked chicken soups, following Doc Gospod's instructions. Every time dark Sinna showed up in the sitting room to suckle the baby, she stopped by the sick man's bed, smiled and said, "Cheer up, Aggo. I know you'll get well soon."

Now, like so many years ago when she was a small scrawny tot, she kissed him on the forehead.

"I want to ask you, Sinna," Vancha cleared her throat and went on. "Who's your baby's father: Sto the policeman or my son Naum, or Doc Gospod's driver that visited you, too? The guy left fifty levs by the baby's pillow. A dozen high-school students came to see your son. And everyone left the lad money. Even grandpa Simeon, whose wife met her maker a month ago, God bless her soul, even

Grandpa Simeon dropped in and left more than the half of his pension in your son's crib."

"So you're mad at the guys that gave some extra cash to the midget?" Sinna asked as she poured herself some soup, although the nettles were still half-boiled. Then she grabbed the loaf of bread and bit into its crust.

"I'm not mad. All I want to know is if I'm the kid's grandmother or not," Vancha said, snatching the loaf away from her Sinna's mouth.

"Why don't you ask Naum if he's the worm's father? Why are you questioning me? Call Naum tomorrow. I'll give you his cell phone number, if you don't know it."

"Will you marry Naum after he comes back from Germany? Grandpa Aggo and I were saving up our pensions for his wedding."

"Mark my words, Vancha. You don't want to know what I'll do with your pension savings. I've already told you what I did on your money. But I can also tell you what I will do to your son Naum when he comes back from the back of beyond. I won't speak about other things only because Aggo is in this room. Aggo took care of me as if I was made of gold, every inch of me, and I am not his daughter. I'm not telling you those things for Aggo's sake, Vancha, for the sake of his weak legs. And I want you to know it."

Binna went to the crib, took the crying baby and tried to rock it back to sleep, but the little one kept on writhing in his rompers. She brought him to his mother, gently touched his nose and said, "Please suckle him, Sinna, he's hungry."

Sinna grabbed the white bundle, gave him her breast and the whining immediately stopped.

"Tomorrow I'll go to Gypsy Anna. She'll bandage up my tits, and I hope my freaking milk will run dry. I'm fed up with the crusty patches on my blouse, and I am sick and tired of squeezing fat milk from my teats," Sinna grumbled. "You'll feed the worm on goat milk."

"You give money to Gypsy Anna. You pamper her kid and neglect your own son, you fool. Or maybe you go to Gypsy Anna to get something else." Vancha spoke harshly, her eyes glued to the nettle soup.

"You are right. I give her a lot of cash, loads of it. And I'll give money to anybody I take a shine to. I earn the money, and I'll fork out two grand on a guy or a girl I like, whether you mind or not," Sinna said as softly as if she was conversing with the bowl of soup. "I'll make Gypsy Anna bandage my tits. I can't stand the way they run like a runny nose."

"It's a sin to have milk and not suckle your baby," Vancha said. "Dozens of women pray for a drop of milk like yours. Look at the baby: he's as handsome as a picture. Suckle him."

Sinna didn't say anything, her head a thunderbolt above the nettle soup, powerful and self-confident like the North wind. She cut a slice of bread, took a wedge of cheese and drew near to Aggo.

"Are you hungry, old man?" she asked. "You and I will have a bite to eat. Come on."

"I'm full, Sinna, honey," he said his voice soft sand. "But if you've set your mind on feeding me, well...I'll eat."

Bent over the old man, Sinna carefully brought the spoon to his colorless lips. Then she broke off a piece of bread, so tiny as if she were going to give it to her son, and slowly, taking her time, put it into Aggo's mouth.

"I don't want anymore, Sinna, honey. It's enough for me," Aggo said feebly, but opened his mouth for the bread that her fingers had warmed up.

"One more bite, old man. Doc Gospod said that you'll kick the bucket if you don't eat. There's no use dying, is there?" Sinna prattled on, her words as soft at the sky above Radomir in the evening. The sky was good only in June—neither scorching, its stars swooping down and catching you, nor freezing November gray when the clouds were cold water above your hat. The month of June was Sinna's voice, with the clear water of the Struma River, the sorrels in the meadow, the first ripe cherries. She said to Aggo the junkman. "I won't let you die, old man. Don't you ever forget it," she looked him in the eye. "I won't go anywhere before you slurp the last drop of this soup here."

The old man's cheeks were yellow with pain and agony, yet a tiny smile warmed his lips.

"May I eat only half of this, Sinna, honey? I'm tired."

"We'll see," she answered quietly. "Don't tell me that a soldier awarded an order for courage in the World War II can't eat a spoonful of soup now. I won't have this nonsense! Perhaps they gave you the order because you got in your lieutenant's favor? You were fawning all over your boss, so 'Come here, Aggo, take this order for courage, nice boy.'"

"No, I won it honestly. I was badly wounded in an explosion. My leg was splintered by a grenade. Eutim, a guy from Pernik, dragged me three times out of hell. This guy, my old friend, flew to Black Peak years ago. His wife brought me the newspaper with Eutim's obituary in it. 'Tell your pals, Aggo', she said. Eutim dragged many soldiers out of hell at the Drava River, sixty men from Radomir did he carry on his back away from the bullets."

"Then eat this bread for Eutim," Sinna said, carrying a tiny piece to his lips." And three drops of soup."

"For Eutim, may he rest in peace," old Aggo the junkman whispered as he swallowed with difficulty. "For Eutim, and for Stavri... he got killed in Nish... for Ivan Andonov and ...for Ivan Trayanov of my platoon... shot dead in Nish too," Aggo's hands trembled.

"Leave Ivan Andonov and Ivan Trayanov alone, may they rest in peace," Sinna said, patting Aggo on the shoulder. "Brace up,

Sergeant First Class Aggo. We aren't going to bite the dust, not us! You'll live to drink a bottle of wine at my son's wedding. Do I make myself clear?" She carefully pulled up the old man's blanket, wiped his mouth with the back of her hand, bent down—she started doing this after she was three year old—and kissed him on the forehead. "Good night, Sergeant. Tomorrow, I want you to report to me you feel much better! Sweet dreams."

Binna remembered everything.

22.

Vancha had put Aggo Junior's crib in the room where the two sisters slept at night, and the baby's constant fretting and fussing was hard to stand. Perhaps he was hungry or thirsty, or a severe colic seized him. Doc Gospod instructed Sinna to nurse him once every three hours, but she suckled the midget every time he started to wail. In the daytime, Sinna disappeared, but before she went out, the dark hailstorm left a bottle of her milk for him. She came back in the dead of night, her breasts swollen, hard like marble; sat down on the couch, cursing the milk as she made efforts to squeeze it out.

Once in a blue moon, she came back home in a cheerful mood: on these occasions she had suckled Gypsy Anna's latest baby, the Spanish scrawny girl, and her own son's noisy crib failed to catch her interest. She didn't even spare a glance for it. Sometimes Sinna brought a heap of shabby baby clothes with her; Gypsy Anna had thrown them out because she was too lazy to drag them to the trash can. These were old Spanish tot's rompers and socks. Sinna brought expensive bodysuits, pajamas and booties, too; Barren Dana's business assistant, scatter-brained Isabella gave them to her. On all pullovers and little coats a *Made in Italy* label was attached which, translated into Bulgarian, meant *Knitted in Italy.* It was evident these rompers and stuff had been knitted abroad. Sinna's runt—little Aggo Junior—looked magnificent in them.

So magnificent that when Vancha took the baby for a walk in the street and met a guy freshly back to Radomir, Arch neighborhood, from the olive groves in Spain, no matter which trade the bugger exercised he screwed up his eyes and carefully studied the little one's face in the pram. Vancha didn't say anything, but the guy did.

"He'll grow into a strong man."

Then the olive picker or bricklayer fished in his pocket. Sometimes men left fifty levs, sometimes a hundred euro or a hundred dollar bill by the pillow, depending on the profit the worker had made. Some touched the baby's hand; others slightly stroked his small nose, still others just looked, but everybody said, "He's a handsome boy." Most frequently among them all, before the 10th of each month, Sto the policeman stopped his jeep in front of Vancha's house and lugged a big cardboard box of pureed baby foods and a bag of baby skin care products, moisturizers and soaps.

"Why do you bring us creams and stuff, Sto?" Vancha asked him. "We rub pork fat into his skin and the little one's healthy like a horse, god bless his soul."

Sto changed his tactics. He bought baby diapers and rattles. When the cardboard box Vancha had prepared for his gifts was full to the brim, and he couldn't cram in a single jar of baby powder or an anti-colic bottle, Sto left a fifty lev bill instead.

"Hey, Sto, man, the child is wonderful. He doesn't look like you anymore," Vancha said one day to Sto, but the policeman was mild-mannered, quiet, and went on leaving his presents in the new big cardboard box by the front door.

Vancha was convinced that Sinna still cleaned Sto's living room and the whole house as well. Every night the snake served the drunks brandy in the pub at the highway rest stop, Sto the policeman made a patrol of the taproom, his old Niva police jeep a crawling cockroach in the shadowy neighborhood. Sinna's work shift ended in the morning, at midnight or at noon on the following day, and the policeman picked her up, saying, "Sinna, it was pure chance that I just passed by, you know. Accidentally, I'm on my way to Aunt Vancha. I can give you a lift if you want."

At times Sinna said, "Okay", but more often than not she remained in the pub with a client. Various crowds honored barren Dana's pub: highway maintenance workers, truck drivers, pipe fitters, mechanics and locksmiths, jobless guys, masons, millwrights and welders from Zenith metallurgical factory that was on the verge of bankruptcy. They came from Pernik, Dupni, or from the capital Sofia, but geography was of no consequence to Sinna. All places were alike to her. Men ogled her, the patches and crusts of dried milk on her dress, and the smell of an unwashed baby Sinna exuded attracted them the way a bloody bone enticed a pack of stray dogs. Sto waited until she finished with the client. The policeman sat in his cold old Niva jeep, trying hard not to think of what they did or said to each other, and when at long last the client emerged, all smiles at the pub's front door, flaccid like the cold soup Sinna served at all times, freezing Sto finally got out of the Niva jeep. He strode across the yard to the pub, knocked at the door on which someone had scrawled *Personnel*. Sinna and grandma Lazara, the cook, were the personnel. Grandma Lazara's soups were discussed and revered along the length of the highway to Greece and beyond, while Sinna was the specific topic of interest, stirring up heated discussions in Pernik, Dupni, Radomir, Kustednil and numerous other towns, villages and helmets in Bulgaria. Even Sofia, the capital of the country, was obsessed with Sinna and her pub Barren Dana had proudly named *Motherland*.

Sto the policeman knocked at the door of the Personnel office, and after Sinna shouted, "Come in!" he came in, but very often she didn't shout anything at all. The dark girl Sto cared about lay in the rickety bed she had made out of twenty-four plywood beer crates, covered with empty bags of synthetic fertilizers. Sinna slept on the fertilizer bags, no sheets, no blankets, nothing. Sto was worried sick about her; she might catch cold and then who would look after Aggo Junior, who would breastfeed the infant? Sto wanted to cover her, but found only a couple of torn fertilizer bags. In his opinion, a fertilizer bag could hardly warm up anybody, so he took off his coat and very carefully wrapped it around Sinna's chest and shoulders. He felt like waking her up on the spot, anxiously asking himself who'd breastfeed little Aggo. The policeman knew very well she ran all day long, bringing bean soup, pork stew, spinach pasta, fish with rice and fried chicken to drunks and other clients, so he let her sleep on—half an hour more, often forty-five minutes more. Then he woke her up, touching her shoulders carefully like a thief and saying, "Your shift is over, Sinna."

She goggled in amazement at him.

"You're nuts, Sto," she grumbled, but he gently, very gently indeed, touched her shoulders and repeated, "Your shift is over."

Finally, Sinna awoke, and he added, "It was pure chance that I just passed by, and my day on duty is over. Accidentally I'm on my way to Aunt Vancha's and I can give you a lift, if you want."

Vancha saw the screeching old Niva jeep stop at the front door of her house and got scared. Something's brewing, she thought, panic surging in her chest. Idiot Sinna has robbed a wretch at gunpoint, or bitten a guy black and blue, or has gnawed his poor throat through and through. She's got blood on her hands now, and Sto the policeman is here to take her into custody. That was what Vancha thought in the beginning, but soon got accustomed to this spectacle. She watched as Sto the policeman, most gentlemanly, opened the Niva door for Sinna as if the weasel was the secretary of state. The uppity cabinet ministers acted like her on the TV. Sto offered her his hand, and Sinna got out of the car, their Sinna, dark as the bark of the damson tree, black like the tires of the Niva jeep, and Sto clung to her, holding her hand as if she was the Prime Minister and couldn't find the way to Vancha's house by herself. Often the screeching Niva jeep went on towards Sto's small house, a tiny gray two-room affair. If one asked Vancha's honest opinion, the poor policeman shouldn't bring baby creams, lotions and fruit purees, he'd better plaster his poor dilapidated hut instead.

This time, Sto's Niva jeep with Sinna in the passenger seat continued towards the policeman's ramshackle house. He was an orphan boy. After his grandma who had brought him up met her maker and the young man had no roof above his head, he bought this two-room wreck. The Niva jeep waited in the street while Sinna and Sto patrolled inside the place for a long time. At a certain point, Sto drove her back to Vancha's house and said, "I am sorry Mrs. Vancha, I know she has to nurse young Aggo and is a little late. It is my fault, please, forgive me."

"If I had waited for Sinna to suckle Aggo Junior, the baby wouldn't have put on an ounce on him," Vancha, a woman of precision and rectitude, said. She knew that short reckonings made long friends. "I taught little Aggo to drink goat milk. You can't imagine what great kid he is, a tiny bit on the thin side, I admit, but..."

"I'm thin too, Mrs. Vancha," Sto the policeman said. "I've been toothpick thin all the time, it's God that's made me that way."

"It's not God's fault," Vancha objected. "You don't have a wife to make soups for you, that's all there's to it. Find yourself a bride. She'll cook veal stews and pump out the poor starving bones you have."

"Well..." Sto the policeman started hesitantly. "I've proposed to Sinna six times already... If she agrees, I'm ready."

"If you rely on Sinna to cook soup for you, Sto, you'll never put on any weight. Skin and bones, that's what you'll be."

"I thought… I mean I thought, you know," Sto the policeman hummed and hawed, then blurted out, "I believe she wants to marry me. I know she's promised to marry your son Naum after he comes back from… I don't know the country, sorry."

"Neither do I," Vancha said. "Naum proposed marriage to her a dozen times. If she had accepted, we'd have known where my son was gadding about. Now what? I listen to the weather forecast every evening. Is it cold in Berlin? Is it raining? Naum is in Berlin, I say to myself. Then I wonder if it's raining in Brussels. Naum is gone traipsing around Europe or Africa. Who knows where he's collecting designer rags at symbolic prices?"

"Sinna is the most beautiful girl I've seen, Mrs. Vancha," the policeman heaved a deep sigh. "I'm sure you are happy that she lives in your house."

"This means you haven't seen any girls worth their skirts," Vancha snapped. "You don't understand anything about girls, Sto, although you are a good police officer." It was Vancha's pleasure to talk to this young guy ever since he brought Aggo Junior the first gift of an endless series. The policeman called her "Mrs. Vancha", not "Grandma" and that was a sign of his deep respect. She felt warmth for him, compassion, too, as if she had given birth to the orphan boy constantly on patrol in this neighborhood of burglars and conmen. Not many guys stayed in Radomir, young and old preferred picking olives in Spain instead. The ones that still didn't go away were construction workers and thieves: Derrick operators during working hours, burglars and drunks on Saturdays and Sundays. Vancha felt like Sto was her son, not the big strapping straggler who delivered second-hand clothes from Europe at symbolic prices.

At a certain point, Sto returned to his Niva jeep and went to make a patrol of another area. Vancha went back into the house, took a peek at the living room, checking to make sure Sinna suckled the little one, but the snake hadn't suckled anybody. She slept with her dirty clothes on, one shoe in the farthest corner of the room, the other one in the middle of it. Sinna breathed softly, sprawled out on the couch like an old crumpled coat. Vancha felt sorry for blue-eyed Binna. Her bed sparkled, clean, silver-white. The baby's crib sparkled too. It was Binna that took care of it.

"Sinna, won't you squeeze milk for your son?" Vancha asked, although she knew the snake would hiss, "Go drown yourself."

The old woman shook the dark weasel as hard as she could. "Nothing's better for a baby than his mother's milk," she muttered under her breath. Vancha didn't have a drop after she gave birth to Naum, and was ready to crawl on her belly from Radomir, Arch neighborhood, to London if this could fill her teats with milk for her son. She could do nothing and Naum used to be a sickly child.

"Sinna, squeeze milk for the kid," Vancha said.

"Milk for the baby" and "go hang yourself" were bandied about a number of times until Sinna, a furious lake of rancor, jumped to her feet, unbuttoned her blouse, started squeezing and cussing, "Beat it! Lump of lard, run to Sto and…" she mentioned a lot of cavities in Sto's body into which Vancha could thrust her head, but at long last the snake expressed about a pint of breast-milk.

After a week, Sinna ceased to return home or talk to Sto. Some neighbors said she slept in the *Personnel* office at Barren Dana's *Motherland* pub. There, no one made her squeeze milk for the worm that wailed at the top of his lungs and throat in his crib. If anyone cared about Sinna's views on breastfeeding, she'd state she wouldn't pander to a brat's every whim. The worm was doing just fine on the milk of Lena, their goat, so Sinna didn't intend to squeeze her teats every evening as though she were a mangy dog. Mothers' milk, you talk some flim-flam. As if you and I drank mother's milk every day!

It was common gossip—and Vancha had heard it, too—that a woman married to a highway maintenance worker had a baby and no milk. Every afternoon, she took her daughter to Sinna and the snake nursed the little one, charging fifty levs per feeding. The baby was as big as a flea, so puny and frail she hardly had the strength to open her eyes. Sinna suckled the flea and didn't allow Gypsy Anna to tie her chest with a woolen scarf in order that her milk ran dry—the fifty levs the snake pocketed were just a cover. There must have been something else apart from the money, Vancha thought: it was the woman's husband who gave Sinna the bills. Neighbors said he was as tall as a house and his shoulders were massive airplane wings.

If he's so massive and tall, how come his baby can't open her eyes, Vancha wondered. Men like him set tongues a wagging; a lot of retired folks lived in these parts, offering both Doc Gospod and Matey, the local undertaker, ample business opportunities. Matey not only sang in the church, but also dug the most wonderful graves, and everybody was perfectly happy with his efforts. So far so good, the woman who took her baby to Sinna for her milk often had temper tantrums for a very subtle and deep reason.

It was true Sinna's milk was as strong as concrete, and the baby girl gained two pounds within twenty five days. Not only did the little angel open her eyes, but learned to roll over, flipping from back to front. But on the twenty sixth day, the woman found Sinna and the airplane-wings man in the narrow *Personnel* office.

While the baby girl was putting on more than two pounds in the course of these twenty-five days, Sinna and the Airplane wings gained weight in the narrow *Personnel* office, or at least most town folks thought so. Could you hide anything from the herb-gathering ladies? No way. Forget it. They noticed the most miniscule blades of grass as clearly as if they were using a microscope and knew everything worth knowing. These ladies not only supposed, but proclaimed far and wide that Airplane wings planned to ditch his wife, the reason being a distinct lack of milk for their baby. The Wings intended to beat it, accompanied by Sinna, for Spain, and find a place in the warm country where the two of them could pick wonderful olives and other fruits. The winged nitwit obviously lacked in brains—and grew taller than a hut—he believed that Sinna would pick olives with him, the moron!

She told the Wings crystal clear, "Go pick olives by yourself."

The man, his mouth drooping sadly, said, "I won't go if you don't come with me. I want to be with you in the *Personnel* office all my life."

"I'll stay in the Personnel office, yes, but not with you," Sinna explained to him, and not a word more was heard about this man along the highway to Greece and beyond, at least no one visited Vancha to brief her on the hottest news about the luckless fellow.

The wife and her scrawny baby came to look for the Wings in Sinna's office; the poor woman spent a fortune to travel from Dupni where she lived at her mother's place, languishing in obscurity and thinking of a nitwit! Sinna was willing to suckle her baby girl free of charge, but the wife blustered and shrieked, "I trudged the last two miles to your office to kill you!"

"You want to kill me on account of your spouse, or I got your meaning wrong?" Sinna asked the woman. "It's true he's got shoulders, but nothing else. Cool it, fretting won't solve anything."

The woman left her baby girl on the ground, snatched up stones and rocks, and took to hurling them at Sinna. She got so carried away with throwing that she totally disregarded her skinny suckling although she was bawling her heart out. Finally the construction workers came, big men who often stopped for lunch at

Motherland pub. They captured the woman, thrust the baby into her hands and declared, "Leave pretty Sinna alone. Run back to your 6-foot-Something bonehead. Scram!"

The woman cussed, sobbed, hollered and choked, foaming at the mouth, but the construction workers put her, complete with her suckling and two rocks in her pockets, on the bus to the town of Dupni.

Vancha wondered where Sto the policeman could possibly find free space for his raw-boned backside if one considered the facts and the stories, revolving around Sinna. Why should the poor man bring more gifts for Aggo Junior? Vancha, a woman of punctuality and integrity, stopped racking her brains on this issue; she plodded down to the policeman's house and asked him a simple question, "Hey, Sto, where's your place among the constructions workers, the highway maintenance guys, the mechanics of Fiat Car Service and the foodstuff suppliers, I mean with respect to Sinna? I'll be honest with you," Vancha was a woman of accuracy, too. She hated bushes and beating about them, minced no words and didn't go in for the twists and curves of idle talk. "I'll tell you the truth, son. Sinna doesn't care about you."

"Aggo Junior looks like me, Mrs. Vancha. He's thin like me, isn't he? And his eyes are brown like mine."

"All guys in Radomir have brown eyes, Sto," Vancha said.

"Little Aggo's are brown" the policeman said full of hope, paused then added quietly, "See you soon, Mrs. Vancha. Please take this Gummy Bear and give it to Aggo Junior. He's starting to teethe. I hope that the lad will have good strong teeth when he grows up. Maybe he'll bite like his mother.

23.

Binna remembered everything clearly. It hurt. It had never stopped hurting.

"I got home from work early today, Binna. Do you want to know why?" the dark young woman sat by the door of the room with the two beds and the crib, ignoring the baby in it. She had chosen the warmest and cleanest place in the house for her chair.

"Your son's left eye is inflamed and irritated, perhaps you dripped some of your milk into it," the blue-eyed girl said. She touched the baby's hand, adding, "Yes, his eye is inflamed, the eyelid is swollen. Don't worry, Sinna. You've got to give it time to heal."

"I'm not worried at all. Let's leave Aggo Junior's inflamed eye and Aggo Junior's wet pants alone. The more you pick at a baby, the bigger nuisance he becomes. Let me see the ring," Sinna took a step to her sister, caught hold of her hand and pulled it hard. The blue-eyed girl groaned.

"This engagement ring costs at least eight grand," Sinna declared confidently as she tried to wrench it from Binna's finger. "Don't moan. If you don't want me to break your hand, remove the thing and give it to me."

It was a gold ring with a huge ruby, reflecting the bright light of the electric bulb.

"When did the schmuck give it to you?" Sinna asked.

"His mother gave it to him first then he put it on my finger," Binna said.

"So he put it on your finger? You'll be weeping with joy now, won't you?" the dark-haired girl chuckled. "Today, you are no longer a shabby midget. A wealthy guy's fiancée, that's what you are, Sis. Nikolay will no longer bring paper flowers to you, Granny Raina, the bitch, won't pay you gold pieces to roll in the hay with him. It's so sad. I'll start sobbing right this minute."

Binna kept quiet. Her face, softer than the breeze, burned. The same color was the grass in Space's backyard when summer walked away from Radomir, or winter brought Christmas to town and the evenings glowed, happy with the children's smiling cheeks.

"You are pretty, damn it!" Sinna growled. "You are the prettiest woman I've seen. You know what? That's why I decoyed Nikolay. He couldn't walk, didn't have the strength, after me; lost twenty pounds within a fortnight, poor kiddo. I scratched him and bit him. Every time he said your name, I plucked a wisp of his hair."

Days were anguish. Binna's past caught up with her every time she thought of this long cold year.

"I wish you sewed up your foul mouth," Vancha said heatedly. "You're marrying my son and you tell us what you did with Nikolay. Aren't you ashamed of yourself?'

"Not at all, you stale cheese pie. You know what? I'll sew up my thing below if your son comes back. And he'll want me; you can take my word for it. I'll never marry him. I wouldn't breathe the dust of his old rags. I don't want a man in tatters. My husband won't be a junkman."

The baby screamed his head off, kicking energetically in his white rompers.

"Unbearable!" Sinna shouted. "If I had known he'd be such a nuisance, I'd have aborted him." Then she turned to her blue-eyed sister. "Look here, Binna. Don't make it hard on yourself. Give me the ring of your own accord. Do you care to know why? Do you? Because I'll marry your big wig who put that ring on your finger in Sofia."

Binna could not forget. The dark minutes flowed into her blood.

..."Sinna, pretty girl" a quiet voice faltered in the corner. It was so slow and weak it resembled dry sand. Old sand that the wind would soon carry away, all the grains lost for good, and no one would remember a thing about Sergeant first class Aggo Aggov from Radomir, Arch neighborhood. "Don't say that, please."

"I'll marry the big cheese from Sofia, and will marry his father if the old grouch is still at it. I'll give birth to a couple of worms, Number One by Big Cheese Junior, Number Two by the old boy, two wailing caterpillars like scrawny Aggo Junior in this crib. I produce moppets with ease. After I ditch them, Binna the kind sob sister, will wipe snot off their honkers. I will clean their dads' sitting rooms. Come on, give me the ring."

"Sinna, girl," once again echoed the voice that the wind took and scattered far from Radomir, Arch neighborhood, a voice that had loved Vancha all days and nights, but was afraid to tell her.

Aggo, their father... He had taught her Binna to read when she was four years old.

"Sergeant first class Aggov, say one more word and I'll bite Binna so hard that even Doc Gospod's pink pills won't help her to get rid of the bruises I'll give her. They'll stay for years to come."

"Sinna," the junkman whispered desperately.

The baby that after twenty years might have a quiet voice as beautiful as summer sobbed helplessly. Sinna didn't even glance at him.

"You know what," she said as she took a step to her blue-eyed sister. "Yesterday I cleaned the forest ranger's sitting room."

"Space doesn't have a sitting room, you liar. Somebody has to poison you and throw you out of town."

"You're right. Space doesn't have a sitting room," the swarthy-complexioned weasel said. "Day in, day out, Binna drags herself all the way to his place, so I went and cleaned it up. Do you want to know what Space said, Binna, sweetheart?"

Binna kept silent. Her face bloodily glowed like the sunset above Space's rugged backyard when jackals howled against the sun. Her face died like the moon eclipsed by a cloud heavy with a hailstorm.

Binna kept quiet.

Space was like Aggo. Poor Space. Her dearest poor father Aggo the junkmen.

"Space the forest ranger said, 'I want her.'

24.

IT WAS A POSTER OF the most famous Bulgarian pop stars. Directly on the stars' faces, all of them platinum blond and more than well-endowed, a message had been printed: shaky block letters, blue ink, a hundred crossed out words, printed bold again, and again crossed out.

"Hi DANA,

Today I, made my mind to write you, a letter, because I ran away, on you. On the contrary! I didn't run! I want to tell you—u, something. I felt, VERY SAD. I got, the BLUES for You. I got drunk, like every other guy But I still got the blues, for you and bigger blues, for the KIDS. For my girl MUMMA and my Boy Kalcho. I didn't believe I'd get the BLUES, for You DANA but shit I did. I was running, away and, something was pulling, me back hard. I say to, myself, it's the wine for FRIzzes that pulls me, back, that crazy Isabella gave, me to drink. She s crazy all, over her crazy head you MUST KNOW THIS. She beat me hard with, a mettle post and she, nasty bitch shoot at my … buttoks Therefore I don't hate the bitch, FOR she moreover takes good care of, the kids.

Wonderful. She reads to them, fairitales, about golden

apples, and Tsar Trayan. If Mumma, didn't love, her so mutch, and if Kalcho didn't love, her so mutch, I d have strangled her like, I strangled that, stupid goat which, grazed down the peppers in the garden. Therefore, Dana I am running away, from you and, you canot catch me, but I got the, BLUES for you, gal, and I stop and, I myselfe, run back to YOU. When, I count to five I see, five times the KIDS. Mumma who IS NOT, AT ALL short witted, and more and more often I see Kalcho. You gived birth to Him for me, thanks so mutch. But, therefore, Dana I want to see You. When I count, to five I want you. In our toolshed. I will drink no drop, NO DROP, I will not drink even on Sunday!!! Come to, our toolshed Dana. Isabela will , lie to the kids about, Golden Apples, and stuff.

I won"t drink. Dana I m sorry you're that filthy rich. Can't you, be poor like normal folks??? Therefore you will not, keepe me penned in the toolshed and Sto the Police guy will nott chase me, I can do HIM IN and he's, my best friend. We'd better, have a drink, I and Sto, but he gets drunk very easy and I carry him to, his place. Danna I, don't want FROG BAR I want YOU. You, look like Dora. She died. You know, my Dora. She gave birthe to Mumma Sinna and Binna. I am running with my chums but, I cannot run!!! I say to myself, you shithead, why did you escape From the shed imbecil??? Somebody will, steal, your Dana from you, imbecil. She's a pretty woman, and she looks like, your gal Dora, and she looks like Dora more than Dora herself does. DANA gave birthe to your boy. Therefore the pretty woman shall give birthe to, one more boy hopefullly! She can hit a hawk in his foule head when the bastard, flies like a rag in Heaven thinking like a professore on how to snatche Dana's hens.

Therefore Dana, sell everything to the smallest nail but KEEP our toolshed. It's the best! The first and best!!! Sell the dairy. Sell the forest. The lake… I suspect you must NOT sell the lake. Where will you swim like a crazy imbecil, if you sell the lake??? We can fill the tub, with ice and you, can lie in it. We shall drink therefore two, days and two, nights and bitch Isbela shall pull the wool over the kids eyes about Tsars and apples, and stuff. I wants to marry you, like everybody else with a priest and, church and stuff. Makes no, sense, running away on you, DEAREST DANA. Because, I run and something pulls, me back. I want to sea the kids. I have Mumma and Kalcho. **MY LIITLE GIRL!!! AND MY LITTLE BOY!!!**

Above all, above heaven I, want to sea you, therefore I stop running and get drunk. And I say to myself,,,, let me pawn this sonof a bicth, **kidney,** get some money and go home to this pretty woman! MY DANA But I, hit my head with my fist and start thinking hard and deep. Hard and deep and frank. I have to work, my ass, off, to feed the kids and I want, my kids to know chalk from cheese and give them education. Dana, you are not simple and , not stupid. Let them talk the imbecils. Listen to me. Sell everything or give, it to bitch Isbella. I AM strong I shall, pick, olives like every body else, and I shall care about My woman DANA, and, my Kids. I'll give them education, I shall. I shall give, you, Dana, education too. You won't go simple like a bag, of beans.Dana, don't chase me. My hearte bleeds for poor Sto. When I'm drank, I can clobber him on the, head. I can breake his poor head. Who then, will go, calm down the crazy Grandmas in the fieldes? Marry me Dana, BUT don't keep me penned in the shed. Stay with me in the Shed. We shall teach Muumma to become a doctor. She shall make a good doctor like Doc Gospod. We shall not torture Kalcho to study. He shall make a football player.

I am Okay. I feel very fine. Don't call Sto to chase me. You chase me. You. You. **9 pm in the toolshed!!!** Don't get the, kids, to go to bed, so early. Bring them to me! MUMMA

and KALCHO Bring to me. I run, and I see, them, all the time
and I can't run.

Kissess. See you in the toolshed. Can t wait.

Yours truly,
Tano V. Tanov

.... "You're thoroughly off your rocker, Miss Dana. Why are you whimpering, tell me! Who made you sob? Tell me. I'll go skin him!"

Isabella, angry yet sympathetic to the tall woman's plight, did her best to cheer up the sturdy lady by shaking her shoulders as hard as she could. Barren Dana wouldn't budge. The business assistant studied her carefully and at a certain point wrenched the poster from Dana's hands. The sparkling galaxy of pop stars, all blond, left the business assistant unimpressed. She didn't give the stars another thought, she slapped her boss's face instead.

"The worst will blow over soon, Miss Dana. You'll brace up like our bitch Blizzard after they killed her lover mutt. She bayed and growled for a week then found another mutt, more beautiful than the first one. Don't turn on the waterworks again, Miss Dana, please. Who are you weeping bitter tears for? Tano the jerk! Oh My! Miss Dana, stick a pin into my eye and I'll cry with you. Let's sob together, or I'll die laughing. Miss Dana, I say it in your face: your sharp wit is going to seed."

But the tall woman in a dress made of an ordinary bed sheet went on crying.

"I can't live without him," she sobbed, pressing the pop-star poster to her heart.

"The poor girl," Isabella whispered. "Her wrong thinking is all over the place," the business assistant pondered on the situation, scratching her neck then resolutely turned to her employer, "Miss

Dana, do you want me to pour a bucket of freezing water over your head? No? Listen! Let's go for a swim. I'll jump in the son of a bitch lake with you. O, man, I hate the bastard water's guts."

25.

THE ROOM WAS HUGE AND very bright, a picture supposedly painted by Vermeer hung on the wall to the east; a dozen mahogany African witch-doctors sparkled under it, fabulously graceful and expensive. Books in English, German and French arranged in a gilded bookcase gleamed in the dusk; there was a mahogany bed and on the high wall pictures of a woman were affixed. The woman was young, dark and exceptionally beautiful. The photographer had taken multiple nude photos of her. A portrait of the same woman painted in oil, original gold frame, hung on the opposite wall, and under it glowed a watercolor painting of the dark woman, a man and a boy who looked more like the man.

In the mahogany bed, the young man of the portrait had buried his face in the lap of a plump, middle-aged woman. Her clothes, immaculately clean and elegant, gave out a discreet perfume of jasmine. The young man's shoulders were shaking, and on the woman's milky-lilac dress large wet patches could be discerned. There, the young man's tears were seeping through the soft fabric.

"Greta, oh, Greta," the young man sobbed. "It shouldn't have happened. Where did I go wrong? What was my mistake?"

"Nothing's gone wrong, my dear boy," the woman answered, carefully kneading his back. "Everything will be ok, we'll forget all the bad things and then…"

"It will not be ok. My father! My own father! He wanted to steal my wife from me? My Sinna. Why? Why, Sinna!"

"At the end of the day, he hasn't stolen anything from you. It was she…. I mean, she chose another course of action, and nothing important happened, absolutely nothing," the woman went on, her voice moth-eaten woolen yarn that didn't know how to soothe his nerves; it found no convincing arguments to set the young man's mind at ease. She simply offered him sympathy and warmth. Yes, something had happened. But good loyal Gretchen had witnessed much more objectionable phenomena in the course of the long years she had been working for the Markos. "Your father simply… he couldn't have taken another course of action. Your wife was… how shall I put it? She was ravishing. She was too beautiful…"

"She is so beautiful now! She is magnificent!" the man cried out.

"Yes, she is magnificent," the mature lady agreed. "She is exceptionally beautiful, yes, she is. How shall I put it, Sammy…I hate hurting your feelings, you know, my dear boy. Like every exceptionally pretty woman she… she'd prefer to have a lot of choices, or options, or alternatives at her disposal and… and this is only natural. She'd like to get acquainted with multiple aspects of life, and to get to know many human beings. The more they are, the richer her experience. Time flies, you see. Her high criteria were… proverbial indeed. For this reason, all gentlemen succumbing to her irresistible charm, were, let me put it this way… they all have acquired high financial status, all without exception, your father too. He has a very strong personality… and suffered a lot. You have to forgive him."

"Oh, Greta, tell me that she will come back to me... My Sinna..."

"She will come back to you," the woman tractably repeated, absorbing the moisture on the young man's eyelids. For a split second, he raised his gaze to meet hers. She continued kneading his back gently, skilfully and competently. "We are sensible guys, you and I, aren't we, Sammy? So we need to arm ourselves with patience... courage, I have to keep my head... and you have to keep your head, my dearest. Yesterday, I visited your father at the clinic. He was very upset by the whole thing. Thank God, doctors say his life is out of danger. Chest pain, short of breath, so they thought he had a heart attack. Thank God, he didn't, only mild pain and discomfort. He said a few words about Sinna."

"About Sinna? Of all the nerve! After all he did to me! His meanness knows no end."

"Actually he... he informed me that... Listen, Sammy, you and I have to be prudent... in the best sense of the word. You and I will be wise, yes? Promise me please. Yes? Good boy! Greta's sweet clever boy... I gave your father some advice in the same vein, Sammy. He also suffers deeply within himself and..."

"Suffers deeply, does he! Who's to blame for all this? He is. Who was mean?" the young man shouted and his shoulders that have gradually calmed down twitched again. His frame shook. "You say he kissed her and that was all. Are you sure, Greta? Greta, look at me!"

"Let us arm ourselves with courage, my dear boy," she said softly. The fragrance of jasmine had touched his wet face, and she hoped it had steadied his nerves a little. "Man has to keep cool in explosive situations. Equanimity and poise are keys that open all doors, Sammy, dearest. Man has to show understanding and sympathy. Your father could have died of heart attack. Thank God, the doctors got his disease totally under control. I am glad they did!"

"You're not helping me, Greta!" the man screamed. Rivulets of sweat trickled down his face. The woman made great efforts to absorb his tears in a silk handkerchief, but unfortunately didn't rise to the occasion. "Sinna will come back to me, won't she... our son remained with me. She loves her son, doesn't she? She loves him so much, doesn't she, Greta?"

"Maybe she does," the middle-aged woman heaved a sigh. "David is a very sweet child, a wonderful boy," her hand flitted to her dimpled chin: a reddish scar gaped there, several deep dents as if someone had stuck a fork into her jaw.

"David is the most magnificent child in the world," the man sobbed. "I know he has bitten you many times. It is his way of showing how much he loves you. She used to bite me, too, do you remember? She used to bite me so beautifully. My God, will she come back? Do you think she will come back to me?"

"Listen, Sammy. Listen, my dearest boy, my sunshine! Sinna got engaged a week ago. That's what your father told me at the clinic. Don't worry; the doctors assured me that he will fully recover. He will live through it, and it is not serious... She got engaged to Mr. Miron. Your father thinks it's too much pain to bear. But his life is out of danger. Your mother stayed an hour with him in his hospital room... Perhaps you and I should visit him, too... Of course, it's only if you agree to accompany me to the clinic, my dearest. "

"Miron?" Sammy groaned. "Who was that Miron guy, the bald-headed old grouch from my father's law firm? Shit! She got engaged to this... fossil... mummy... corpse... How could she?"

"The fossil was Senior Investment Strategist and now chairs the board of trustees of Southeast European Development Bank," good loyal Greta sighed, massaging the desperate man's shoulders. "Actually Mr. Miron is my age, perhaps a year or two my junior. And of course he's bald, bone-dry, and the wrinkles on his face are as deep as the Valley of Death. That's what happens when a guy smokes, my dearest. It's a difficult habit to break, I know, but I'll give you a hand, Sammy. I promise. You should quit smoking. We'll fight it together, you and I."

"Miron... Miron the moron! She'll marry this mummified slug. She'll marry him. My God, Sinna, where did you find this moldy skeleton?"

"He used to be your father's close friend, Sammy. Miron and your dad got on quite well together," good loyal Greta explained. She was certain she could ease the pain if she found *les mots justes* no matter how complicated the situation at hand was. Her task was to come up with these soothing words now. "Your father introduced him to Sinna at a party he threw in your mother's honor. At that time you were at a conference in Köln, my dearest. I was happy you were away; it was an unbearably boring event. I served the VIP guests... Sinna didn't enjoy it. Miron talked to her. Perhaps this explains why your father finds it so hard to bear."

"She won't live with him for long, will she, Greta? Live with this rat! Smelly maggot! She'll come back to me," Samuel's eyes gleamed and the moisture gave their irises sharp, dark beauty.

"They say Miron is very rich," the woman said.

"I'll kill him!" the young man sobbed as he buried his head in Greta's lap. "I'll kill him tomorrow!"

"We have to be sensible, Sammy, dearest. You and I have to calm down, go on living and occasionally relaxing a bit," the woman was whispering now, and gently, as if her life depended on it, pulled the beautiful linen-silk sleeves, setting the young man's arms free of his shirt. "Please, Sammy, stretch your legs, slowly, gradually. We are not in a hurry, are we? Do it for Gretchen. Good, good! We have to be reasonable, my dearest sonny boy. You will calm down, won't you, Sammy? Or our hearts will burst the way your father's was about to do. Do not judge him too severely… It's not worth dying for a woman."

"But this woman is Sinna," the man groaned.

"Yes, this woman is Sinna," the mature lady said. "Sinna married you and burned her sister's clothes in your fireplace. And you were engaged to her sister. If I have to be honest, that blue-eyed girl was the most beautiful creature I've seen… Do you remember how Sinna arrived at your house in Boyana? It was Sunday, and it was raining."

"She looked as pretty as a picture," Sammy whispered.

"She, pretty as a picture, gripped her sister's throat and threw her out of your room, this very room. You didn't ask Sinna where she'd take your blue-eyed fiancée. You didn't stop Sinna, didn't even try. And I know why you didn't. You, my dearest, spent a couple of minutes with Sinna in the corridor. I saw her. I saw what she did to you. Didn't it hurt? I saw dents like these all over you," the woman pointed to her dimpled chin still red as if someone had stuck a fork or an awl into her soft flesh.

"My God! It was magnificent! I had never been happier. This corridor is my favorite place in this house… Her teeth… They are magnificent. Do you remember, Greta? I took you to this corridor too. It was magnificent, wasn't it?"

"Yes, it was," the woman sighed, but her voice hardly expressed any admiration. "The marble on the floor was very cold," she added, but the man didn't hear her.

"Sinna came back," he murmured dreamily. "I don't know where she'd taken her sister. Sinna came back and this was… O, my God, it was awesome. It was unbelievable. She was great!"

"Great?" the mature lady allowed the yellow streak of doubt to weave its way into her voice. "She pushed you to the floor, Sammy. She rammed into you. She hurt you. She didn't even pretend to hide from me, did it before my very eyes as if I were a piece of dirt on the floor. She threw her sister out, a girl you were engaged to be married to. She didn't let you eat, didn't let you stand up or get some rest."

"It was magnificent. Oh, Greta, Greta! Please find her! Go to her! Ask her to come back to me. Take the child and the two of you cry at her feet. Convince her to come back. Fall on your knees and ask her!"

"Yesterday Sinna and Mr. Miron met me on the street," the housekeeper said. "Sinna tossed me a fifty-Lev bill, and didn't deign to utter a word. The gentleman formally threatened to call the police if I set foot in the vicinity of their gorgeous house. He ordered me to stop pestering them, or I'd be taken into police custody."

The mahogany witch-doctors glittered above the bed, bathed in sunlight. Vermeer's picture uneasily shook all its subdued shades. The man scrambled to his feet. His hand, trembling, uncertain, touched one of the dark woman's photographs that was smiling at someone outside the picture or was simply happy amidst the uneasy blush of the sunset. The dark young woman was smiling in all her pictures, and loved sunrises that had escaped from this room for good. He bent down and kissed the dark glowing ankle in the photograph. His lips left a wet stain on the strap of her high-heeled sandal.

"Sinna!" he called out, but the photograph didn't say anything. Her ankle sparkled, hot, exquisite, stronger than the mahogany magic of the statues. "Sinna, I will forgive you for what you did with my father. I'll forgive you for Miron. I'll forgive you everything. Come back. I forgot everything."

"My dearest, dearest Sammy, calm down, please. We have to be sensible. Your father meant nothing to her. I suppose that Miron, her new fiancé, is just a slight delay, heralding her rise to power.

Miron is not an object of interest or concern to her, apart from the purely financial aspects of his portfolio.”

“Yes, the financial aspects,” the young man said, relieved. “She will come back to us soon, won’t she, Greta?”

“Perhaps she will,” the mature lady answered vaguely. “But why should we think of her now? We should be astute judges of character, and we have to think of your son. We should raise the boy, Sammy. We have to provide a future for David and we will do it. He is such a wonderful young lad. David will have his mommy and his daddy. Two must take care of a child, his mommy and his daddy. Don’t you think so? You and I will nurture David and will love him. Sit up, please, just a bit. That’s a great boy. Give me your foot. Good boy. Good for Sammy, my handsome sonny man. The other foot now, it’s ok. Let’s get rid of this belt. We don’t need this belt of yours now, too tight on your stomach, isn’t it? Come on.”

“Sinna will come back to me,” the man repeated. “And you’ll stay with me, Greta. Will you?”

“Sure,” the middle-aged woman responded and gently, with consummate skill accepted his lips that had turned quite irresolutely to hers. Her fingers knew very well what they were doing.

“Greta! Greta! Greta!” the young man said in a frantic gasping whisper. His skin burned, his breath broke down, bursting onto the glen between her soft white breasts. “Greta! You know… I told you long time ago, Greta. I think I love you. I love you!” he shut up, sinking pacified, happy into her warm jasmine-scented flesh. She was the most beautiful, the safest and the most peaceful haven for him in this room where the dark woman’s smile saw everything and was more powerful than his blood.

26.

THE MONTH OF JULY STILL lingered in the air, but it was not one of these warm and endless days when the wind was a small boy, and the sun set at midnight. It was cold, from time to time the sky tore at the horizon, hissed and growled and dripped a handful of rain enough to turn the dirt roads into mudslides and spatter mud all over the cracked tiles on the sidewalks in Radomir. The town folks remained at home and so did Vancha. Her pans and cups sparkled, everything in its place, and even the frying pan looked beautiful in the cupboard where her grandson Aggo Junior could easily reach it. The lad often had to wash the frying pans. Grandma Vancha had given him a kitchen sponge, but Aggo hated its guts. He preferred to leave the chunks of bread in the pan and keep them for Vasko the drake.

Vasko was being silly on Saturdays and on Sundays. On the workdays, he was wise because Grandma Vancha let him go pick worms and bugs in the field behind the house. In the open, the drake gobbled down vitamins directly from the grasses and the nettles, but on weekends the feathered pirate was locked in the chicken yard with the hens and the two small ducklings. On Saturdays, the kids of

Gypsy Anna—his grandma called her "the mean ghoul"—sneaked into the backyard to steal geese and hens. Gypsy Anna had many kids, three boys and a girl, as thin as Vasko the drake's neck. Aggo Junior approved of this girl. In his opinion, to approve of a kid meant to call this kid, share with her your buttered toast and keep a piece of meat in the frying pan for her. Aggo hoped every day that Saturday would come any minute now and Vasko the drake would make a fool of himself. Then if you were lucky, you could pull out two feathers from his tail and adorn yourself like Old Shatterhand.

"What's your name?" Aggo Junior had asked the girl.

"Toast," she had answered.

Young Aggo could not believe his ears. He came up to the child: she wore a dress that was three times longer and five times wider than her. The girl stepped on it, and it was a miracle she didn't come crashing to the ground after each step she took. While Aggo was studying the kid's dress, she darted across the backyard and snatched the buttered toast out of Aggo's hand. Junior was shocked. He wanted to play with somebody so much. No other kids lived in the Arch district. On Monday, the girl's brothers gave him a sound beating, and after that chucked him into a mud puddle, but last week he ran in the field with them. It was true Vasko the drake was an interesting companion, but playing with kids of flesh and blood was the best thing in the world.

Aggo Junior devised a method for finding someone to play with. He took two slices of buttered toast from the kitchen, but didn't tell Grandma Vancha about it. She disliked Gypsy Anna, her children and people of her ilk. The kids had stolen Vancha's lettuces and cabbages, and had picked the cherries in her orchard. Aggo Junior carried the slices in his hands, his arms outstretched, and Toast, the girl, showed up at once. Two dogs, scraggy and thin like worms, followed her, driving Purring Cloud, the tomcat, crazy, and even more so Steffa, Vancha's dog. Aggo gave one slice to the girl and gobbled the other one.

It was so wonderful to eat with another child! Grandma Vancha didn't tell you, "This one is for Binna, treasure. This one is for Doc Gospod. She saves men's lives every day, and this one is for Daddy." Aggo Junior chewed and swallowed the food only when she said, "This one is for Sto, the policeman."

Sto didn't have a dog or cat, so from time to time Aggo Junior took Purring Cloud the tomcat to Sto's place, a tiny house on top of the hill where the policeman lived by himself. There were only two interesting things there, a broken motorcycle and two photographs.

"This is my mother," Sto said and showed the boy a woman in a white kerchief. "And this is your mother," and Sto showed little Aggo another woman who didn't have a kerchief. Aggo Junior had seen this woman before. It was not exactly clear to him when this happened, but it surely was more than two hours ago, at Christmas last year. Then the woman on the picture brought him ten sweaters and ten pairs of jeans. Aggo Junior wanted to give one of the sweaters to Toast, the girl, but she stole all the ten as they lay on the big gray stone in the middle of the yard. Aggo had left them there, a favorite place that Vasko the drake loved to climb. Once on top of the stone, the arrogant fowl quacked how clever he was.

Toast lifted all the ten pair of jeans as well and several days didn't come to play with him. Aggo Junior was very sad.

"Sto," he said to the policemen as he made up his mind not to beat about the bush. "Toast stole my pants and my sweaters, but you won't take her into custody, will you? I'd have given everything to her all the same."

"How come she stole these?" Sto the policeman asked.

"Are you my friend?" Aggo Junior asked him and Sto answered in the affirmative right away.

"Then you won't take her into custody because she's the only child that plays with me. Hey, Sto, why don't you take me and Toast to Sun Sweetshop? It's ok if you don't have enough money. I won't have a piece of chocolate cake. Only Toast will."

Sto listened carefully and declared he had money for ten pieces of chocolate cake. My goodness! That was what Grandma Vancha said when she was impressed by a particularly stunning episode of the TV series *The Black Widow*.

"My goodness!" Aggo Junior exclaimed as he witnessed Toast wolfing down eight pieces of the chocolate cake. She crammed the remaining two into the pocket of her enormous dress.

"This child should not go about in this eh... long outfit," Sto the policeman remarked and took the children to the clothes shop, but not to the one where twenty-second-hand pants, skirts, bathing suits, hats and shoes were sold. Aggo Junior's dad transported all the above from Germany, from another Germany to the south of the first, and from yet another Germany that was the most German of the three. Aggo Junior saw his father at Christmas two years ago; his dad dropped in for ten minutes in Radomir and left Aggo two sports cars he had bought dirt cheap in the warmer part of Germany situated in Africa where black smiling kids lived. The sports cars were second-hand goods and that meant they were rusty, so Grandma Vancha took the red one and made a hencoop for Vasko the drake, then turned the blue automobile into a rack for old slippers. Sto the policeman took Aggo Junior and Toast to an expensive first-hand shop and bought Toast a dress, the most beautiful new outfit in the Radomir, and the minute the girl put it on, she started to sparkle like Vasko the drake on Saturdays. Grandma Vancha saw Toast and stood her mouth gaping open.

"Oh, my Goodness!" she exclaimed just like the countess in *The Black Widow*. "I can't believe you are such a beautiful girl!"

This girl was a thief. She filched a cap from Vancha's second-hand shop and while the old woman was repeating "My Goodness!" Toast pilfered a cup with Vancha's new pair of dentures in it. Grandma Vancha didn't notice and treated Toast to baked potatoes. Aggo Junior knew his grandmother baked the best potatoes in Radomir, and this meant, Oh, My Goodness, the best ones in the world! She chopped the potatoes into wedges, sprinkled a little salt on them and put them directly on the hot cooking plate. It took a century to bake the potatoes—Oh, My Goodness!—and everyone wanted them. The ducks and the hens sneaked past the kitchen, weaving their way through grasses and shrubs, Vasko the drake, all ears, paced the yard as Gypsy Anna often did when she planned to lift the sausages Vancha had hung to dry in the wind under the eaves. Their goat Lena ran to the kitchen too, willing to try the baked potatoes.

Grandma Vancha baked more potatoes and told Toast, "Eat, little girl! How could this Gypsy Anna give birth to such a beautiful child?"

"I can steal very well that's why I'm beautiful," the child said.

"What's your name?" Grandma Vancha asked.

"Toast," the girl answered. "That's how Aggo Junior calls me. He doesn't beat me. He gives me slices of buttered toast which he pilfers from you. It's good to steal. I can teach you to, if you want, Grandma Vancha. I like "Toast" better than my own name. You can eat it, and it smells good. Toast is a better name than the one Mom calls me."

"How does your Mom call you?"

"She calls me, 'Monique, I'll skin you, you mean bed-bug."

"Okay, Monique," Grandma Vancha said. "Have some cheese cake too. Monique is a beautiful name."

"Grandma Vancha, you're a good woman. I'll give you back

your teeth," the girl said as she produced the glass with the new pair of dentures she'd been hiding under her magnificent dress, the best and most expensive one Sto the policeman had bought her.

Everybody stared. Even Vancha could not imagine where the kid had hidden this glass with a pair of dentures in it under the wonderful dress from the expensive shop. And when Grandma Vancha baked potatoes, Oh, my Goodness—so delicious, smelling gorgeous, but still underdone, and if by accident Grandma Vancha baked the best potatoes on Sunday, Monday, Tuesday, Wednesday, Thursday, Friday or Saturday – then always before she distributed the scorching hot potato wedges, Sto the policeman arrived. He arrived this day, too.

"How are you, Toast?" Sto asked. "And how are you, Mrs. Vancha, and you, Aggo?"

Vancha was the most wonderful old woman the wind in Radomir had run into all the time he'd been blowing in these parts. Vancha was a grandma every inch of her although when Sto addressed her as "Mrs. Vancha" she smiled even if she'd taken the dentures out of her mouth. And it was true all her meals tasted as lovely as cotton candy.

"Hey, Sto, this is for you," Toast said, giving the policeman a baked potato wedge. "You're not nutty as Mom says you are. I stole two of your T-shits, a blue one and a black one. Now I can't give them back to you. We swapped the T-shirts with a cowherd for a pound of apples and half a bottle of brandy. But the brandy was no good. Mom didn't sing after she drank it. She sings like a nightingale if the brandy's good. Uncle Sto, I'll steal nothing, I tell you—nothing—from you. Honestly! I'll be as good as my word. I always am!"

Aggo Junior thought of the pair of sandals Sto had bought him, then of the penknife with the red handle, the watercolor box and the sketchbook, of the toy truck that had genuine lights. Sto gave him all these awesome things and said, "Eat a lot, boy. Please! Then you'll grow up as big as me."

"Mom says you are as small as a hazelnut, Sto. Don't worry, I like hazelnuts very much, and you still are my friend," Toast tried to calm him down.

"You have to drink this, Sto," Grandma Vancha said, pouring a cup of tea for him. "This is the best tea in Radomir, son, you can take my word for it. I myself picked the blossoms off my linden tree. In the second half of June, I picked blossoms for Doc Gospod, too. This tea will do you good. The doc has cured dozens of babies of sore throat with it. Grandpa Aggo bought the linden tree for 2 levs at the market place and we planted it just for fun."

"Will you give *me* a cup of tea?" Toast asked. "I like linden blossoms, but I don't know a tree to steal them from."

"You must not steal, girl. Tell me what you want and I will try to buy it and give it to you."

"Mom's right, you are crazy, but I love you all the same, Uncle Sto," Toast's whole face smiled, forehead, eyes, cheeks, ears, chin and all. Her new dress smiled too. The sky and its cold moth of July that flooded Radomir a week ago beamed with joy, oh my Goodness! "Don't be silly, Sto. You mustn't give anybody anything. How will the poor kid learn to steal if you do? No way. She'll go hungry or thirsty. When Mom's thirsty she doesn't sing. The only one Mom doesn't steal from is a lady called Isabella…"

"She's a bad egg through and through," Vancha barged in. "I won't listen to anything about her."

"If I didn't know you were Aggo Junior's grandma and Sto's friend I'd set fire to your barn. I'd set fire to your lousy clothes shop, too, for calling Isabella "bad egg." She's the best! Isabella is like Uncle Sto, but she isn't silly like him," the child said hotly. "She gives me bread every day. I love her. I love her even more than you, Uncle Sto. Mom loves her too."

"Drink your tea, Sto, drink it slowly," Grandma Vancha poured some tea for the policeman. The blossoms were hand-picked of her linden tree that Grandpa Aggo bought for two levs forty-seven years ago. Then Grandma Vancha, without asking Sto first, dropped two cubes of sugar into his cup.

"He doesn't like sugar in his tea, Grandma," Aggo Junior said. The boy visited Sto every day and the policeman often gave him a lift in his jeep. At times, the two of them caught criminals. These were invisible bandits, entirely transparent, but one learned to catch invisible criminals first then seized the real ones.

"Drink, Sto, drink, son!" Vancha said. "You're a good police officer, sugar or no sugar, what difference does it make?"

Sto, a mild man, tried hot peppers once just to please Mrs. Vancha, and wouldn't say no to linden tea with two cubes of sugar in it. He slowly raised the cup to his lips. The tea was as sweet as maple syrup.

"You don't like sugar, Sto," Aggo Junior turned to him. "Even Vasko the drake knows that."

"Oh, I do, I do," the policeman said, taking a tiny sip.

"My son Naum hasn't come back to Radomir for two years now," Grandma Vancha muttered under her breath. "When he was a little boy, he used to like linden tea. It's a pity he's not here with us."

"Sinna is not here..." Sto whispered above his warm cup. "I wish I could see her for a minute, Mrs. Vancha. Surely, she's become more beautiful. Do you think she remembers us?" his voice broke and ran dry, so dry and helpless was his voice that Toast pulled his trouser leg, and Aggo Junior got scared his friend Sto had choked on the air he'd breathed in. "I wonder if she ... if she asks after... after me?"

"No way!" grunted Grandma Vancha. Then she looked up at the little weedy man, the kids looked up at him too, and saw something on his face. Grandma Vancha saw it too, although she didn't have her glasses on her. The old woman stopped grunting and her voice was suddenly soft. What wonderful words Grandma Vancha said! She sounded as if she was speaking to Aggo Junior, her grandson. "Well, I'm sure Sinna often asks after you, Sto, son."

Sto the policeman choked and coughed. The two children patted him on the back. One never knew what a cup of linden tea with too much sugar in it could bring you.

27.

I WAS COLD ALL THE time, shook like an aspen tree and hated the wind's guts. And right I was! It blew great guns, and the climate was a son of a bitch, the month of July rainy all over the place. I said to Miss Dana, "Miss Dana, something's eating my blood. I'm sure something's gone terribly wrong with my red blood cells. Take me to Doc Gospod."

"Something's gone terribly wrong with your head," she said.

"It blows great guns all over the place all the time," I explained to her. "And I'm always cold."

"Isabella, you've got a bee in your bonnet, girl. Where's the wind, tell me. Blizzard the bitch nearly had heatstroke yesterday, and I thrust her into the barrel of cold water to cool her off. I put on wet T-shirts and Tano huffs and puffs...."

"Tano always does huffing and puffing."

"I pushed him into the barrel, too. The lake is as warm as mulled wine, like the one you and I love drinking at Christmas. You're not all there, Isabella, the field cleaves with heat."

"Didn't I tell you I'm not all there? I'm seriously ill." I said to her. "Take me to Doc Gospod, Miss Dana."

"Okay, I will," she said. "Let me bring you the Fritzes wine first. We'll drink a bottle each, and you'll be as good as new. Do you want me to knead your back for you?"

"I am not that crazy, Miss Dana. Last time you kneaded my back, the bruises you gave me were as deep as the British Channel. Let's down a bottle each as becomes gentle and intelligent ladies."

"Who will keep an eye on Mumma and Kalcho?" Miss Dana wondered.

"Why on earth should you ask? Tano will. He teaches them to spit into an empty yogurt cup, but the kids don't care about it. I'll make him read fairytales to them."

"You brain is totally off the track, Isa, totally and thoroughly. The man stutters even when he doesn't read, and when he reads he chokes. Then the kids scream at night during sleep."

"Don't I know how they scream at night?" I told her. "Last week, it was my turn to look after them and they slept in my room. They shrieked and whimpered, asked me to give them water seven times each! Tano, the imbecile, read a tale to them, something about Sue, the blood sucking dragon. 'Isa, dearest, there's blood-sucking dragon in the cupboard,' little Mumma sobbed. "May I come and sleep in your bed?' Kalcho screamed, 'Isa, Isa, the dragon is hiding in the corner. I, too, want to sleep in your bed with you and Mumma.' You can't imagine what happened, Miss Dana. Kalcho was pulling my left ear, and Mumma tugged at my sleeve. I broke my back singing lullabies, sons of bitches slumber lyrics all of them."

"Which lullabies did you sing to them, Isabella? You go to sleep before the lullaby starts, and you never wanted me to sing anything to you. You sleep like a log."

"Are you implying that I am a log?" I was outraged indeed. "Who breathes close to your head, driving away your bad dreams, eh? I do. Who breathes for little Mumma and Kalcho, kicking Sue, the bloodsucking dragon, in the ass? I do. You are a log, Miss Dana. I breathe like a swan for you to calm down and sleep well."

"Okay, I agree I'm a kind of a log. Okay? Which song did you sing to help the kids fall asleep?"

"Don't you know? *Fairyland*, of course! First, I didn't feel like singing at all. And I was cold like a January night. Then I downed one of our bottles, the ones you and I drink as all intelligent ladies do, and then the kids and I danced the waltz."

"And the kids fell asleep?"

"Not at all. We danced Lambada, the three of us, and then we opened our mouths, the three of us, and an awesome *Fairyland* did we thunder in the night, driving crazy all bloodsucking dragons in the cupboard. I don't remember what happened next. At a certain point, the kids were lulling me to sleep, singing *Sleep My Little Baby.* You're an incompetent instructor, Miss Dana. I tell it to your face. How could you teach these lovely kids to sing *Little Baby* so flat and off key? Their tune turned my spinal cord inside out! I made up my mind to teach the little angels to sing properly and suffer no longer harm and musical distress under your guidance. But you know me: I sleep like a log. At a certain point, I perceived that they were covering me with a blanket and then both Mumma and Kalcho cuddled by my side."

"I know the way they cuddle. They do it to me, too. And they pull my ears. But I don't let them blackmail me with Sue, the blood sucking dragon."

"You're so strong, Miss Dana, that a dragon is a louse compared to your fists," I pointed out. "And if you dance Lambada with the kids, you'll step on their toes. They don't have iron thread reinforced shoes like me. You remember the pair you bought me from Milan, Italy?"

"I don't let them lead me by the nose and I don't dance Lambada with them!" Miss Dana said filled with indignation. "I'm not as nutty as you are."

"Oh, you are nutty as a fruitcake," I said honestly. "After you down a bottle from the special ones you and I drink like intelligent ladies, come and see what happens! The lake is insufficient to please your ambition. You cut dry beech trees like a lumber-mill."

"Hello! Are you suggesting I am lumber? I take offence at it, you know."

"Of course you are not," I lied to her. "Tano will stay with the kids. He'll take them quail hunting or might teach them to pump on a swing. Well, Kalcho doesn't like the swing and hates hunting. He sits across from Mumma, watching her. If she nods, he nods, if she sneezes, he sneezes too."

"Stop prattling, Isabella, it won't help you feel warmer. Here is wine and aspirin for you. Are you Okay?"

"No, I'm not. I'm cold."

"Do you want me to sing to you? Or perhaps we should dance Lambada, what do you say?"

"No offense, Miss Dana, but you dance like a steam shovel. Last week, you stepped on my toes ten times when we danced the waltz. My toenail is still bluish-green. And when you sing... Oh, I feel like cutting my own ears, frying and eating them. You are a very bad singer, I tell you the truth."

"What shall I do then? Shall daub some brandy on your neck?"

I knew her daubing well: she pressed your neck hard then made you run like a jackal, telling you stories so that your poor skin would absorb the brandy more quickly. Quickly my foot! Oh gosh, arguing with Miss Dana was the same as teaching a worm the Theory of Relativity. She took to daubing my neck with brandy, then opened her mouth and sang like Sue, the bloodsucking dragon, screeching as if she were swallowing hazelnuts together with their shells.

"I feel much warmer now," I told her. "Stop singing," but she suspected me of cheating on the spot.

"I suspect you!" she said. "You don't feel warm enough. I can't leave you exposed to danger like that. I'll sing the song to the end. Get up. I can see you are still cold. We'll dance Lambada. Its rhythm is full of ambition."

Ambition is a son of a bitch. I hated ambition. Miss Dana stepped on my toes again. But it was very perspicacious of her to make me put on my reinforced shoes beforehand. In Milan, Italy, metallurgy workers wore reinforced shoes, fearing that a metal rod would fall on their feet. Miss Dana declared she couldn't be sure where she'd step while we were waltzing. She forked out a lump sum for my safety and my feet were no longer badly bruised. Each shoe weighed a ton, and I despised the footwear industry altogether for the sake of this nasty pair. When I wore my reinforced shoes, I felt like tangoing: didn't move at all, jutted out like a lamppost, and if Miss Dana wanted to lift or put me somewhere else she was welcome, since I could hardly budge in my cumbersome brogues. After I imbibed a certain quantity of the Fritzes wine, a drastic change in my behavior occurred: I gamboled, frolicked and hotly admired Miss Dana's song, responding with thunderous applause and multiple shouts "Encore! Encore!"

"That's a great girl! Great Isabella!" Miss Dana sighed happily. "You regained your health and now you're as fit as an iron rod. It's good I didn't take you to Doc Gospod. I'd have made her do all sorts of tests, A—Z, to check for your medical conditions."

The two kids slept soundly, and I was amazed when Miss Dana said, "Hey, Isabella, why don't I marry you off to some handsome guy? I know you can't stand Sto the policeman; every time you utter Space the forest ranger's name, your lips turn blue. That guy makes your mouth grow small and dark. We have to attract somebody, you and I. I'll give him a cash prize, if he marries you. Look at you. How pretty you look! Give birth to a kid. I'll raise him to be smart and tough: I have very rich experience and I can teach the lad to shoot hawks, to fell oaks..."

"Come off it, Miss Dana! If you sing the kid a lullaby to the end, you'll frighten the poor midget out of his wits."

"Okay. I'll pay a professor from the Conservatory of Music in Sofia to come and get your baby to sleep."

I thought that Miss Dana and I were just shooting the breeze, but the truth was different. She'd got it into her head to marry me off. I had to only choose a guy and I'd have him no matter how much it cost. The issue would be settled within a week. Then we had to wait for the baby to start kicking in my stomach, and Doc Gospod would take care of the rest. Miss Dana would buy orchids for me, and the two of us would swear at them together; she'd rub grease into the skin of my belly and make fresh-squeezed orange juice for me. She'd make me swim in the son of a bitch lake, so the kid would love to swim after he was born. Well, if the baby was a girl, we wouldn't fret, not in the least. She'd become Kalcho's wife. If I gave birth to a son, perfect again. He'd be Mumma's fiancé, although the kid would be a couple of years her junior. This fact was of no consequence nowadays. Today the world didn't care about one's brains and intellect, Miss Dana concluded. Intelligent ladies like me and her were comparative rarities.

I exerted myself to explain to Miss Dana that as a matter of priority, I ranked men as valuable as the mud under my reinforced shoes; the best thing you could do was to chuck your fiancé to our bitches Fury and Blizzard and have his neck bitten off.

"If I had wanted a man, Miss Dana, all guys in Sofia, from the bigwigs down to the shabbiest pauper, would have left Sofia to settle in Radomir, Arch district. Moreover, they would have learned to speak Italian in order to win my heart. You didn't throw caution and money to the wind, Miss Dana, when you sent me to Milan to study Italian culture. I *parlare* Italian *perfetto*, and a guy who doesn't speak *la lingua Italiana* doesn't stand a chance with me. But even if the bloke was born in Rome, he'd hit a snag in my case. Miss Dana, a man holds no surprises for me. Guys are drawers under a kitchen sink. You could find only junk and rubbish there. Men are the rugs on which you step to clean your reinforced shoes. What does a guy give you—flea infestation and nauseating smells, neither more nor less."

Then I asked her, "For example you, Miss Dana, what do you see in Tano? A mangy mutt is a higher being than him."

"No way," she exploded. "He's no mutt. He's my man."

I had a lot of other issues to clarify, so I gave Miss Dana more roasted chicken to eat, I gobbled some, too, otherwise the wine would drive its alcoholic teeth into my brains, throwing me off balance like a corpse by the empty bottle box. Miss Dana went to bring two more veal sausages for us.

At that point, we heard voices: the first one as thin as a stem of a cherry: a low and very familiar child's voice. If I hadn't paid such close attention to the sausages, I'd have guessed earlier who spoke in this thin cherry voice. I knew right away the other voice, sweet as honey, rich and warm. The wine that cut the Fritzes in two halves even before they removed the stopper from the bottle evaporated in a flash from my head, leaving me stunned and speechless. What was this honey voice looking for in our house?

In front of us, in a green Italian dress from Milan, the most truly Italian attire I had given somebody in my life, Anna stood. I stared at her and stopped breathing, gasped for air, but the air was a heap of stones. So gorgeous she looked, magnificent in the Italian dress and Italian shoes. But neither the dress nor the shoes could compare to the thinnest of her eye-lashes, to the dust under her heels, to her pinkie nail. Oh, my God, why couldn't I think that she too was a drawer under a kitchen sink! She held her youngest child by the hand, the Italian schmuck's daughter, a tot as small as a paving stone, in a dirt cheap pinafore like the ones I'd seen in the *Radomir Forward* discount store. Anna had three more children, boys all of them. Neighbors said she gave birth to the first one when she was fourteen, after a year had another one with a tramp, a suspicious character even in Radomir, Arch district. Anna was not sure whose spawn was responsible for her third offspring. *Does it make any sense to remember a guy's name? No, sir. A guy's cheaper than a doormat.* You could give your dog a doormat to sleep on, so the beast wouldn't freeze in February. Could you do a useful thing with a guy? They all wanted one thing, then took to their heels, didn't even say "Good bye", and you howled like a dog, no money, no bread, a new baby in your lap.

"Anna," I had asked her one day. "How can you be so pretty after you gave birth to four kids?"

"And how can you be so pretty," she asked me back, "After you gave birth to none?"

"Listen, Dana," Anna said.

The Italian dress that I had bought for her from Sofia was beautiful like a jewel on her. I was feeling pretty peeved. Couldn't she say, "Hi, Isabella, the children and I were happy when you bought us a bag of sausages and cheese. We didn't go hungry two long days. Thank you."

She didn't even look at me. I had bought her Italian shoes, too. She was looking Miss Dana in the eye. "Barren Dana, don't just stand there, gaping at me. Listen to what I say."

"Why should I listen to you?" Miss Dana said, a bludgeon

shaking in her voice. It happened like that every time she got mad. Miss Dana's anger was rapid and black. It thrust its way into her voice first. I had to do something, had to save Anna from the black pit in Miss Dana's voice.

"I'm leaving for Italy, Dana," Anna said. "I'll be picking olives like the rest of them."

"I don't care if you'll pick olives or pockets," Miss Dana said, the bludgeon between her teeth already clobbering Anna on the head. But Anna didn't give a damn. She was not scared of bludgeons. Wasn't I proud! This woman didn't frighten easily.

"The boys will come with me. I leave tomorrow."

She's leaving. She'll go tomorrow. I... What will I do? Where will I go? Her Italian dress glows and her skin glows too. Anna goes away tomorrow. What will I do?

"I'll leave my daughter Monique with you, Dana. Isabella will take care of her. You'll take care of her, Bella, will you? You'll take care of Monique together with Dana's kids."

Miss Dana was so amazed that she almost choked. I thought I knew what had astounded her: Anna's insolence. I suspected Miss Dana had bitten her tongue.

The backyard was as smooth as the bottom of a frying pan, we had mown the grass and everything was clean and gleaming. Most beautifully gleamed Anna's dress and Anna was leaving for Italy. Anna was leaving for Italy and I had to live without her. The world went deaf. I went blind.

"I'm not Monique," shouted the voice as thin as a stem of a ripe cherry. I remembered. A searchlight swept back and forth in my mind and I knew: in a thin cherry language spoke Anna's only daughter, her youngest child. Anna had had her with an Italian thief. The idiot hadn't bothered to travel to Radomir to see his little princess, the shabby Italian wretch!

"Child, how come you are not Monique?" Miss Dana asked. There was no bludgeon, not even a wood splinter in her voice now. She spoke as if she was giving Mumma and Kalcho a glass of milk to drink at breakfast. Whenever this woman saw a child, she grew totally weak in the head. "You are Monique. Why can't you remember your first name?"

"I'm not Monique," the cherry voice insisted. "My name is Toast."

The kid's mind must have become unhinged by hunger. I liked the girl, she was Anna's child, and half of the little one's blood was Anna's. The father, the lousy Italian... God knew where the wind had dumped him, the mean rat.

"Are you hungry, Monique?" Miss Dana asked. "I'll give you a big sandwich, kid. Just wait a sec."

"I am not hungry, Dana," the girl said. "Don't you understand that my name is not Monique? My name is Toast. Don't make me angry. Or I'll steal everything from your castle, to the last grain, even the hairs in your head. Do I make myself clear?"

While the kid was giving Miss Dana that stuff and nonsense, Anna, his mother, threw herself at me. She kissed me, not on the lips, she kissed me on the cheek, and her face was wet. Was I whimpering like a puppy, or had she started crying? She pressed her cheek against mine, and I could not imagine how I would live without her.

I'd be always cold. The winter would never go away from my bones.

"Bella! Bella, dearest!" three tiny voices suddenly rose in the air, as thin as cherry stems all of them.

Kalcho and Mumma had rushed to me from the meadow and grabbed hold of my trouser legs.

"Isa Bella, Bellissima!" shouted the thinnest voice, the one of the smallest cherry. "Tell them my name is Toast. I am Toast. Let them remember this!"

28.

Binna was going away from the library. She didn't turn back to the shelves where she used to arrange the books printed before 1940, novels, stories and poems that followed the old rules of spelling and punctuation. *Tobacco* by Dimitar Dimov, Elin Pelin's *Windmill* haunted her thoughts. Although the big wooden book-cases were empty now, her mind's eye saw the faded colors of the covers, the pale letters of the titles. She wouldn't be able to go if she turned one more time to the cold dark room. *Nights at Antimovski Inn* still lingered in it, all endless summer and quiet rains, *The Iron Lamp* glowed and its subdued light was a sigh of a motherless child.

They had informed her that the library was closing.

"You have been working hard, Binna," the Mayor of Arch district told her. "We are short of money. There is no funding, please understand. I did my best and failed, couldn't preserve the library. You have to go. It saddens my heart. We can give you the books with edge-marks and shelf-wear, the worn copies with contents possibly loose. I know how many times you had saved these books. They are for you. Take them."

There were four big cardboard boxes: books with front covers torn off, novels with missing pages that no one had read for years, their dust-jackets moldy and damp. Binna had to go to Spain. Naum, Vancha's son, had found a job for her: she would look after two aging sisters, spinsters in their late eighties. They donated women's clothes to their local church, but the priest could not collect the jackets, pullovers and coats. Naum acted rapidly, scavenging everything, clothing and shoes, from the boxes and containers of *Caritas International.*

"I found a regular job for you in a village near Barcelona. Even if you speak Spanish you won't understand a word of what they tell you," Naum had said to her. "Get your luggage ready."

It was about time she left. She'd been standing by the four cardboard boxes until her eyes clouded with the dusk. Binna took only *Nights at Antimovski Inn* for that village near Barcelona. She could not go anywhere without the inn's darkness. Then she took *The Iron Lamp,* snatched up Geo Milev's *September* and wanted … all the four cardboard boxes. She had to bring them to Spain… and that was impossible. There was a way. She would give everything to high school students. Binna hoped they'd accept the books, these old tired soldiers with worn pages, the ancient suns that had set in the shabby cardboard boxes. She had no fairytales, no king's daughters, no princes, and no heroes anymore. Quietly, deep inside the humble fragile paper Binna could hear Aggo's old voice, so soft that her heart grew as small as a hazelnut. She could not leave the four boxes in the empty room. She remembered the dusk on the spines of the books, the hours she had spent by the rickety electric heater, the happiest in her life.

How could she leave Vancha behind? Who would read fairytales to Aggo Junior in the evening…Binna had made up her mind. She had to tear herself away from Radomir, Arch district, had to see other lands, other houses, other folks. The sunset above Vancha's house was in her eyes. The moon was thin, small, and Grandma Vancha slowly walked with it into the night. Binna didn't want to let her go, she had to cut the loaf of bread and choose the softest slice for Vancha. Binna could not leave Vancha and the cold sunsets behind. She hated to go. She loved the yellow grass in the backyard: in the night it glowed with impatience that Aggo Junior's young steps gave it, and in the daytime it was one of Sinna's wild songs.

It was about time. She had to go.

She'd take the books to the local school. Perhaps a kid would read a couple of them. A short story might land in a first grader's heart. Then an impossible white sparrow would fly to Radomir, and young and old would dance for days as it came to pass seventy years ago. But even if the white sparrow didn't show up, a young day would dawn. All children in Radomir were white sparrows of joy. They had grown up under the most miraculous sun, in the greenest of summers. Binna grew up here, too, the warm sunset in her bones taking her to Vancha and young Aggo along the narrow road of hope.

She could give the books to Doc Gospod. The doctor would write her patients a prescription and together with it she'd give them back the voices of the people that meant everything. In these parts, even the babies knew that what Doc Gospod wrote in her prescriptions was good for you. If you summed up the years of life she'd given the folks from Arch district, infants and herb-gatherers all told, you'd come up with five centuries. But all you remembered was the hours when the guys kept their fingers crossed for the old doctor, the smile the mother gave her after the little baby recovered from pneumonia, the sigh of relief after pain took its leave of the house, and at last the father noticed that the sun was shining in Arch district, too.

Binna had to go.

Stripped of their books, the naked walls of the library looked dark, but she could still see them: the faded tomes of *Young Students Series*, the shabbiest of all, the ones she loved, the sweet murmur of the *Windmill*, the sparkling *Iron Lamp*. Binna made for the door.

She opened it and could not believe her eyes. Boys and girls from the high school, first-graders from the elementary school smiled at her, each hand holding a humble and ordinary flower. The kids had plucked them from the nearby hill: bluebottles, dandelions and crane's bills—so many wild colors in their young hands. Some high school boys had plucked roses from the school garden, most of them drooping and faded. Peonies from the small gardens shone in girls' and boys' fingers, dahlias and hollyhocks glowed, simple Bulgarian flowers, the grandest thing in Radomir.

"Binna, that's for you," the kids said.

Dahlias lit up the earth beneath her feet and the sky over her head. She opened the first cardboard box. She didn't have books for the kids; she gave them her Radomir nights. They knew that Radomir was a warm inn, and on arriving in the town, hope crossed your way. Binna showed them quiet afternoons. It was in the afternoon that Doc Gospod gave the dark homes hope. Binna gave the kids grass that grew full of wind. One couldn't compare summertime in Radomir to summers anywhere in the world, even if one picked the best olives in Spain or made a fortune in Toronto. In July, warm magnificent days were born.

"Binna, this is for you," it was Nikolay from the tenth natural sciences class, with a bag of paper daisies that looked like airplanes, so many paper airplanes that all first-graders in Radomir, Arch district, could fly on them until the daybreak. Nikolay muttered under his breath, "They are all for you. Take them to Spain."

Peonies were everywhere, dandelions and poppies smiling at

Binna. How could she leave them behind? Could Spanish hills give birth to beauty like this?

A big, sharp voice echoed amidst the flowers.

"Binna!"

Behind the boys from the tenth natural sciences class and the crowd of first-graders, behind Nikolay's paper daisies, even behind Nikolay himself, a man stood—totally out of place amidst the bright flowers and the strong voices—a tall man, his hair bleached almost white by the sun, his shabby green uniform with patches on the elbows. He had mended a hole below the left shoulder with white thread, another in the lapel with blue sewing cotton, already quite soiled. It was Space, the forest ranger. He was not drunk.

"Binna, listen to me!"

He thrust his way through the crowd.

The flowers were suddenly silent. Nikolay's paper daisies that looked like airplanes stopped whirring. The first graders froze in their tracks.

The forest ranger was clean-shaven. Without the thick beard, his face looked so clean, so handsome that guys who knew him could hardly believe their eyes. None of the students from the natural sciences class had imagined a man's voice could be so thirsty, impatient like a hand that had been waiting for help that never came.

"Binna, stay with me!"

29.

Are you trying to order me about? Me, wicked Sinna, the rag that the old crone Vancha called "low-down skunk"? Do you plan to wind me around your little finger? Wait a minute. I adore the good and smart mama's boys. I adore bad boys too. I comfort unfortunate worms, pull out predators' teeth and tame savage beasts. Look at them, sprawled out on floors, couches, four -poster beds, drained, spent, and ecstatic that I'd allowed them to kiss the mud I'd stepped on. Ten days with me then feral dogs become bone-dry turtle shells. Do you still want me? Be careful. You'll be on cloud nine, but it's extremely dangerous there.

I'm sure it is my mom that raised me from a high place embedded in heaven, not dumpy Vancha that was itching to fatten my buttocks, buying me the cheapest twenty-second-hand dresses. Didn't she curse me! Called the children in my womb *moles!* My birth mother is in my bones, in my words, under my nails, not fat Vancha. My mom, thin and sick, made truckers forget where they were bound for. Summer came in January to warm her up and then men went crazy for the perfume of her dress. Her thoughts were poison and blessing. I don't have a drop of my father's blood.

He must have been a schmuck, or his heart was muck. To ditch a woman like my mother! The minute she showed up by the highway, the air caught fire and the drivers forgot they had to move refrigerators to Athens. They couldn't leave her side, lingering long after she'd forgotten their names, their last penny spent on her, and blessed.

I can imagine men's ten dollar bills burning her skin. I know what she did to wring every last cent from them, and I'm sure that even a sigh my father had heaved did not stay with me. How could he dump her? Must have been insane or was a cockroach, not a human being. Or perhaps mom didn't want him. She didn't care for a cesspool, for a garden slug's slime. She must have got drunk a lot. It's a pity I don't know her name. Was she Nevena or Sonya? I wish she was called Binna like my sister. I want my third child to be a girl and I'll name her Binna. I will love this kid. If someone tries to hound her, pester her, I'll grind his eyes with my teeth and I'll bite off a piece of his neck.

I have two sons. So what? I don't give a hoot about their fathers.

I do what I want. I can crush them or give them one more son. I choose my men. I decide what I do to them. It's up to me if they'll groan, listening to my lies in rapture, or whimper, their tongues lolled out, dead snakes in the night. I tell them how much they'll pay me. I get ten times the price I'm worth. I pick and choose. They depend on my whims and vagaries. You depend on me. Your life depends on me. I am your Everything. Write that down on the wall and read it ten times a day. Learn it by heart. I won't have mercy on you. No one had mercy on my mother.

I wish I could see her photograph.

I can do it like her.

I can bring a man more happiness within a minute than a lifetime of triumph. Or I can give venom that feels like a black century.

Some folks can paint pictures, others can tell you tales still others fly to the moon. I can have my way with men. So did my mother. The air in her blood smelled of honey. They rushed for her, white guys, black guys, yellow guys, from Radomir, from Belgium and Greece, from Qatar and Dusseldorf... I sneered at the dudes, I hated their guts, I crushed them and I could move in with Gypsy Anna if I wanted to.

I gave her money every week to dye her hair blonde lying to her I loved blonde women. Year in, year out, I could give birth to a wailing bundle of diapers, and soon after that I could beat it for Spain or Germany if I liked. The proud dad would get into the soup with the bawling bag of nappy rash and a heap of smelly rompers.

I would if I didn't know old Aggo.

My goodness, how ugly old Aggo was, short, pot-bellied, his face brown like the dust on the street. He sold ancient rugs and bought old clothes dirt cheap. He laid aside black, slow bucks, and told me, "Wait, little Sinna, please wait another day. I'll save up enough money and I'll take you to the sea. It's big and blue."

That's how old Aggo and I called it, 'The big blue'. "We'll collect money for the Big Blue, Sinna pretty girl. I'll show you what the sea looks like," and he made a sea in a glass jar for me and my sister Binna. He poured water into the jar then added blue watercolors, and I sprinkled a handful of table salt over it.

"Hey, snake," Vancha shouted. "Do you drink the salt or will you lap up the blue mud in the jar?"

I told her I put salt below, on my thing she hated most, and men were dying for. The old shoe squirmed and writhed. We sent for Doc Gospod. She inserted tubes into Vancha's neck and arms and saved her life a dozen times. I don't hold a grudge against the fat doughnut any more. I learned to listen to her for Aggo's sake. He used to make a sea for us in that big jar, built a paper boat for me and let it swim in our Big Blue. I put the sea under my bed and I dreamed of ships, big and bright, of fishes in fine tulle dresses, all gold.

"Tulle is expensive, Sinna pretty girl. If we have tulle, we'll have bread," Aggo said. He always had a splitting headache, but in the evening I kissed his bald pate. He didn't have a hair on his skull, the poor guy, and his head looked like a whitewashed wall, but to me it was beautiful like a ship in the blue distance. Every day, I dropped cents into a box. I was collecting money for the motorcycle that would carry Aggo and me to the sea. I kissed boys behind the post office and they gave me everything to the last coin in their shabby pockets. I came to know I could have my way when I was thirteen. Boys followed me like crazy wolves, and I saved up pennies for Aggo's motorcycle that would take us to the Big Blue.

"You can sing like a bird, Sinna pretty girl," Aggo said to me one day. "Binna, your sister, has a heart of gold, but she can't sing like you. Vancha, who is the kindest woman ever and cooks the best nettle soup in Bulgaria, can't sing either. But you can, Sinna!"

Songs are like men. You either can sing or cannot. My mother's blood has taught me to set fire to the stones and songs. I found out by myself everything I had to know if wanted to keep Naum or another Naum tractable the way you kept a dog on a leash, to sap him of his strength and arrogance, to ruin him and make him kiss the boot that has just kicked his face. And if I felt like it, I might give him a baby, a little howling worm, and then go away.

The songs… they are fog. It covers everything, roads and rivers, and you can't see where you're going. They want you all the time. Songs are blood. If you lose it, you die. Songs are everywhere. They stay on your teeth, and the minute you open your mouth they go away. You don't know why they come back. But they always do.

"Take that money, Sinna," Aggo told me. "They're running a

competition in Sofia. It's competition for folks that can sing. Go there. Show them what big voice has grown up in Radomir, Arch district."

"But we are going to the Big Blue, aren't we, Dad Aggo?" I said. "We've been saving up cent after cent in this jar for years to go to the Big Blue."

"You are my Big Blue, Sinna, pretty girl," he said. "Take the money. I don't want a motorbike. We'll make our Big Blue in the jar again, and you'll sing me the song about the girl who sews a shirt for an old happy man. This song will be our ship, what do you say?"

I sang and he listened, his bald head wet, glistening with sweat, his swollen face opening, a big smile in his dark eyes, and I knew we were there, at the Big Blue, and he was in a big brightly lit ship. I kissed his forehead.

"Your headache will go away, Dad Aggo," I told him. Binna brought him Vancha's nettle soup, and I prayed that one day soon he'd agree to buy a motorcycle, and we'd go to the Big Blue.

He gave me the money from that jar. I didn't take part in the singing competition, left for the Black Sea coast with Naum, Vancha's son, instead. We didn't make it to the sea. He stopped at Rally Motel, a mile from Radomir, we spent the money on booze, and after two days the last cent was gone. Naum kept on telling me I was magnificent and none of the women he'd been shacked up with could compare to the worms in the mud under my shoes. They all could drink water from my old trainers for all he cared, and I was so young, almost a child. After Vancha's Naum, another Naum came, then a third one, a tenth. All Naums said the other women had to drink water from my boots. I came to know that everything depended on me the way a chicken depended on Vancha as she squeezed its neck, pressing the trembling feathers against the log, an axe in the other hand. This is what I feel for all Naums.

I fear no one.

At a certain point, Vancha's son that had ditched me returned to Radomir and I did make him drink water from my boot. Then I took him again to the same motel, a mile or so from Radomir.

"Did you win the competition, Sinna, girl?" Aggo asked me after I came back from that motel the first time.

I couldn't bring myself to tell him that I and his dumb son Naum frittered away the money Aggo had been saving for a rainy day, the coins he got for the old clothes, the shabby rugs, the chipped plates he sold in Pernik, Kyustendil, Melnik as far as the Greek border. I couldn't look him in the face, couldn't sing to him that evening. I wanted to melt in my shoes and burn, watching how he made our Big Blue. Couldn't sing, my heart was in my mouth, I wanted to die as he said to me, "Cheer up, Sinna, pretty girl. There will be another singing competition. You will win. Your voice is as big as the sky. It's deeper than Doc Godpod's knowledge. The woman has cured young and old in these parts, and your voice is a thousand times stronger than that, Sinna. One can gain knowledge, but cannot gain a voice like yours. It is like the Big Blue. There is no end and no shore in your voice, girl."

Aggo was gone. He didn't find out I had not participated in that competition. I didn't enter any other contest in Sofia. But there is still no shore and no end to my voice.

I gave birth to a boy, thin tapeworm, Naum's kid. I did it to make Aggo happy. The old soul smiled like crazy at his grandson.

Naum was like everybody else, cigarette smoke.

Naum is a heap of autumn leaves.

I decide what we are in for. I have my way with him exactly as Vancha when she cuts the chicken's neck on the log.

Aggo has taught me that there are different people under the sun, ones that can see the Big Blue inside you. They throw away the motorcycle they've been dreaming of all their lives. Dad Aggo, you are not my father, but you are more precious than that, you are worth a hundred fathers, a thousand fathers to me. You are my most precious Big Blue, Aggo.

I tell you now. I brought the sea to your grave. Put it in a jar. But the sea is nothing, Dad Aggo, the sea's nothing. It has salt and shores. Our Big Blue, Dad Aggo, has no shores and no end. You have no end and no shore. I want you to know that to me Doc Gospod is a lake because she saved your life so many times. I've forgiven even Vancha because she took care of your swollen legs and quietly saw you off when you left for Black Peak, the biggest place full of old clothes and cheap chipped plates.

No one can order me about, Aggo. You taught me that if you and I had the Big Blue, I was not to be scared of anything. Binna has Big Blue in her eyes, too. It feels as if a part of you stayed there for good.

She's so silly, the poor thing. To bury herself in Space's poky place, give up on Spain's rich summers! But perhaps this is it, the Big Blue in a man, Dad Aggo: to meet a guy like Space, the forest ranger, and find something in him that has no end and no shore. Binna can do that. It's in her bones; she's got it from our mother. It's not a voice to listen to and not a picture to look at. It's like your motorcycle...you dreamed of taking us to the Black Sea. But the Black Sea is not worth a dime, dad. It's not worth a speck of dust compared to the sea you made for us in the jar: tap water, blue watercolors and salt.

I hope that somebody will make a sea of watercolors for my sons. I hope that their fathers will find their Big Blue. I will not lead them there because the air I breathe is dangerous and I press their necks against the log the way Vancha did to the chickens. I won't have any man order me about. If somebody tries to, he simply doesn't know what lies in store for him tomorrow.

Dad Aggo! Dad Aggo!

Fomite

A fomite is a medium capable of transmitting infectious organisms from one individual to another.

"The activity of art is based on the capacity of people to be infected by the feelings of others." Tolstoy, *What Is Art?*

Writing a review on Amazon, Good Reads, Shelfari, Library Thing or other social media sites for readers will help the progress of independent publishing. To submit a review, go to the book page on any of the sites and follow the links for reviews. Books from independent presses rely on reader to reader communications.

For more information or to order any of our books, visit
http://www.fomitepress.com/FOMITE/Our_Books.html

More Titles from Fomite...

Novels

Joshua Amses — *During This, Our Nadir*

Joshua Amses — *Raven or Crow*

Joshua Amses — *The Moment Before an Injury*

Jaysinh Birjepatel — *The Good Muslim of Jackson Heights*

Jaysinh Birjepatel — *Nothing Beside Remains*

David Brizer — *Victor Rand*

Paula Closson Buck — *Summer on the Cold War Planet*

Marc Estrin — *Hyde*

Marc Estrin — *Speckled Vanitie*

Zdravka Evtimova — *Sinfonia Bulgarica*

Daniel Forbes — *Derail This Train Wreck*

Greg Guma — *Dons of Time*

Fomite

Richard Hawley — *The Three Lives of Jonathan Force*

Lamar Herrin — *Father Figure*

Ron Jacobs — *All the Sinners Saints*

Ron Jacobs — *Short Order Frame Up*

Ron Jacobs — *The Co — conspirator's Tale*

Scott Archer Jones — *A Rising Tide of People Swept Away*

Maggie Kast — *A Free Unsullied Land*

Darrell Kastin — *Shadowboxing with Bukowski*

Coleen Kearon — *Feminist on Fire*

Jan Englis Leary — *Thicker Than Blood*

Diane Lefer — *Confessions of a Carnivore*

Rob Lenihan — *Born Speaking Lies*

Ilan Mochari — *Zinsky the Obscure*

Andy Potok — *My Father's Keeper*

Robert Rosenberg — *Isles of the Blind*

Fred Skolnik — *Rafi's World*

Lynn Sloan — *Principles of Navigation*

L.E. Smith — *The Consequence of Gesture*

L.E. Smith — *Travers' Inferno*

Bob Sommer — *A Great Fullness*

Tom Walker — *A Day in the Life*

Susan V. Weiss — *My God, What Have We Done?*

Peter M. Wheelwright — *As It Is On Earth*

Suzie Wizowaty — *The Return of Jason Green*

Poetry

Antonello Borra — *Alfabestiario*

Antonello Borra — *AlphaBetaBestiaro*

James Connolly — *Picking Up the Bodies*

Fomite

Greg Delanty — *Loosestrife*

Mason Drukman — *Drawing on Life*

J. C. Ellefson — *Foreign Tales of Exemplum and Woe*

Anna Faktorovich — *Improvisational Arguments*

Barry Goldensohn — *Snake in the Spine, Wolf in the Heart*

Barry Goldensohn — *The Hundred Yard Dash Man*

Barry Goldensohn — *The Listener Aspires to the Condition of Music*

R. L. Green When — *You Remember Deir Yassin*

Kate Magill — *Roadworthy Creature, Roadworthy Craft*

Tony Magistrale — *Entanglements*

Sherry Olson — *Four — Way Stop*

Janice Miller Potter — *Meanwell*

Joseph D. Reich — *Connecting the Dots to Shangrila*

Joseph D. Reich — *The Hole That Runs Through Utopia*

Joseph D. Reich — *The Housing Market*

Joseph D. Reich — *The Derivation of Cowboys and Indians*

David Schein — *My Murder and Other Local News*

Scott T. Starbuck — *Industrial Oz*

Seth Steinzor — *Among the Lost*

Seth Steinzor — *To Join the Lost*

Susan Thomas — *The Empty Notebook Interrogates Itself*

Sharon Webster — *Everyone Lives Here*

Tony Whedon — *The Tres Riches Heures*

Tony Whedon — *The Falkland Quartet*

Stories

Jay Boyer — *Flight*

Michael Cocchiarale — *Still Time*

Neil Connelly — *In the Wake of Our Vows*

Fomite

Catherine Zobal Dent — *Unfinished Stories of Girls*

Zdravka Evtimova —*Carts and Other Stories*

John Michael Flynn — *Off to the Next Wherever*

Elizabeth Genovise — *Where There Are Two or More*

Andrei Guriuanu — *Body of Work*

Derek Furr — *Semitones*

Derek Furr — *Suite for Three Voices*

Zeke Jarvis — *In A Family Way*

Marjorie Maddox — *What She Was Saying*

William Marquess — *Boom-shacka-lacka*

Gary Miller — *Museum of the Americas*

Jennifer Anne Moses — *Visiting Hours*

Martin Ott — *Interrogations*

Jack Pulaski — *Love's Labours*

Charles Rafferty — *Saturday Night at Magellan's*

Kathryn Roberts — *Companion Plants*

Ron Savage — *What We Do For Love*

L.E. Smith — *Views Cost Extra*

Susan Thomas — *Among Angelic Orders*

Tom Walker — *Signed Confessions*

Silas Dent Zobal — *The Inconvenience of the Wings*

Odd Birds

Micheal Breiner — *the way none of this happened*

Gail Holst — Warhaft — *The Fall of Athens*

Roger Leboitz — *A Guide to the Western Slopes and the Outlying Area*

dug Nap— *Artsy Fartsy*

Delia Bell Robinson — *A Shirtwaist Story*

Peter Schumann — *Planet Kasper, Volumes One and Two*

Fomite

Peter Schumann — *Bread & Sentences*

Peter Schumann — *Faust 3*

Plays

Stephen Goldberg — *Screwed and Other Plays*

Michele Markarian — *Unborn Children of America*

9 781942 515708